ALSO BY GREG RUCKA

Keeper
Finder
Smoker

SHOOTING AT MIDNIGHT

GREG RUCKA

BANTAM BOOKS
NEW YORK   TORONTO   LONDON   SYDNEY   AUCKLAND

SHOOTING AT MIDNIGHT

A Bantam Book

PUBLISHING HISTORY
Bantam hardcover edition published October 1999
Bantam mass market edition / July 2000

ISBN 0-553-57827-8

Published simultaneously in the United States and Canada

Bantam Books are published by Bantam Books, a division of Random
House, Inc. Its trademark, consisting of the words "Bantam Books" and
the portrayal of a rooster, is Registered in U.S. Patent and Trademark
Office and in other countries. Marca Registrada. Bantam Books, 1540
Broadway, New York, New York 10036.

PRINTED IN THE UNITED STATES OF AMERICA

OPM 10 9 8 7 6 5 4 3 2 1

This book is dedicated to the friends.

They know who they are; they know what is never spoken.

ACKNOWLEDGMENTS

Thanks to the following:

Sergeant Pete Kerns, Eugene Police Department; Detective Bill Golodner, Sixth Detective Squad, NYPD; Detective Daniel O'Connell, Sixth Detective Squad, NYPD; and Officer James Gombach, Midtown South, NYPD. At FDNY EMS, Elizabeth Rogers, paramedic, and Jack Carlson, paramedic.

Additional recognition goes to Steve (The Mystery Man) and to Jerry Hennelly.

Enormous gratitude to Sister Regina Bechtle, SC, at the College of Mount St. Vincent in the Bronx, for showing through word and deed the beauty of being a religious. May we return to the Overlook soon. Thanks also to Sister Janet Ryan, SNJM, Thomas More University Parish (Newman Center), in Eugene, Oregon.

A fountain of praise to the following: N. Michael Rucka, Corry Rucka, Carol Lea Benjamin, Evan Franke, Alex Gombach, Rachel Leonhardy, Mighty Mo, Brian Donnelly, Café Roma, Morgan Wolfe, Bryan Swanston, The Gang of Four, Mike Arnzen, Nic Witschi, Daria Penta, Kate Miciak, Amanda Clay Powers, Ben Moeling, and the others who asked not to be named, only remembered.

Special thanks to Scott Nybakken, who has been there when needed each and every time. The Best Man.

Finally, to Jennifer, who has pretty eyes.

A man always has two reasons for what he does—
A good one, and the real one.
—*J. P. Morgan*

Persons are fine things, but they cost so much!
For thee, I must pay me.
—*Ralph Waldo Emerson*

Opiate, *n.* An unlocked door in the prison of Identity.
It leads into the jail yard.
—*Ambrose Bierce*

SHOOTING
AT
MIDNIGHT

For my thirteenth birthday, Da gave me a Midtown South sweatshirt that was too big for me, NYPD shorts, and a pair of running shoes.

It was just what I'd asked for.

The next morning, bright and early, I put them on and drove with my Da to Van Cortlandt Park on the north edge of Bronx County, just the two of us. He used orange traffic cones stored in the trunk of the car to set up a small obstacle course while I stretched. When he was finished, he showed me how I was supposed to run it.

"Is it like this at the Academy?" I asked.

"No, but this is a good place for you to start," he said.

I put everything I had into running that course, and when I had it mastered, Da made me run it in reverse.

I loved every minute of it.

From then on out, usually once a week, Da would take me to Van Cortlandt Park and I would run whatever course he set for me. I'd run it in snow and rain, sunlight and humidity. Couple times his partner, Uncle Jimmy, would join us, and they would smoke and drink beer and watch and heckle and give me pointers.

Couple times that year my sister, Cashel, went with us too, but she hated it and, after the third time, didn't come back. So Saturdays became days for my Da and me, for my Ma and Cashel.

Which I thought was just great.

For my fourteenth birthday, Da gave me a new pair of running shoes and a set of boxing gloves.

Just what I'd asked for.

We went out to Van Cortlandt Park and Da set up the same course as he had a year ago to the day, and he timed me as I ran it, and when I was done, he showed me the records he'd been keeping in his little notepad, showed me how much I'd improved.

"That's my girl," he said.

Then he put on sparring mitts, and he taught me how to throw a punch that would knock a man down. From then on out, we always ended our sessions with me wearing the boxing gloves.

"They'll make it hard on you. You're a woman, and they'll make you pay for it every inch of the way. But we'll fix it so they never know what hit them. You're smarter than me. You'll be tougher too. You'll get the gold shield I never got; hell, you'll get your own command. You'll have all the education and all the ability, and you'll have the heart and the strength, and that's the most important thing."

"Yes, Da," I said.

"That's my girl. Now . . . let's see that uppercut."

For my fifteenth birthday, Da gave me new shoes, a new MTS sweatshirt, new shorts, a sports bra, and a copy of the cadet's handbook. When I opened the sports bra, he blushed and said, "Your Ma picked that out."

We went to Van Cortlandt Park and reviewed my progress, and Uncle Jimmy came along, and when I was done working out that day, Da and Uncle Jimmy gave me a beer. Then they gave me another one, and another, and I made it through most of a fourth before I got sick-drunk and passed out.

Da joked about how well I could hold my alcohol.

He hadn't figured out that I'd been sneaking beers after school for months already, drinking with friends.

He hadn't figured out that I'd begun smoking pot.

Even when I started missing my dates with him, either spending the night at a friend's he thought he could trust or claiming I was sick because I'd caught a bad bug rather than a savage hangover, he didn't see it.

He was disappointed, but he never said so.

And by the time he suspected, by the time he was willing to admit what his eldest daughter had gotten herself into, I was gone.

I spent my sixteenth birthday living in an abandoned apartment in Alphabet City, trying to steal enough money to score.

Three months later it was over, Da and Uncle Jimmy bringing me back home to the Bronx at four in the morning, laying me in my bed. I was screaming and shouting and Da held me down while Jimmy got Ma and a basin of hot water and some towels.

"Jesus Lord," Ma said when she saw me, and she crossed herself.

"Jimmy, go sit with Cashel," Da said. "Keep her out of here."

"I'll be down the hall with her, Dennis," Jimmy said.

They waited until he had shut the door, and then Da held me still while Ma stripped and bathed me. When she saw my arms, she started to cry.

When they were finished, they left, locking me alone in my room.

———

Six days later Da woke me at seven in the morning, dropping my sweats and shoes on the end of the bed.

"I'll meet you by the car," he said, and left without locking the door behind him.

When I put on the sweatshirt, it hung looser than it had before. The shoes pinched at my ankles. When I came down the stairs, I had to use the banister for support.

Ma and Cashel were in the kitchen, having waffles for breakfast. They asked how I was feeling.

"Better," I lied, and went out to the garage, where Da was waiting by his Alfa Romeo.

We drove to Van Cortlandt Park without exchanging a word. It was winter and I was shivering, trying to keep my teeth from chattering. Da turned the heat up higher, but it didn't help.

He set up the obstacle course in the snow and told me to run it.

I put everything I had into running that course, and I couldn't do it. My legs wouldn't work, my coordination was shot. I could barely stand straight. I was sweating after only five minutes, my stomach cramping, my hands shaking. I tripped and fell again and again, and Da just watched.

I got sick, doubled over with dry heaves.

Finally he said, "Come here."

He put the gloves on my hands, the sparring mitts on his own.

"Jab," he ordered.

"Da . . ." I said. "Da . . . I can't."

"Don't cry."

"I'm sick . . . I can't."

"Jab."

"Da . . ."

"You throw that jab now, goddamn it, or so help me I'll make you fight back!" When he shouted his voice rumbled across the parade ground, echoing off the snow.

I tried to punch at his extended hand, and the glove on the end of my own felt like it was full of wet sand. There was barely a sound when leather met leather.

"Jesus Christ! Jab! *Jab!* Use your left, for fuck's sake!"

I brought my left up and missed. I was crying and the mitts were hard to see.

"Again."

I tried again. I tried every time he ordered me to. When I hit, it wasn't hard enough, and when I missed, he swore louder and louder. Finally he ordered a left cross that I just couldn't raise my arm to give him.

"I can't, Da, I'm sorry I can't do it." I was sobbing when I said it, choking on tears and frustration. "I'm sorry I'm sick, I'm sorry I'm weak—"

Before either of us knew what had happened, the mitt on his right hand shot forward and caught me in the left eye, and I was on the ground in the frozen-sharp snow, feeling my sweats soak with icy water, my gloves hiding my face. I tried to swallow the noise I was making, tried to stand up, and I slipped and fell again.

Da took off his mitts and looked at me, his mouth half open and his eyes almost shut, his breath blowing away from him like steam from a train engine.

I saw what he saw then.

There was never going to be a cadet's handbook or a command or a gold shield all my own. It was never going to happen.

Da crouched down in the snow in front of me, helped me off with my gloves. He took my face in one huge hand and checked my eye where he'd punched me. Then he helped me up and put me in the car to wait while he stowed everything in the Alfa's trunk.

We never went back to Van Cortlandt Park.

That was thirteen years ago.

PART ONE

September 2 to October 17

CHAPTER ONE

I woke up to find I'd been sharing my bed with Mr. Jones.

He fought me when I threw back the covers, and he fought me when I pulled on my sweats, and he fought me when I snapped on the light in the kitchen and turned the water on to boil. He whispered in my ear as I waited for the steam to rise, and he lurked behind me as I made my cup of herbal cures-what-ails-ya swamp water, and he mocked me as I sat in my easy chair and watched the sky debate color-coding with the coming dawn.

Mr. Jones is a smug motherfucker, and he wouldn't take the hint. So I spelled it out for him.

"I am not going to do it," I told Mr. Jones. "So you can just go fuck yourself with a fork."

Mr. Jones smirked and then slowly faded away, and as he went so did the memory and the ache and the itch. I caught my breath and waited for my heart to slow to normal, and when I felt safe enough, I checked my arms.

Clean.

Of course.

I was eighteen when I'd had the cosmetic surgery, expert skin grafts layered to hide my track marks. Good work, too, that had my father moonlighting at all the worst hotels to make certain we could pay for the operations. I've told myself a million times that it's impossible to know what the discoloration only I can see hides.

I toyed with going back to bed. Six minutes to five in the morning. I had to be at work at nine. What was the point? I could use my early hours productively; I could exercise, or read the *Times,* or listen to the entirety of *Morning Edition*. I could lay out my clothes and make my bed and act like the domesticated animal I now was.

And, of course, if I stayed awake, I'd be unlikely to dream another smack attack.

When I'd first kicked, my nights had been fast and furious with the dreams of using. As I've stayed clean and put more distance between my life and my habit, they've faded until, at times, I've almost forgotten I'd had them at all. Nearly five years had passed since my last run of drug dreams, but in mid-August they'd returned with a vengeance, two or three nights a week. Today's had been the worst in as long as I could remember.

My drug dreams are like my sex dreams, and I'm talking about the really good ones, not the ones that fade by the time you hit the shower. No, these aren't so kind; these are sensory delights, filled with the memories of sight and sound and scent and most of all touch, the kind when, in the moment of opening your eyes, you can still feel the kiss on your lips or the hands on your hips.

Or, in this case, the needle in your arm and the rush of heat into your head.

These are the kind of dreams that make me suspect that there is, indeed, a good chance that the whole godforsaken mass called Humanity is, in fact, the dream of a Great Intergalactic Space Iguana. These are the dreams that make me question reality.

Something like that, at any rate.

I hate them. They make me feel weak.

I finished off my herbal infusion and resolved that I was now, in fact, officially awake, that there was no going back, and that it was time to switch to coffee. I filled the pot and looked at the phone, and even though it was early, seriously considered calling the Boy Scout. If I did, I'd wake him up. I wasn't certain how it made me feel, knowing that he wouldn't mind. Atticus would listen to what I had to say, and we'd talk, and then he'd ask when could he see me, and I'd lie and say soon.

So when the phone did ring, I nearly started half out of my skin.

But it wasn't him. It was Lisa Schoof, and she said, "He found us."

"I'm coming over," I said.

She opened the door for me with one hand, her other pressing a dirty pink dish towel filled with ice to her bottom lip. Vince was a righty, and he'd worked with that fist almost exclusively. Lisa's left eye and cheek were swelling too. She was dressed in boxer shorts and a tank top, and best I could tell, Vince had contented himself with her face.

"Are you all right?" I asked before I'd even made it through the door. "Is Gabe all right?"

She motioned with her free hand toward the kitchenette. I saw Gabe, in thin green pajamas, watching my arrival. He was wearing once-ivory-colored sneakers.

"I made him hide in the bathroom." Lisa sounded like she was reading me a message from Western Union, still angry and still scared, and she spoke slowly to conceal it. "As soon as I knew it was Vince, I woke Gabe up and told him to hide in the bathroom."

"I had to lock the door," Gabe said. "I couldn't come out until he left."

"What'd he want?" I asked Lisa.

"Money." She put her back to me, went the eight feet across the apartment to the kitchenette, and reached for the whisk broom wedged between the refrigerator and the wall.

A bright crayon drawing of an ambulance was stuck to the door with a magnet. Wedged between the magnet and the drawing were coupons from Fine + Fair.

I looked over the whole apartment, a process that took all of two seconds. Three rooms, counting the bathroom, and I almost didn't because it was so small the only person who could use it without asphyxiating was Gabe. Lisa was balanced on the poverty line, and closer to falling the wrong way than into money. The apartment mirrored that—a decrepit couch that served as her bed, a card table that was both desk and dining surface, two white plastic chairs that were reluctant to take on any weight other than their own. Gabriel had his own room, a real bed, even a particleboard bookcase.

What the apartment lacked in furnishings, it made up for in dignity.

Except that Vince had been through it, and done his best to cause as much damage as possible during his visit. There were shards in the kitchen, glasses that he'd shattered and two or three plates. The few pots and pans Lisa owned had been yanked from their shelves. Otherwise, most of the mess was paper, Lisa's textbooks thrown from the table, Gabriel's homework scattered on the floor.

One of the benefits of not having much is that the mess is smaller.

"You're going to suck at that," I told Lisa, taking the broom from her hand. "Get the dustpan."

She let it go without comment, and Gabe moved out of the way to let us work, watching. When you see them together, it's clear they're from the same Scandinavian end of the gene pool, the straight blond hair and the almost gray eyes. But where Lisa's face is broad, with a wide mouth and a nose that's almost beaky, Gabriel's features are more condensed and narrow. He'd grown too, maybe as much as an inch and a half, and I guessed that by the time he was done, he'd be taller than his mother's five six. Now, though, both of them were slender and small, and in comparison, I felt like a giant, especially in the claustrophobic apartment.

We finished in the kitchen and Gabriel and I set to work

gathering the strewn books and papers. Lisa used the hand not holding the dish towel to convert her bed back into the couch, a process that consisted of folding a blanket that had once been gray. Now it was almost white.

Gabe and I replaced his collection of Matchbox cars in its blue-and-yellow plastic case. He showed me a tiny midnight blue Porsche and said, "It's not yours, but it's the closest I could get."

"Boxster," I said. "Not bad. Mine's better."

He looked at me thoughtfully. "Did you bring it?"

"How do you think I got here, buster?"

Gabriel considered, looking to where his mother was now sitting on the couch before he turned back to me. "I think you drove your car."

"You're a smart kid," I said, and dug into my jacket pockets. I had a roll of Wint-O-Green in my left, Tropical Fruit in my right. "Guess."

A smile crept onto his face, chasing Vince's shadow away. "Left."

"You win." I pulled the Life Savers from the requested pocket and pressed them into his hand.

"Thanks," he said with careful politeness, and began fighting with the foil.

"Don't open that," Lisa told him. "You can take it to school with you, have some after lunch."

Gabe stopped trying to unwrap the candy. His smile flickered out. "I'm not going to school. I'm staying with you."

"I've got to go to school too."

"I'll come with you. I won't leave you alone."

The ice had long since melted away, and when Lisa dropped the towel from her cheek, water trickled along her jaw. She wiped it with the back of her hand, then extended her arms to her son. He scrambled off the floor and went to her hug like he was being chased and, as soon as her arms closed around him, began to cry.

I had no place in a mother-son moment, so I waited. Next door an alarm clock announced morning with a shocking blast of salsa music; the noise cut off as a fist slammed into a snooze bar. Walls this thin, the neighbors must have heard everything that had happened here, and yet there was not a police to be found. Lisa certainly hadn't called for one.

Instead, she'd called me.

First time we'd spoken in a year, and I began wondering what exactly she wanted me to do now that I was here.

Lisa rocked Gabriel against her, crooning in his ear, telling him that everything would be all right, that Vince wouldn't come back. Her eyes didn't believe a word she was saying, but Gabriel couldn't see her eyes, and he stopped crying and pulled back. She stroked his forehead, trying to calm his fear with her fingers, and it worked, because finally Gabriel nodded.

"Go take your shower," she said. "Get dressed. Then we'll talk about breakfast."

"I know a great pancake house," I said. "You want a ride in the Porsche?"

Lisa looked about to object but Gabriel asked, "Will you drive me to school?"

"It would be my pleasure."

He wiped a trail of shiny snot from his nose and went to his room, shutting the door quietly behind him. Lisa cocked her head, mother-radar sensing for misbehavior, and when the water in the shower came on, looked back at me.

"I can't pay for breakfast," she said.

"It was my invitation. I'll cover it."

Pride twitched at the corner of her mouth. "Thanks." She stood. "I've got to change too. I've got an EMS class at Fort Totten this morning."

"You want me to wait outside?"

"Nothing you've never seen before."

"True enough."

An old suitcase was wedged between the wall and the back of the couch. She crouched and flipped it open and revealed the entirety of her wardrobe. She pulled out clean clothes and draped them over the arm of the couch. Tan slacks, blue blouse, bra, panties, socks.

She changed clothes while looking at her feet, and I suppose modesty should have kept my eyes off her, but it didn't.

We'd first met when Lisa was fifteen and I was just-turned seventeen, and I'd easily weighed twice as much as she did even then, and not just because I was already six feet tall. All of her scars seemed to be the same, although it was hard to tell with her forearms, where the tracks were. But the cigarette burns still clustered at the base of her spine, and when she turned while slipping on her bra, I could see the thin puckered line where Vince, years ago, had run a knife up her left breast.

For a minute there, anger closed my throat like I was being choked.

When she was dressed, I asked, "Why did you call me? Not that I mind, but I'm not certain what you need from me here. Moral support? Money? An extra set of hands?"

She used a blue barrette to clip her hair back. "Help."

"With what?"

She shot another look at Gabriel's bedroom. The door was still closed, but the shower had stopped.

"With what, Lisa?" I repeated.

"Killing Vince," she told me.

CHAPTER TWO

At the Royal Canadian Pancake House on Second Avenue, Lisa and I watched Gabriel work his way through a flapjack about half his size. Lisa drained two cups of coffee, but she didn't eat anything. I had a glass of orange juice and a bowl of mixed fruit, some of which was actually fresh.

By the time his food arrived, Gabriel had been returning to the kid I remembered, animated and talkative, and that allowed his mother to get away with a fair silence during the meal. Gabriel monopolized the conversation with me, asking about my car, mostly.

"It's the '97, right?"

"The '96," I said.

"How fast can it go?"

"About 190."

He dropped his jaw in an exaggerated gape, and I got to see what half-masticated pancake looked like in a ten-year-old's mouth. "Have you ever done that?"

"Driven that fast?"

He nodded.

"Nope," I said.

"What's the fastest you've ever drived?"

"I took her up to 170 about a month ago."

"Was it fun? Was it cool?"

"Really fun," I admitted. "Really cool."

"Next time you go that fast, can I come with you?"

Lisa's face lost some of the color she'd gotten back.

"Sure," I said.

That had made him almost as happy as the looks he'd gotten when we dropped him off outside of P.S. 64, into the crowd of kids just arriving for school. Lisa left him with a hug and a kiss, and then Gabriel disappeared into a circle of children who stared at us in the Porsche as we pulled away. I gunned it for good measure.

Small thrills are what make life worthwhile.

"Where do you have to be and when?" I asked Lisa when we'd put a couple blocks between us and her son.

"I've got a class at a quarter past ten," she said. "I should catch my train around nine."

"That gives us an hour," I said, and swung us around and up until we reached Tompkins Square Park. We came in on the east side, and I found a space just below Eighth Street, opposite St. Brigid's Church, which I thought was appropriate.

We got out and I set the car alarm, and we headed into the park together. There were a few people out and about, several elderly couples reading newspapers and sharing cups of coffee, and I saw a boy in his early twenties, his face tattooed like a Maori's, playing with his pit bull in the dog run. A sector car from the Ninth was stopped just inside the park, and the two officers within were keeping a close eye on the parents and children in the secured playground.

"Okay," I said when we'd settled on a bench. "This is what's going on in my mind, just so you know, sort of FYI. I haven't heard from you or Gabriel in, what, thirteen months? That's one. Second, you call me in the dark hours of dawn. Me. Not the police. And finally, you say you need my help. To commit murder, no less.

"So any time you want to explain, I'm listening."

"Not murder." She settled back on the bench, drew her knees up to her chest. "Self-defense."

"I said I'm listening."

Lisa pressed her right cheek against her thigh so she could face me. The swelling on everything but her lip had stopped and begun to recede, so I figured the ice had worked. She'd tried a little makeup too, but it wasn't really doing much but highlighting the fact that she was trying to hide her face. Her lower lip still looked like she had a gumball fused into her flesh. She shut her eyes.

"We were so close," Lisa whispered. "We were almost there, Bridgett, and then this happens. This happens and it all goes to shit, and it's like I've done nothing, like it's all been for nothing. And I can't protect myself. I can't protect my son."

"When was the last time you'd seen Vince?" I asked. "Before this morning, I mean."

"Five years or so . . . yeah, five years."

"Not since then?"

"No."

"So you're clean?"

Her eyes shot open. "Fuck you, Bridgett Logan."

"Answer me or I'm walking," I said.

She unclasped her knees and angrily began yanking back on the sleeves of her blouse. "You think I'm that stupid? You want to check for fresh tracks? You think I don't know that if I fall I lose it all for good?"

"I think you're a junkie just like me," I said.

"Recovering junkie. Struggling junkie. Former junkie." She shoved her left forearm, bared, in my face. The old scars made my hidden ones itch, and I pushed her wrist away.

"You can hide it, Lisa. You're smart. You know how. You'd shoot between your toes if you wanted to fix bad enough. I would too."

"I haven't had so much as a sip of wine in over sixty months. Nothing." Lisa jerked her sleeves back down. "If I use I'll lose Gabe. Children's Protective Services will yank him from me so fast even you and your fancy Porsche couldn't catch them. Do you think I'm so fucked up I would put my habit before my son?"

"You did once before," I said.

Her mouth opened to bite back, then she turned away. The cops had been joined by another car, parking parallel to them, and there was laughter coming from the lowered windows as the four officers bantered. I couldn't make out their words. For a moment I felt the suspicion that they were laughing about us, that they knew our histories and our shames.

Lisa and I went back over ten years, back to the rehab program my parents had put me into after I'd first kicked my habit. The program had been run by the Sisters of Incarnate Love—probably still was—and when I'd entered it, the Sisters saved my life. I have no doubt that without the support of both them and my family, I'd have gone back to using.

I'd been in the program six weeks when Lisa showed up, fifteen and three months pregnant, terrified of using, of destroying the life she was carrying within her. We were both Bronx girls. I came from a solid middle-class family, Irish-Americans who broke their backs daily and, hate to say it, savaged their livers at night. Lisa was South Bronx all the way, the broken-family story that's all but cliché, her only living relative her mother's sister. And Aunt Vera hadn't been enough. Lisa started running the streets early, and she stayed there too long, and when either she or I stopped to think about it, we agreed it was a miracle she had survived.

I know that there are a lot of people who think that there's no excuse for using drugs; certainly, I didn't have a good one. But drugs are an escape from a brutal reality, and that's a fundamental truth. Lisa's reality had been one worth escaping, full of all those talk-show staples from abuse and molestation to rape and hooking.

All of this is to say that things had never been easy for Lisa. She'd had school trouble and money trouble and law trouble, some of it just honest bad luck, some of it bad luck she'd made for herself. Since Gabriel had been born she'd gone back to using twice that I knew of, the last time, if I was to believe her now, five years past. The first time, she hadn't been high long enough for Children's Services to figure out what had happened. The second time, they'd "relieved" her of Gabriel. He'd been seven before Lisa could convince the state to give him back.

She cleared her throat. "I'm not using, Bridgett. I didn't yesterday, and I'm praying that I won't tomorrow. I have done everything I could to get away from it, to be legit, and I've done it all for Gabriel. If you don't believe me, then we don't know each other anymore. If you can't believe me, then I'm sorry I bothered you. I'll take care of Vince myself."

I looked at her hard, and she returned my stare with just as much stone in her eyes. Then she nodded and started to get up. "I won't bother you again," she said.

"Don't be a fucking martyr," I said. "Sit down."

She wouldn't. I watched her ears turn scarlet. "Not everyone's as tough as you are, Bridgett."

"What the fuck do you mean by that?"

"It means some of us don't get it right the first time, that's what it means." Lisa was looking at the kid with the Maori tattoos. "It means some of us make mistakes and go back to using, and it means that for some of us, every day is a fight. You don't know what it's like being poor, being on welfare because you *have to be*. You don't know what it's like to turn on the fucking radio or pick up the fucking paper and read about Rudy or Schumer or any of those smug shiteaters calling you a waste of space and money and life."

That hurt, and made me angrier, and I ended up speaking faster than I'd have liked. I said, "That's not what I think of you, and that's not what I called you, and if *you* believe I think that, then you're right, we've got nothing in common anymore."

What I'd thought would be indignation and fury in her expression was instead hurt and pain. "Then why would you accuse me of using, Bridgett?"

"I didn't accuse. I asked. It's been a year since I heard from you, Lisa, and now Vince is back and you're talking about *killing* him. What am I supposed to think?"

"They're not related," Lisa said.

"All right, I believe you. Now explain it."

One of the sector cars had left, leaving the other behind, and now the driver was having an animated conversation with an ancient Hispanic man with a cane. In his other hand the old man held a brown paper bag, and my guess was he was a drinker. The cops in the car didn't seem to care. Lisa sat down again beside me.

"Which do you want first?" she asked.

"Vince. What happened?"

"I don't know how he found us. He wouldn't tell me, and I didn't have much of an opportunity to ask. I opened the door and the first thing he did was punch me in the face."

I thought, but did not say, that she should have kept the door shut, but Lisa caught my look.

"He said he'd break it down. You saw the damn door. It wouldn't have kept him out."

"It would have bought you time," I said. "You could have called the cops."

"If he came in and found me on the phone, he'd have killed me." Lisa said it evenly. "And even if he didn't and the cops managed to get there in time, so what?"

"He gets arrested."

"And then he's out again in sixty days and he comes back and this time he really does kill me."

"So you want to kill him first? That's your plan?"

"He wanted money," Lisa said. "He wanted twenty-eight hundred dollars, and he gave me until tomorrow night to give it to him. He says it's what I owe him from when I was using. Plus interest, of course."

I pulled out my remaining roll of Life Savers. Lisa took one and I took one and we each sucked for a minute while I thought.

"You can't give him the money," I said.

"No way. I mean, even if I had it, which I don't, he'd just keep coming back. I was stupid, I thought he'd forgotten about me. I really thought I'd left him behind. But Vince said that he'd never lost track of me or my 'brat.' "

"Was that all that happened?"

"He said if I was willing to go back to work for him, he'd settle for only a grand. Said I could work the rest off. Said it could be like the old days."

From what I knew, the old days had consisted of Lisa spreading her legs for Vince in exchange for a supply of clean needles and good smack. She'd also been expected to help run Vince's "business," counting cash, loading the glassines, cutting the dope down.

"Did he threaten you and Gabriel or just you?"

"Just me. He plans to rape, then kill, me if I don't pay up." The way she said it, it sounded like a program listing from *TV Guide*. Tonight's episode of *Lisa's Life*.

"Inventive," I said.

"Doesn't need to be," she countered. "I know it's only a threat and I know he's just trying to scare me . . ."

"But he found you," I finished.

She nodded. "And if I can't make him go away, he'll just come back again and again."

I broke the remainder of my Life Saver with my molars. "We have to talk to the police."

"As far as the blues are concerned, I'm just a junkie whore. I'm only worth their attention once I'm dead, and then not much."

"You have to stop talking that shit," I told her. "You're clean, you're a good mother, you're legal. You're in school, you're going to be a fucking medical technician, for Christ's sake. The only person who doesn't think you're legit is you."

"You're wrong," Lisa said. "The cops will take one look at my arms and call me a junkie. Then they'll take one look at Gabriel and they'll call me unfit." She spat out the remainder of the Life Saver she'd taken.

"And I won't take that chance. No cops, Bridgett."

"Let me look into it," I said. "I know some people, maybe I can—"

"Listen to me!" Lisa was shouting. "No. Cops. None. If there's even a remote chance I could lose Gabriel, forget it. I mean it. Just forget it."

I held up my hands to show that I had no intention of

pushing that button again. Lisa's chin dipped in a short nod, pleased that I'd understood her point.

I said, "If you get arrested for murder, you'll lose Gabe anyway. Have you realized that?"

"That's why I called you." She whipped her head around, checking the position of the people in the park. The remaining sector car had moved on. The Hispanic man was admiring my car. "With your help, we could get away with it."

I started shaking my head, but she didn't even give me time to argue.

"You could work it." She had lowered her voice, leaning forward. "You know how cops think, what they look for. You could fix it so we wouldn't get caught."

"You're maybe giving me too much credit there, Lise."

"No, you could, Bridgett, and you know you could. I realize what I'm asking, I really do, but there's no other way. If I do this alone, I know I'll get caught. If I don't do this, I'm going to end up losing Gabe. One of these days Vince will kill me. Or he'll kill Gabe. This is the only way to solve the problem, to make sure that Vince won't ever come back."

"There are other options."

"Name them. Name one that guarantees he won't do this to Gabe and me again."

I started to open my mouth, then realized I was about to say "Shooting him" and that such an answer was counterproductive to the argument. I ran my hands through my hair, felt the accumulated city. I had to go home. I had to change, get ready for work.

I had to find a way to convince Lisa that there were other solutions to her problem besides murder.

Unfortunately, I wasn't coming up with anything, and I had the murmuring suspicion that that was because I agreed with her: the only way to make certain Vince didn't come back was to put him down for good.

"Are you going to help me?" Lisa asked.

"You know I'll help you."

She didn't smile, but her mouth stopped looking like a line chiseled into marble.

"But we're not going to kill him," I said, and before she could interrupt me I wagged my index finger at her. "It's too risky. I'll come up with something, something that'll put a good scare into him. Something that will keep him from ever coming back. But we can't kill him, Lisa. Murder's too far to go. You do a murder, you'll never be a citizen. You'll lose Gabe forever."

"We need to be sure."

"And we will be, I swear it. Give me today to think about it, call me at home tonight. I'll have an idea by then."

She raised an eyebrow slightly, but kept her doubt confined to that. "Whatever you say."

"I need his full name too."

"Vincent Lark."

"That's not an alias?"

"Don't think so. He's called himself other things since I've known him, but Vince Lark is the name he always returns to."

"All right."

"I should go, catch my train."

"You want a lift?"

"No, I can walk over to the station on Astor. I just need to get my bag out of your car."

We walked back to where we'd parked and I zapped the alarm and Lisa pulled her book bag from the floor on the passenger's side. It was a vinyl satchel, embossed to look like it was made out of leather cured from a sick green cow, and the plastic was tearing in places, revealing the cardboard reinforcement in the side panels.

She shut the passenger door and said, "I'll call tonight."

"You still owe me another answer."

Lisa looked at me over the roof of my car. "I'm going to be late, Bridgett."

"Why haven't I heard from you until today?" I asked. "Why'd you cut me out of your lives?" I was doing a really good job of sounding like I didn't care, like I just wanted answers. That I hadn't been hurt when she'd ignored my messages and didn't return my calls.

"Not now."

"Now," I said.

Lisa sighed, then hefted her old vinyl book bag and rested it on the roof of the car. Her face had fallen again, and she looked thoroughly unhappy.

"What's wrong with this picture?" she asked.

I looked at the dingy, cheap bag resting on the top of my shiny, expensive auto. I said, "I'm not going to apologize for who I am."

Lisa slid the bag off the car and pulled the strap onto her shoulder. Only the right side of her mouth curled in a smile. Her left stayed immobile, swollen and anchored.

"I don't want you to apologize, Bridgett. Who you are is what I need to help me right now. I'll call you tonight."

I nodded and watched her head across the park, and when she disappeared from view I slipped back into my car and pointed the Porsche toward my apartment. I jockeyed with the cabs and the vans, wondering if any of the other drivers needed a junkie private eye to commit murder.

CHAPTER THREE

A dozen red waited on my desk, the blooms clustered tight a good nine inches above the edge of their fluted green glass container. The roses cast a shadow on the card propped against the vase.

I knew who they were from and my stomach went silly for a couple seconds. I took off my jacket and turned to hang it on the back of my door, and I almost stepped on one of my bosses, who had entered my office right behind me.

"From him?" Laila Agra asked.

"Gotta figure."

"Martin gave me flowers as often as you're getting flowers, I'd be smiling." Laila squinted up at me. "Why aren't you smiling?"

"I'm smiling on the inside," I said, and waited for her to get out of my way. She stepped aside and took the chair in front of my desk, and I reached around and hung my jacket on the hook on the back of the door. Then I took my seat opposite her and slid the vase out of the way, toward the phone.

The envelope holding the card fell flat on the blotter. My name was printed on it in block capitals.

Laila looked at the envelope and then at me, expectation and glee dancing in her almost-black eyes. She's Indian, forty-three years old with not a wrinkle to show for it, with skin the color of fallen autumn leaves. Her hair is as black as my own, and it curled around from the back of her neck in a braid that dangled down the front of her shirt, ending in a pile in her lap. She's all of five one, a full foot shorter than me, and that ponytail is almost as tall as she is. She's fiercely proud of the fact that she had her last haircut the day after she turned thirty.

She's also happily married to my other boss, Martin Donnovan, and therefore believes she's entitled to full and forthright reports about my romantic life.

"Where's Marty?" I asked.

"Hartford. Looking at birth certificates in the Wilkes case."

"And how's that going?"

"So far, so normal, and you know Marty. The chance of reuniting a family always lights a fire under his tubby ass."

"Nice way to talk about your mate."

"A detective must always be objective." Laila looked pointedly at the card again. "I'll wait quietly while you read it."

"I'll wait until I'm alone to read it."

She pouted. "You'd deny me my vicarious thrill?"

"It's the only thing I can deny you at all."

Her pout ceased and she rapped her knuckles on the edge of my desk. "I want to meet him," she said. "It is a him, isn't it?"

"It's the same one, so it's still a him," I confirmed. "And you'll meet him when he's been suitably prepared for the vicious gauntlet you and Marty will run him through."

"We'll be angels," she objected.

"You'll grill him like he's a T-bone."

"I don't eat meat." She bounded out of the chair and rapped her knuckles once more on my desk. "I need your write-up of the Bremmer Insurance investigation before tomorrow. Otherwise you may consider it a quiet day." She waggled her eyebrows at me. "You could call your boy and arrange a midafternoon quickie."

"You're going to make an excellent lecher someday," I told her.

"Memories for me to cherish when I'm in my twilight years. I'll be in my office if you need anything."

"Yes, boss."

She shut the door after her and I listened to her flats click down the hall, then the rustle of her voice as she gave Charice, our receptionist, the update on my social life. I don't know how or when or why my social life had become the pet project of Agra & Donnovan Investigations, but it'd been this way since I started my apprenticeship. When I was involved with someone, Laila wanted all the details. If I was single, she wanted me involved with someone.

I let my chair rock back, wincing at the inevitable squeal of the springs, then sighing up at the ceiling. I stared at the frosted-glass cover over the light in my office that has always looked like a giant tit, and tried to plan the day ahead in my mind. But the agenda was already screwed, and it was no great deductive leap to explain why.

The chair returned to level with a creak, and I reached for the envelope with my name on it. The card was plain cream-colored paper. *Thinking about you. Hoping to see you. Atticus.* The *A* in his name was small and precise, and I could tell he had thought long and hard about what he was writing, even down to how he would sign it.

Simple is best.

He'd sent me roses, and I thought that it really was very sweet of him. It made me want to see him.

I didn't like that just by sending roses he could make me want to see him.

I looked at the card and looked at the card and looked at the card some more.

Then I threw it into the trash.

I was supposed to be downtown for lunch around two, which left me most of three hours to actually do some work.

I typed up what I had on the Bremmer claim in about forty-five minutes—two-car accident, claimant demanding compensation for further medical fees. I'd interviewed doctors and chiropractors and observed the claimant himself, and had personally concluded that the guy was telling the truth. The Bremmer people wouldn't want to hear it, but that's what I'd discovered, and so that was what I wrote. I intranetted the report to Laila when I'd finished.

Rolodex time.

I had one number that I was certain could give me the lowdown on Vince Lark. I had another number that might. If I went with the sure thing, I'd feel guilty, but I'd get something I could use. If I went with the potential, I'd probably end up having to call the sure thing.

So I called the sure thing, because I'm lazy and don't like having to do the same thing twice unless I absolutely have to.

"Group 37."

"I'm calling for James Shannon," I said.

"Hold on. I'll transfer you."

"Thank you," I said, but the voice of reception was already gone and there was more ringing.

"Shannon. Go ahead."

"Uncle Jimmy," I said. "Long time no see."

There was a moment's pause before Detective James Shannon said gleefully, "Cashel? Is that you?"

"The older one. Remember?"

He sputtered, then cried, "Bridgett!"

"How you doing, Jimmy?"

"Fair to piddling, and you, girl, how are you?"

"Solid and sober," I said, and then wished I hadn't.

His silence was abrupt and came through the phone like a lump of lead.

"I'm good," I said.

"Haven't seen you in quite a while," he said. When Jimmy spoke, it always reminded me of my Da. Both put the same core of authority in their tone. "Neither has your sister."

Gritting my teeth, I opened my desk drawer and delighted myself by finding a container of Altoids. "I've been meaning to call Cashel."

"You can lie to me all you like, Bridie. Don't lie to Cashel."

"I wouldn't dare," I said.

"Last time I saw you was up on East Eighty-fifth, wasn't it? At Ryan's Daughter? When was that?"

"March."

"So six months, then."

"Sounds right. I'm sorry I haven't called."

He chuckled, a sound that started traditionally in his belly and then vibrated through his throat. The phone only made it all the more impressive. "Have I got you feeling guilty yet?"

"Something fierce," I replied. "Especially since I'm calling for a favor."

"I doubted you were checking on my health, my darling. What do you need?"

"Anything you've got on a guy named Vincent Lark. He's a dealer, mostly smack, and he's been working the city for at least ten years, maybe longer."

There was a pause, and I assumed he was taking notes on what I'd just said. I waited. He didn't say anything. I opened my Altoids and enjoyed a curiously strong mint, and still he said nothing.

"Uncle Jimmy?"

"Bridie, why're you asking?"

"I've got a friend who's having some trouble and Vincent Lark may be a part of it," I said.

"A friend? Friend have a name?"

"I'd rather keep her out of it."

There was more silence while he thought. I could only guess what was going through his mind, but it probably had something to do with his dead partner's daughter—the junkie—calling him up at the Joint Drug Taskforce and asking about a smack dealer. He was probably trying to figure out if my friend was fictional or not.

Because once a junkie, always a junkie.

"I'll have to call you back, Bridie," Jimmy said. "I'll dig and see what I find. You're at work?"

"Yeah," I said, and gave him the number. "If you could get back to me before one I'd really be grateful."

"If I get back to you before one, you have to promise me that you'll call your sister. I spoke with her last week, she told me you haven't talked to her in almost a year. She said you've stopped going to church."

"Thanks for this, Jimmy," I said. "I'll wait to hear from you."

And I hung up, and I looked at the roses, and I ate some more Altoids.

At one-thirty I was putting on my jacket to leave when Charice buzzed me through the speaker on my phone. "Bridgett? There's an NYPD detective named Shannon calling for you. He won't say what it's regarding."

I pressed the com button and said, "Put him through," then picked up the handset and added, "Uncle Jimmy?"

He coughed politely. "You hung up on me."

"I thought our conversation had ended," I fibbed.

Jimmy sighed like a put-upon parent. I could hear voices behind him, Taskforce cops cracking wise, most likely. "Vincent Lark. Still interested?"

"Very." I reached across the desk for a Bic ballpoint and a pad, and got a hefty whiff of the roses.

"You'll call your sister?"

"Jimmy," I snapped. "You're not my mother."

"Nor am I your father, may they both rest in peace. But I'm obligated to look after you all the same. Dennis would've done as much for me and mine."

"You going to tell me what you've got?" I was already tired of the guilt game he was playing. "I'm running late."

"I can call back."

"*Now,* Jimmy."

"I ran the name," he said after a second. "And Lark's a grade-A asshole dealer fuck. Rotten, rotten guy, Bridie. Record like you wouldn't believe, arrests for possession, possession with intent, assault, menacing, armed robbery, attempted rape. Not a fucking conviction. He's either very lucky or he's got one hell of a lawyer."

"Anything current?"

"Nothing on paper. But I talked to some other guys on the Taskforce and they say your boy's tied into the Alabacha Cadre. Heard of them?"

I perched myself on the edge of my desk and scrawled more notes on the pad. "Only in the papers."

"I'm glad to hear that," Jimmy said, and the vehement sincerity in his voice told me just how worried he had been over me. Before I could say anything, he went on. "Alabacha is Nigerian, part of the generation of distributors that have taken over from the Chinese. Bad news. Rumor is that he was part of the Nigerian police force, and they've never won any international awards for honesty or incorruptibility. Came here after being dismissed from his post, apparently, started moving dope using the connections he'd made as a cop. Runs most of the smack on our fair island, and has his fingers into most of the other boroughs as well."

"Lark's working with someone who has that much juice?"

"Nobody here can say for sure. But Lark's got staying power, that's a given. Most dealers don't last more than five years on the street. Your guy, he's been around at least three times that long. Maybe longer."

He paused and I took the opportunity to ask for the spelling of "Alabacha," then scribbled it down.

"Got it," I said. "Thanks. I got to go."

"Your friend," Jimmy said. "How much trouble is she in?"

"Enough," I said.

"Vincent Lark looks like bad news, Bridie. Anyone who's survived working a corner as long as he has, he's going to have serious balls. Not someone who is ever going to back down easily."

"Maybe he's just had good luck."

"His kind of good luck tends to come from another's bad. You go careful if you're dealing with this guy."

"Nah," I said. "I won't go near him. This is background information, that's all."

"You want me to believe you?"

"I'd like it if you did, yes."

"Call your sister, Bridie."

I almost hung up then, but I had to say it even if Jimmy wouldn't just come out and ask. "I'm not back on the horse," I told him. "Don't worry about me."

He said, "Somebody's got to."

CHAPTER FOUR

I tried to make up the time on the drive, and still ended up twenty minutes late for my date. It was probably subconscious; I wasn't looking forward to the meal or the conversation, and was uncertain how I felt about the company. The odds were that I was speeding to attend the postmortem on a friendship that had been in a coma for almost a year.

Parking was a bitch—always is when you're in a hurry—and I ended up paying eighteen bucks to put the Porsche in a garage three blocks from where I needed to be. Then I ran and attracted stares.

She had picked Chanterelle for our meal, the sort of eatery that I, for the most part, make it a point to avoid. The food is expensive and good, and the crowd is that Wall Street and politico detritus that plays squash instead of racquetball and manages to turn a profit on every S&L that goes belly-up. I took off my sunglasses when I got through the door, and even though they'd been shaded, my eyes needed a moment to adjust.

She had already been seated at a table near the rear of the

restaurant but away from the kitchen, and had turned the back of her chair to the wall. Like every bodyguard I know, Natalie Trent perpetually rides a mild wave of paranoia. Doesn't matter if she's on the job or not, if she's in public she's always looking to cover her back, and it's the same with the rest of them. If you get four or five of them in the same place, you're in for a real laugh; they shuffle about like lost chicks until each of them believes they have the best view of every entrance. If you want to make them really nervous, ask to meet them somewhere with a lot of open spaces—a park or a stadium.

So she saw me the instant I entered, and she raised a hand, and I started for her table and was promptly intercepted by the maître d', who didn't like what he saw one bit. It might have been my nose ring or it might have been my biker jacket or it might have been my blue jeans or it might have been my boots. It might have been my Hothead Paisan T-shirt, which is white with Hothead herself stenciled on the chest, dancing a little jig with her cat, Chicken.

Hell if I know.

"Can I help you, madame?"

"Mademoiselle," I corrected. "I'm meeting my date."

He looked where I was pointing and Natalie nodded, and the maître d' looked me over again. He struggled with his mouth and managed to not scowl, probably because I'd be sitting far enough away from his honored guests that my odor wouldn't offend.

"If you'll follow me." He scooped up a menu and we threaded our way past the tables. It was busier than I'd have guessed for a quarter past two, and heads turned as we went by. When we reached Natalie's table, the maître d' went so far as to pull my chair out for me. "Enjoy your meal, mademoiselle."

"I'm savoring the cuisine already," I said.

Casting one last glance, he headed back toward the ordered safety of his podium.

"I was wondering if you had changed your mind," Natalie said.

"I told you I'd come. I came."

"Thank you."

Around us was the clinking of glass and silverware, the voices of monied men talking about money. Natalie had a glass of ice tea in front of her with a crushed quarter of lemon floating with the ice at the top. She looked nervous but at home. With her red hair folded up in a bun at the back of her head and her tailored black blazer, I thought she looked quite the executive. She'd kept her jewelry to a minimum, just small pearl studs, one in each ear. With the table between us, I couldn't tell if she'd gone for slacks or a skirt and couldn't bring myself to lift the tablecloth and peek. Probably a skirt.

We looked at each other, taking stock and checking what we saw against the pictures in our memories. It'd been November when we'd seen each other last, and I don't think either of us had known at the time what was coming. No big explosion of rage and feeling followed, not even a fight, really. Natalie had slept with Atticus, or Atticus had slept with Natalie, and then Atticus had told me, and that had been that. Friendships had just stopped as I cut the lines that tied our lives together, let my hurt and anger seal the space between us. A separation of company was probably the best way to put it. Natalie had tried getting in touch with me twice in late November and then once more in early December; I'd returned each effort with silence.

Then, last Friday, she'd called Agra & Donnovan and asked if I was free for a Monday lunch downtown.

"I want to clear the air," Natalie had said.

I'd surprised myself by not slamming the receiver down and instead saying yes. With Natalie across the table from me now, my anger still sparked like a third rail, made me nervous and drew tension along my shoulders and up my back.

Natalie Trent had put back some of the weight she'd lost after her boyfriend died, and her pallor had passed, and she looked good and happy and healthy and I wasn't going to guess about wise. But then again, Natalie always looked good, always dressed well, blessed with five feet eleven inches of height and a body that clothing designers imagined when they toiled in their workshops. The two inches I had on her made Saks a totally different experience for each of us.

"You're looking well," Natalie said.

"I was thinking the same thing about you."

"I'm feeling good. It's been a long time since I felt this good."

"Glad to hear it."

It sounded snide, even to me.

Natalie glanced at the menu in front of me. "Do you want to order first . . . ?"

"I'm not very hungry," I said. It wasn't really a lie.

"Let me buy you a drink, then?"

"I'll take an ice tea."

"It's good," she said, then raised a manicured finger and of course managed to summon a waiter with it. Natalie ordered and the waiter gave me another one of those looks that said I didn't belong before tending to his duties. When he retreated, Natalie gave the room another of her almost paranoid surveys. She was careful to exclude me from it.

"I'm right here, Natalie," I said after her gaze had missed me for a third time. "Why don't you say what you want to say?"

Natalie made certain her fork, knife, and spoon were perfectly parallel. Then she looked at me and said, "I'm sorry for how I treated you. Please accept my apology."

I opened my mouth to tell her where she could put her apology. She saw me do it, braced for impact.

Then my back felt suddenly looser and my stomach felt suddenly calmer, and my precious anger, the fire I'd nursed for the better part of a very long year, died.

Gone.

Just like that.

Everyone at all the other tables seemed so much louder. I could hear someone complaining about their rabbit, how the sauce was too much mustard and not enough pepper. Someone at a nearby table was trying to calculate how much to leave as a tip.

"What a fucking waste," I said.

"I needed to say it," Natalie said quickly. "I needed to say it to you, in person. I know you can't just forgive and forget and I— What?"

I was shaking my head. "Wrong. You're wrong. Forgiven already. Not forgotten, but . . . I think I was just waiting on your apology."

She looked uncertainly at me, her left eyebrow arching gently. "If this was all it was going to take, I'd have apologized sooner."

"If you had apologized sooner, it probably wouldn't have been enough."

Natalie rested her forearms on the table, leaning in closer, searching my face. After a second she reached for my hands, and I let her take them.

"I never did it to hurt you," Natalie said. "It was a mistake. If I could undo the damage and the decision, I would in an instant. Do you believe that?"

"I do," I said.

"You can accept it? My apology?"

I really thought about it, and it took me the better part of a minute to be certain of my decision. But the fact was that, of all the things I was feeling, anger at Natalie wasn't one of them, at least not any longer. I wasn't even certain I was angry at Atticus anymore. The memory of the hurt and the betrayal, that remained. The slap of knowing that Natalie had gone to his bed, that Atticus had welcomed her there, that still stung.

But the anger I had was directed at someone else.

"I accept your apology," I said, and then squeezed her hands, just to prove it.

When she smiled she straightened up in her chair. She let go of me and pushed my menu towards my side of the table. "Does that mean you'll let me buy you lunch?"

"I will let you buy me lunch," I said.

We stayed at Chanterelle until close to four, and the crowd around us morphed and changed from the Late Lunchers to the Market Closers, and the martinis flowed like the waters of Niagara. It was nice to have my friend back, nice to be able to talk again, and by the time we finished our main course we had reassured each other enough that we were even willing to try joking a bit, and by dessert were making each other laugh so hard I was in danger of shooting coffee from my nose.

I'd missed her, and I'd missed her humor.

"We've gone round and round on it," she was saying. "Red Bear and then Bear Securities and even worse than that, and none of us could come up with a name until last night."

"And?"

"KTMH Security," Natalie said.

"Sounds like a radio station."

"All security, all the time. Kodiak, Trent, Matsui, and Herrera. That's what I was down here doing, filing the name and finishing up our business license. Dale and Atticus are supposedly picking out stationery."

"And Corry?"

"He's looking for office space. As of now, we're running the business out of Dale's garage in Forest Hills." Natalie rattled what was left of the ice in her glass, making the lemon quarter spin. "Which is easy as far as rent goes, but a pain in the ass when we want to meet clients."

"You've got clients already?"

"Are you kidding? We just got a name."

"This is the voice of KTMH radio," I said in my best announcer tone. "All the hits, all the time."

Natalie winced. "Very bad pun, especially since July."

I laughed because I hadn't intended the joke. Atticus hadn't told me much about the events of July, only that he and Natalie and the rest of his security crew had tangled with a professional killer. I assumed the good guys had won, because the good guys were all still alive, but I'd heard none of the details.

"Why haven't you seen him?"

"Who?"

"You know who." She took a sugar cube from the service bowl and used her coffee spoon to knock it into my lap.

"Not ready," I said.

"If you can forgive me, you can forgive him."

"I already have forgiven him."

She checked the maître d's position, then hit me with another sugar cube. "So see him already. You can't kiss and make up if you won't see him."

"I'll see him when I'm ready."

She leaned across the table and gestured for me to move closer, so she could whisper her secret. "The poor boy's in love with you," Natalie said.

I moved back against my chair. "Maybe that's the problem."

"More, please. Explain."

I blew out enough air to lift the hair off my forehead for a second.

"All right," I said. "A year or so ago, Atticus and I, we get together. Then, before even a week is out, you and he are in the sack. And I spend ten months or so trying to get past this, and after a while, I think I'm doing it. It's not easy, but I think I'm doing it."

Natalie had taken another sugar cube from the now near-empty bowl and was nibbling on it like a mouse eating cheese. I could tell she was listening because she was actually looking at me.

"Then, eight in the evening on the last weekend of July, he calls me and he says, 'Hey, it's me. . . .' "

I stopped, sipped my ice tea, which was now so diluted from the melted ice that it tasted neither iced nor tea-ed.

"And?" Natalie prodded.

"And I know it's him just from his voice. Just from those three fucking words, Natalie, and my heart's suddenly in my throat and then he says he's sorry but I almost miss that. I almost miss that because I think I'm going to cry, I'm so glad he's finally called."

Natalie said, "Go on."

"No," I said. "That's it."

Natalie nibbled her sugar cube away to nothing. Then she licked her fingertips and gestured to the waiter and the bill was on our table before her hand was back to her side. She took a wallet from her bag and selected a credit card. The waiter scooted away to ring up the sale.

"Well?" I asked when she still hadn't said anything.

"Well what?"

"Aren't you going to say anything? Tell me to get over it. Tell me I'm tormenting myself for no reason."

The waiter returned and Natalie deftly calculated the tip, scribbled her signature on the end of the paper, and then put her copy and her card back in her purse. She rose, putting the bag on her shoulder, and waited for me to get up as well. After a second I did, and we walked to the door, passing the maître d', who very conspicuously did not say "Come again."

We exited onto Harrison Street and Natalie looked up and down the block, then asked, "Where'd you park?"

"Not here. Why won't you answer me?"

She rolled her green eyes at me. "Because there's nothing I can say, Bridgett."

"You can come up with something."

She tugged the ends of her blazer down. I had been right; she was wearing a skirt. "It was great seeing you. Give me a call, we should go out later this week."

I practically hopped up and down on the sidewalk. "Natalie! Tell me what you think!"

She looked me over with a sigh. "You're fucked."

I searched my pockets for something curiously strong.

CHAPTER FIVE

So I got home and took a shower and put on my sweats and cleaned out the sink and the coffeepot. I checked my messages and sorted my mail and threw out the fourth Victoria's Secret catalogue that had come in as many days. I have never shopped from them and I don't know how I got on their mailing list and I wish they would stop; the number of trees they could save staggers the mind.

When the clock above my sink read six exactly, I reached for the phone. It was a cheap dime-store plastic clock, and its face was a mismatched collage of colors, decorated by hand. The clock was a present, and the person who had given it to me answered the phone.

"Ahoy, matey," Erika Wyatt said.

"Hey, brat."

"Hey, wench," she said with glee. "You want the boy?"

"Not yet," I said. "I want to know how the first day of college went."

The breath Erika Wyatt blew at the phone hurt my ear.

"It's just extension courses. I don't start college for real until the spring, and that's if I get accepted full-time."

"You're going to get accepted full-time, Erika," I said. "You're smart and you're capable and if you develop some discipline you'll be fine."

"I have wonderful discipline. Ask anyone in the S&M scene."

I laughed and heard Atticus in the background saying something about the bondage scene. Erika said, "He's threatening to paddle me if I don't hand you over."

"Talk about needing discipline," I said.

"Uh-huh. I think it's high time you tied him down and taught him a lesson or two."

Atticus's protest was loud.

"You better put him on," I told her. "You're scaring him."

"One frightened slave-to-be, coming right up," Erika said, and I heard the phone switching hands and it wasn't more than two seconds before he came on the line.

"Hey, you," Atticus said.

"Hey yourself," I said, then added, "Thanks for the flowers."

"You didn't mind?"

"I've never really been a flower girl. Not that I don't appreciate the gesture."

"Don't worry, I'm not offended. I'll just send you cases of Life Savers instead."

"Flamboyant, but certainly more useful. Tell me about your day."

"You first. I already know all about my day."

"Your logic amazes," I said, and told him a little about what had happened. About Lisa I said only that an old friend had called me early in the morning and that she was having trouble with a guy named Vince.

"How old a friend?" he asked.

"Very old. Ten years old."

"You've never mentioned her before."

"Lisa Schoof. We've been out of touch."

"This Vince guy, you going to need any help?"

"No, we'll handle it just fine," I said quickly.

He misinterpreted my speed. "I don't mean to press. You know you can call if you need an extra set of hands."

"I know," I said, and didn't correct his assumption, in part because it wasn't entirely wrong.

I've got two worlds of friends and associations, and I've done my best to keep them apart. Once people know you're a junkie—even a recovered junkie—they can never treat you the same. They treat you the way Jimmy treated me on the phone, with that cloying suspicious concern. Either that or they treat you with some kind of pity, going on about how awful it must have been, about how brave and strong you are to have defeated your awful addiction.

Atticus, Erika, Natalie, none of them knew, and none of them needed to know. Simple as that.

And I didn't feel guilty about keeping it to myself.

"Your turn," I told him. "Tell me about the birth pains of KTMH Security."

"It's all very exciting," Atticus said, and then told me about his search for appropriate letterhead, about how he and Dale had combed the city for the right logo, the right paper, and the right stationery, all at the right price. He told it like an epic, including—for my benefit—three gunfights and one car chase that resulted in Dale putting his van on two wheels to facilitate their escape from Mutant Nazi Frogmen pursuers.

"My hero," I said, when he was done.

"All in a day's work, ma'am. Any chance I can wow you some more over dinner?"

"Tonight's bad."

"Maybe tomorrow?"

"I'm going to be busy."

He almost managed to keep any frustration from crossing through the phone, but a little evaded him. "Well, let me know when you're free."

"Sure."

"Talk to you later," he said, and hung up.

After a second I did too, feeling like a heel.

My stereo was turned up way too loud and I didn't have any idea how long the knocking had been going on before it finally made it to my ears. At first I thought it was my neighbors demonstrating their dislike for L7—some people have no taste—but then it hit me that it was the door, and I zipped from my couch to my peephole and looked out.

Fish-eye view of Gabriel and Lisa Schoof.

I snapped back my locks and shouted, "Let me turn the music down," then went back to my main room and paused the CD. Gabriel came around the corner from the hall, dressed as I'd last seen him, the strap of his backpack slipping off his shoulder. Lisa was right behind him, and she had her same bag too.

"An unexpected surprise," I told them. "What's up?"

Lisa ruffled Gabriel's hair and said, "I changed my mind and decided to take you up on your invitation. If it's still okay, we'd like to spend the night."

"Great," I said, and then, "That's . . . great. You hungry, Gabe? How about a pizza?"

"Can we order one? Is that okay?"

I looked pointedly at Lisa and she moved her chin just enough to make sure the nod was clear.

"Sure," I said. "Why don't you get settled and I'll make the call. Pepperoni and mushrooms?"

"I like olives," he said.

"Then it'll have olives as well," I said, and made for the kitchen and the phone. I hit the button with the preprogrammed number for Sy's Pizzeria and ordered the pie, smiling all the while, watching over the counter while Lisa and Gabriel looked around my front room. Lisa pointed Gabriel to the couch and put her bag on the floor, then turned to look at me. She put the apology in her eyes and mouthed the words "Thank you."

I finished with the order and said, "It'll be forty minutes or so. Lisa, you want to help me make up the spare bed?"

"Can I try your PlayStation?" Gabriel asked. He was

staring at the game console, where it was positioned beneath my television.

"You betcha." I went to the television and set everything up, handing him one of the two controllers. "I've got Tekken 2 and—"

"No fighting games," Lisa said.

Gabriel rolled his eyes at his mother. "Please?"

"No fighting games. I don't want you beating on anyone, not even for pretend."

"It's just a game, Mom."

"I've got a driving game," I said, and found the CD. "Here you go. You can race a Porsche."

He took the CD and said, "Thank you," and I waited until the cars came on the screen before grabbing Lisa's arm and pulling her after me down the hall, to my bedroom.

"Am I suffering a memory lapse and I actually did invite you to spend the night?"

"I'm sorry about this." She sat down on the corner of my bed and looked at me like she was completely and utterly lost. "He was at work. Vince."

"I thought you went to school."

"After school. I'm working by Port Authority, at one of the peep shows. I've got to make the rent somehow." She ran her hands through her hair. "I was in the box and dancing and the blinds went up and Vince was in one of the cubes, just fucking sitting there, showing me his knife."

I sat down next to her.

"Totally fucked my set," Lisa muttered. "I'm probably going to get fired."

"Did he approach you at all? Try anything?"

She shook her head. "He just wanted to be sure I saw him. He didn't need to say anything. Then the blind dropped and when it came up the next time there was some other guy in the booth, some fat ass jerking off."

"Where was Gabe?"

"My aunt's been taking care of him after school when I have to work. He was with her." Lisa wrapped her arms around her middle and leaned forward. "I didn't see Vince when I punched out, so I went to Vera's and picked Gabe up and then got really scared. What if Vince was already at our place? What if he was waiting there for us?"

I put an arm around her shoulders. "Yeah," I said.

"I didn't want to impose." Lisa's control finally crumbled and she started crying. "I really didn't, but I didn't know where else to go and I was afraid Vince was following me, that if we stayed at Vera's he'd just show up there . . ."

"It's all right," I said. "I don't mind, and you're not imposing."

Lisa nodded and coughed and fought to stop crying, and I got off the bed and grabbed a box of tissues from the bathroom. She used a handful to blow her nose, then another handful to wipe her smudged face, and then looked around for a place to dump the trash. She'd put on a lot more makeup to cover her bruises, to hide them while she showed her body at work, and her mascara was running, mingling with the foundation and blush.

I took the tissues from her and threw them into the trash can by the toilet, then dropped a washcloth into the sink and ran hot water over it. I wrung it out, then brought it over to Lisa.

"I can't let him do this to me," Lisa said. "I can't let him destroy my life."

"I know."

"Then it's like I said."

"No."

"He won't stop, Bridgett!" She squeezed the washcloth hard enough to force new drops of water out and between her fingers.

"He will stop, Lisa," I said. "Once he understands that it's more dangerous to come after you than to leave you alone, he'll back off. That's what we've got to do. We've got to scare him. We've got to teach him a lesson."

"He won't learn," she muttered. "He won't listen, and he won't change. He is what he is, and he won't stop."

"We'll make him listen."

"How?"

"I'll come up with something," I said. "Trust me."

"I do trust you, Bridgett. I always have."

Dragging the washcloth over her face, she wiped more of her makeup away. The remains of her mascara gave her the hollow eyes of a war refugee.

The pizza came while Lisa was in the shower, and after we'd finished dining from the box, we all got ready to retire for the night. By the time the pie was gone, Gabe's eyes were unfocused and his yawns profound. Lisa and I made up the small futon in my office for him, and while she tucked her son in bed, I got out a spare blanket and pillow and made up the couch in the front room.

"I'll take it," Lisa said. "I'm used to sleeping on a couch."

"You'll take my bed," I said. "You're a guest in my home and that's the end of the discussion."

She tried arguing with me but I was fierce and adamant and finally won out. Lisa went down the hall and offered me a final "Sleep well," before disappearing into my room.

I yawned and stretched and contorted myself onto the couch, and even though I was truly tired, failed to fall asleep. The last time I'd slept on my couch, I'd had an Atticus to keep me warm, which is almost as nice as an afghan, or had seemed that way at the time. We hadn't even fooled around that night—not for lack of trying—and I'd ended up sleeping more on than beside him through an amazing act of contortion. But we'd somehow fit, and it'd been a nice way to sleep together and, in my memory, very romantic indeed.

All that was almost two years ago, and the couch no longer fit, and very little else seemed nice. I could practically hear Mr. Jones already, looking for a nice spot where he could sit and watch and bide his own sweet time until I fell asleep.

But when I did, I didn't dream of anything at all.

And when I woke up, I was looking up the barrel of my father's gun.

CHAPTER SIX

When my Da was one of New York's Finest, all cops carried the Model 10 Smith & Wesson with the blue steel finish and a two-inch barrel. They don't much anymore, because for many, six shots just aren't enough to get the job done, especially when the return fire is coming from some sort of fully automatic weapon. The NYPD now lets its officers pick from a choice of department-approved pistols, and most of the younger cops carry semiautos with ten-plus shots.

My Da would've been disgusted. He would've said, "It's not the number, it's the placement."

Then he would've added something unkind about department standards, about how low they'd fallen, about how much trouble rookies cause. Then he would've had a Guinness and complained about that too.

"Put that the fuck down," I said. I did not screech, but I did not sound like my normal smoke-and-whiskey self either. I probably sounded a lot like a woman who'd woken up to find a gun pointing in her direction.

Gabriel jumped at the sound of my voice. His arms came

down quickly and he stopped himself from trying to hide the Smith & Wesson behind his back. His face ran through three distinct phases at having been caught—surprise, guilt, and then a passable attempt at innocence.

I sat up and glared and held out my right palm.

"Sorry," he muttered, and started to hand the gun over.

"Not that way," I said. "Never barrel first. You let me take it by the butt, by the handle."

He nodded and quickly turned the pistol in his hand, and I took it by the butt and pointed it at the floor and swung out the cylinder. It was empty, just as I'd left it. I snapped the cylinder closed and put the gun beside me on the couch and pulled my blanket off my legs. I'd slept in shorts and a T-shirt, and didn't feel an overpowering need for modesty. Gabriel was wearing only his pants from the day before.

According to the sunlight shining on my parquet floor, it was morning. According to Erika's collage clock on the kitchen wall, it was sometime around six.

Gabriel wasn't looking at me. He was looking at the edge of the coffee table by my knee. The attempted innocence had passed, and he was biting his lower lip, anticipating my scolding.

"If you know you shouldn't have been playing with it," I said, "why'd you take it out of the box in the first place?"

"I didn't know it was in the box," he said, and his eyes darted to the open closet, then to the open shoe box, and then back to my knee. "I was looking for games."

"You thought I might have games in my closet?"

"I wanted to play Tekken. You going to tell Mom?"

I rubbed my eyes and felt my hair sticking out and imagined how awful I looked. I thought about being ten and being fascinated by my father's gun, and I tried to remember what Da had done under similar circumstances. Admittedly, he'd never woken up to me waving my .38 around the house. No, I'd been waving it around the backyard at my baby sister and he'd been up for hours already when he caught me pretending I was a miniature version of Kate Jackson.

My ass had literally stung for a week.

Didn't think I had the authority to issue a spanking to my friend's son.

I patted the couch on my right side, away from where I'd set the gun. "Sit," I said.

Gabriel took a step, stopped, then finished the journey. After he was seated he resumed staring fixedly at my knee.

I picked up the revolver, still pointing the barrel at the ground, and swung out the cylinder again. "This was empty," I said, showing it to him. "And that's why I'm not going to knock your block off, buster. But you don't ever pick up a gun unless you're under supervision. Never, ever, because you don't know if it's loaded or not. A gun is not a toy. A gun is something that is used to kill people. *Comprende?*"

Gabriel nodded.

"Okay," I said. "I want your promise that you're never going to pick up a gun again, not even as a joke, unless you've got an adult supervising you."

"I promise," he said quickly.

I looked at the top of his head and thought about thumping it. When I was his age, I didn't really listen either.

"I just wanted to see what it was like."

"And?"

"It's scary," he said, and risked glancing at me. When he saw I wasn't going to eat his face, he added, "It's heavy. Is it yours?"

"It is now. It used to be my Da's. This is the gun he bought when he joined the police."

"He let you have his gun?"

"I got it when he died."

His eyes widened. "Did he get shot?"

"No. He had cancer." I snapped the cylinder closed again and turned the pistol in my hand. The blued finish was replaced on the right side by a piece of stainless steel.

"Why's it like that? Two different colors?"

I grinned, remembering. "What handed are you?"

"Um, left."

"So am I. So was my dad. See this piece, the stainless steel piece? That's called the side-plate. When my Da wore the gun in his pants, that was the part that rested against his hip." I poked Gabe in the matching part of his anatomy. He giggled and squirmed.

"So?"

"Well, when I was your age the summers were always really hot—"

"They're hot now."

"Not like then, buster. And my Da would wear the gun in his pants when he was off-duty, and he'd sweat like a horse. All that salt, it corroded the steel. See these, the bolts?" I turned the gun in my hand, showing him the four blue steel screws that held the stainless steel plate to the gun.

He nodded.

"Well, this piece, that used to be like the rest of the gun. But my Da sweat so much, he had to order a replacement. He ended up needing to order three, maybe four replacements for the side-plate. And finally he decided that he was just throwing his money away, so he paid for this new piece, which is stainless steel and won't corrode."

"But it makes it look . . . well, weird, kind of," Gabriel said.

"Yeah, it does, but when it was in his holster, you couldn't see that part, because it was against his body. And if it ever came out of the holster, it probably came out because there was trouble, and if there was trouble, that meant that people weren't really looking at his gun."

"You mean like he had to shoot it."

"Yeah, like that."

"Did he ever kill anybody?"

"Not a soul," I said. "Thirty years and he never had to shoot once."

It wasn't the answer he had wanted, and it showed in his face. "Never? Not even to stop somebody from hurting somebody?"

"Never. He didn't need it."

"But how did he get them to stop doing it?" In his lap his hands had turned to small fists. "If he saw someone hurting someone, how did he stop it?"

"Different ways," I said. I knew what he was after and I wasn't going to give it to him, same as I wouldn't give it to his mother. "Mostly by talking. My Da was a big man, and he had a loud voice, and people listened to him."

Gabriel's mouth twisted into a frown as he looked away again. "That wouldn't work," he muttered.

"I'll tell you a story," I said. "This is a story my Da used to tell all the time, anybody who'd listen, he'd tell it. It's about this Irish poet, a guy named Thomas Moore. He was really famous in his day, and rich too. Famous and rich.

"So anyway, Thomas Moore is out one day looking at the Meeting of the Waters, this meeting of rivers in Ireland, and he's just staring because it's so beautiful, it's all he's seeing. It's *so* beautiful, get it? He's totally into the way the lights look on the water, stuff like that. Doesn't see anything else.

"And this bum comes up behind him, and he's in sad shape. Holes in his shoes, clothes filthy and torn, head to toe, this guy's dressed in rags. And this bum, he asks Thomas Moore if he can spare a little change."

"Like on the subways," Gabriel said.

"Exactly. And just like on the subways, Thomas Moore ignores this bum. Pretends he's not even there, just keeps staring at the beautiful water.

"So the bum, he knows Moore's a poet, right? So he clears his throat a little and then he makes up a little poem right then and there.

" 'If Moore was a man without place of abode,' says the bum. 'Without clothes on his back, and him walking the road, without food in his belly or shoes on his feet, he wouldn't give a damn where the bright waters meet.' "

Gabriel smirked, probably at the "damn."

"And Thomas Moore, he just turns around, and he reaches into a pocket, and he gives the bum half a sovereign, which is way a lot of money back then. And he says to the bum, 'I couldn't have done better myself,' and he thanks him. And off they all go on their separate ways."

"That's it?" he asked, looking skeptical.

"Sure," I said. "That's it."

"Why'd he thank the bum?"

"That's the whole point of the story," I said.

Gabriel considered. "Stupid story," he said.

I shook my head and started to get up and saw Lisa at the end of the hallway, watching us. Before I could wish her good morning she snapped, "What the hell are you doing with that thing out around my son?"

"I was showing it to him," I said.

"Dammit, Bridgett! Put it away. I don't want Gabe near it."

"I'm putting it away," I said mildly, reaching for the shoe box. I wrapped my father's pistol in its cloth and closed the box and took it over to the closet.

"Put it on the shelf," Lisa said, sounding a little shrill. "Out of the way of little hands, all right?"

I tensed my shoulders but didn't turn around, just stored the box on the high shelf, next to my collection of baseball caps.

"God, you just leave it lying around?"

I closed the closet door and turned to face her. "I don't normally have visitors under the legal drinking age," I said. Both mother and son were looking at me, and while Lisa's stare was crammed with maternal indignation, Gabriel's was dousing me in gratitude. We both knew I'd just saved his hide big time.

I said, "Lisa, why don't you take your shower and I'll start making breakfast. There are towels already out."

Lisa turned her head to her son, then looked back at me, and I thought she'd probably guessed what had really happened. She kept her lips tight together like she wanted to keep her mouth entirely closed while she thought about what to say, just in case something slipped out prematurely. The swelling on her lower lip looked pretty much as bad as it had the night before. Then she turned and made for the bathroom.

I went into the kitchen and started morning coffee, got down three bowls and a box of Froot Loops. Gabriel wandered into the kitchen and I poured him a glass of orange juice. He drank it while standing, wandering out of the kitchen again to look down the hall at the closed bathroom door. Then he returned and handed me the empty glass.

"It's still a stupid story," he said.

"Don't ever go near that gun again," I said.

CHAPTER SEVEN

Fort Totten is on the north edge of Queens, and I drove Lisa out there after dropping Gabriel off in front of his school. Lisa fretted all the way.

"They'll think I'm not taking care of him. They'll think I'm ignoring his needs again. If one of his teachers calls the City and says—"

"You really need to relax," I interrupted. "He is well fed, he is clean, he has had a full night's sleep. Lots of kids wear the same thing two days in a row. You're wearing the same thing two days in a row, for fuck's sake."

"That's totally different."

"Not totally," I said.

Lisa swore at me, then swore at me again as I took a sudden and fortuitous opportunity to pass a garbage truck on the Cross Island Parkway. "Would you slow down?"

"I am going slow," I soothed. I was too. We weren't even doing sixty.

"I can't believe I'm worried about tonight. I'm not even going to live long enough for Vince to kill me."

"He's not going to kill you. Stop worrying, I've got a plan."

"Which is?"

"I'll tell you when it's time."

Lisa was upset enough that she actually looked away from the windshield and at me. "No, I want to know. This is about me, remember?"

"You've got school to deal with first," I said. "When it's time, I'll let you know. What's your day like?"

She glared at me, then cringed in her seat as she thought she saw me nearly miss an ancient Chevy that was trying to crowd our lane. "I'm done with class around one. Then I've got to dance again."

"Where?"

"Same place as yesterday. I'm there until five."

"Skip it today. Vince may show up again."

"I can't afford to lose the money."

"You want me to stop by? Just to be there? You know, moral support."

Lisa watched the traffic for the better part of a mile before nodding.

"I'll be by around four, then," I said. "Gabriel's going to your aunt's?"

"Yeah."

"You should call her, tell her that he needs to spend the night."

"I can't do that," she protested. "He'll end up wearing the same thing three days in a row."

"I'm sure there's clean clothes at your aunt's."

"No, there aren't." She sounded awfully shrill. Worrying about Gabriel's clothes was easier than worrying about Vince's impending visit.

"When I drop you off, give me your keys. I'll go by your place, pick up some clean clothes for both of you, and take them to your aunt's, okay? Just tell her that I'll be coming by."

"He's got a Knicks shirt that he really likes," Lisa told me. "Ewing's on it. I washed it on Saturday so he could wear it this week."

"I'll bring the Knicks shirt. Where's your aunt live?"

"Vera's got a place on the Lower East Side." She gave me the address.

I stopped at the security shack at the entrance of Fort Totten, rolled down the window and told the middle-aged and clearly bored badge that I was dropping Lisa off for a class. He waved me through, and I drove up past the parade ground, where a flock of birds were clustered in its center, then along a narrow road until Lisa told me to stop. She unsnapped her belt and opened the door, getting out of the car before grabbing her bag. I leaned across the seat and looked up at her while she searched for her keys, setting the green bag on the roof of my green car.

"Relax," I said. "Chill. Everything's going to be fine."

Lisa dropped her keys into my waiting palm and met my eyes. I tried to look assured and confident, to show her a face full of hope and resolve.

She shook her head and walked off without another word.

I stayed at the office until noon, going through the motions of business while developing a plan. From what I knew of Vince, any subtlety I tried to bring to tonight's meeting would be wasted.

I'd met him once, years ago, when I'd gone looking for Lisa after her last fall from the wagon. He'd been working a corner around Powell in the high One-Twenties, identical to his thousand-plus brothers who slung dope and coke from corner perches, rolling wads of bills tight until they could finally fit the money into their pockets.

I closed my eyes and conjured his face, and my memory supplied nothing. I couldn't even remember what Vince Lark looked like.

A nasty-looking pit bull was taking a shit in Lisa's hallway by the mailboxes, and when it had finished its deposit, it growled ominously at me. I kept my eyes on it as I made my way up the stairs, and it followed from a distance. When I reached the door, it barked indignantly, then trotted down the hall.

Two of the letters were clearly bills and marked OPEN IMMEDIATELY, and I pocketed both, leaving the rest of the mail on the card table with its split vinyl top. I went through Lisa's suitcase and pulled out some clothes for her, then found the Knicks shirt in Gabriel's room. I picked out clean underwear and socks and pants, and all of the clothes were well worn, though none of them had holes. I put them all in a plastic shopping bag.

No one stopped me or asked me any questions coming or going, and when I came back out, three teens were lurking around my Porsche. No harm, no foul, at least not yet, but I thumbed the alarm in my pocket and my car started screaming. The teens retreated, probably wondering what they had done to enrage my automobile, and they stared at me as I drove away.

Vera's was next, a third-floor apartment only fifteen blocks away, by the post office on Grand Street. Her place was nearly twice as big as Lisa and Gabe's, which meant that it was merely small rather than degrading. It took her only a minute after I rang the bell to open the door.

"Bridgett Logan?"

"That's right," I said.

"Lisa said you would be coming by. Vera Grimshaw. You don't remember me?"

"How could I forget Lisa's only caring relation?"

"Hell, it's been ten years." Vera held the door open and gestured me inside, but I shook my head and stayed where I was, handing the shopping bag of clothes over. She had a Newport burning in her mouth, and her voice was cigarette-cured. "What can I tell Gabriel?"

"Lisa will be by in the morning, before he has to go to school," I said. "I brought some clothes for her too. She'll probably want to change."

The cigarette twitched in Vera's mouth. "That girl just goes from shit to shit. She's been clawing at the world for years now, just doesn't get a break."

"She's getting one tonight," I said.

For the evening's activities, I had some shopping to do, so I took the Porsche back to the garage and locked it up good and tight. I'm paying more money than God to keep the damn car off the streets, but I don't really have a choice, and I knew it would be like that when I bought the damn thing. Every morning when I check the space and see that the car is still parked where I left it, I marvel at my luck.

Back home, I opened Lisa's bills and paid each in full, one to Visa and one to Con Ed. Visa was killing her with interest. Then I took a quick shower, changed into suitable work clothes, and made for the Kmart next to Madison Square Garden. I bought what I needed, took a cab to the U-Haul place on Eleventh Avenue and Fifty-second, and picked out a truck. The guy I rented the truck from was twice my age, five foot ten, and greasy. He was also all over me, offering me first an appliance dolly, then a selection of cardboard boxes, and finally, himself.

"You need help moving, hey? I'm strong, could help you out. Easier when you've got friends, know what I mean?"

"I've got it covered," I said.

He glanced at my shopping bag. "Playing ball?"

"Softball league," I said.

"Hardball's the way to go," he said. "You should play basketball, WNBA shit, you're tall enough. Really tall. How tall are you?"

Suppressing a groan, I said, "Six one."

"No shit?" He wiped some of the shine off his forehead with a corner of his work shirt and smiled at me until I suppressed another groan. "Kidding me. I'm six one."

The second the words came out of his mouth, I knew how the conversation would end. It happens to me all the time, at least twice a month, more if I've been hitting the bars or the clubs. Every fucking male over five feet ten inches believes himself to be six one. I don't know why they think this, what sociological reasons are hard at work in the culture to urge men taller and taller, but they always ask, and I always answer, and it always ends the same way.

No way in hell this bozo was six one.

"No, I don't think so," I said.

"Sure I am, yeah. Here, let me check." He stepped close enough so that I could smell the bologna he'd had at lunch, and his nose didn't even meet my chin. He put a hand on his head and moved it forward until it bumped my forehead. I stared at him.

"Fuck," he said. "No way you're six one. You're six three, at least."

"How could I have been so wrong for so long?" I asked. "How much for the truck?"

He finally took the hint and backed off, taking care of the paperwork. I paid and then got the keys and the hell out of there and was at Dance Girls Dance by ten of four. At least I think it was called Dance Girls Dance, because that's what the sign above the door screamed at me, but it might have been an order. Or perhaps a plea, or maybe even a polite request. I really doubted the last, but I try to keep an open mind.

I've noticed that such signs never say Dance Women Dance. It's the sort of thing that could keep me up nights if I let myself think about it for too long.

Inside was spotted with the usual porn buffet, racks of videos and magazines, shelves of toys that are euphemistically called marital aids. If an inflatable sheep or a two-pronged vibrator or a four-inch-thick, three-foot-long double-headed dildo is a marital aid, then I'm of the opinion that the whole institution of marriage is in trouble.

Deep, dark, dank fucking trouble, at that.

I looked at the consumer base, a no-no in shops such as these where a meeting of eyes can mean either a proposition or an accusation. No sign of anyone that I remembered as Vincent Lark. One man returned my gaze, and he had enough sense to look away quickly. But I felt the stares on my back and my body, and I bit down hard on a Life Saver to keep from doing anything I'd regret later.

I worked my way to the back of the shop and up a flight of steps to where the floor show was running. My boots were loud and the place felt quiet, but I know that the quiet was my imagination. I don't have a problem with sex and I don't have a problem with masturbation, but the problem I have with porn is quite simple: There's no joy in it whatsoever.

A row of doors ran the length of the floor, most of them shut, with one at the end of the hall marked Private. It was a lot cleaner than I'd thought it would be. At least my boots weren't sticking to the floor.

I took a breath and a booth, shutting the door behind me, and checked the chair before taking my seat. The chair was hard black plastic and clean, with a small black plastic trash can at its side filled with discarded pieces of toilet paper. The dispenser was mounted on the wall, the kind that spits out sheets rather than holds a roll. The room had that almost-bleach smell.

"Come one, come all," I muttered.

The music was audible in the booth, but barely, some funky, bass-heavy rhythm designed for gyration. I fed a five into the money-sucker on the wall, and the blinds shot up and the speakers in the little booth kicked on, the noise immediately tripling. The window was tinted but was not one-way glass, and I wondered how hard it had to be to dance and see the faces and the working arms and nothing else.

There were two on display in the box, an African-American woman in the midst of shimmying out of her red short-shorts, and Lisa, clad in a black G-string and long black gloves and black fuck-me pumps and nothing else. Lisa's back was to me at the start, and she was giving most of her show for a viewer on the opposite side of the stage. Body makeup covered the scars that her gloves didn't.

I ate another Life Saver, the strawberry mingling with the other scent, then leaned forward, hoping she would see me through the tinting, just to let her know that I was here. It took another twenty seconds before she worked her way back to my window, and she dropped her stage face and grinned and waggled her tits my way. She tossed her hair and I saw her mouth move as she spoke to her partner, and the black woman glided closer. Lisa said something else out of the corner of her mouth; the other woman arched an eyebrow, then laughed and nodded.

They glided their way back to the center of the box and began a tandem act, pointing most of it at my window, really mugging for my benefit. The music had changed to something slower, and both women altered their moves to match it, sliding over one another provocatively. I sat back and told myself not to blush, and they continued to rub and play against one another for almost two minutes before Lisa caught something out of the corner of one eye, jerked her head, and froze for a moment, missing the beat.

I bolted from the booth and went left, trying to figure out what she had seen and which room it had come from. The doors down the hall around the corner were all closed. I tried the knobs on three back to back, catching one guy with his hands working furiously in his lap, another with his fingers in his mouth, and then, in the third, an empty room with the window shuttered. I dug my fingers in at the edge of the window and tried to get the blinds open, but they had locked tight and I had no purchase. I forced a buck into the reader, and the blinds shot up, and there was a piece of paper taped to the glass. I tore it off and read what had been written.

P.S. 64 is a nice little school.
Tonight. All my $$$.

I crumpled the sheet and left the booth, checking the hallway again and thinking that if I'd been on my toes and out of the box, I'd have caught Vince at his game. The man with the busy hands was looking at me, his cheeks bright red. He hadn't bothered to zip his trousers.

"You're leaking," I told him as I went past.

Lisa was wearing a robe, had just come out from the end of the hall as I turned the corner. She was sweating and breathless and she shouted, "Did you see him?"

"Gone," I said.

"He's going after Gabe! We've got to call Vera—"

I took her shoulders and stopped her from trying to get past me. "It's a warning, that's all. He's just spooking you."

"But he knows!"

"Of course he knows," I said. "He's pushing your buttons, Lisa. Don't let him."

"It's my son!"

"It's just a scare, it's nothing. Even if he's got the stones to try anything with Gabe, he won't until tomorrow. He wants his money first."

She bit down on her lip, eyes fried with fear, trying to believe me.

I said, "If he tries anything with Gabe, he knows we'll bring the police into it. He doesn't want that any more than you do. He's just scaring you, just pushing buttons, making certain you'll pay up. That's it, that's all it is, Lisa."

The sweat on her brow trickled along her temples as she shut her eyes and shook her head, leaning into me. Behind her, the African-American dancer leaned her head past the opened door at the end of the hall, saying, "Lise girl, you okay?"

"She's fine," I told her.

The woman frowned, concerned, leaning out a little farther. She hadn't bothered to cover up. "You want to go, I'll take the rest of the set. Ain't no thang for me, Lise."

Lisa shrugged my hands from her shoulders. "Would you do that, Meg?"

"I'll square it with Baker," Meg promised her. "You go do what you've got to do, we'll all be fine here."

"I'll owe you for this. I'll pick up one of your dances, if you want."

"That'd be fine. Come on back in here, you're giving the boys a free show."

Lisa and I looked around. Most of the doors had opened, and, in fact, there were plenty more eyes on us than necessary. When Lisa turned, I followed her back down the hall, into the little dressing room. After we'd gotten inside, Meg leaned her head back out and said, "You all want to see girls, get back in the booths."

Sweat and cigarettes and alcohol stank up the dressing room, and as Lisa began hunting for her street clothes, Meg offered me her hand. "Megarth Lee Tabor," she said. Her lack of clothing did not translate to a lack of manners. "You her special friend?"

"Not that special. Bridgett Logan. It's a pleasure."

"She's helping me," Lisa said.

Megarth Lee Tabor crossed both her arms beneath substantial breasts. "You going to put that boy down, the one who's been scaring our Lisa here?"

"Like the dog he is," I answered.

"You do that shit. You put him way the fuck down." She squeezed Lisa's shoulder. "You don't worry about Baker. I'll fix him for you."

"Thanks, Meg."

"Girls got to stick together," Meg said, then headed back into the box.

Silently, Lisa wiped away most of her makeup and then changed her clothes. The music had never stopped, and in the dressing room was louder than it had been with the speakers on in the booths. I nibbled away two Life Savers after offering the roll to Lisa. She just shook her head at me, like I was insulting her with the offer of candy. When she was finished dressing she wadded her G-string and gloves into a tight ball and thrust them deep into her bag, following them with her shoes.

"I'm going to call Vera," she told me. "There's a phone on the corner."

Lisa showed me a back way out of the building, down a flight of stairs that dropped us onto Ninth Avenue, around the corner from where I'd left the U-Haul. We opened the door into a group of tourists who dodged us wordlessly, and Lisa marched straight to a beat-up pay phone. She searched her pockets for a quarter, and I offered her one but she refused, continuing until she found two dimes and a nickel in the side pocket of her green vinyl bag.

While she made her call, I looked at the street and didn't see anyone who looked to me like a Vincent Lark. I saw people I didn't like the looks of for sure—folks who'd been driven out of Times Square in the last few years, looking for greener pastures for their wares—but there weren't that many. I remembered a time when I could hit Times Square and be hooked up with some really good shit in less than three minutes.

Lisa was off the phone and saying, "Vera says Gabe's fine. I told her that I didn't want him going out and she said she'd make sure they stayed inside together."

"I told you he was fine."

Lisa opened her bag again, shielding it from the pedestrians around us, and found her sunglasses inside, cheap black wannabe Ray-Bans that were enormous on her tiny face. "You gonna tell me now?"

"Follow," I commanded her, and led the way back around the block to where I'd left the U-Haul. It was still parked safe and sound, though a flyer for Dance Girls Dance had been stuck under the windshield wiper. The flyer was bright yellow and I crumpled it, tossing it into the gutter before unlocking the cab. I waited for Lisa to get in, then started the engine and pulled out. The truck was nothing like my car, but that didn't stop me from trying to drive it like it was.

"Where's the Porsche?" Lisa asked.

"Wouldn't work for what we need," I said. "Vince is going to be riding in the back."

Even behind her oversized sunglasses I could tell she'd arched her eyebrows. "And how the hell are we going to convince him to come for a ride?"

"Who said he had a choice?"

From five o'clock, when we reached her apartment, until a quarter of eleven, I went over it with Lisa again and again, making certain she had it all down, and had it down good enough so that if things went wrong she'd fly on autopilot. She gave me grief about almost all of it too, from who would have the bat to who would drive the truck to how we were going to move him.

What if the neighbors hear us? she asked. What if they call the cops? What if it doesn't work, if it doesn't take, if he just comes back again and again?

"I'm not going to kill him," I said. We were laying the plastic down over the carpet, and the sheets crinkled and fluttered whenever either of us moved.

"Then I'll do it," Lisa hissed. She'd been whispering since it had grown dark. "It's got to be done."

"It does not got to be done," I said. "And you won't do it. I won't let you. Now, you let that go, or I'm packing all this up and heading home and getting a good night's sleep."

She fumed at me, then went to tear the duct tape strips. I finished laying out the rest of our things, and at twenty past eleven, told her to change and get into position. I laid down the cotton bedsheet I'd bought, spreading it over the plastic so the glare wouldn't show. The noise would give the plastic away, but by that time, my hope was that Vince would be worrying about too many other things to ask why he was standing on plastic sheeting.

Lisa made her bed and changed into her nightclothes— boxers and tank—then mussed her hair with both hands.

"Look like I've been asleep?"

"Bad dreams and all," I assured her.

Lisa parked on the floor. "Why can't I just be on the couch? We want him to think he woke me."

"Because if you get on the couch you might really fall asleep. Uncomfortable is good."

Lights off, I put my back to the wall by the door and sank down on the floor, the Louisville Slugger in my lap, listening to my heart beating over the sounds of the other apartments. The pit bull barked once in a while, and every time it did, Lisa cursed it softly. Either right below us or right above us, some very noisy love was being made.

"You been seeing anybody?" Lisa asked.

"Not really," I said.

"Meg thought you and me, we were together, you know?"

"I always thought you were cute. You currently unattached?"

Lisa nodded. "Where'm I going to find a good guy, huh? Single mom, ten-year-old son, living here. Not going to happen. Maybe after I graduate, get posted to a crew, maybe then. What about your sister? Cashel married now?"

"She's in a committed relationship. I haven't seen her in a while."

The lovers' song hit its crescendo, then faded. I thought I heard a couple of roaches scrabbling across the counters in the kitchenette and the ticking of the old alarm clock on the table.

"I'm so tired of being afraid," Lisa whispered.

By the luminous dial on my watch it was one forty-three when he showed up. I heard the tread coming down the hall, stepping like it was trying too hard to be light. The whole building had gone silent and perhaps to sleep in the hours before, and the sound of footsteps in the empty hall was surprisingly loud.

"Up," I whispered to Lisa. "Get ready."

She scrambled to her feet and shook her legs awake, then climbed onto the couch, spreading the blanket over her as if she'd been sleeping. The streetlight hit her just enough to keep her visible, but it fell short of the floor in front of her. The plastic didn't show.

When he started pounding on the door, I stood, checked my grip on the bat.

"Pay time, Lise! Open it or I'll break it fucking in!"

Lisa glanced at me and I nodded and she called, "It's open." The quaver in her voice sounded a lot like sleep and a lot like fear.

"You're a smart cunt," I heard Vince say.

The knob twisted and the door swung open with force. I'd positioned myself carefully and the door missed me when it hit the wall, but only by half an inch. The light from the hall fell in a short shaft that didn't reach Lisa, but illuminated the dark blue sheet on the floor. I could see the edge of his shadow.

If he figured what the sheet was for, we were screwed. But I didn't think he would. I didn't think that he had even considered that Lisa would oppose or refuse or fight him.

And I was right.

He stepped into the room, saying, "I hope you got my money, Lise. Else I'm going to . . . have to . . ."

He looked down at his Nikes, probably wondering why his expensive sneakers were making such a sudden and strange crackling sound.

I kicked the door gently shut with the toe of my boot.

Vince turned his head, still not getting it. He looked right at me, his eyes widening, white and dumb. That one look at his face was all I needed to remember him, and he didn't look different at all. Narrow white face with no chin and black hair that collected grease like the fan over a quick-order grill.

"What the fuck is this?" he asked.

"Batter up," I said, and then swung away.

CHAPTER EIGHT

I rolled him out of the back of the U-Haul at seven past five, and Vince hit the Hudson shore like a big sack of trash. The Manhattan skyline sparkled with predawn lights in distant windows.

I pulled the pillowcase off his head and stuffed it into the trash bag that contained the items we'd taken from his pockets—his knife, his disposable lighter, a great big Philly blunt packaged in a Ziploc bag. I dropped his wallet beside him and sliced the duct tape on his hands and feet with the knife. Then I wadded up the tape, put it and the blade back into the trash bag, and chucked the lot into the river, following it with the bat. I turned away before the splash.

The pulse at Vince's neck was steady enough. His right foot was turned ten degrees the wrong way, though no bone was popping through his skin. When I pulled my hand back, Vince made a sound like he was about to awaken with a hangover.

When I was in the cab of the truck once more, I looked back a final time and thought I saw him move, but I didn't wait and tried not to care one way or another. Lisa kept her silence up, just stared straight out the windshield and over the engine cowling. I drove us into Union City, then turned south, angling for the Lincoln Tunnel.

"Did he say anything more?" she asked.

"No."

"But he'll stop? He'll leave us alone now?"

I nodded and Lisa didn't add a follow-up question. By the time we'd cleared the tunnel the silence was getting to me, so I turned on the radio and caught the morning news, kept it on until I found the car wash I wanted off Houston, one that opened early. Lisa got out with the remaining trash, the plastic, and the sheet, and after the truck went through the water I opened the back and hosed out the bed. Some of the water ran brown, but that could have been rust as easily as blood.

Didn't keep me from asking the Blessed Mother's forgiveness, though.

We turned back uptown when we were finished and returned the U-Haul. It went smoothly, the guy I'd dealt with the day before nowhere to be seen, and I handed over the keys and got my deposit back. Lisa asked the attendant about which kind of dolly was needed to move a refrigerator, and when he moved from the counter to show her how the straps worked, I reached across and took his copy of my bill too. We left, grabbed a cab, and rolled back to my place.

"You want coffee?" I asked, and when Lisa just shook her head I nodded, took a book of matches from the drawer by the sink, and headed to the bathroom. I burned all the receipts over the toilet, flushed away the ashes, and then took a shower quicker than I wanted to. When I dried off, I felt marginally cleaner, but no better.

Then, dressed for work and with Lisa following silently behind, we got the Porsche and I drove over to Vera's. It was only seven when we arrived.

"You want me to come up?" I asked before she got out of the car.

"No." She didn't move, looking out the window at her aunt's apartment building. "Gabe's probably still asleep."

"Maybe just getting up." I opened a new roll of Life Savers, took one, then another. Hot Cinnamon ran a nice burn along my tongue.

"He won't come back?" Lisa asked.

"No."

She turned in the seat, unfastening her belt, facing me. "I didn't think he'd beg."

I kept myself from saying anything, especially from saying that I'd known he would.

As far as execution, it had gone exactly as I'd planned it. When the tables had turned, Vince had caved quickly, his initial threats of revenge turning to protests turning to pleas. He'd tried explaining himself, tried explaining that he'd only come back for Lisa because he'd had to, that he was desperate for money, that he had people after him who wouldn't take late payment as an option. He'd been skimming from his package, he'd told us, and now his connection wanted the missing money.

"Tough shit," I'd told him, and used the bat on his ribs, and Vince had stopped trying to explain then and had finally started to listen. I'd spelled it out as plainly as I could, and I'd used violence to emphasize the lesson, and I'd underlined the whole package with the implicit threat—I could kill him if I wanted to. That I hadn't was an act of capricious mercy and nothing he could count on for the future.

To my mind, what we'd dumped on the shore was broken and finished. There was no way Vincent Lark would ever find the courage to come after Lisa or Gabriel again.

"He comes again, he's dead," I told Lisa. "If he knows nothing else, he knows that. He'll leave the two of you alone."

Lisa's teeth worked on her lower lip, carefully avoiding the swelling, before she finally shook her head.

"Maybe this has just made it worse."

"He's a coward, Lise. He's gone for good."

Her teeth released her lip, and she tried a nod that was only a little more perceptible than the shake before. "Gone," she echoed.

"For good."

She reached out across the seat for me and I put an arm

around her shoulders and gave her a hug, and she put her face against my neck.

"Go see your son," I said in her ear.

She sniffed and nodded and I felt resolution in her posture, the flow of a deep breath and then the squaring of her shoulders. Lisa had made a decision, and it showed in her face when she pulled back, and when she planted a little kiss on my lips, it surprised me more than it embarrassed her.

"Thank you for this," she said.

"I'm your friend," I said.

Lisa reached for the handle on the door and started to get out of the Porsche.

"Give Gabe my love," I said.

"I will."

She was inside before I'd pulled away, and I drove uptown, thinking about the warmth of company that loves unconditionally. I imagined her going through Vera's door and tiptoeing her way to Gabriel's side, and I tried to picture the expression on her face as she looked at her son asleep.

My Da had smiled that way at me, once upon a time.

On my seventeenth birthday, I tried to cap myself.

I'd been in a rehab run by the Sisters of Incarnate Love for almost four months at that point, living in a dormitory residence in New Paltz. The program there was a cross between juvenile detention and college prep, all girls, housed together in a single dormitory where we exercised, learned, ate, and "came to terms" with our addiction under the supervisory eyes of the nuns. We weren't allowed to leave the grounds until we had passed the program, and the only time we were allowed visitors was on Saturday—family or close friends with parental consent only—but we couldn't leave with them, not even to get a burger in town.

Every Saturday Ma and Cashel would be waiting for me. And every Saturday my Da was nowhere to be seen.

Six weeks after I'd entered the program Lisa Schoof arrived, barely fifteen and already in her second trimester, thin and small. It was as if the life in her belly was the only thing anchoring her to the ground, as if without it a strong wind could lift her into the sky like some sort of junkie weather-balloon. The other girls in the program immediately took to calling her Virgin Mary, mostly as a dig at the nuns who were held in unearned contempt. I didn't call Lisa anything; we never had reason to speak to each other, not even in group.

In group we'd talk about our experiences on drugs—how we'd begun using, why we'd begun using, why we stopped. We talked about pasts and presents, difficulties with families and friends, our current struggle against our addictions.

In group, Lisa never said anything at all.

When I was pressed by the Sisters I'd talk, but only about my time on the street, my experiences on smack, and if the conversation turned to anything more personal, I'd drop out like a soldier going for cover in a foxhole. I never talked about my family, or about how I had betrayed my Ma and sister. I never talked about how I couldn't throw the punch, or about the eye that had swollen shut from Da's right cross, or about how I was crying myself to sleep every night.

I never told them why either.

It had been the traditional post-Mass Sunday drive with a twist, the twist being it was just Da and me. Ma and Cashel were visiting relatives in Boston, and Da drove his Alfa Romeo faster without them in the car. With Ma away, I got to sit up front beside my father as he flew through the gears and sped us along the thruway.

I was twelve and we'd been studying the saints in confirmation class, and so I asked, "Da, why'd you name me Bridgett?"

"Because Mike Pat isn't a good name for a girl," he said, reaching over and mussing my hair.

"I was going to be Mike Pat?"

"Named after my Da. I was certain you'd be a boy, didn't even consider girl names at all. Figured you'd end up like the rest of us, another son to follow in his father's footsteps, then one day passing his old man by. Your Grandda, he was a cop, you know."

"I know." I scrunched further down in the front seat. My paternal Grandda had been a police like all good Logan males since The Famine. The year before I was born he'd been killed in a shooting while on the job. Sometimes people who had known him would tell me there was a resemblance, that we had the same eyes.

"He never made sergeant," Da said. "And here I am—— Sergeant Logan. Maybe one day you'll have a son, and he'll be lieutenant or captain. Hell, commissioner even."

It was hot and the smell of exhaust potent. It took several quiet miles before I understood what he'd said.

Then I told him what I wanted for my thirteenth birthday. He just laughed and rumpled my hair again.

I turned seventeen on a Saturday, a visiting day, and I was sure Da would be there to meet me in the garden with Ma and Cashel.

"He had to work," Ma told me.

I heard the lie in her voice, and I knew they'd fought about it. Da wasn't at work. He was at home, watching the game, slamming back brews with Uncle Jimmy. Comfy in his old chair watching college ball rather than visiting his junkie daughter in rehab.

I got two presents, a new Walkman from Cashel and Ma, complete with a tape my sister had made from the LPs strewn about my room. The other was a blue cardboard garment box.

"From Da," Cashel told me.

It was a sweatshirt, and when I saw it I thought it would be all right, that he had forgiven me. But there was no Midtown South silkscreened on it, no NYPD embroidered crest. Just a gray sweatshirt, size XL.

I put it on and thanked my Ma and Cashel, then told them I was feeling tired and had to go back to my room. I left them in the garden without another word.

———

Because the Sisters trusted us, they didn't lock our rooms at night.

Because they knew better than to trust us completely, they kept the medications and sharp objects tightly locked away.

That was all right; I knew how to get up onto the roof.

It was almost dawn when I went to do it, cold, the wind edging easily through the new XL sweatshirt. I had written a note and put it in the front pocket of my jeans, an insincere apology, a heartfelt fuck-you.

The sky was turning from black to the color of a bruised plum. Over the ledge I could see the deep shadows on the front steps, sharp and far below. I stared down into those shadows, thinking that I wanted it all to be over. My life had ended months ago; it had just taken me this long to realize it.

I was crying and so I didn't hear her come out, didn't hear her crunching along the gravel roof, coming up behind me.

"Hey?"

I spun, guilty, saw Lisa Schoof standing ten feet away, a flashlight in one hand, a closed book in the other. The flashlight was off.

"You okay?"

I nodded, wiped at my eyes and nose.

She didn't move for a couple of seconds, then came closer and sat down on the edge of the roof. She didn't look at me. She dropped the book to the ground first, then lowered herself carefully and let her feet dangle. She moved the book back onto the big curve of her belly and opened it, turned on the flashlight to examine a page she had marked. The gloss on the paper made the light bounce, and I saw that she was looking at a star chart.

I wiped my nose again and tried to ignore her, hoping she'd go away.

"You know which one's Orion?" Lisa snapped off the flashlight. When I didn't answer her, she added, "Which constellation, I mean."

"I know what you mean."

"You know which one it is?"

"I wanted to be alone," I said.

"Oh, sorry. I just wanted to see Orion."

I snuffled and looked up, found the three stars in the belt, and pointed. "There. The three in a row, that's Orion's Belt."

Lisa craned her head back and searched the sky. "Okay, I see it, I think."

"Fine."

She didn't move. When I shifted my weight, the gravel scraped, loud in the shadows.

"That's Orion," she said.

"I know."

"I wasn't talking to you. I was talking to the It."

"What?"

"The It." She indicated her belly. "That's what I'm calling the baby. The It."

"You don't know its sex?"

"No."

"It?"

"Yeah."

"That's lame."

"You got a better name?"

"Brat," I said. "Bastard," I added, thinking of the nuns.

"No. I like It. If it's a girl I'm going to call her Sharon. If it's a boy I'm going to call him Nick."

"Yippee for you."

She nodded without seeming to take offense and the flashlight clicked on again, and she checked her star chart once more. "What about Pegasus? You know how to find Pegasus?"

"No, I don't know how to find Pegasus." It came out nasty. "What are you doing out here anyway?"

"I told you. What are you doing out here?"

"Nothing."

"Well, yippee for you."

"You better go down," I said. "They'll be doing a bed check and if they find you're gone you'll get busted."

"And you won't?"

"They already checked my hall. They check it at two."

Lisa didn't say anything. She leaned back on her arms

until she could lie down on the roof and look at the sky. Then she sighed.

"Go away," I said.

"No. Why?"

"I was here first."

"Too bad."

I thought briefly about jumping on her swollen belly, and then thought about the other jumping I'd been planning to do, and perspective suddenly imposed itself.

We both watched the bruised sky start to lighten.

"Fuck," I said, and sat down next to her on the roof.

Lisa said, "I thought about it a couple times. Never up here, though."

"Shut up," I snapped.

She sucked in a breath quickly, and I thought it was in response to me, but then she did it again.

"What?" I demanded.

"It's kicking," Lisa said. "Hard. Wanna feel?"

She grabbed my right hand and pressed it against her stomach. Even through her sweater I could feel the heat under my palm. I started to open my mouth to say I didn't feel anything, and then It kicked.

"Feel that?"

"Yeah."

"Neat, huh? It'll do it again. Wait."

I waited for the baby to kick again, watching as the darkness in the sky began melting away. Under my palm, I could feel Lisa breathing. I think I could feel the beating of the heart in her belly.

"We should go back in," she said after a while. "They're going to bust us."

I helped her stand. We went back inside, splitting up when we reached the fourth floor, each sneaking back to our room.

I gave it two nights, then went back up on the roof. I hadn't even made it to the edge before I heard her footsteps on the gravel behind me. She hadn't brought the book this time, and I knew she'd appointed herself to be my friend.

"You can't keep coming up here," I snapped. "It can't be good for the It. Pregnant women need their rest."

Lisa nodded. She didn't move.

"Fine," I told her. "But only so you'll get your sleep."

She nodded again, and I followed her off the roof and away from the shadows.

I never said thank you.

When It was born I was named his godmother, and I swore to myself that I'd be there for Lisa and her son if times got bad, whenever they needed me—for the rest of my life, no questions asked.

CHAPTER NINE

Almost three weeks after we dealt with Vince, on the second to last Monday of September, Erika Wyatt was over at my place, looking for a fight. She kicked me once in the knee, once in the stomach, and then executed a perfect back flip that caught me under the chin and put me flat on my ass, out cold.

"Nina Williams wins!" the television said.

"Kicked your ass," Erika echoed. "Give it up, old girl, you're meat for my grinder."

"One more round," I said, and pressed the button on my controller to start another game. "You're going down, child, you're going down in a bag of broken bones."

"Talk is cheap. Let's see your moves."

Together we leaned in toward the television, working our controllers furiously, making our PlayStation warriors inflict improbable damage upon each other. I got lucky and caught her in a neat little hold that had my fighter literally walk up her animated warrior's chest and then kick off backwards, sending her flying across the screen. When she came down again, I jumped on her, landing with a fist in her character's stomach.

"I win," I said.

"Bee-itch," Erika said, then laughed and tossed her controller to the floor. "I don't want to play with you anymore. You cheat."

"Sore loser."

"Uh-huh. Want a soda?"

"I'll take a beer."

"Me too." She sprang from the floor and made for the kitchen, and I reached over and turned the machine and the television off.

"You ought to get one," I said. "You could practice at home, learn how to fight a real master."

"I've tried," Erika said, head in the fridge. "Atticus doesn't want a video game console in the apartment. He says it's a waste of money and time. Says I can just play games on my laptop."

"Atticus says this?"

"He thinks video games are stupid and pointless." She brought two beers to the counter and, finding the opener, popped off the caps. "I think he just sucks at them, and he doesn't want to constantly lose to me."

"Maybe I'll get you guys one for Christmas."

"Hanukkah, for him."

"Well, Hanukkah and Christmas, then."

"It's not the gift I had in mind," Erika said.

"Is this where I ask what you want for your present?"

Erika beamed and nodded, and when she did, blond hair flopped and clung to her cheek. She swiped back the strands to cover her ear. Reflex, the way I scratched at my forearms until I discovered the benefits of a steady supply of mints. And like the grafts on my arms, Erika's hair hid a secret, a left ear that had been cut almost in half. The missing piece had been sent to Atticus special delivery. The cut had long since healed, and her hearing on that side hadn't suffered much, but Erika hid the scar whenever possible, and she'd been doing it for so long now that I doubted she realized it each time she reached.

"Ask me what I want for my present," Erika said.

"What do you want for your present?"

"I want a biker's jacket, like yours."

"Huh," I said.

"Huh? What do you mean, huh? It's not an unreasonable request."

"Have you told Atticus this is what you want?"

"It hasn't come up yet. I want you to tell him. The two of you can buy it for me together." She leaned a little closer to me over the counter, narrowing her eyes. "You can take him shopping."

"Nice try," I said.

She put on a pout.

"That's very good. Can you make your bottom lip quiver too?"

Erika exaggerated the pout, crossing her eyes. When I finally laughed she stopped and fixed her face. "When are you going to see him?"

"When I'm damn good and ready," I said, and took my beer and myself back to the couch. Erika followed me.

Since Lisa's departure from my life, things had returned to a normal stability that included the nightly phone calls to Atticus, but still no visits, social, conjugal, or otherwise. Natalie and I had hit the town a couple of times in the past weeks, meals, movies, café meetings over cups of joe. I'd been busy at work, making money and proving to Laila and Martin that I'd be a good choice for partner in the firm. Summer was rapidly dying, the first chills growing stronger in the breeze. Mr. Jones was still residing in my dreams, but his visits were getting more and more inconsistent, and I figured I wasn't long away from him going into hiding once more; maybe hibernating during the winter months, or so I hoped.

"Should I stop bugging you about this?" Erika asked, taking the chair.

"If you want to live to your eighteenth birthday, yes."

Erika shrugged and tilted her bottle to her lips, swallowing the beer like she was training for a college frat party. She burped heartily.

"Classy."

"Eat me," she said.

"Lick me twice."

"I would but I haven't had my shots."

I raised the back of my hand as if to strike and then there was a rapid-fire series of knocks at the door.

"Never even touched me," Erika said.

I hoisted myself up once more and made for the door, wondering who would be calling at ten of eight in the evening. Before I hit the end of the hall another six knocks had been used, and it sounded like meat hitting the door rather than knuckles, and I thought it was a cop-knock and checked the peephole before turning the latches.

There were two of them outside, both men, both about the same height. One was Asian, the other Caucasian and fair, with hair that was in fast retreat from the threats posed by his forehead. Suits and slacks, and no way to see the shoes from where I stood. Hands both at their sides.

"Evening, Officers," I said, once the door was open.

The white one looked momentarily surprised, but the Asian one just reached for his pocket and flashed me his badge. "Detective Lee," he said. "This is Detective Ollerenshaw."

"How do," I said.

"Are you Bridgett Logan?"

"Think so."

"May we come in?"

I moved myself into the space between door and doorframe, keeping one hand on the knob. "Why?"

Detective Ollerenshaw smiled sincerely. "We're hoping you could answer some questions for us about Lisa Schoof."

"Is she here?" Lee asked.

I shook my head, then realized that wasn't going to do it as long as I was blocking the door, so I backed up and let them inside. Both detectives said "Thank you" and headed down the hall, and I shut the door and used the ten seconds alone to try and keep the falling sensation in my stomach off of my face.

Nothing but trouble, this was.

"And who are they?" Erika asked me when I reentered my main room.

"Cops," I said. "You should probably head home."

Erika cast a dubious glance over Ollerenshaw and Lee, then sighed. "I'll give you a call tomorrow?"

"That would be fine."

She got her coat on and the detectives occupied themselves by wandering around the space, looking at the pictures on the walls, my selection of CDs, the books and magazines that were lying around. Erika zipped her coat and sighed at me, and I walked her to the door.

"You in trouble?"

I shook my head.

"Better not be."

"Or else?"

"Or else I'll tell Atticus, and he'll come over here."

"Then it's good that I'm telling the truth," I said. "Talk to you tomorrow."

Lee was still prowling the corners when I returned. Ollerenshaw had taken the easy chair. He gave me a big, broad, dirty-teethed smile and gestured with his thumb over his shoulder, at the wall. The photograph he was indicating was five years old and showed my whole family together. It had been taken the year before my mother died.

"That your old man in blue there?" Ollerenshaw asked.

I nodded and sat on the couch.

"Knew a Dennis Logan, maybe fifteen, twenty years ago. Sergeant at Midtown South."

"The Busiest Precinct in the World," I said.

Lee chuckled and looked away from my selection of videotapes at his partner and me. Ollerenshaw nodded, smiling, happy. "Great motto, isn't it?"

"It is a great motto," I agreed.

"Better than this new one we've got, this 'CPR' bullshit. I keep forgetting what it stands for. What does it stand for again, Kevin?"

Lee said, "Courtesy, Professionalism, and Respect."

"You believe that bullshit?" Ollerenshaw asked me.

"It lacks panache."

"So what happened to your old man?" he asked. "He retire?"

"Disability leave," I said. "Then he died."

His face fell, honestly sorry to hear the news. "Aw, Christ. That stinks. He was the best."

"Yeah, I miss him a lot," I said. "You guys want to tell me why you're here?"

Ollerenshaw was shaking his head, still dealing with the news of my Da's death. Lee stuck his hands into his pockets and leaned against my bookcase.

"Dancer named Megarth Tabor told us you might know the whereabouts of Lisa Schoof," Detective Kevin Lee said. "We're trying to find her."

"Might I ask why?"

Lee looked at his partner again, who was now rubbing his eyes. I wondered if Ollerenshaw was going to start crying.

Lee sighed, said, "We've got a warrant for her arrest."

I nodded and was about to ask the charge when Kevin Lee supplied it for me.

"She killed a dealer named Vinnie Lark."

My stomach plummeted, heading down five floors and straight to the sewer.

Vince dead.

And I'd beat him down. Beat him down hard.

Maybe too hard.

The possibility that this was my murder spun into my head, then partnered up with Mr. Jones, who took the opportunity to casually mention how nice a shot would be right about now.

"How'd he die?" I asked, keeping my voice even.

"Schoof shot him in the head."

I didn't know if I should feel relief or more gut churning. "No, that can't be right. . . ."

Lee sighed and moved over to the other chair in the room, taking a seat. "We understand that you helped Schoof work out some difficulties with Lark a couple weeks back."

"He'd threatened her," I said. "She came to me after he'd torn her place apart."

"Yeah, that's what Tabor says. Says that you and Lisa are close, maybe . . . uh, well, maybe you're lovers? And as such, you might know where she is?"

"No, we're just friends. Lisa's straight."

"No offense."

"None taken."

Detective Ollerenshaw wiped his nose with his fingers and resettled his weight in his seat. When he spoke his voice was thicker than it had been. "You have no idea where she might be?"

"If she's not at home, no."

"She a good friend?"

"Pretty good."

"You know she's a junkie?"

"She's recovered."

The detectives exchanged another glance, and Lee said, "Lark was killed in a shooting gallery way uptown. Washington Heights."

"You guys are out of the Three Four?"

"Three Three," Ollerenshaw said, then cleared his throat. I tried to look him in the eyes, to see if there had really been tears, but he avoided my gaze, staring instead at my kitchen. "We've got one witness who says Schoof was spending some time around the gallery in question over the past week or so."

The gallery in question. "She's clean," I said. "She wouldn't use. She's got a kid and she's terrified of losing him."

"When was the last time you saw her?" Lee asked.

"The fourth."

"Have any idea where she might be if she was trying to avoid us?"

I shook my head.

Ollerenshaw swiveled to look at Lee, and they shared silent partner-speak for a couple of seconds, and then both of them rose. Ollerenshaw dug out a business card and handed it to me.

"She calls you, you know what to do."

"Yeah."

I walked them to the door.

"Your pop," Ollerenshaw said. "I was a rookie at MTS.

He and his partner, Shannon, they were good to me. Made me the police I am today. You're going to do the right thing here, aren't you, Miss Logan? If your friend contacts you?"

"I'll do the right thing," I said.

Ollerenshaw gave me a last look-over, then sighed and shook his head. "Dennis Logan's girl. You have a good night."

"Good night, Detectives."

They left me alone to do the right thing.

CHAPTER TEN

"She ain't here." The end of Vera's Newport poked through the space between door and frame. "Cops already been looking."

"They'll be back," I said. "They'll come with a warrant."

"That's what they told me. You give her up?"

"Would you have?"

Vera squinted through the smoke, then shut the door on me. The chain rattled and fell. The door opened right into the apartment, dumping me between ill-defined kitchen and ill-defined multipurpose room. NBC's newest sitcom sensation chortled away. Windows onto the fire escape and the alley were at the back of the room. Another door was on the left wall almost down at the end, shut.

Vera moved past me, crushing her cigarette to death in an ashtray she'd grabbed from a table, then took a seat before igniting a new one. The remnants of dinner were on the table, several hours old, dirty dishes and utensils, set for two. Grease filmed the bottom of a plate like gelatin, and a mostly empty bottle of ketchup was capped and on its side.

"Gabe's in bed," Vera said on an exhale. "Not asleep, though. Trying to get him to close his eyes, but he was out here when the cops came, heard all of it."

I took a seat and checked my watch. It was twelve minutes to ten. "When'd they come by?"

"Around six."

"And when did she drop Gabe off?"

"Around four." Vera puffed, looking down the shrinking length of her smoke at me. She had long fingernails, press-ons, hot pink. "Told me she'd be picking him up when she got off work."

"So she said she was going to work?"

"What she said, yes. Didn't, though, did she?"

"No. The cops would have picked her up there. They went by, talked to one of the other dancers and God knows who else. Probably went from there to my place."

"One of the detectives, he told me they were getting a warrant for her arrest. Said that she'd killed Vince. Shot him in the brain, this detective said. They should give her a fucking reward, that's what they should do."

I kept myself from nodding.

"Think she did it?" Vera asked gently, knocking ash onto the plate of grease.

"I don't know."

"Cops have a warrant, that means they think they've got a case, right?"

"Sometimes." I got out of the chair. "Means Lisa's in trouble for sure."

"Where she damn well lives."

"I'm going to look in on Gabe," I said.

"Right ahead, dear. I'll make some coffee. Figure you'll want to wait till she comes back, right?"

"If she comes back here."

Vera hacked and swallowed, then took another draw off the butt. "She's coming back, Bridgett. Her boy's here."

He was lying in a bed far too big for him, on his back and on the covers, arms crossed behind his head. A rickety lamp cast weak wattage from a corner. He was in thin cotton pajama pants with New York Jets helmets up and down each leg and an old black T-shirt. Three weeks hadn't altered Gabriel Schoof much but for a trip to the barber's. The short buzz shear made his blond hair stand like current was running through him, like in some cartoon. His eyes didn't move to me when I came into the room, just stayed on an invisible point beyond the ceiling.

I shut the door and started searching my pockets. "Hey, Gabe."

"Hi, Bridgett. Have you seen her?"

"No."

"She'll be back soon."

"That's what Vera said."

"She will," Gabe affirmed.

The mattress was soft, and when I sat on the edge of the bed, the whole thing listed enough to almost get Gabe sliding towards me. He sat up, putting his back to the wall, looking out the window.

"You're a very serious-looking kid," I said, and dropped a roll of Tropical Fruit Life Savers in his lap. "Have a sweet."

"I brushed my teeth already."

"I won't tell. Do you know where she went?"

"She said she had to run errands and go to work, but she was lying."

"How do you know?"

"It's Monday and she doesn't work Monday. It's the day when she's got to go to school all day, so she's too tired to go to work at night." Gabriel pulled the Life Savers from where they had rolled under his thigh and regarded them as if they might tell him a secret. Then he tried to hand the roll back to me. "Thanks anyway."

"Keep them. I've got dozens."

"I know. Mom says your teeth are going to rot."

"No way. I brush twice a day and floss after every meal."

That actually got a lip to turn, the beginning of a smile to show. "You so don't."

"No, I don't, and yes, they will," I conceded. "You should try to get some sleep. You've got school tomorrow."

"I can't. I've been trying. They said she shot Vince. They're going to arrest her."

"I know."

"She didn't do it. Even if she did, she had to. Even if she did it, she had to do it."

I put a hand on his head, felt the hair like bristles of a brush. "Gabe, are you telling me that Vince came back?"

"No. I don't think he came back, I mean. I don't know, maybe, maybe Mom saw him, but if she did she wouldn't tell me. And she would have to do something, if she saw him again."

He was using his thumbs to hold the roll of candy, pressing on each end, watching his hands work. With his fingernails, he traced the outline of each individual Life Saver in the paper, digging at them hard.

"You want to tell me something more, Gabe?" I asked as gently as I could. I don't know how gently it was, because frankly I don't think I'm good with kids; my urge is to talk to them like I talk to everyone else.

Gabriel had gotten his mouth open for an answer when there was a rattling from the fire escape, and he bounded out of bed and over to the window before I'd finished turning. Outside, a specter in the glare on the glass, Lisa was trying to force the pane up. It took Gabe and me some muscle, but we got it open far enough for her to slip through, and she slid over the sill on her belly, rolling onto the floor and then up onto her knees almost as quickly as her son was in her arms.

The swelling and bruising had gone away, and her face was flushed but unmarked, and sweat was running along her hairline, down along her neck. Shirt and jeans were filthy, and wherever she had been there had been puddles, because her sneakers sounded like sponges and leaked water with the slightest pressure. No lumps or bumps or shadows beneath her clothes, and I hoped for her sake she wasn't packing.

I'd seen the unmarked outside, although I hadn't seen the occupants. I wondered if the cops would wait for backup. It made no difference; whoever came, the cuffs would look the same.

Still hugging Gabriel, Lisa said to me, "You shouldn't be here, Bridgett. You're not involved and you shouldn't—"

"Shut up, Lisa," I said. "The cops came by my place, and they're on their way up here right now. We need to talk about the trouble you're in and how we're going to get you out of it."

Gripping Gabe, she started shaking her head. "No, I've got this, it's okay. They would have stopped me coming up if—"

Vera had pushed back the door and stood just outside the room, Newport ablaze. "She's right. They're coming."

"They let you get in so it'd be easier to catch you," I told Lisa. "There's a unit already blocking the alley, I guarantee."

The pounding started at the front door. Vera's head snapped to the noise, then back to me. "Them?"

"You better open it, or else they'll break it down."

Vera went for the door as Lisa lost her color like it was money on rent day. She let go of Gabe almost as fast and lunged at the window, but I caught her arm. Lisa tugged and spun back on me, face set to wild. Gabriel had backed off a couple of steps, his hands twisting the bottom of his shirt to knots.

There was a bang as the door got forced back and the sounds of cops, footsteps, shouting. I heard Lee shouting the litany, that he had a warrant, that Lisa Schoof was under arrest.

Lisa stopped struggling, and I dropped her arm, and they came into the room, three uniforms and Ollerenshaw, guns out. "Up against it!"

I could see the other uniforms, one of them turning Lisa and throwing her onto the floor. Hands ran across my neck and down my back, between my legs to my ankles, then back up.

"Cuff the one on the floor," Ollerenshaw said, and the anger in his voice said I'd betrayed his trust. As far as he was concerned, I'd known Lisa was here all along.

The hands on me dropped, and I turned to see the cuffs snap on Lisa's wrists. Gabriel had gone as far back as he could, into the corner, looking like he was dying inside. Vera pulled him against her, trying to turn his face away, but Gabe wouldn't play, wouldn't avoid the scene.

"Told you to do right," Ollerenshaw said to me. "Stand off and stay out of the way."

Lee had made it to where Lisa was still on the floor, talking as he came. "Lisa Schoof, I have a warrant for your arrest."

"Not in front of her son," Vera snarled. "Jesus Christ, don't do it in front of the boy."

"Mom—"

"Keep that kid back there," Ollerenshaw said. "Get her to her feet, get her up, get her out of here."

A cop helped Lee pull Lisa up and Ollerenshaw stepped out of the way, giving passage from the bedroom. They man-handled her past, shoves instead of guidance, and I pursued. Over her shoulder, Lisa was straining for a last glimpse of Gabriel, and when that was denied, burned her focus into me. Her eyes looked blank, like they belonged on a big china doll. She said my name like there was actually something I could do for her.

"Just keep quiet," I said. "Nothing, just ask for your lawyer and don't say anything else—"

"That's enough!" Ollerenshaw bellowed and swung a finger my way. "I don't care if your father was the goddamn commissioner, you shut up, and you shut up now!"

"It's your right," I shouted to Lisa as they got her to the door, bumping up against Ollerenshaw as he blocked me. "Stay silent, just stay silent until I get there."

Ollerenshaw growled and pushed his finger into my breast-bone, then spun and went out the door with the rest. Vera came out of the bedroom, still anchored to Gabe.

"I'm following," I told her. "I'll call."

Then I hot-pursuited the bastards.

CHAPTER ELEVEN

They didn't care that I followed, went straight to the Three Three on Amsterdam. I parked fast, wedging the Porsche between squad cars, but they were quicker and Lisa was out of sight, as were Ollerenshaw and Lee, by the time I made the lobby. I spun in place, trying to spot them, and failing that, located the nearest pay phone. A fat black man with the road map to misery on his face was parked on the bench beside it, and when I grabbed the receiver he whimpered that he was waiting for a call.

"Won't take long," I assured him, and fed the phone a quarter. By now Erika was back with the Boy Scout, and I hoped that he was up and awake and, better still, in.

"Hello?"

"Hey, it's me."

"Hey, you," Atticus said. "Erika said you had some trouble with the police?"

"Cops just bagged a friend of mine. We're at the Three Three and she needs a lawyer in the worst possible way. You got a counsel I can call for her?"

"My attorney's good, I can give her a call and we can meet you there."

"Not you, just her," I said.

"If it's trouble—"

"Then it's my trouble and there's nothing you can do about it. Stay clear, Atticus."

"Bridg—"

"Just get me a good lawyer down here as fast as possible," I said. "I'll call if there's something you can do, I promise; otherwise, I need you to leave me alone on this."

He took a silence, then said, "Let me find her home number."

He put the phone down a little too hard, and Erika's muffled voice asked him what was up. He didn't answer and I heard silence on one side for most of a minute, the precinct sounds on the other. Cops were flowing through the lobby, and phones were ringing at the main desk. The black man on the bench was watching me imploringly.

Atticus came back. "Her name's Miranda Glaser," he said, then gave me a number. "And she's very good."

"Fine," I said. "Thanks."

I hung up as he was saying good-bye, gave the phone another quarter to munch on, and dialed the number from memory. It rang four times and I was tapping my foot and looking for Altoids when the click came.

"Hello?"

"Miranda Glaser?"

"Speaking. And this is?"

"Bridgett Logan. Atticus Kodiak gave me your number. He says you're a good attorney and that's what I need right now."

"Atticus gave you my home number, did he?" Miranda Glaser said. "What precinct?"

"Thirty-third. But it isn't me, it's a friend of mine."

"Is this something that can wait until morning?"

"It's a murder charge," I said.

"Of course it is. I'll be there as soon as I can."

"I'll be in the lobby. I'm wearing—"

"Oh, please, don't," Miranda Glaser said. "I'll recognize you, I'm sure."

The sad black man's name was Bill, and he was waiting for his daughter to come off shift. Turned out his wife was in the hospital and they were going to pay her a visit. He never told me what the call he was waiting on was about, and it never came, and he and his daughter left at six past eleven, according to the precinct's lobby clock. At nine past, a mid-sized white woman with brown hair in a shag-shell cut blew into the lobby, wearing jeans, blue Chuckies, and a Guatemalan sweater that was a rainbow gone ballistic. She was toting a light tan barrister's case, and I started off the bench to hail her. She saw me before I was all the way up and came straight over, right hand extended. She was younger than I'd expected, maybe low-thirties, tops.

"Miranda Glaser," she said. "Bridgett Logan?"

"Right."

She looked at my boots first, then worked her way up. When she reached my eyes, she said, "So much for introductions. Who's your friend and what's he or she not done?"

"Her name is Lisa Schoof. She's been arrested for the murder of a dealer named Vincent Lark, but I really don't think she did it. Problem is, she's got a bad history and a spotty record, and the cops have already made up their minds."

"Bad how?" Her right eyebrow went up with her query, cresting the gold rim of her eyeglasses.

"Some arrests, all misdemeanors. Drug history. She's clean now, been clean for over five years."

"Where is she?"

"Interrogation, I think, or holding. I told her not to say anything until she had counsel, but I don't know if it took."

"You were there when they grabbed her?"

"Yeah. She was at her aunt's with her son. Gabriel's ten."

"How old is she?"

"Twenty-six."

Glaser frowned. "Unwed mother. She white?"

"Does it matter? She's a recovered junkie. She's had a rotten fucking life and she needs help."

"Don't worry. I just like to know the politics of a situation before I jump in." Glaser turned and looked toward the desk. "This could take a while. Will you be here?"

"Yeah."

"Then I'll see you when I come back down."

She headed to the desk, got directions to Interrogation, and went up the stairs without once looking back.

In my pockets I found two half-eaten rolls of Life Savers but no more change, and ended up getting four quarters from the desk sergeant. I had to use Information to get Vera Grimshaw's number, and it didn't make it through one complete ring before she answered the phone.

"Vera, it's Bridgett. I'm at the police station. Lisa's still being questioned."

"When will you know?"

"Couple of hours. I got her a lawyer. How's Gabe?"

"He hasn't said anything since the cops left and now he won't go back to bed. Will Lisa be coming home?"

"Not tonight," I said. "She's going to get held for arraignment. Maybe we can get her bail."

"Bail," Vera echoed. "Shit, how's that gonna get paid?"

"I'll handle it."

"Call when you have more, you do that, all right?"

"It could be late," I warned. "Close to dawn, probably."

"I'll be up. We'll both be up."

"All right," I said. "Give Gabe my love. Tell him it's going to be fine."

"He won't believe me."

"Convince him."

By one I was out of Life Savers and at war with the bench, with the way it made any position impossible to maintain with comfort. My hips hurt, my head hurt, my mouth swam in an ocean of mint aftertaste, and there had been no sign of

Lisa or Glaser. The shift had changed, the parade of perps had slowed, and my optimism had bottomed out.

It was entirely possible that Lisa was facing a charge she had earned, that she had found a gun, tracked Vince down, and busted the cap that would end her relationship with him once and for all. She'd made it clear that, for everything I'd done, Vince's death was the only security she'd accept. I knew she believed it was the only way to break his hold over her.

If she'd killed him, she'd given Vince in death as much power over her as he'd held in life. If she was going down on a righteous charge, I didn't know what I could do.

More, I didn't know what I should do.

I was twisting on the bench, trying to get the blood flowing to my backside, when Lee said, "You call that attorney? Glaser?"

Ollerenshaw was with him, both partners looking rumpled and ready to roll home, both wearing the kind of triumph that comes from having scored one for the system.

"She's a friend of the family," I said. "Can I see Lisa?"

"Already on the way to the Tombs for the night."

Ollerenshaw waited until I made eye contact, then said, "There's nothing you can do, Logan. It's going all the way."

"We'll let this shake down," I said. "Bring it to a jury, see what they say."

Ollerenshaw started shaking his head. Stubble shaded his jowls and upper lip, and he was beginning to waft the sour body odor of a hard day's work. Most of the antagonism he'd thrown around at the arrest had gone.

"Won't ever get that far," he said. "Schoof's being a stubborn girl, but that Glaser woman isn't. She'll plead it out. This won't see a jury."

"Thanks for bringing me up to speed."

They hovered a second or so longer, wondering if there was going to be something else, then each mumbled a good night and went on their way. Glaser showed up by the desk about then and, when she was finished signing out, made her way over.

"I'm parked out front," she said. "Walk with me."

It was almost cold on the street, and a little fog had descended. Water vapor did S-turns in the streetlight.

"Your friend's gone to the Tombs; they probably already told you that," Miranda Glaser said as we made our way to her car. "We didn't have much of a chance to talk, but she assures me she did not kill Mr. Lark. I got a copy of the police report from Corwin, the assistant DA who was sitting in, and I'll review it before the arraignment this morning."

Her car was an old Toyota that was probably red, but in the night and with the years, it looked closer to pink, like a cooked salmon. She kept her keys in the briefcase and had to set it on the hood to search for them.

"Way they're talking, it's a done deal," I said. "They made it sound like you were going to take a plea."

Still searching for her keys, she shook her head. "Too early to say. I'll look at the police report and take it from there."

"What's the damage look like?"

Her hand came out of the briefcase, holding the shining keys in a clenched fist. "You talking about my fee or their case?"

"Their case."

She exploded an exasperated breath but kept her voice kind. "I told you, I don't know. I'll read the report, I'll have an idea. Whatever they've got, it was enough for the arrest warrant."

"When's the arraignment?"

"Criminal court, sometime after nine."

"I'll be there."

Glaser put her key into the lock, then had to tug on the Toyota door to get it to open. Rusted metal showed on the frame. She threw her briefcase across the seat, then got into the car.

"We'll talk more then," she said. She started to turn the key in the ignition, then stopped. "Your friend Lisa, she a fighter?"

"Big time," I said.

"That's good, because the one thing I can say as of now, even without reading the report, is that she'll need to be."

She left me on the street, watching the car disappear, a metallic salmon thrashing its way upstream, and I made my way home too, thinking about baseball bats and dead dealers.

I called Vera and told her the news when I got home, kept it brief, told her about the arraignment, then hung up.

There was a message from Atticus on my machine. I didn't call him back.

CHAPTER TWELVE

Lisa didn't make bail. The ADA, Corwin, argued that she was a flight risk, that she had been preparing to flee jurisdiction when the police had apprehended her the previous night, and that she had no direct ties to the community. Glaser came back at him with arguments about Lisa's schooling and her young son, but His Honor wasn't willing to take that argument. He was kind enough to offer a hearing on the subject of bail, though, and gave the attorneys two days to prepare. Then the gavel did its bang, and the judge decreed that Ms. Schoof would be remanded to Rikers Island pending the outcome of that hearing.

Lisa hadn't slept, and the one night of state hospitality had been enough to start wearing her down. When the bailiff led Lisa away, the look on her face was identical to the one she'd had after Vince's first visit three weeks ago: the horror that it was all going to pieces, that she had fallen far already and still couldn't see the bottom below. Her eyes found me and Vera, but they couldn't rest on her son, and then she was out the door and out of sight.

None of us got to exchange a syllable with her.

As the next case was called, Glaser peeled off to have words with Corwin, and I caught up with Vera and Gabe just outside the courtroom. Vera already had a cigarette primed but not fired, and Gabriel waited, mouth shut, fists balled, back to the wall, five feet from her side.

"That lawyer of yours, that chicky lawyer, she had damn well better get my niece bail," Vera barked at me.

"It's not her fault the judge wouldn't grant," I said.

"She's got a kid, don't they understand? Gabriel needs his mother." Vera reached a hand to Gabe, beckoning him closer. The boy didn't move. "She's innocent, she didn't do this thing."

"You heard the DA's case. There are witnesses."

"Then they're lying, Lisa's being set up. Fucking prick drug slinger gets shot, the cops arrest a good girl doing her best to stay straight, what the hell is wrong with this system?" She pivoted away from me, catching sight of Glaser and Corwin as they emerged. With a book of matches she lit her Newport, ignoring the No Smoking sign over her head. "What the hell is wrong with them?"

I crouched in front of Gabe, offering him both of my closed hands. "Pick," I said.

He looked straight through me.

"We're going to work this out, Gabe. You'll see your mom soon." I opened my left hand, showed him the roll of original Life Savers. "Here."

"I don't want your stupid candy."

"Keep them for later."

Gabriel turned away, moving to Vera, into her bubble of protection. I put the Life Savers back into my pocket and stood up, finding Glaser waiting for me. I made introductions, and when I was done, Vera pounced.

"You get my niece out of jail, girl. You do that quick, she can't stay in there."

"I'll do everything I can," Glaser said mildly. "I'd like to call you at the hearing, to vouch for Lisa."

"Just tell me where to stand."

Glaser looked at Gabe, then back to Vera, then took a breath before saying, "Gabriel is staying with you?"

"That's right," Vera said, challenging Glaser to contradict her.

"Someone from Children's Services will be coming over to interview you and Gabriel later today."

"Why?"

"They have to, Vera," I explained. "As far as the DA's office is concerned, Lisa is a killer. They need to make certain that Gabriel is all right, that she's doing well by him."

"And how the hell does she do that, locked in at Rikers Island? How do they expect her to mother when she can't be with her own son?" She dropped an arm around Gabriel protectively. He snaked out of the grip but didn't back away.

"Just answer the questions and tell the truth, it'll be fine," I said. "Lisa's done nothing wrong."

Vera plucked her cigarette from her mouth. Softer, she said, "They take Gabriel again, it'll kill her."

"I need a phone number I can contact you at," Glaser told her.

Glaser offered a slim leather-backed notepad from within her blazer and a pen, and Vera printed out her name, address, and phone number. Gabriel was watching the attorney the way a mouse watches a snake. When the pad and pen had been replaced, Glaser turned to me.

"We should talk."

"Whatever you've got to say, I want to hear it," Vera said.

"I'll keep you informed," I told her. "You should take Gabe to school now."

"School? You think school's going to do him any damn good today?"

"School will do good for the CPS folks."

Vera tossed her butt onto the floor and stamped it flat with the heel of her ratty sneaker. When she nodded, she didn't stop frowning. "When can we visit her?"

"I'll try to arrange something as soon as possible," Glaser said.

Vera took that with another nod but not another word, and led Gabriel away. When they'd turned the far corner of the hall out of sight, Glaser sighed.

"Let me buy you lunch," I said.

It was a long lunch, and I talked a lot more than I thought I would. There was a lot Glaser didn't know about Lisa, and I laid out almost everything for her, Lisa's history with heroin and Vince, his reappearance in her life, her coming to me for help.

"And what did you do then?" she asked, gnawing on a leaf of Caesar salad.

"I'd rather not say."

"If it has bearing, I should hear it."

I shook my head. "If Lisa wants to tell you, fine. I can't."

"Will she?"

"I think so," I lied, and drank some diet Coke. "Have you had a chance to hear her side of the story?"

"She says that she never went near him, didn't even know he was dead. It's an obvious lie."

"How obvious?"

"She was fleeing the police, or at least actively avoiding them. It's circumstantial and some might think an admission of guilt. Her entry into Vera Grimshaw's apartment via the fire escape only makes it look worse."

"You can explain that."

Glaser speared her last piece of chicken and ate it, then set the utensils aside and wiped each corner of her mouth. Her glasses were gone, and her eyes were blue, and I was fairly certain that they had been brown the night before.

"I can," she said. "What I can't explain—as yet—are the three witnesses listed in the police report."

"Three?"

"Could be smoke. Cops tend to write up their cases stronger than they actually are, but if those witnesses are for real, it'll make things . . . interesting." Her smile was sour. "According to the report, two people can place her at the scene at the time of Lark's death—or at least within seconds of hearing the shots. One claims to have seen her with the gun, firing into the room."

"This is all news to me," I said. "I know none of this. I don't even know the timeline."

"Four days ago Vincent Lark was shot in a gallery up in

the One-Sixties. Once in the shoulder, once through the head. The police say that Lisa Schoof got herself a .38, found her man, and opened fire. Then she fled on foot. They pulled three rounds from the back wall, shots that missed."

I thought about how common thirty-eight-caliber guns were, how easy it was to buy one in the five boroughs. "They find the gun?"

Glaser shook her head. "She didn't speak to you about any of this?"

"We didn't have time to talk last night, and before that I hadn't seen her in nearly three weeks. Cops came to my place, didn't find her, I went to Vera's, she showed up. Bang, boom, click, cuffed and stuffed. Then I was calling you. Is there more?"

Glaser waved for coffee, and the waiter filled our cups, then removed the dirty dishes. She stirred half a packet of pseudo-sugar into her cup before sipping. I popped a mint, telling myself to be patient.

"I don't know you," Glaser said finally. "I'm not certain how I should be treating you with regards to this case."

"I'm the person who's paying for Lisa Schoof's defense," I said.

She set the spoon on the tablecloth, and a drop of coffee spread into a stain. "Fine. Nice to know I'm not working for free. But that doesn't entitle you to privileged information."

"I'm also a licensed private investigator in the state of New York," I said. "A good one. I'm offering you my services, and I'll eat my fee. I'll be working for you on this. I'll help with the defense. And, as such, retained by you for this case, I will be covered by your privilege."

"You're a PI?"

"With Agra & Donnovan Investigations."

Glaser's not-really-blue eyes got a little wider. "Oh, so you're *her*."

"What her? Who her?"

She dismissed the direct question with a shake of the head, saying, "Atticus has mentioned you. I hadn't realized you were the one he was talking about."

I defeated the urge to ask what he'd said. "Yeah, her am I. We clear on this now?"

Glaser shook her head again. "There's still an ethical question you have to address."

"Any conflict of interest is on my end, not yours. I want to do the investigation, I can bring it to you on my own dime. You don't pay me, *you're* not retaining me."

"But you're paying *me*. Any impartiality you have is therefore gone."

"I'm not going to pretend to be impartial. I won't even fake a play at being objective. I don't believe that Lisa murdered Vince, she wouldn't have, she's got too damn much to lose. I won't let her go to prison on this."

Glaser set her hands in her lap and slid back on the seat of her chair just a fraction, as if the half-inch of distance would give her a better look at me. "What's your involvement?"

"I'm her friend."

"And that's why you're pushing so hard?"

"Someone has to speak for her. The system sure as fuck won't. Vera can't do it, Gabe can't do it, and after that, she's out of people."

"I'm suddenly on a crusade?" Glaser asked.

"That's right."

"And you, you're willing to toss your license in the chute if this goes wrong for you? You get reviewed on this, you're out of business."

"Someone has to help her."

"You."

"And now you."

"Why?"

For a moment I had to just think, to see if there was a way to answer simply. There wasn't.

"True story," I said. "Lisa is fourteen, she's been on the streets for four years, the only family worth speaking of is Vera, and that's not steady lodging. Parents are long out of the picture. Fourteen, get it? And she falls in with a heavy crew from the Bronx that's distributing coke. Serious dealers, these guys, not the corner slingers. One of them likes her age, understand?"

Glaser arched a single eyebrow, but I took that as a yes.

"They get the bright idea that, at fourteen, she's an ace mule. They fix her with papers and fly her down to Bogotá solo, and there she meets up with two cartel boys in a hotel room. This is all she sees of Colombia, because the moment she's in the hotel, these two boys feed her twenty bags, tied condoms, one after the other. She chokes them down.

"That night, she sleeps in this room with one guy wrapped around her, hands clasped at her middle, to keep her from running off. The other with an Uzi, watching. If she didn't know this was serious, she does now, right? She knows if she falters on this, she's dead. She doesn't sleep that night, she's so scared, and you can bet her stomach is killing her. Next morning, they take her to the airport, put her on the plane."

"I've heard the story before," Miranda Glaser interrupted.

"Not this part," I said. "See, that stomachache, it gets worse. Not a bag bursting, of course, because if that happened, we wouldn't be chatting, but something bad. Virus or something she ate or maybe nerves, she doesn't know, but it's agony, and she's got to use the toilet. She fights it most of the flight, grinding her teeth, but finally she's so afraid she's just going to shit her pants where she's sitting, she goes to the bathroom.

"She perches on the counter and goes in the sink. Twenty bags. It's a given that she's dead if even one bag is missing, and here's twenty of them in the sink, and she's just starting the descent to Kennedy.

"So she washes them off, one after another, and then she swallows them again, all of them. Washes her own feces from these things, puts them in her mouth, and swallows them."

I bit down on the remains of my mint, then chased it with some coffee. Glaser hadn't doctored her second cup yet, and looked adequately ill.

"She did it to survive," I said. "And that's why I'll go to the wall for her."

A lot was going on behind her stare, but she was good at hiding it, and I couldn't tell what Miranda Glaser was thinking. When the check came she let me pay without comment, watching the way I opened my wallet and laid out the cash. I also took out one of my business cards and slid it across the table to her.

"I have to prepare for the bail hearing first," she said, looking at the card without taking it. "But I'll send a copy of the police report to you at your office before the end of the day. We'll talk tomorrow about where you should look, what I'll need you to do. Will you be free in the afternoon?"

"For this, I'll always be free."

She stuffed the card into her briefcase, and I slipped my jacket back on and rose. I offered her my hand. Her shake was feminine, but not too soft, and she dropped it quickly.

"I hope Lisa Schoof knows what you're willing to sacrifice on her behalf," Glaser said.

"Whatever I sacrifice," I said, "won't come close to what she's already lost."

I needed to go to the office, to work, but had to know, and so went home first. I hit the answering machine as I went to the closet, listened to messages from Erika, then Atticus, then Laila Agra, all strumming variations on the theme of Where Are You? By the time Laila's voice had vanished, I was in the closet and reaching for the top shelf, for the box beside my fitted Yankee cap.

I knew the moment my fingers tugged the edge, the way the box came down too light, missing its pounds of metal. It wasn't really necessary to open it, but I'm thorough in my work, and so I lifted the lid and looked inside, at where my father's Model 10 should have been but wasn't.

In a way, I was glad.

It meant that, like the cops and Miranda Glaser, I didn't know where the murder weapon was either.

CHAPTER THIRTEEN

The day of Lisa's bail hearing, I called in sick to work and drove out to Kingsbridge in the Bronx. It was a lane of memory I hadn't traversed seriously since making good my escape to college, though I'd been back when Da was dying, and again after my mother passed away. The last time I'd seen the house where I'd grown up had been over four years ago. Cashel and I had gone together to clear out the space, to meet with the realtor, to put our old home on the market.

Out of sheer masochistic perversity, today I decided to drive past it again, taking the Porsche slowly along the streets where the trees were a little bigger, the houses a little more shabby than I remembered. It was sunny and bright, shady where limbs heavy with leaves were starting their change to autumn colors. The neighborhood had changed its color as well, going from white to shades of brown and black, all here for the same reason we'd been, families struggling into the middle class.

My home had been repainted and an addition had been built on the south side, where my parents' room had been. I parked and let the car idle. A mailman was making rounds, and down the block an Asian homeowner was pushing a manual lawnmower across his plot of grass. From behind my sunglasses, I watched one woman walking a Dalmatian, another pushing a stroller. Mr. Jones asked me if I thought any of them were doing dope, and I told Mr. Jones to behave himself, and started a new tin of Altoids.

Domestic bliss.

When I couldn't stand it any longer, I put the Porsche in gear and turned a U on the street, heading north again. The houses ended abruptly, residential turning to commercial with a vengeance, and now the changes were more apparent. Mom-and-pops had fallen prey to the chains. I watched the numbers and passed fast-food restaurants and video rental stores, dry cleaners and stab-and-grabs, until I found the right address in the back of a new minimall, wedged between a hairdresser's and a defunct travel agency.

Parked, engine dead, I sat for almost a minute longer, giving myself all the time I needed to commit or go chicken. I checked my logic, checked my reason, tried once again to talk myself out of what I was going to do.

But I really didn't think I had another choice. I needed the help, and there was no other way to keep my past and my present in their separate boxes.

Inside the dojo a lunchtime class was in progress, seven men and four women, all in their *gi*s, mostly yellow and green belts sparring on the big white mat that covered most of the hardwood floor. I got no attention when I entered and slid along the wall to the corner opposite the mirrors, where I had a full view. I watched the punches and throws, listened to the rustle of cloth and the *whap* of the strikes, the easy, practiced drawing of meditative breath.

Andrew Wolfe made me think of a priest, the way he moved barefoot among his students, watching, criticizing, offering praise in their pursuit of Seibukan jujitsu. His *gi* was spotless white, his *hakama* as black as the silk belt on his waist. I'd heard he was a fourth-degree black belt, but that had been well over two years ago, perhaps even three, and my information was certainly out of date. Students assailed him and he caught wrists and sent them easily to the floor. Taller than I remembered, dirty-blond hair in a ponytail to just below his neck. I looked, but under the sleeves of his *gi,* couldn't see the scars. I saw the shine of a claddagh ring glinting on his left hand, and that was unexpected enough that I stared, trying to be sure I was seeing straight.

The class wound down and Andrew clapped and the students formed up into three ranks of four, facing him. He bowed and they bowed, and he said he would see them tomorrow. Then the group broke, heading for gym bags set in a line against the wall of mirrors, and Andrew began replacing equipment, sliding one *boken* after another onto their racks, restoring everything to its proper place. One wall held the weapons, the wooden swords and *jo* staffs in horizontal lines.

He waited until the last student had left, the last weapon had been stowed, before turning to face me. He did it on the ball of his left foot, so smoothly and so precisely it made me think of water running through a curve in a pipe.

I took off my sunglasses and hung them from the neck of my T-shirt and tried to smile.

"Bridie Logan," Andrew Wolfe said. "Holy shit."

"Holy shit, Andrew Wolfe," I agreed.

A dance bar ran along the wall of mirrors, and he pulled a short white towel from it, wiped his face. When the terrycloth came down, his expression had softened to something less wary than before, but nothing I could mistake for delight.

"Last I heard you were living in the big city, making good for yourself. A private investigator, I heard."

"If you can believe it."

"I was thinking about you just last week. Ran into your sister . . . she's really turned into something."

"I suppose she has."

Andrew put the towel back over the dance bar, then crossed the room to me. His feet were soundless on the hardwood floor, and he moved with something approaching a glide, the way the sentinels at the Tomb of the Unknown walk without seeming to leave the ground. He stopped just outside my personal space, his arms relaxed at his sides.

"Jesus," he said. "You look great."

"You're looking good too. Going a little gray."

"Just the temples. It gives me *shihan* clout."

"Very distinguished."

He chuckled and offered me his arms and I took them and we shared a hug. Taller he may have seemed, but somewhere along the line I'd outgrown him, and in our hug I discovered he was shorter by maybe an inch. We didn't hold the hug for long, just enough to make certain each of us was really there.

"I don't have a class for another two hours," Andrew said. "You want to get a cup of something?"

"Cup of something would be great."

"Let me change and lock up."

There was a Starbucks three doors down, and we got cups of coffee and sat out front around a little black metal table, sipping in silence for most of a minute.

Finally I said, "You got married."

"Uh, yeah." He glanced at the claddagh on his finger, where the hands were joined on the heart. "Kelly, as a matter of fact."

I scalded the back of my hand with spilled java.

He couldn't hide his grin. "Yeah, it was a surprise to me too. We've got a little boy, and another kid on the way, due in November."

"When did all this happen?"

"Uh, four years ago? Frankie was born May before last. Why you looking at me like that?"

"You're married and a father, how do you expect me to look?"

"Less shocked, more pleased, maybe?"

"I'm pleased," I assured him. "Really. But shocked, yes. Kelly? Kelly Phelan? The same Kelly Phelan who spray-painted 'Free Leonard Peltier' on the walls of the cafeteria?"

"She's just the same," Andrew said. "And she's a paralegal now, getting ready to finish it off, become a lawyer. After the baby comes, of course. You really *are* stunned, aren't you?"

"I think, perhaps, I have glimpsed life passing me by," I said, and drank my coffee. The skin on the back of my hand was a candy pink, but it didn't feel like much of a burn. "And a wave of guilt is crashing too, with bottles full of messages that are accusing me of being too long out of touch."

"We went our separate ways, Bridie," Andrew reminded me.

Silence.

He kept his hands on the table, on the coffee cup, unmoving. Ten years ago he never could have managed the stillness, would have been jittering in the chair, tapping his toes, talking with his hands. Out of the *gi,* he was wearing a white T-shirt advertising the dojo and black BDU pants, and his arms, exposed, showed ancient tracks puffed up on his skin, lifted by muscle.

"Nine years since I last saw you," he said. "You're bringing back a lot of memories."

You too, I thought.

"Why're you here, Bridie?"

"I need some help."

"I don't look for fights, not anymore."

"I'm not asking you to bust heads for me, Andy. I need someone to cover my back, and you're my first choice."

"Me? After this much time, you need my help? Why?"

"I've got a case I'm working, looking into the murder of a dealer. The places I need to go, the questions I need to ask, I won't be welcome. With you, I've got a chance of getting some answers."

"What sort of places are we talking about?"

"The sort of places where you and I once lived," I said.

He ran his blue eyes over my face. "I don't use anymore. I haven't for seven years and four months."

"I don't either."

"I go to NarcAnon meetings three, four times a week, Bridgett. I'm the sponsor to a recovering addict."

"I'm not trying to get you to use again," I said, breaking a Life Saver beneath my molars.

Andrew's head shake was as precise as each of his other movements. "No, that's not what I'm implying."

"What, then?"

"Why do you want to walk through that temptation?"

"I don't want to. I have to. I have a friend in trouble, and she needs me."

"Perhaps you should explain a little more."

"The dead dealer, the cops think my friend did it. The best way to break their case is to find a better suspect. I know this dealer—his name is Lark—was working for some big guns, Nigerian shippers. But the cops didn't pursue that angle, they just made a nice, tight case and hung it on my friend's neck."

"And if you can find a better suspect, they'll drop the charges?"

"The best way to prove her innocent is to give them some-body who's guilty. But I can't do that without looking, and I can't look alone."

"Which brings us back to the Why Me." Andrew said it gently. "Nine years late, why me, Bridie?"

I felt myself starting to flush, surprised myself with the growing anger. "You want to know why you haven't seen me for nine years, Andy? The same reason you haven't looked for me. The people in my life now, they don't know what I was, what I did. They don't know where I slept or why or with whom or for what. And I don't want them to know. They don't need to know. If I'm going to be swimming in needles again, I can't have them with me. I need to have someone who shares the fear and the longing."

The sorrow in his face was only making me angrier, but I didn't want to add more, so I opted for the rest of my can-dies. He watched me chew them, hands motionless on the table, one on each side of his cup of coffee. I knew he was breathing because his lips weren't turning blue.

"You should tell them," Andrew said. "You can't heal it if you don't share it."

"It's healed," I said. "It's healed and not the issue. If you don't want to help me, Andy, fine, say so. But don't try to lay a line of Twelve-Step crap on me, because I didn't need it then and I sure as hell don't need it now."

I was already out of the chair and ready to go, but Andrew brought one hand up, the gesture asking me to stop and to wait.

"I'll do it," he said.

"I'm not sure I want your help now. I'm not sure coming here was my brightest idea."

"But I want to help you."

My laugh was unintentionally derisive, out before I could cork it. "You sound like Cashel."

Andrew rose, taking his coffee with him. "Bridie, I owe you. If this is what you want from me, I'm willing to do it."

"I don't need a chaperon, Andy, just backup."

"Understood."

"I'm not looking to score."

"I know."

"I'm *not* looking to score," I repeated, harsher.

"I believe you."

"Good," I said. "I'll give you a call this afternoon, we can start tonight."

I tossed my half-empty cup into the trash can, went to the Porsche while snapping on my shades. Andrew was heading back to the dojo, but he stopped to watch me go when the engine purred to life. He had the same centered, calm look on his face, the same leveled, at-peace-with-the-world, Twelve-Step look that made me want to kick his ass.

I reversed out of my spot and spun the wheel and pushed the pedal, zipping out onto Irwin Avenue, leaving him well behind. Andrew Wolfe and Kelly Phelan and their little kid Frankie and another on the way, his dojo and life.

When my Da found me, brought me home and locked me in and began cleaning me out, Andrew had been gone for two months. It wasn't until I was clean and clear for five months that I even heard what had happened to him. That day all those years ago Andy had gone to score, left me in the gallery to wait, and he'd hit trouble almost immediately. I didn't know it all, but I knew there had been violence and blood and, finally, the police and an arrest for aggravated assault.

Once Andrew was in the system, his father—also a cop, but unlike my Da, an SOB—had done the only good deed he'd ever managed for his son: he'd gotten Andy into a juvenile facility, rehab, the works. Out of the city and away from the crowd, Andrew had kicked and come back to life and, in the process, found jujitsu through a teacher who used the martial art as a means of therapy. Andrew had found salvation in the use of weight and strength, motion and stillness.

I shouldn't have come back, I decided.

I should have let it all lie dead and decomposing. Andrew had gotten himself straight, and he didn't need me coming back and kicking the corpse of the gone life.

But I told myself that I really hadn't had any other choice.

"Lisa's bail was denied," Glaser told me over my car phone. "She's staying at Rikers until trial."

"Motherfuckers," I said.

"Ms. Grimshaw's reaction was much the same. I did everything I could."

"What were the grounds?" I asked, looking for an opening in the left lane.

"Pretty much what Corwin argued at the arraignment."

"What about the CPS people? What happened there?"

"That's the one bright spot. They're allowing Vera custody of Gabriel for the time being. If Lisa's convicted, there'll be another proceeding to determine the boy's placement. Worse comes to worse, I think he'll end up staying with his aunt."

"You think?"

"The Children's Services people aren't ogres," Glaser said. "Whenever possible, they try to keep families together. They'd rather place Gabe with a relative."

"I'm sure that's a load off of Lisa's mind." A pickup truck was dawdling in my lane, and I couldn't find a way around it. I used my horn to no avail.

"It should be the least of her worries. I'm sure that Corwin's going to call for a meeting after the grand jury indictment. I think he'll offer a deal."

"No deal," I said. "She can't do time."

"Listen, Logan, this is not a good-looking case right now. I'm getting no help from Lisa, and if I have to go to a jury with the story she's sticking with, we'll lose."

"Can you arrange a meeting for me? I need to see her."

I slowed to pay the toll on the Triborough, then accelerated out again. Along my right was the strip of East River off of Ward's Island, called Hell Gate. Seemed appropriate.

"If I get you to Rikers, will you talk some sense into her?" Glaser asked. "Tell her to quit fighting me?"

"Absolutely, Counselor," I said. "I'm on my way out there now."

I drove north through Astoria in Queens and onto Hazen Street, following it across the water of the East River, thinking about the empty shoe box in my closet.

Either Lisa or Gabe had taken Da's gun when I wasn't looking, had brought it back to their home. Afraid of Vince, unsure of what I would do, one of them had decided the gun was an option and had stolen it. Probably Lisa.

And it had stayed in the apartment, and the business with Vince had been concluded, and she couldn't give it back to me, embarrassed and ashamed. She couldn't leave it in her home where her son could find it. So she'd dumped it somewhere, in a trash can or in the river, someplace it would never be found.

There were other .38s all over the boroughs, easy to get and easy to lose.

The gun that killed Vincent Lark didn't have to be my father's pistol.

Prison gray made Lisa look sick and small, like the junkie she once had been, and that leaked into everything. She shuffled into the interview room like a convict, fingers laced before her, eyes down. Only after she'd parked in one of the provided chairs did she lift her eyes. She ignored the social niceties.

"You've got to get me out of here, Bridgett."

"Believe me, I'm doing everything I can."

"I can't stay in here. I can't do it. I hate it here."

"I know you do."

Her expression tightened like a guitar string about to snap. "No, you don't. You've never done this. This is hell, it's cold and lonely and everyone hates everyone else, and I can't do the time, I don't have the strength to survive in here."

"Then you've got to start helping us, helping Glaser and me."

She unlaced her fingers and scratched at her right elbow, through the gray sleeve. "I can't abandon Gabe," she said, ignoring me. "He's already had to be without me once, and I can't do it to him again. Do you see what's happening? It's the same thing again, just all over again, with him alone and me in here. The cycle has got to end, it's got to end with me and him. I won't be like my parents, I won't abandon him."

I took the chair opposite her. "Glaser says you're not giving her anything to work with."

"I don't like her."

"She probably doesn't much like you," I said. "But I'm told she's a good attorney, certainly better than the PD you would have gotten stuck with. She's our best chance of getting you acquitted."

"But I didn't do it!" The shout collided with the metal doors that clanged shut down the hall, and when its echo died, Lisa put her face in her hands.

I gave her a moment. Then I asked, "Did Vince come back? Did he threaten you again?"

"Aren't you listening? I didn't do it!"

"Then why can three witnesses put you at the scene?"

"I don't know. I wasn't even there."

"Don't lie to me, Lisa."

"I'm not lying to you! God, why doesn't anyone believe me? Glaser doesn't believe me either."

"There are three—" I began again.

"I know, damn you! But they're wrong! I wasn't there, I didn't shoot him!"

"You ran from the police, Lisa. Why?"

She didn't answer.

I reached across the table and caught her chin with my hand, forced her face up. She hadn't been turned into such a convict that she'd lost the ability to cry, but the tears weren't quite ready to spill yet either. Her eyes were bloodshot and rimmed with the red of sleeplessness, but the pupils looked good. Then she realized what I was looking for and jerked her face away.

"Were you looking to score?" I asked. "Is that why you were at the gallery?"

She shut her mouth tight, lips beginning to tremble, but whether that was anger or fear, I couldn't read it.

"Were you holding, is that why you ran?"

She didn't answer.

"Show me your arms."

"Go to hell," Lisa said.

"Show me your arms or you're on your own. I swear it."

She didn't move. I reached for her right wrist, pinned it to the table, and she tried to yank back and couldn't free the hand.

"Show me."

"You are a bitch, you're a fucking bitch," Lisa said, and she yanked once more with feeling and I let her wrist go. She smacked into the back of her chair, tears dribbling down her cheeks. "You're a self-righteous bitch."

I got up. "Better self-righteous than self-pitying."

"You're going to leave?"

"You're not giving me a reason to stay. You're giving me nothing, Lisa. I'm here to help you, I'm doing this because I'm your friend, and you're giving me dick back."

"If you were my friend, you'd believe me. You wouldn't want to check my arms, check my eyes, and you wouldn't ask where I was or why I ran."

"Did you take my father's gun?"

If I'd slapped her, her cheeks might have colored just a little faster. "No!"

"Did Gabriel?"

"You know what, Bridgett Logan? I don't want your help." Lisa used her fingers to swipe the tears from her cheeks and jaw. Her nose was beginning to run, a bulb of clear mucus shining just below a nostril. "Leave me the fuck alone."

"God, you just love being a martyr, don't you?" I said.

Without warning, Lisa came out of her chair and around the table, pushing herself into my face. From the corner of my eye I saw the screw just outside start to move for the door, but I waved my right at her, motioning her off.

"You're no better than I am, Bridgett Logan," Lisa said. "You think you're all hot fucking shit but you're just as dirty as me. Well, I don't want your help or your fucking fancy lawyer. I don't want your money or any other piece of shit you've ever gone near."

She put her right finger into my chest, shoved the rest of her anger into my breast. "And you stay the fuck away from Gabriel and from me."

The guard had opened the door and begun to reach, but Lisa spun off me and turned, presenting herself to the corrections officer before she could be grabbed.

I waited until the door clanged before making my exit.

■CHAPTER FOURTEEN■

Andrew called me that evening to arrange our meeting and I told him it was off, that I didn't know if I'd be needing him after all.

"That's a quick one-eighty," he said. "You're sure?"

"Sure I'm sure."

"Okay. Call if you change your mind again."

"Say hi to Kelly," I said insincerely, and hung up. After a moment I turned on my stereo and then turned it off again. I turned on the television, then turned that off. I searched my pockets for Life Savers and didn't find any, so I checked the cupboard, and saw that the carton was empty. I got my keys and coat and headed for the door, and as I was on my way out the phone began to ring. I didn't stop for it.

I'd thought I was going to the deli down the block, my traditional mint supplier, but passed it without breaking stride. The sun was setting and the foot traffic was nothing to speak of, mostly couples or people who'd saved their grocery shopping and so on for the end of the day. Six blocks

north of my place was a minor drug corner, nothing super-
evolved, just a slinger or two working the street.

"Dream's Death, baby, got Dream's Death."

I stopped and stared and the dealer saw what he wanted
and gestured me over to where he was supporting a parked
Ford Explorer. He was black and in his thirties, wearing a big
navy winter parka and denims that were just a little too large.

"How's it?" I asked.

"The bomb," he said confidently. "And fresh, baby. Not
that Red Sky beat, this is the bomb." He checked the street,
quick looks in both directions. "You got business?"

I extended my index finger, telling him I wanted a
single bag.

"Ten."

I dug the money out of a pocket, slipped it in a closed
hand to him, and the bill vanished like water vapor. Without
another word he turned and went for the apartment building
across the corner, disappeared inside. Traffic on the street
was steady. A sector car came along the avenue, stopped at
the light, and the officer at the wheel looked my way and
didn't see anything he felt the need to stop.

The light changed and the traffic rolled away, and the
dealer came back, offering me his hand. I took it, took the
deck he palmed off, and without a word he continued past to
his post, and I stuck my hand in my pocket and continued
merrily on my way.

By the time night had claimed the city, I'd walked a total
of thirty blocks, the glassine Baggie in my hand, hands in my
pockets. Up Sixth, near the main branch of the public library, I stopped for half a meatball sub from a pizza shack.
Then I turned back towards home, one foot in front of the
other, listening to Mr. Jones tell me where I could get a
spike. Everything else I already had back at my apartment,
he told me, but if I was going to do this right, I needed
a spike.

It felt like he pointed at every drugstore I passed.

Back home, four messages were waiting, two from the Boy Scout, one from Glaser, one from Uncle Jimmy. Atticus kept both messages short, calling to check if I was in and around to chat, and the invitation to call him back was open and he managed to keep any pressure for me to do so from his recorded voice. Glaser's message wanted an update, but said it could wait until morning, when I should call her at her office.

Uncle Jimmy wanted to know why I hadn't called my sister, and when I was going to see him.

I took a shower and washed the street grit out of my nose and ears, then put on my cotton pajamas and made a cup of herbal helps-ya-fall-asleep tea and picked up the Toni Morrison novel I was reading. I drained my cup after twenty-odd pages and turned off the lights and crawled into bed, setting the alarm for seven, trying to forget about the deck in the right-hand pocket of my favorite jacket.

Like acid, heroin gets named on the street, labeled by the different dealers who sell different batches. After receipt from the wholesalers, the dope gets stepped on—cut—and repackaged, then sent out onto the corners, sporting its advertising name—Mighty Dawg or Savage Cunt or Fuck Me Please or The Beast. The names differentiate batches for different crews and generate hype for the product, but they also promote a perverted little economic warfare. If a fiend scores Dream's Death and it's a mighty blast indeed, then he or she tells all his dope-fiend friends, and Dream's Death is the flavor of the hour and the crew that slings it is suddenly rolling in cash.

The junk at the start of a run is almost always purer—and therefore better—than the stuff at the end of the sell; fresh Dream's Death may be in the 50-plus pure range; by tomorrow you could be buying twice as much baby laxative as smack, expecting the same blast, and barely getting off the ground.

Dream's Death, I thought.

When I was living for the blast, heroin was anywhere from 4 to 10 percent pure. Maybe you'd score a bag that was 12 or 13, if you were lucky, but you'd shoot more shit than shit, if you get my meaning, and you had to shoot it if you wanted the hit.

Nowadays it's not unheard of for a batch to reach the street with a mean purity of 40 percent. In some places, I'd heard it was up to 80. Purity like that will kill you if you aren't steeled for it.

Dream's Death.

I rolled the words around in my head, even tried them out loud.

Sounded like one hell of a high.

There were no flowers from the Boy Scout waiting when I made it into my office the next morning, and for some reason I'd imagined there would be, and the lack made me grumpy. I wasted most of the morning pretending to actually work, until, just before noon, I motivated myself enough to call Miranda Glaser's office, ran the gauntlet of receptionists and assistants, and finally achieved contact via speakerphone.

"Is there a particular reason your friend is making this so hard, or is she always like this?" Glaser sounded like she was shouting from deep within some cave.

"She's scared."

"Of what? Of me?"

"Of the system," I answered. "It's never worked for her before, and the last time she ran into trouble, it took her son."

"She's not helping us."

"She needs time."

Glaser cursed. "She doesn't have the luxury of time, Logan. Corwin's got the grand jury set for Monday, that's four days from now, and he'll get the indictment, guaranteed. After that it's either Let's Make a Deal or we go to trial."

"No deals," I said, and finished to hear her saying it along with me.

"I know, I know, she can't do the time. That's what they all say."

"This time it's the truth."

There was silence for several seconds, no noise at all over the line. Then Glaser gave a sigh. "Can we agree that she's lying about what happened? That she was at least there around the time Lark was killed?"

"Maybe."

"I'm thinking that a self-defense plea will get us a lot farther than this flat denial Lisa's foisting on us, and I suspect it's closer to the truth as well. We know there's a history between her and Lark, that he threatened her with violence, threatened to hurt her son. If we can determine that he returned, issued another threat, then I can say she was acting to protect herself and her son."

"You're thinking she did it, that she killed him?"

"Don't you?"

"Not yet."

She didn't say anything. The speaker on her end picked up the sound of a door opening and a man's voice, asking if she was ready to go. The man called her sweetheart, and she called him honey and asked him to give her another five minutes.

"I asked if Vince had come back when I saw her yesterday," I said after hearing the door shut. "Lisa didn't give me much of an answer aside from a 'Fuck you.' "

"She's used that line on me too. I've never met anyone who can make those two words sound so much like a one-two jab."

"And you haven't even heard her warmed up. When she really gets going, she swears like a Bret Easton Ellis novel," I said. "What do you need me to do?"

"No matter how we're going to formulate the defense, we need to know what really happened that day. The police ran Lisa through a lineup, and all three of the witnesses scored ten out of ten, so it's unlikely that we're ever going to be able to prove she wasn't at the scene. Why she was at the scene, and what happened when she was there, those are the questions we need to answer."

"I can start with the witnesses."

"Then do so."

"With a self-defense plea, if you win, she'll get out without time, right?"

"If we win, yes. She'll walk."

"Vincent Lark was a veteran dealer," I said. "A guy like that is going to have a lot of enemies, a lot of people who'd shoot him for the cash he was carrying or the dope he was dealing. Why is it that nobody seems willing to consider that someone other than Lisa might have killed him?"

"We're back to the witnesses," Glaser said. "Look, Logan, if you find a better suspect, I'll be all over it. If you can prove Lisa just happened to be there at the same place and at the same time as the murder, I'll run with that. But it's not how it looks right now, and I've got to say that I don't think you'll find anything along those lines."

"I can find other suspects."

"Preferably another suspect who actually pulled the trigger."

"If you insist," I said.

"I do," Glaser said sharply. "Let's be clear on this. I will use everything in my professional and ethical toolbox to see that Lisa goes free, but that's as far as I can go. I won't break the rules and I'm loath to bend them, and we can't work together if you don't share that, no matter how unconventional you may be."

"Unconventional? Because I have a nose ring and a tattoo?"

"Never mind."

"No, I mind. Where did that come from?"

"It's the word—one of the words—Atticus used to describe you."

"When did you talk to him?" I asked, and I asked it with a big bitch coming on, and I didn't even feel bad about it.

"I called him after meeting Lisa. I needed to know who I was working with."

"And what did he say? Aside from calling me unconventional?"

"He said I should trust you. I didn't tell him anything about the case, if that's your concern. I left that to you."

I kicked my chair back and swung my boots onto the desk and stared at the tit on the ceiling. "You can loosen your chastity belt, Counselor. I won't present you with any evidence or testimony that isn't legit."

"As long as we understand each other."

"Oh, perfectly," I said.

I did the two interviews I could the next day, starting in the early afternoon with Mr. Kim Su-Kim. Mr. Kim was in that middle age where everything was starting to slide—his jowls, his middle, even the skin around his forearms, all of it baggy from gravity. His English was limited and my Korean was worse, and our interview was something from a Pinter play. On the street, pedestrians pretended to move through their daily routines, but it was a bullshit dance and nobody in the know bought it. Kim Su-Kim owned the bodega on a major drug street in Washington Heights, and all four corners were alive with the cycle of addiction.

"The woman you identified for the police," I said. "What was she doing when you saw her?"

Blast of Korean.

"I'm sorry, I don't understand."

"On corner."

"She was on the corner? What was she doing?"

Another blast of Korean, and then Kim pointed out the window, past the sunbaked poster of the Budweiser Bikini Babes taped to the glass. The neighborhood was mostly Dominican, but the buyers were truly American in their ethnic diversity, and I saw a Honda Civic pulling away from a sale, its driver white and happy to be hooked up.

"She was over there?"

Mr. Kim ignored me, glaring at three young Hispanic men as they entered the store, making for the candy racks. None of them looked older than thirteen, each dressed for the hood, and the only thing that threatened was their color and their number. I bit my tongue and fiddled with my nose ring, and waited while Mr. Kim watched for potential theft.

The three young men came to the counter, buying bags of Doritos and Snicker bars, and a surly exchange of money took place. Mr. Kim didn't try to hide his expression from them and counted the money carefully, as if expecting to be shortchanged. The three left, talking among themselves in Spanish. Before they went out the door, one of them said something that made the other two laugh.

Mr. Kim muttered something in Korean that, at the best of times, would have been impossible to catch. But the meaning was clear.

"What was she doing on the corner?"

"Over there." He pointed again.

"But what was she doing? Watching? What?"

More Korean.

"I don't understand."

"Drugs. Buying drugs, huh?"

"Did you see her buying drugs?"

"On the corner," he said, exasperated.

"Did you see anything in her hands?"

Again with the Korean.

"Was she carrying anything?"

He shook his head, moving down the counter, reorganizing the cigarettes he sold as singles for a quarter a butt. When he was done with the smokes he moved on to the counter display of high-energy vitamins. I cleared my throat and he shook his head and looked back at me.

"Told police," he said. "On corner. It was her."

"And that's all? How long was she out there?"

"Long?"

"How much time?" I tapped my watch.

"Long time, hours, sure. Long time."

"How long?"

Mr. Kim's hands went up in supplication to the gods of comprehension. More Korean, and then, finally, "You buy something now?"

"Sure," I said, and grabbed a roll of Butter Rum Life Savers and plunked down a buck. "Thanks for your help, Mr. Kim."

He took my dollar and shook his head. "Bad corners," he told me. "Bad, bad corners."

———

"I don't have a lot of time for you, I'm afraid," Esther Brand said by way of welcome. "I've got to get my grand-daughters from school in fifteen minutes or so."

"Whatever time you can spare will be fine, Ms. Brand."

"Have a seat, then. Would you like something to drink? It's Indian summer out there, or so it seems to me, and I expect you are thirsty if you've been walking about."

"I'd love a glass of water," I said. "Thank you."

"I'll be right back."

Esther Brand pointed me to the flowered couch in her narrow living room and then scooted into the kitchen, where I heard water begin running from the tap. The apartment was clean and tidy and very cluttered, too much stuff in too small a space, and I watched my legs as I sat, trying to keep from kicking anything. There were some books and a small television set, a window with homemade pink curtains drawn back revealing the housing projects across the way, other pieces of furniture pressed against each wall. A couple of dolls shared space on the couch with me, in their own corner, minding their own business.

Photographs were everywhere, including a shelf with no less than fourteen snapshots in frames. The center picture was of three African-American men, all in the dress uniform of the United States Marine Corps, all three looking polished and smiling broadly. I put the youngest at around twenty and the eldest just shy of thirty, and they were good-looking men, made more handsome by their pride. The picture had me thinking of Atticus without meaning to, and I realized I'd never seen a picture of him in uniform.

Probably just as well. Maybe it's because of my Da, but I'm a sucker for men in spit-and-polish.

The tap shut off and Esther Brand returned with a glass of water and ice cubes, which she offered to me. I took the drink with another "Thank you," and she turned her head to find where I had been looking, then said, "Those are my boys."

"You've raised good-looking young men," I said.

"Oh, yes! And smart, they're all smart as tacks. I'm very proud of them." She sat opposite me in a small cloth-covered chair, smoothing the hem of her summer dress down over her knees. The dress was yellow and white and blue, floral print, the sort of thing I'd rather die than put on, but it looked charming on her. She was a tiny woman, a little chunky, her black hair just turning gray, with smart eyes that settled with parental kindness on me. "They sent me that photo this last Christmas."

"Do you see them often?"

"They get home about once a year now. But my daughter is still here, and her husband, so I have family, and I don't get too lonely." Her smile was small and wistful, and perfectly maternal. Then it resolved and she asked, "Now, what was this about again?"

"The woman you identified for the police," I said, getting out my pad and pen. "I'm working for her attorney, trying to get all of the facts."

"I don't know very much about what happened. I only saw the girl for a moment."

"Can you tell me about it?"

"This would have been last Thursday?"

"Friday," I said.

Crows landed on either side of her eyes, leaving footprints. "Right, that's right. Friday, it was looking like rain." Her eyes opened again, following another smile. "I was walking the girls to school. My daughter, Frances, and her husband—his name is George—they head to work early, so they bring their two little ones here and I walk them to school each morning and back each afternoon.

"We'd been walking down the street, and this girl, the one I identified, she comes running out of one of the buildings on the way, and she's not even looking where she's going. Came down those steps like the Devil was calling her name and nearly ran right over Dede—she's the youngest, she's just seven now. Turned seven beginning of September."

"Then what?"

"Well, I got a little short, I'm afraid. Started shouting that she ought to look where she was going—shouting at the girl, not at Dede—but she didn't pay me any mind at all. Just ran down the alley running alongside that building. She grabbed a bag out from behind the Dumpster about halfway down the alley, then kept running."

"What kind of bag?"

"I can't exactly say, I'm afraid. Not too big."

"Like a book bag?"

"Maybe bigger than that. I didn't see much more because that's when the other fellow came out, down the stairs, looking all around and asking if we'd seen anyone run past. Deana—she's my eldest grandchild, she's ten—she pointed and the man looked and by then the girl was gone."

"You think this man was chasing her?" I asked.

"That's how it looked, but that apartment building, it's full of drugs and so on, and there's always someone doing something there they shouldn't, then running for it. He didn't follow after her either, just went back in the building like he'd forgotten something."

I worked with the pad for a couple of seconds, taking notes, then asked, "Can you describe him?"

"He was a white man, big, and I don't mean just tall like you, but big in the shoulders. I don't remember his face that well, but I seem to recall that he struck me as an older man."

"Anything more?"

"No, I'm afraid that's all I can remember," Esther Brand said. "I took the girls the rest of the way, then came back up the street, maybe it was a half hour later, and by then all the police were there, and I heard about what happened."

"And how'd the detectives find you?"

"Oh, I went to them."

"You volunteered?"

"Yes, dear."

Ollerenshaw and Lee must have nearly fainted, I thought. Witnesses to anything these days are hard to come by, but outside of a shooting gallery? They'd caught themselves some grade-A luck with the sudden and unbidden approach of Esther Brand, an honest-to-God, living and breathing good citizen.

The kind of citizen whose testimony would be pretty much unimpeachable.

I finished scribbling my notes and Esther Brand cleared her throat, then said, "I am sorry, Miss Logan, but I should get ready to get my grandkids."

"Not at all. You've been very helpful, and I really appreciate you taking the time to speak with me."

"You know, I have to head that way to get the girls. If you'd like, I could show you where it happened."

"That would be great."

"Just give me a minute to change," she said, and disappeared into one of the rooms off the hall.

I stowed away pen and pad, then finished the water and took the glass into the kitchen, where I washed it. The kitchen was spotless, and the toaster on the counter was chrome and shiny and would have looked great in my apartment, and I made a mental note to do some shopping, to pick up a loaf of bread before heading home.

When Esther Brand returned she had replaced the summer dress with a maroon blouse and white slacks, and was wearing plain blue canvas tennis shoes. She picked up a small black pocketbook and held the door for me, and I waited in the hall while she locked up, and then we descended the six floors to the street. The halls and stairs were uncluttered and nothing creaked.

Outside, I put my sunglasses back on, and together we headed south along Audubon Avenue. My strides had her struggling to keep up, and after half a block I realized what was going on and slowed my pace. Lifelong needle freaks sat on the steps outside of buildings, their limbs swollen from years of vein abuse, watching the street, waiting for the chance to score and fix.

At first I thought it was simply our combined visual impact, the tall white girl and the short black woman walking side by side, that was keeping the business at bay. But then I realized that it had nothing to do with me. Esther Brand had the neighborhood's respect, and the dealers and junkies alike gave her room and peace, the steerers falling silent as we approached. Esther, for her part, seemed to walk oblivious to the nature of the business around her, a generous smile for everyone who looked our way, devoid of judgment.

Waiting to cross at 163rd, she asked, "That ring you've put through your nostril, why'd you go and do that?"

"Um," I said.

"I imagine it hurt."

"A bit."

"Why'd you go and do it, then?"

"I like how it looks."

She shook her head as the light changed, and we started across the street. The bodega of Mr. Kim Su-Kim stood, windows grated, doors shut, on the opposite corner. In the window was a small sign that read YES! WE'RE OPEN!

"Putting holes in a perfectly nice face," Esther Brand said. "That's craziness. Deana, she wants one too. Says it'll make her look sexy. Child's not much past ten, and she's looking to be sexy. What'd your parents say when they saw what you'd done?"

"My mother laughed and told me I looked stupid," I said. "My father told me that it was my nose, and I could do with it what I wished, but that he'd thought I was smarter than that."

She chuckled, then stopped on the sidewalk. "It was right here."

It had once been a nice building of apartments and was now, lock, stock, and barrel, a nest for users, even though most locks, stocks, and barrels had long since been sold off for drugs. Most of the windows were missing or boarded, and the front door looked barely stable on its hinges.

Esther Brand took a couple of steps back and extended each arm, holding the invisible hands of her grandchildren. "We were right about here, Dede was on my right." She turned slightly, indicating the alley. "The girl ran down that way."

The alley was all I'd expected it to be, cluttered and filthy. The rusted and broken frame of a bicycle was crammed behind a Dumpster on the left-hand side, and the ground was carpeted with broken glass and sodden paper, wrappers for cheap food and drink. A small mound of crack vials, most of them broken, was piled below a shattered window about twelve feet up.

I couldn't hear anything over the street noise, but I knew damn well what it sounded like, what it looked like inside.

Even in the alley, the smell was strong, the burning mixture of fecal matter and rotten food and languishing junkies and burnt-out crackheads, all within, wandering in near darkness, set to blast, looking for a clean spike or a drop of water or the dregs in an almost empty bottle cap.

The last thing I wanted to do, I told myself, was go back to living like that.

"I hope this is helping," Esther Brand said.

"More than you can possibly know," I told her.

CHAPTER FIFTEEN

On the following Monday the Manhattan District Attorney's Office convened a grand jury and indicted Lisa Christina Schoof for murder in the second degree, one count. After the indictment, they trotted out a standard plea arrangement; Lisa could say she was guilty, swallow a reduced charge of man one, and go away for five to fifteen. Or she could gamble on the jury system, on a trial where her track marks would be People's Exhibit 1.

Lisa, still on course and full speed ahead, told the ADA to take his offer and stuff it.

That afternoon Miranda Glaser and I had another strategy session where I gave her the witness testimony I had gathered. Lisa's trial was scheduled to start in mid-January, and Glaser was already complaining about how ninety days just wasn't going to be enough time. Then she sent me out once again to find Witness Number Three, Colin Downing.

It was Downing's account that could turn the circumstantial testimony of the other two witnesses into something harder, because, according to the police, it was Downing who could put the gun in Lisa's hand as its bullets were entering Vince's brain. He hadn't shown when summoned to the grand jury, but then his testimony hadn't been necessary for the indictment. At trial, however, he would be critical for the prosecution and damning for our defense.

And, of course, because Colin Downing was a junkie fuck, he had vanished from the face of the earth.

"I was afraid I'd offended you," Andrew Wolfe said.

"I got over it."

It was Tuesday night, the second day of what was beginning to look like a long week ahead, the day after Lisa had been sent back to Rikers to await trial. I beckoned Andrew through my front door, then led him down the hall. He posed on the ball of one foot, shifting his balance forward, then turning in a controlled three-sixty to take in the surroundings. It looked like he was still wearing the same BDU pants from four days ago, but the T-shirt had been changed, and now was black, and unadorned. He wore an Australian-style raincoat, the kind advertised as being from the Outback, and the oilskin surface was dark green from the rain.

"You take the subway?" I asked. "You look like a drowned rat."

"Walked," Andrew answered. "This is a nice place you got, Bridie. You're living large."

"Big as can be. I appreciate you coming out tonight, Andy; I know it was short notice. Kelly didn't mind?"

He shook his head and his ponytail did a flip-flop from one shoulder to the other. "She asked if you'd like to come to dinner, maybe next week. She'd love to see you again."

"And I'd love to see her. Do I get you for the night or do you have a curfew?"

"I told Kelly I'd be late. Got as much time as you need." He looked around my living room again, hands thrust in his pockets, relaxed, then crossed to the far window. The view isn't great—mostly other buildings, and you can't see the Hudson even. In the darkness, though, lights shone on rain-slicked pavement and rooftops.

"Pretty out," he said.

"Autumn," I said. "Make yourself comfortable, okay? I've got a couple things I still need to take care of."

"No rush."

I left him standing there and headed for my office. It'd been four days since I'd been blown off by Lisa, four days since I'd passed the blow-off on to Andrew. I'd done a lot of thinking over the weekend, keeping to myself, canceling a date with Natalie Trent and another with Erika Wyatt to spend the time alone with my thoughts.

Lisa would come around sooner or later, I knew. And when she did, I'd be there to help, and that meant that I had to keep helping now.

Tonight's course of action wasn't one I'd come to without deliberation. To find Colin Downing I was going to have to search the corners, and if I was searching the corners, it wouldn't hurt to find out more about Vince's business. But Vince's business had been with violent men, and I fully expected that, no matter how sweetly I asked, I'd be told to fuck off.

I expected to be told to fuck off repeatedly, as a matter of fact.

And since I wasn't going to oblige, there would probably be harsh words followed by the pushing and the shoving. In which case, I felt, a weapon of my own was warranted. It wasn't that I doubted Andrew's abilities—if I did, I never would have contacted him—but more that I wanted the certainty of being able to take care of myself.

So tonight I was going to sport my grungiest blue jeans and my meanest black T-shirt and my boots and my jacket, and I'd top the ensemble off with holster by Galco and gun by SIG-Sauer.

The phone started ringing as I was loading the clip, and Andrew called out, asking if I wanted him to get it.

"Yes, please!" I hollered back.

I slipped the clip into the gun and slapped the butt but didn't chamber the first slug, then headed down the hall, trying to get the holster over my shoulders. Andrew was holding the phone out to me.

"Some guy named Atticus," he said.

I put the gun on the counter and took the receiver, wedged it between my neck and shoulder. "Hey, you," I said.

"Hey yourself," he said, and goddamn it but his voice did it to me again. "This a bad time?"

"It is," I said. "I'm just about out the door. Sorry."

"I won't keep you, just wanted to say hi, see that you were okay. Haven't heard from you for a couple of days."

He was being generous. We hadn't actually spoken since Lisa's arrest. I hadn't returned any of the messages he'd left, and over the weekend, when he had called once on Saturday and once again on Sunday, I'd just let the message play.

"I know," I said. "It's been really busy."

"Working?"

"Yeah, pretty much."

"Anything I can do?"

"No," I said. "I've got some help already, so I think I'm okay."

"That your help who answered the phone? He sounds big."

"Yeah, that's Andrew. He is big."

"Call when you get a chance, okay? Erika is missing you."

"I'm missing her. I'm thinking she and I can catch a flick at the end of the week."

"I'll let her know."

"Okay."

"Okay," he said, and hung up.

I put the receiver into its cradle and worked on the straps of my holster for a minute, getting everything tied down and comfortable. I suppose I should wear a hip holster, but the SIG's a big gun and my anatomy makes it easier to conceal under my arm than on my waist.

Besides, I think shoulder holsters look cool.

"So, who is Atticus?" Andrew asked when I didn't say anything.

"A friend."

"Uh-huh. So, how long you been seeing this 'friend'?"

I glared at him. "Shut up, Andy."

Andrew leaned against the counter and moved his attention from me to the pistol. "You don't need to bring that."

"We're going to stick our noses where they don't belong. I want to make certain that our noses remain safely attached to our faces."

Andrew reached around under his raincoat and presented me with a cylinder of polished wood about a foot and a half long, perhaps an inch and a half in diameter. He tapped it gently on the counter, where it made a solid and heavy knock.

"I'll have this."

"A stick," I said. "Wow. I've never seen one this close before. Can I touch it?"

"*Tanbo,*" he said. "It's all we'll need."

"Put your *stick* away, Andy. I'm not planning on speaking softly tonight, and I'm bringing the gun. That's that."

"*That's* asking for trouble."

"No, arguing with me is asking for trouble. Doing what I say, that's a way to avoid trouble. Hasn't Kelly taught you anything?"

He slipped the *tanbo* back under his raincoat. "We're trying a new kind of relationship, Kelly and me. Where each person approaches the other as an equal."

"It will never work, Andy, and such radical thinking can only lead to trouble down the road."

"Not as much trouble as you will," he muttered.

"I beg your pardon?"

"I said you're probably right."

"You grow in wisdom, Grasshopper." I patted his shoulder. "Now let's go bust some heads."

As far as that went, the first head didn't actually get busted that night, nor the next, nor the one after that. From Tuesday to Thursday we worked the street, night after night, eight in the evening until four in the morning, moving from corner to corner asking our questions and facing the street-freeze and eyefucks with growing fatigue and frustration. Ostensibly I was trolling for Colin Downing, but in reality I was looking for anything that would lead to another suspect, a suspect I could turn into Vince's killer.

But nobody was talking to the two white folks who were asking the wrong questions on the wrong corners.

"Seen Colin?"

Quick shake of the head, sullen slink away. Young slingers and steerers with street names like Munchie and Pepper and Bang-Bang, old fiends with swollen limbs or malnourished frames, Betty and Linda and Tobias.

"Know Vince?"

Empty stares, then a request for twenty bucks, or ten bucks, or five bucks, just to "get straight."

"Talk to me now, I'll give you the money."

A junkie shake of the head, eyes nervous and jumping, plotting a way to separate me from my money, a scheme to reach the next blast. "Don't know nothin'. You give me some cash to make it through, I can ask around, though."

"No dice."

"You ain't shit."

Over and over again, until by Thursday night nobody would even acknowledge our presence, let alone answer our questions. Andrew and I had proven we weren't cops—therefore not an immediate threat—and had done nothing to disrupt business. We weren't even filling empty palms.

Best to be ignored then.

Thursday at two in the merciless ayem, finishing our fifth and final cups of bodega-brand coffee of the night, I said to Andrew, "This is fucking useless."

He drank his coffee with both hands, and lowered the cup from his mouth just enough to say, "I could have told you they wouldn't open up."

"Then why didn't you?"

"You wouldn't have listened," he said.

We drained our drinks and tossed the trash. "This sucks. This fucking sucks."

"At least we've put the word out."

"Optimist," I accused. "About us, not about who or what we're looking for. This is getting us nowhere."

"We're discovering what doesn't work," Andrew corrected.

"You're lucky you're a black belt. Talk like that gets broken faces."

"One surrenders oneself to life."

I showed him my teeth in a glare. "For all we know, we could have talked to Colin Downing himself and not even have realized it."

"This is true. Are we doing this again tomorrow night?"

"We're doing this until a lead turns up."

"I have a family," Andrew reminded me. "I'd like to actually see them, you know, just to remember what it's like."

"Family is overrated."

"No comment."

"Tomorrow night, same hours," I said. "Then you can take the weekend off."

"Promise?"

"Promise."

"And tomorrow night we'll do the same?"

"Something else," I said. "Something different."

"Like what?"

"I'll come up with something."

"Suddenly," Andrew said, "I'm very afraid."

Dealers on the street for the most part don't carry their product with them, afraid they'll be caught with intent to sell. It's the same reason most don't actually pack heat, but instead keep their guns at home for retrieval later.

So the dealers hide their product along the street, beneath trash piles or in mailboxes or under the blankets in baby carriages. This creates another problem, of course, that of the fiend who's looking to fix for free. Junkies will lie in wait, watching a dealer work a piece of sidewalk, tracking movement until they can locate the hidden stash. And then the obvious happens.

It's never good to mess with a slinger's stash; it's their

money you're threatening, and in these parts that's a skull-cracking offense. More often than not, the offending fiend is severely beaten, an attempt to impart a lesson that will never take. Junkie logic sez, hey, if you let your dope out of *your* sight, it's already mine. So the theft continues, and the beatings continue, and occasionally someone dies.

Stealing a stash, like I said, is dangerous.

But it's a hell of a good way to get someone's attention, to make certain they'll answer your questions.

It took us until midnight before we could find the right slinger married to the right stash, and almost one-thirty before we figured out where the dope was hidden. The dealer's name was Goldy, an ethnic mix of African and Latin American descent, stocky and shaved bald, and doing mediocre business.

"I'm going around behind him," I told Andrew. "When you see me, move in and back me up."

"This is a really bad idea, Bridie."

"Nah, it's a good idea. It's just dangerous."

"We must talk about relative definitions of good, bad, and risk," he said softly.

"Later," I said, and went down the block, left, and then up again to 155th Street.

Goldy hadn't put much thought into his choice of alley, picking one that was open on east and west ends, and poorly illuminated at that. His stash was wedged under a pile of bricks, guarded by the fiercest of urban watchdogs, the New York City rat. I took position, waited until Goldy had completed another sale, and after he exited the alley, made my move. It took two kicks of the boot to clear the rodents, and another to move the bricks, and then I had my hands on twenty glassines stuffed into a rusty can of Alpo.

Can in hand, I waited, my back to the wall, for Goldy's return. I thought about munching a mint or two, but didn't want to put my hands near my mouth until I'd found hot water and antibacterial soap.

By my watch it was one fifty-three when Goldy came back

to the alley, saw me standing over his stash, and pulled up short. My heart started thumping full steam and the adrenaline ran fast and free, and I knew I was scared and I loved the moment. He took a second, then began approaching me, wariness in every step. In the shadows, I was hard to make out, and he wanted to know what he was dealing with before deciding on action. He could safely guess I wasn't a junkie— I wasn't running away.

About twenty feet from me he identified my face.

"You," he said. "Fucking bitch."

"Hey, Goldy. Lose something?"

"You touch my stash, I'll fuck you up."

"Got it right here," I said, and raised the can in my left hand.

Goldy went to the pocket of his Nike athletic wear running pants and pulled out a long butterfly knife. Each finger on each hand was decorated with gold rings, and they shone almost blue and orange in the poor alley light. He flicked his wrist and the blade came out and he flicked again, showing off, and made the metal clatter.

"Cool," I said. "You practice that?"

"Drop the tin, I'll only cut you once."

"I bet you do practice. In front of your mirror, maybe? I mean, that was really neat, that was all fluid and sleek, like you were born with the blade in your hand."

His eyebrows tried to knit together as he fought through my commentary. I risked looking past him and his blade, trying to spot Andrew, and got an eyeful of nothing but alley and street for the effort. When I looked back at Goldy, he was still in the same place, in the same pose, and still trying to make sense of what I'd said.

"Sarcasm," I clarified. "I'm insulting you."

"Bitch, I'll fuck you up." He extended the blade. "You want that pretty face with a split lip?"

"What I want is for you to answer a few of my questions."

"I told you already, you ain't worth my time. Drop the fucking can, or I'll cut you all the way open."

"Put the sharp thing down, Goldy. You're only going to get hurt."

Goldy smiled. His nickname came from his two golden incisors rather than his penchant for digital ornamentation. "Yeah, you're gonna get hurt now."

"Oh, shut up and attack me already," I said.

He did, bringing the knife up for an over-the-shoulder downstroke that was never finished, because Andrew reached around from behind him, gripped the wrist, and suddenly Goldy was on his back. Andrew had the butterfly knife in his hand, and he clattered it shut with a blur, stowing it in a raincoat pocket.

"Stay down," he advised.

Goldy didn't listen, scrabbling on hands and knees back to his feet, lunging at Andrew's middle. He wasn't all the way up before Andy had the *tanbo* out and ready, and Goldy surged up and to target. Andrew sidestepped, caught the near elbow with a blow from the stick, and Goldy wailed and went back down on his knees, clutching the wounded joint.

"Motherfucker!" Goldy screamed.

"Stay down," Andrew repeated.

"I'll kill you both, I'll kill you both, I'll blast your fucking heads off!" Goldy turned his look from Andrew to me and back again, over and over, his eyes watering from the pain. He did not, however, try to get up again.

I stepped over to him and dropped the can of decks beside him. "You can kill us later," I soothed. "Right now you can answer questions."

"Fuck you, I'm not saying anything, you just fuck yourself with your—"

"Hurt him again," I told Andrew.

"Anywhere in particular?"

"The eyes."

Andrew started to reach for Goldy, and Goldy flinched and shut up, and Andrew looked my way for a final confirmation.

"All right!" Goldy said. "All right, all right, motherfuckers, back off, I'll tell you something."

"Something about Colin Downing?" I asked.

"I don't know that freak!"

"I believe you, Goldy, I really do. But my friend here, I don't think he does."

Goldy rocked back and forth on his knees, on the ground, biting back his pain. He looked mostly at Andrew, and there was as much frustration in his expression as anything else.

"You got that kung-fu shit going on, man, that ain't cool," he said.

Andrew didn't move.

Goldy switched the gaze to me, then checked each end of the alley for witnesses. We'd put him in a bad place, one where he was losing respect, beaten down in his own alley. Sooner or later what we'd done to him would demand an accounting, and it was in his eyes that Goldy was already planning his payback.

"Colin Downing," I said. "Vincent Lark. Either name, anything you've got. I'm losing patience here, Goldy."

He released his elbow and looked at his arm, as if the damage to flesh and bone could become visible through his coat. "That guy, the white son of a bitch who got blown away, he was moving stuff for Alabacha's crew."

"I know he was a slinger," I said.

"Nah, bitch, that ain't it. He was *moving* the shit, get it? He was handing out the daily packs to different crews."

"Your crew?"

"Never touch his shit. That Lark motherfucker, he's a rat, he fucking had it coming."

"And Downing?"

"Don't know him."

"I want you to look between your legs, Goldy," I said. "Just look down and think a little about all that the good Lord gave you."

He didn't follow the instructions, but his face changed and so did his tone, and he said, "He's a skinny son of a bitch, real tall, like you. Got holes all along his arms, he's a fucking needle freak. You see him, you'll know by the smell."

"Where?"

"He docs at a place on One Seventy-first, that's all I know."

"That's not enough."

"Nah, that's it, all right? That's it." He gave his elbow a tentative squeeze and winced, the tears once more bubbling up in his eyes. "Shit . . . that's it, bitch. Just leave me off."

"Get a better corner," I said, and turned and headed for the east end of the alley. Andrew fell in with me, and we were almost at the street before Goldy started shouting after us, shouting how once he got his crew together he was getting his Tec-9 and going to fuck us up but good. He added a couple other things that were gender specific and fairly violent, but I didn't turn around for any of it.

Andrew and I headed south, looking for a street where the cabs weren't too afraid to stop for a fare. After a minute of silence, observed perhaps out of respect for Goldy's pain, Andrew sighed.

"How seriously you going to take his threats?"

"I'll watch myself but I'm not going to worry about it," I said. "These guys threaten to bust caps as a matter of course. Doesn't mean anything."

"Hope you're right."

"Yeah, well, me too."

We crossed the street and dodged an open palm from one of the doorways. A shrill voice cursed us and our ancestry. Andrew asked, "If Downing's a needle doc, that means you'll find him in a gallery."

"One expects."

"You'll wait until Monday to look for him, right? Until I'm with you?"

"Sure."

He stopped and a step later I followed suit, turned back to catch his look, all serious with concern.

"You shouldn't go in alone."

"I'm not going to fall on a loaded needle," I said.

"I know what it's like, Bridie," Andrew said softly. "I'm feeling it too. You chase this alone, you're looking to fall."

"I'm clean and sober, Andy, and I'm staying that way."

"There's a meeting I usually go to, tomorrow night. If you—"

"I leave steps for climbing ladders. If you're having a hard time with this, I'm sorry, Andy. I don't mean to put you through pain. But I'm holding just fine."

"If you say so."

"I do," I said. "I'm doing just fine."

CHAPTER SIXTEEN

I scored early Saturday morning a couple blocks from my home, then headed uptown, and was on my stakeout before seven, all puffy-eyed and hating life. Addicts don't take the weekend, so neither do the dealers, and business is always as usual. The street that Goldy had fingered was dotted with shooting galleries, old tenements where the rent was cheap and the amenities nil. Even in buildings where the whole structure hadn't surrendered to drugs, there was always an apartment or two given over to being a safe place to use.

If Colin Downing was a needle doc, like Goldy had said, he wasn't going to be out and about. He was going to be nesting in a gallery somewhere, waiting to ply his very particular trade.

Finding him was only a matter of patience and knowing where to look.

I watched the tester lines beginning to form across the street, against the chain-link fence that surrounded a battered playground, cracked concrete and rusted seesaws and merry-go-rounds. It was easy to spot those junkies who'd managed their pick-me-up blast versus those who'd started the day dry. The dry fiends listed to either port or starboard at angles that nearly defied gravity.

This morning there was a group of three dispensing the joy, and they passed out decks to grateful junkies, and I counted off ten free samples before they began charging, then switched my attention to those who had managed the freebies.

There were two men, one Hispanic, the other white, and both ravaged by their lifestyle, heading together down the block. They walked slowly and with pain, their free samples tight in their hands. The white one's limbs were fat like sausages, veins scarred deep and impossible to hit, and his companion was reed thin, as if wasting away with every breath.

Fiends like these need a miracle worker, I thought.

I followed them from half a block back for nine minutes until they reached their building, entering through a narrow doorway squished between a liquor store and another apartment building. I waited until they disappeared from view before crossing the street, and even with the head start, they were only halfway up the stairs when I stepped inside. The white one heard the door open and craned his head to look back at me. Whatever he saw made him grunt and mutter something to his companion. The Hispanic man's laugh was thinner than his body.

I followed them up the stairs, down the hall, catching up to them outside of their destination. The white one knocked. Neither paid me any mind.

The door was opened by a Hispanic woman who, like the men, was ageless.

"You get it?" she asked.

"Big Glass," the white one said. "Don't know if it's any good."

"Let me see."

Each man opened his palm, showing the woman his freebie.

"You all set," she told them. "Make sure you leave the tax."

"Carla, you're all sweet," the Hispanic man said, and then he went past her, into the apartment. The white man followed, and I moved up to the doorway.

Carla gave me a look over, suspicion in her eyes until they met mine. Then she saw something that told her I wasn't a police, that I wasn't government or social work.

"One bill," she said. "One more, you need a spike. You need help, you pay the tax."

I gave her a twenty.

"What's your name, girl?"

"Bridgett."

"I'm Carla. You go on to the kitchen, Bridgett." She moved aside to let me pass.

The hallway into the apartment was dark, and I was wondering if there was any power running to the place at all until I heard the television coming from another room. The floor was fairly clean, some trash crumpled against the baseboard. Roaches cheerily skittered up the wall on my left.

I could smell him before I saw him, the stink of necrotic flesh, rotting from abuse and disease. More than the cooking heroin, more than the infinite supply of fast food and vomit and waste, I could smell Colin Downing.

He was a pale white man, sitting at a table in the kitchen, and even so I could see he was taller than me. His hair was either black or brown, but I couldn't be certain, not even with the light from the candle that flickered on the table, or the beam of fall sunlight that slivered through the window. He wore a stained gray T-shirt, Bart Simpson posed defiantly on his chest, and it was too small for him, the sleeves barely over his shoulders. His arms were bare and horrible, lesions and abscesses up and down the right and left, holes in the skin the size of quarters that would never heal, not as long as there was a dose to shoot.

The white man I had followed was already on the nod, standing by the window, looking out, humming. His friend was seated opposite Downing, handing over his bag.

"How's it today, Beau?"

The man at the window nodded and said, "Fine. It's fine."

I moved away from the door, waiting my turn, and Carla came in behind me. She stopped at the table, watched as Downing opened the bag and measured out the Hispanic man's dose, then saved some for himself and some more for Carla. This was the tax, the fee for services and lodging.

Downing's hands were steady, working his equipment. A jerry-rigged cooking base had been assembled on the table, a short metal stand with a spoon tied securely in place. Downing measured powder and added water and began cooking the dope.

"What's working for you, Lemon?"

Lemon presented his left arm, tapped a point just above his wrist. "That's been good, Colin."

Downing picked a thin plastic syringe from the table, a needle that was as far from being sterile as I was from acting smart, and with a wisp of cotton as a filter, loaded the shot. He ran his free hand gently over Lemon's arm, touching his way, as if divining for water. No need to tie off the arm, to slap up the vein; I watched Colin Downing perform his miracle, find a sure vessel in an arm where nothing was left.

Straight and true, a shot worthy of William Tell, Colin Downing slid the needle into Lemon's arm, saw the blood wash back, confirming the hit, and let the plunger fall. Lemon's sigh billowed through the room.

Downing's teeth were yellow and black, and he showed them all in his smile. "You're all set, my friend."

Lemon sighed again, and Carla helped him from the chair. Beau, at the window, turned to watch, and laughed at the sight.

"Good shit, right?"

"Oh," Lemon sighed. "Yeah, this works fine."

Carla offered the chair to me, like she was the maître d' at Chanterelle. My stomach was rippling, as if caught at sea, and my head felt light. I tried to slow my breathing, tried to remember why I was there, all the while fingering the deck in my pocket, feeling the powder shift between pressing fingers.

I took the chair, and Carla told Colin, "She needs a spike."

"Let's see what you've got," Colin told me.

I handed over the packet of Little Big One I'd scored that morning. My hand was shaking, and he noticed.

"You came to the right place," he said. "Tremors like that, you'll end up hurting yourself. This one of the testers?"

"Little Big One," I said. I sounded hoarse.

"That shit's no good," Carla muttered. "You got burnt, girl. That shit's been bad all week."

"Maybe this one's got some juice to it," Colin said, opening the package. "You need to take off your jacket there, sweetheart, and tell me where you want it."

I started to take off my jacket. The sleeves of my black T-shirt were short, ending mid-bicep. I figured for a traditional hit, just up the forearm, below the elbow, inside. That used to work well for me.

"Her name's Bridgett," Carla said.

"Where you want it, Bridgett?"

Anywhere you can find a vein, I thought. Anywhere you can hit and work the miracle and make me feel fine again.

Beau and Lemon were both back at the window, all their pain gone, wearing their pleasure the way a peacock shows off his feathers. They'd shot gold, and didn't have a care in the world, didn't feel anything but good through and through.

Holy Mother, help me, I prayed.

I'm going to use.

I put my right arm on the table and opened my mouth to damn my soul and instead heard myself saying, "I just want to ask you a few questions."

Carla and Colin looked almost as surprised as I felt. For almost ten seconds there was just quiet and shock, the gentle sound of Beau's doped murmurings.

"You're not a police," Colin said.

"No."

"What the hell you doing here?" Carla demanded.

"You *are* Colin Downing?"

He barely nodded.

"I need to ask you about the shooting you witnessed," I said. "I've been looking for you for over a week now."

"Aw, shit, this is that thing?" Carla cried, hands flying to her hips. "You get the fuck out of my house now, girl. You don't come in here with that, it's just not *done*."

"This won't take long," I told Downing. "I really need to

talk to you. Please, you can keep the stuff, it's all yours. I just need you to answer a few questions."

"Not here he won't!" Carla shrilled. "You get your skinny ass out of here, girl!"

Colin looked at Carla, then back to me. Then at the bag on the table. "Little Big One ain't all shit," he said softly. "This mine?"

"All of it," I said. "Share it how you like, whatever you want."

"It's mine too," Carla said.

"You let me get my friends hooked right, then we can talk," Colin Downing said to me, ignoring Carla. "Just stand over there, give me some time."

I got up, pulling my jacket back on, and Carla swung into the empty chair. "Crazy white girl," she muttered to Downing.

He nodded agreement and set about cooking another shot, which he placed high on Carla's forearm. The blast took her the way it took Lemon and Beau, and she promptly forgot to care that I was still there. Then Downing loaded a final shot for himself, using the same needle, and fired it into one of the holes in his right arm. When the needle went in, his face shone in pain. Then the dope hit, and his eyes rolled back, and the needle clattered from his arm to the floor.

Oh, fuck, don't die, I thought. Please don't die, Mr. Colin Downing.

For a long stretch of five seconds he didn't move, not at all, not even to draw air, in full narcotic freeze. Then came a rustling wheeze, and his head tilted languidly forward, and he smiled a smile born a million miles away, one that traveled like light from a distant star.

"You okay?" I asked.

He raised his awful left hand to me, gently dismissing my concern. "Don't . . . ruin . . . it . . . girl . . ."

"We need to talk."

"In a . . . bit. . . . Just . . . just wait."

And he closed his eyes and left on his nod, joining the rest of his companions as they took their trips.

"I'm not testifying or nothing like that," Colin told me. "No way, doesn't matter how much food you buy me."

"I understand."

"You get me another one of these?" He held up the wedge of remaining taco. "Chicken?"

"First talk to me."

He shrugged, then popped the last bit of tortilla and meat into his mouth and began chewing. He'd pulled on a filthy zip-up sweatshirt for our excursion outside, and it trapped some odor and hid most of his wounds. Still, the scent coming off him was fierce enough to kill my appetite; I couldn't even bring myself to suck on a candy. But if it bothered him, it didn't show, and he had three empty taco wrappers on the table before us to prove it.

"Need to get back soon." He chased his final bite with a slurp of lemonade from a paper cup.

"You're fixed for now, right?"

"I'm feeling fine."

"Then talk to me."

" 'Bout what?"

" 'Bout the death of Vincent Lark."

"That man was a cold-assed motherfucker who got what he deserved," Colin said. Venom practically dribbled down his chin. "Surprised it took as long as it did for his number to get called."

"Lot of people gunning for him?"

"Oh, I don't know about that. But lots of folks didn't like him, wanted to see him take some comeuppance."

"Got any names?"

Colin shook his head. "Just every dealer he worked over 'cause the money wasn't right, every soldier he fucked over with beat. He's been giving us soldiers grief for years now. And he was a rat, turning corners against each other, maybe even wagging his jaw to the cops."

"You an old vet," I said admiringly.

"I've been in the war for twenty years, Bridgett," Colin Downing said. "I'm going to soldier on until I can't soldier no longer."

"You ought to get yourself checked out. Get some antibiotics for your arms."

"I know all about hospitals. Used to work in a fucking hospital. There ain't a thing hospitals can do for me." He looked briefly at the back of his left hand, where a circle of skin glistened dangerously pink. "Lark had himself in some trouble."

"More than normal?"

"He got himself beat pretty bad about a month before he died. Word was that Alabacha got tired of him skimming."

Wrong, I thought. Or at least wrong about who delivered the beating.

"I've been hearing Lark's name in connection with Alabacha a lot," I lied. "Who is he?"

"The man with the best shit in this neighborhood." He gave me another view of his teeth when he smiled. His eyes had been blue once. "You score some Alabacha dope, you'll be happy all day."

"Big operation?"

"Big enough. Keeps a lot of us healthy. Guys like Vince, they move the dope to the street crews. Couple of the crews always selling Alabacha dope."

"You think Alabacha had Vince killed?"

"Shit, yeah," Colin said. "She could have been working for the Nigerians, easy."

"She? You mean Lisa Schoof?"

"That the girl they had me ID?"

I nodded.

"Sure," he said.

"What did you see that morning?"

He sighed, looking down at his empty wrappers. Then he rattled the ice in his near-empty cup. Then he sighed again and looked at me.

"How much?" I asked.

"Forty?"

"Twenty."

"Thirty, and I won't tell you any lies."

I grinned and reached for my wallet, laid out a twenty and a ten. Colin folded the bills into tight little rectangles, one inside the other, and put them carefully into his pocket. Once the money disappeared, he seemed to relax a little more, settling against the bench, getting good and comfortable.

"Let's hear it, Colin. And no lies."

"No, I'll give you the truth, just like I saw it. You going to take notes?"

"I'll remember."

"Fair," he said. "Week or so ago, everyone at Carla's went out, they'd heard about some really good shit being sold on the West Side, they all leave me alone. I figure I'm going to be fine until they get back, but it turns out that the bag they left me with, it's shit, total beat, it does nothing for me.

"So this old soldier has to go out to the front, so to speak, looking for his action. And I end up buying over on Audubon, and I'm not feeling too well. I know this pad over that way, so I head on up and cook and settle in, talking with friends. We're all in the room at the end of the hall, feeling just fine."

"Where was Lark?"

"Further down, different room."

"So you didn't actually see him?"

"No, I saw him, all right. He came limping on up the stairs at some point, leg all fucked up. I watched him go in. He was talking with someone, or something. Probably collecting fees."

"Who from?"

"No idea. Anyway, little later, this blond thing comes up the stairs, wired for sound. She's slinking in the halls, got a big motherfucking gun in her hands, and I figure somebody's going to get into trouble. My friends, they back off, out of the way, but I'm not as fast as I used to be. Didn't get up in time."

"You saw the gun?"

Colin Downing nodded, and the movement blew more of his scent my way. I tried to keep my face neutral and my breakfast down.

"What'd it look like?" I asked.

He heard the import of my question, and his eyes narrowed, looking into memory. "Blue. Big blue. Like the cops used to carry."

I nodded and found the need for a Life Saver outweighing my mild nausea. I chewed three back to back, and they all tasted like shit.

"Blondie gets to the door," Colin continued. "Peeks around, and she sees him, because she just turns and starts shooting. Blam blam blam blam! Noise! Blam! Screams! Running, yelling!"

"And?"

"Fuck if I know. I was hiding by then."

"You didn't see her running?"

"I was ducking, Bridgett," he said. "When I looked up again, there were people running this way and that, and I figured it was time to head back to Carla's. I'm on my way out when a couple police grab me, tell me I've got to wait until the detectives show up." He held up his hands, showed me the backs. "Even with this, and they kept me there until the detectives showed."

I actually put my elbows on the filthy table and leaned forward. "This is vital, Colin. Did you see anyone else?"

"Else like who? There were friends there, like I said."

"I'm talking about a white guy. Taller than me, maybe in his forties or fifties?"

"Nah—"

"No," I insisted. "Think about it before answering. Did you see anyone else, anyone else who might have shot Vince?"

"Blondie had the gun, Blondie did the shooting, and that's the truth, lady. That's what I saw."

I backed off, sucking in a deep breath of mixed air, sorting my thoughts as fast as I could manage. But it didn't matter which ones I tried to throw into the discard pile, I kept getting the same damn conclusion, the one that made me feel stupid and frustrated, and maybe a little closer to tears than I wanted to admit.

Lisa had done it. She had lifted my father's gun, waited for her opportunity, and shot Vince in the head. She had lied to me.

She'd lied to me almost as much as I'd been lying to myself.

"Come on, Colin," I said, getting up. "I'll walk you back to Carla's."

CHAPTER SEVENTEEN

I wasn't paying attention, and that's how they got so close. At least, that's the story I'm sticking with.

I walked Colin back to Carla's and thanked him for his time and help, although I only meant it about the first part. He told me to come back anytime, I expect because he'd labeled me a soft touch with plenty of cash. I was heading down the stairs again before he was through Carla's door.

Lisa, I thought. Lisa, you and I have to have a nice, long talk. And then I'm going stomp on your head for a half an hour, and then I'm going to talk some more, and then I'm going to have a nice, long cry.

And I'm going to ask you why you did it, why you didn't come to me first. I'm going to ask why you wouldn't let me help you when there was something I could do.

I got outside into the sunlight, snapped on my shades, and turned and stared down the street. At the end of the block stood Goldy, waiting for me, another man at his side. The man was black, older and tall and strong, and his clothes set him far and away from being a member of any street crew. A waist-length leather jacket open over a shirt I'd been seeing in the Saks window. Very silk, very nice.

Goldy pointed my way, and the man began walking forward, and suddenly I thought it might be best to stop, maybe even to head in another direction. So I did, turned on my toe to find myself face-to-face with someone entirely new, a white man shorter than me and broad across the shoulders, maybe in his late forties. Brown hair with silver temples and some lines on his face, more when he smiled.

"Excuse me," I said, trying to step around him.

"No," he said, and punched me in the stomach.

The blow doubled me up, and before I could fight the surprise, I'd been hit another three times. The first one was in the face with the guy's knee, and sent my sunglasses to Ray-Ban heaven and my head into a spiral. The second and third ones I'm not too sure about, because I was still flailing from the first.

The white guy caught me by the coat, the world spinning, and threw me off the street, between buildings. I managed to keep from hitting the wall face-first, taking the contact on my shoulder, thinking that my gun would probably have helped equalize the situation, calling myself stupid stupid stupid for leaving it at home; it'd been a judgment call—I hadn't wanted to scare Colin or his cronies.

I got another blow in the lower back, lost the new breath I'd reacquired, and couldn't do much more than keep from falling all the way down. I managed to stop on my knees and he grabbed my hair and twisted, pitching me face-first into the alley wall, so I was off balance and without leverage. There was something wet and slimy on my cheek where it was pressed to the building. I still didn't have enough air, and even if I did, I doubted I could fight back from my position on the ground.

I just hoped it wasn't going to be as bad as it could get, that's all I hoped right then.

He put weight on my back and my left ankle and started searching me, reaching into my pockets and tossing the contents, my Altoids, Life Savers, pad, pen. He didn't speak and his breathing was fast and I felt it on my cheek when he leaned in. He finished searching my outside pockets and then reached around in front of me, inside my jacket. On the way to my inside pocket, he stopped at my left breast and grabbed hold of me, digging his fingers in. I swallowed my voice and tried to force myself upright but I still had no leverage and no way out, and he put more weight on me to prove it, tightening his grip.

"Nice tits," he said.

I felt like I had a horrible fever, could feel the heat in my head, on my face, crawling on my skin. And just as I thought I'd explode into open flame, he let go, moving his hand from my breast to my pocket. When he had my wallet he moved back, letting go of my hair, taking the weight away from my back and my foot, but leaving the pressure inside my chest.

I stayed where I was resting, cheek to the wall, sucking down air as fast as I could, trying to cool. My face felt stovetop hot and I was clenching my jaw and hearing my pulse, and I was thinking about all the humiliations I'd told myself I'd never endure again.

I got to my feet without throwing up, and when I could make my face show only what I wanted, I turned.

Both men were watching me, standing just inside the alley, blocking the exit. The black man was looking through my wallet that had just been handed off, and the white one was lighting a cigarette. Like his counterpart, he was expensively dressed, wearing black pants and polished boots, an open Baltimore Orioles starter jacket, mostly leather. His cigarette lighter was chrome and narrow and electric, and the flame was invisible.

No way these beasts were part of Goldy's little crew. No, these were animals from a different part of the zoo.

"Bridgett Logan," the white man said, pointing his cigarette at me. I could see a tattoo on his index and middle fingers, the ones that held his smoke. Two long and theoretically sexy woman's legs that ended just shy of his nails, black ink faded to blue. At the web of flesh between fingers was a darker patch of ink, and he waggled the cigarette along the thatch of pubic hair like it was an invading prick.

I swiped my cheek, looked at the substance that came away. It was black and green, and qualified as slime. I cleaned my palm on my thigh, then took another swipe, this at the blood coming from my nose.

"Bridgett Logan, private investigator." The white man had a lot of fun saying "private."

The black man closed my wallet, then flicked it back to me. I caught it against my chest and slipped it into my pocket, keeping my eyes on him. His stare didn't waver.

"You're investigating," the white man said. "You're on an investigation. Asking questions. Bugging people. That's what you're doing, bugging people. A private eye. Private dick. Is that you, you one of those chicks with a dick? You got a dick in there, Bridgett Logan?"

"Why?" I asked. "You need one of your own?"

He showed me teeth the way a dog does before attacking. I visualized a point through his sternum where I was going to put my fist. But the black man raised an arm, gesturing his compatriot to remain still.

"Let it be," the black man said.

The white man settled back on his feet without pause, as if he'd had no intention of doing anything else, sucking hard on his cigarette. He didn't stop looking at me, though, and his gaze had weight, and slid to where he'd put his hand earlier. He smiled again and I promised myself I'd kill him.

"Who are you working for?" the black man asked.

"And who the fuck are you?" I snapped.

"Why shouldn't you speak?" he said easily. His skin was very dark, and his diction precise, as if he had learned his English as a second language. "Why not just cooperate?"

I licked blood from my upper lip and my stomach notified me of its intent to rise if I kept that behavior up. I didn't say anything.

"Please," the black man said kindly. "Who are you working for?"

"Who the fuck are you?"

"We're the Welcome Wagon," the white one said.

"You're not from this neighborhood."

"You are mistaken, Miss Logan," the black man said. "Perhaps not the Welcome Wagon, though. Perhaps the Better Business Bureau?"

"You're not Goldy's crew either," I said.

"We are businessmen, concerned about the state of our market. We understand you've been interfering with . . . commerce."

"And that commerce would be?"

"She's either stupid or she thinks we are," the white one told his partner.

The black man smiled gently, and suddenly I was a lot more worried about him than his ill-bred buddy. He was entirely in control of the situation, and he knew it.

"Pharmaceuticals, shall we say," he said.

"I haven't fucked with anyone's dope," I said.

"This is not what we were told."

"We were told you took off with Goldy's stash," the white one said. "Ripped him off good."

"And you believe him? Now who's stupid?"

"Are you saying you did not take Goldy's package?" the black man asked.

"I took it. But I gave it right back. I needed his attention."

The white one whistled while exhaling smoke, shaking his head at my lunacy. "Got ours too, sweet cheeks."

"Goldy's dealing for you, is that it? Are you Alabacha?"

Both of them laughed, and then the white one coughed a couple times, trapped smoke leaking from his nose and mouth. He tossed his cigarette onto the ground, and it landed between the glassine of Dream's Death and the tin of Altoids he'd pulled from my pocket. The tin had popped open, spilling mints into the puddles and grime.

"Neither of us is Alabacha," the black man said.

"So you work for him."

"Perhaps." His smile faded. "Goldy's allegedly false accusation aside, Miss Logan, we are concerned by your presence and attention to this market. We hear that you have been getting in the way of business, asking many questions. You have been asking about Vincent Lark. Vincent Lark is dead. His killer has been caught. If that is your concern, all questions have been answered."

"Not all."

"All that will be answered from these quarters, then. And if your interest does not end with Vincent Lark, but is, perhaps, economic, I urge you now to reconsider any business plan you might be formulating. This is not an open market. Any attempt to infringe on it will be dealt with."

"I'm not looking to set up shop, boys."

"I am delighted to hear that, Miss Logan. I hope, for your sake, it is the truth." He turned his look to his partner. "We're done. Bring me Goldy."

The white man nodded, shot a grin my way. "Hey, now that I know where you live, maybe I'll stop by some night."

"Please do," I said. "I can introduce you to my roommate, SIG-Sauer."

"Women love me," he told his companion, and then stepped out of the alley in search of Goldy.

The black man watched him go, then stepped aside to allow me back to the street and out of the shadows. When I didn't immediately move, he said, "You may go."

"You're fucking kidding me," I said.

"Thank you for your time, Miss Logan."

"You jump me, rough me up, ask your questions, and that's all?"

The black man's expression creased, bemused. "Would you like something more?"

"Answers. I want to know who you two are."

"I will not tell you."

"I can find out."

"Yes. And if you do, and I hear of this thing happening, I will know you have not heeded my warning. Leave it at that, Miss Logan." He gave me another appraisal, then sighed and removed a money clip from his trouser pocket. He peeled a new-style fifty-dollar bill from the top of a thick stack and offered it to me. "For your trouble."

"I prefer to earn my pay."

The money flapped like a stiff flag as a breeze blew down the alley. "You take a beating well."

"And I give one even better," I said. "You can tell that to your friend."

"I shall." He held the bill out for me a moment longer, then folded it one-handed and put it back on his clip. His expression did not change. "Enjoy the rest of your weekend, Miss Bridgett Logan. Hopefully, we will not see you again."

CHAPTER EIGHTEEN

I staggered back through my front door sometime after three in the afternoon, by which time my whole body had discovered the delights of aching. Some of it was surely from the beating I'd caught, some from the adrenaline that had long since run out. But a great big piece of the ache came from something else that I'd seen before, something that always felt to me a lot like rage, but never quite was.

By the time I made it to my living room, I was shedding clothes the way the trees in the city parks were dropping leaves, losing my jacket, kicking off my boots, letting everything fall where it may. My back spasmed twice as I yanked off my shirt. The pain doubled when I removed my pants, stumbling into the bathroom, stopping at the mirror to see nothing that surprised me.

Blood had dried at my mouth and nose, and below my left eye the skin was laying the foundation for a high-rise bruise to be erected before nightfall. My hair was a mess, and I didn't like how I smelled either.

After evaluating my reflection I started filling the tub, then went to the kitchen for a beer and a bottle of aspirin. I chased the three patented pain-relievers with a bottle of Miller Genuine Draft, then returned to the bath. I dumped a packet of Body Shop salts into the water that, according to container copy, would soothe away my aches and pains.

"Fucking better," I warned the empty packet, then climbed into the water.

The old-fashioned tub had been the major deciding factor in my purchase of this place many years ago; it fit me, one of only two I'd ever encountered that could. Just long enough and deep enough that I could keep most of myself underwater if I didn't stretch out completely.

I shut my eyes and felt the lingering pain, sinking in deep, going for bone. Behind closed lids I saw Lisa and her lies, and right after that my own desperate, stupid self-deception. I tried to think about the two men, who they were. Lieutenants in Alabacha's organization, upper-echelon troops who kept the street-level business in line. Why they'd come after me, I didn't know. Goldy's lie about me stealing his stash didn't parse; on street level, if he'd been telling the truth, sure, there would have been trouble. But lieutenants don't chase down every rip-off; they leave that for their crews on the ground. And I absolutely didn't believe that they had thought I was looking to muscle in on their territory, that they thought I was looking to plant my flag and start slinging decks.

So what had I done to call them from their perches? It wasn't as if I'd been bandying Alabacha's name around.

The connection had to be Vince. The bag Lisa had probably grabbed after she blew him away.

I opened my eyes long enough to twist the tap shut, then splashed back, feeling light-headed.

The pain wasn't going away.

The cold woke me, followed immediately by the doorbell clanging for my attention. I shivered in the water and fumbled for the nearest towel. A jackhammer of a headache jumped feetfirst against my forehead the moment I got upright, and my teeth started chattering as soon as I stepped on the tile. I dried myself quickly and inefficiently, got another towel between my hair and the back of my neck, and pulled on my robe.

The bell rang twice more as I came down the hall, and I stopped to wipe my feet on my discarded jeans. The whole apartment felt cold, and my robe wasn't doing anything against it. The clock in the kitchen looked like it was pointing at eight straight up.

The bell rang again, followed by five hard knocks, and then I was at the door and seeing Erika Wyatt through the peephole. I reached for the knob but stopped before turning it, before unfastening the locks.

There was a moment when I thought maybe she'd heard me coming down the hall, when her face changed from impatience and concern to something closer to suspicion. After another second, she actually leaned in and put her good ear against the door.

I didn't move.

After what felt like at least a week, Erika moved back, brow furrowed and lips tight. She gave the bell another, final press, and when nothing happened she turned. She was wearing Atticus's old army jacket, and she dug her hands deep into the side pockets, heading for the stairs, looking at her feet.

For almost another minute I stayed looking through the peephole. Then I went back down the hall, turned on the light in the kitchen. My answering machine indicated two messages, but I went back to my room to doff robe and don sweats. The clothes didn't make me feel any warmer.

I pulled the plug on the tub, then turned on the heat in the living room, hearing the radiator bang its way to life. In my selection of teas I found one that was supposed to be good for aches. I put the kettle on and listened to my messages while waiting for the water to boil.

Both were from Erika, the first asking if we were still on for a movie tonight, the second saying that she'd be by around eight to take me to the Hong Kong film festival that was playing at the Angelika. On the tape she sounded hopeful, both messages long and full of jokes, and I felt like a rat for not having answered the door.

While the tea brewed I picked my things up off the floor,

throwing my dirty clothes into the laundry bag. My mouth was coated with sleep and beer, and when I picked up my jacket, I went through the pockets, trying to find a roll of something to kill the taste.

It took me a second to realize what it was, the soiled little glassine without warning in my hand, and then I dropped it like I was holding toxic waste. I left the Dream's Death on the floor, hung my jacket over the back of a chair.

I'd finished the tea when the phone bleated for attention, just about when I'd expected it to, and I got it before the third ring.

But it wasn't Erika calling; it was Atticus.

"Hey, you," he said. "Thought I'd get your machine."

"Hey yourself."

"Just get in?"

"Little while ago."

"Did you get Erika's messages?"

"Not yet. I just got in, like I said."

"She was hoping you two were still on for that movie tonight."

"We hadn't confirmed anything. I was out."

"Still working?"

"Always working." He didn't say anything for a couple, maybe three seconds, so I added, "She there?"

"Yeah, she's in her room. She went by your place, maybe half an hour ago."

"I must have just missed her."

"Must have."

He fed another silence across the line, then cleared his throat and said, "She, uh . . . she thought you might be there, you know? Might be avoiding her."

"No, no way. I just wasn't here."

"See, because if you *were* there when she came by, she's taking it personally. She's kind of upset."

"Put her on," I said. "I'll talk to her."

"Hold on."

I fought a shiver and waited for a voice to come back on the line. After a long time I heard the clunk of the receiver being lifted once again.

"Erika," I said. "Sorry."

"No, it's me," Atticus said. "Erika told me to tell you she'd call later."

I didn't say anything for a moment. Then I said, "I wasn't here."

He didn't say anything.

"Atticus," I said.

"She's upset. She thinks you're avoiding her."

"Is that what she thinks, just her?"

"What do you mean?"

"Maybe it's what you think too."

"You *are* avoiding me," he pointed out. "Look, Bridgett, whatever I've done to mess things up between us, Erika shouldn't be punished for it."

"I'm not punishing Erika."

"But you are punishing me?"

"You think that's what this is about? That I'm trying to make you pay for what you did?"

"Three weeks ago I would have said things weren't that bad between us," Atticus answered. "Not great, sure, but definitely getting better. I mean, we were talking every night and . . . I thought that . . ."

"Thought what?"

"I haven't seen you for almost a year, you know that?" he said, his voice going soft once again. "And if you need more time, I'll give it to you. But you've got to explain the rules to me. I thought we were making ground, but now I think I was wrong. You're not talking anymore. And it's come out of no-where, and I'm trying not to take it personally, but the fact is that now Erika's getting the fallout."

"I've been busy."

"You keep saying that. But you don't say with what. I call, Erika calls, and we get your machine. Or no answer. Or some guy picking up whose name is Andrew, and that's all you'll say."

"Is that what all this is? You're jealous? You think maybe I'm doing to you what you did to me?"

His silence lasted long enough for me to feel like a witch by the time it was through. Then he said, "Of course I'm jealous. I'm in love with you."

Now I felt like a witch with lots of warts, the kind that kills babies and serves them to their parents.

"I'm not going to say that I haven't considered it," Atticus said. "That I haven't imagined you've moved on and found someone else. And of course that turns me inside out when I think about it. I don't know what's going on anymore, Bridgett. You won't say."

"There's no one else," I said. "Andrew's just a friend. And what's going on would take too long to explain."

"Jesus Christ, Bridgett, I'll stay on this phone until dawn if that's what you want. You should know that by now."

"I'm going to hang up," I said. "I can't tell you what you want to hear. Tell Erika I'm sorry and that I'll call her, that she can call me if she wants, that I'll return any message she leaves. Tell her I'm sorry."

"Bridgett—"

"I'm hanging up," I said, and did.

The silence in my apartment lasted just long enough for my eyes to find the deck of Dream's Death on the floor.

You don't actually need a spike, Mr. Jones told me. I mean, just look at it, you know it's good shit, pure shit. Sixty percent, maybe even seventy. You don't even have to shoot it, no scar, no hole, no way for anyone to know. You can just get yourself some tinfoil, that'll do the trick too. Put it on the tinfoil, let it cook, inhale the vapors.

Go ahead, chase the dragon, slugger.

You'll feel oh so much better if you do, and you know you want to, you know you will.

You'll feel nothing at all but good.

You'll feel so good.

In the end I picked up the deck.

I opened the deck.

I dumped the deck into the toilet.

Then I climbed into bed, shut my eyes, and tried to keep from bawling like a little girl.

CHAPTER NINETEEN

Most of a month of pretrial detention was under Lisa's belt now, and the Rikers transformation was nearing completion. She walked into the interview room with her head level and her mouth set, the least expressive I'd ever seen her face in all the years between us.

Her shoulders seemed broader and were squared, and I wondered if she'd been indulging in the favorite pastime of inmates everywhere, pumping iron. Her contempt for the CO who opened the door and ushered her in blared like she was shouting it from a megaphone. Her hair had been almost entirely shorn, all those locks that had swayed and flown when she danced vanished, and now close-cropped, it showed off the angles of her face. It removed her projected frailty, replaced it with something potentially much harder.

Then I saw her eyes, and knew that Rikers still had work to do on her. She was adapting, sure, but she hadn't gone all the way; the fear remained. Lisa had simply grown better at hiding it.

The door swung shut and the bolt clicked, and the guard

backed off, moving down the hall. Lisa followed her movements with her eyes, not turning her head. When the guard was well beyond earshot, she turned her focus to me.

"I knew you'd come back."

She sounded satisfied.

" 'Twas a near thing," I said.

She crossed her arms over her chest and fixed a convict's stare on me, bored. "The fuck does that mean?"

"Have a seat, Scarface. We need to talk."

She gave me ten seconds of immobility, just to assert her willingness to rebel, then took the chair opposite me. After getting settled she looked me over much the same way I did her. The knuckles at her index and middle fingers on her right hand were swollen and bruised, and there was a discoloration on the left side of her neck.

"Somebody got tired of your bullshit?" Lisa indicated my left eye with a flick of an index finger.

"It's what happens when you look through one keyhole too many. What happened to your hand?"

"I busted some dumb cunt's jaw."

"Nice way to talk," I said.

Lisa shrugged. "She's a cunt."

I sighed. "Yeah, you're turning into a real hard case, aren't you, Lise?"

"I was always hard. Don't you like my new look? What about my hair?"

"Very butch."

"People kept pulling on it." She tilted her face forward so I could see her scalp, the thin line of a scab near the top of her head. "Tore some of it right out. It hurt a lot. They don't pull it anymore."

"You getting a lot of grief?"

The poker face shimmered for a moment, almost let the fear shine through. "I'm surviving."

"You're scaring me," I said. "This isn't you."

"It's who I have to be right now."

"Then I really do hope it's temporary. For Gabe's sake, if not your own."

"It'll last until you get me out of here."

"You're not getting out," I said.

She slammed both hands onto the tabletop, rising out of her seat, body tight with fury. "Bitch! I knew it! I knew you would do this to me!"

I stayed in my seat and didn't speak.

"I knew you'd hang me out to dry!"

Suddenly all of my anger bubbled up and I was speaking before I could think not to, on my feet and face-to-face with my friend without intending to leave my chair.

"You are a fucking piece of work, you know that, Schoof? Copping that fucking self-pity on me. I'm not the one who burst Vince's head with a stolen .38. I'm not the one who's been lying about what went down, playing bullshit games, acting like a fool."

"Fuck you!"

I put my palm on her chest and gave her a shove back. "Sit the fuck down, Lisa, and do it now, or I'll see to it myself that you get a cell for life."

She backed off instead to the opposite wall. There was a grille-covered window there, through which you could see other interview rooms, but nothing of the outside.

I lowered my voice, but kept the intensity just as high as before. "I know what happened. Get this through your crew-cut cranium, girl. I *know*."

Her face was away from me, but she turned it back, and now the fear was flaring up in her eyes the way a dying campfire tries one last time for life in an unexpected breeze. But, like a campfire, it died just as fast as Lisa brought the mask back into play.

"I knew I couldn't count on you."

"Not me," I said. "You. I couldn't count on *you*. I couldn't count on you to tell me the truth or to trust me. You're still a fucking junkie, Lisa. You've used me, taken advantage of me, made me jeopardize my job, my license, my relationships, because I believed you."

Lisa turned her back to me, pressing her fists into the wall, resting her forehead against the grate over the window. "Bitch," she hissed.

"Part of it's my own damn fault," I said. "I admit it. I

wanted to believe you. Convinced myself that you were playing straight with me, or at least as straight as you could manage. That's on me, like I said, letting this go on for so long."

"Bitch," she repeated, louder.

"Where's my Da's gun?"

"How the fuck should I—"

"You held on to it after you shot Vince. It wasn't found at the scene, so you didn't drop it there. Where'd you hide it?"

She spun and tried a last time to refute me. "I didn't—"

"Bullshit!" I shouted.

She tried to match my stare. Then she had to look away.

I sat at the table once more. "Come on, Lisa, stop playing games with me. I spoke to a guy on Saturday," I said softly. "Guy who was in the gallery on One Sixty-first Street when you pulled the trigger. He saw all of it."

"Guy in a gallery, huh? Upstanding fucking citizen witness, I'd bet. A junkie, maybe? You're believing some fucking junkie over me."

I didn't say anything. It took her almost thirty seconds to realize what she'd just said.

"Fucking junkie like me."

"And me."

"Yeah."

When she brought her face up again to meet my eyes, the mask was gone. "I don't know where the gun is. I think I dropped it there, I don't really remember."

"It wasn't found at the scene."

She came back from the window, took her seat once more. "I don't remember what I did with it. Honest."

"Tell me what happened."

Lisa looked past me, to where the guards roamed the halls. "If they hear me . . ."

"It's a little too late to worry about that now," I said. "But they can't use it even if they do hear us. I'm working for Glaser, so her privilege extends to me."

"What part do you want first?" Lisa asked.

"Start with the gun."

She swallowed hard and rested her elbows on the table,

moving her face towards mine as if ready for a kiss. Even that close, it was hard to hear her.

"I took it when Gabe and I were at your place that time. Just in case. You wouldn't tell me what we were going to do, and I thought . . . I was going to give it back, but I liked . . . You've seen our neighborhood . . . it made me feel safer."

I nodded, just to let her know I was listening, that I understood.

"After we did what we did, I thought everything would be fine. But it kept bugging me, and then ˙ . . . I thought I was seeing him places. Picking up Gabe, I thought I saw Vince. Shopping, I thought he was in the aisle, you know, right behind me. I was sure he was following me, that he was getting ready to come back."

"You could have called me."

"No, no I couldn't, don't you see? I tried to tell you back then, tried to tell you what had to be done, but you said you wouldn't do it, and I knew if I told you . . . I knew you'd stop me.

"And I had to be sure. It was the only way."

"Tell me the rest."

"I went up to Washington Heights, started asking around for him. My Spanish isn't too bad, and I . . . I've got the scars, you know. . . . It took me a week, but I found this gallery, the one on One Sixty-first, found out that he was stopping by every few days—"

"Doing what?" I asked.

She hesitated. "He was making runs, dropping bricks off and taking the cash back to his people. I waited and saw him stash his bag outside. I followed him in. And I saw him in the room and I just started shooting and then I ran."

I sat back, and after a moment she did too. I shook my head. "You're leaving out one big piece, aren't you?"

Another hesitation. Then she said, "I grabbed the bag when I was running."

"What'd you do with it?"

"I hid it."

"Where?"

She shook her head, and her lips compressed, as if to stop the secret from coming out should all else fail.

"How much was inside?"

"There wasn't money."

"So what was in it?"

"The bricks."

"How many?"

She just spread her right hand on the table, curling her thumb beneath her palm, showing me four fingers.

"Four bricks. Cut?" I asked.

She shook her head.

"Jesus, Mary, and Joseph."

No wonder Alabacha had his lieutenants roughing up people who talked about Vince. Four keys of uncut heroin. At $250,000 a kilo, that was a million dollars of dope. Compared to what Alabacha was moving regularly, it probably wasn't much. Still, a million dollars is a million dollars, not an easy write-off in any business.

A million dollars that had fallen into Lisa's hands as a fluke.

"What are you going to do with it?" I asked her.

"I don't know. I couldn't just throw it away, and . . . and . . . It's *so* much money, Bridgett! It's more money than I'll make in a lifetime, it's money I could spend on Gabe, we could get out of the city, we could do anything!"

"It's also a motive," I said. "If the DA finds out about those four kilos, you're looking at an amended charge. They'll think you whacked Vince for the smack."

"But I didn't know!"

"Why should they believe you? Why should I? You've been lying about this whole thing since he died, Lisa. Your credibility, pardon my saying so, is for shit."

"Not about this. Not you. Of all people, you should believe me. You know what it's like. You know that I did what I did to survive."

"I don't know that," I corrected, and I heard the ice in my voice.

She shut her eyes tight, as if hit by a sudden migraine.

"There wasn't any choice. He was coming back, he was going to kill me, he was going to hurt my son. It was self-defense. You know it."

"No," I said. "Self-defense would have been if he was coming through your front door with a knife, Lisa. What you did was murder."

She stared at me as if we'd never met before, as if I had a face that was somehow wrong, perhaps equipped with an extra eye or a third nostril. "Don't say that, Bridgett." She said it in a whisper.

I was suddenly aware of how uncomfortable my chair was, how my bruises hurt.

"I did what I had to," Lisa said, and her voice shook. "To be strong, to protect myself and my baby, to stop being a victim. And since I protected myself and my family when no one else would, I'm going to be called a murderer and locked up for the rest of my life. The law wasn't made to protect people like me."

There was a scraping of metal, the sound of the screw returning, unlocking the door. Lisa's expression implored me to understand, to agree.

"Lisa . . ."

"I shouldn't do time for saving my life," Lisa Schoof said. "For saving Gabriel's life." She shook her head, glancing at the screw as she came into the room and held the door open, then shooting me one last glance.

"Bridgett," Lisa begged. "You know I didn't do anything wrong. You've got to help me. Nothing's changed, Bridgett."

"Everything's changed," I said.

And then the CO was guiding her out of the room, and I saw that I'd undone all the lessons Rikers had taught Lisa over the last month.

Lisa left afraid, and more desperate than ever.

CHAPTER TWENTY

Gabriel was sitting on the landing just before my floor, green backpack between his feet, reading a book. The book was *Tales of a Fourth Grade Nothing*, tattered, with all the signs of being from the school library, and he was engrossed enough in the story that he didn't hear me coming up the stairs. I stopped three steps short of him and waited, and then it sank in, and he looked up with that unique surprise that comes from being torn from a tale well told.

"Shouldn't you be at school?" I asked.

"I cut."

"You waiting for me?"

He nodded.

"Waiting long?"

"An hour, maybe."

"Get up," I said, stepping around him. "Come inside."

Gabriel shoved the book back into his backpack and followed me into my apartment. I checked the fridge and found milk that hadn't yet expired, pulled the half-gallon out and set it on the counter. "Cookies?"

"Sure."

Feeling frighteningly domestic, I poured out a glass of milk and opened a bag of Pepperidge Farms, then carried them around to where Gabriel had sat himself on my couch. He went for the cookies first, scarfing down three Mint Milanos back to back, then going with the skim chaser. I took the chair and waited for him to finish. His hair had grown out a bit, and he no longer looked fresh from the recruiting depot. His pants were a little too short for his legs, and in his sitting position, the cuffs rested just below the middle of his shins. His clothes looked clean, and, for the most part, he did too.

When the glass was empty he set it on the coffee table in front of the couch and asked, "What happened to your face?"

"I got punched."

"You've got a black eye. Can you see out of it?"

"I can see enough."

"Does it hurt?"

"Not so much anymore."

"Who did it?"

I sighed. "What are you doing here, Gabe?"

He fidgeted on the couch, sitting on his hands and eyeing the bag of cookies. "I wanted to see you. I haven't seen you in a while."

"I've been busy."

"Working for my mom, right?"

"That's it."

"That how you got punched?"

I thought about how to answer that, decided that I couldn't. "You should head home."

"I can't go home."

"I meant to Vera's."

"Vera's at work. Can I stay here for a while?"

"You can go back to school."

He looked at his sneakers. The white rubber covering his toes was scuffed with black streaks, as if he'd been kicking asphalt. "It'll be over by the time I get back." He looked up at me, and I don't know whether it was intentional or not, but his eyes were wide and innocent and maybe a little frightened, and he looked just like a little boy who didn't have anywhere else to go. "Can I stay? Just for a bit?"

"I have things I have to do," I said.

"I'll be quiet. I'll just sit here and read."

I suppressed an almighty sigh and then the phone started ringing. I reached for it and told him, "Just for a bit, Gabe."

"I'll be quiet," he repeated, going for his book once again.

The phone rang again and I grabbed the receiver, catching it before the bell died. "Logan."

"Finally!" Laila Agra said. "I've been looking for you all day. Why are you at home?"

"Because I live here?"

"You misunderstand me, my feckless and capable employee. I meant, why aren't you here at work?"

"Didn't you get my message?" I lied.

"What message?"

"I had some things to take care of today, I won't be able to come in."

"And you left me a message?"

"Of course."

"With Charice?"

"No, on your machine."

"You're lying to me, Bridgett," Laila said. "What's going on with you? The last two weeks, you haven't been in for more than eight hours."

"I'm working on something for a friend." I took the phone and moved down the hall, out of Gabriel's earshot. "It's eating a lot of time."

"What sort of thing for a friend?"

"I'd rather not say."

She exploded an exhale in my ear. "Okay, listen to me, Bridgett, darling, dear, my fairest employee. I can cut you only so much slack, and you're about to run out. Martin and I need you to come into the office tomorrow. We're getting busy, and I count on you to pick up some of the load."

"I know," I said. "I'm sorry."

"Don't be sorry. Just be here tomorrow, all right?"

"I'll do my best."

"No, don't do your best, just be here. This is your job, remember?"

"I'll be there tomorrow," I lied.

"And I'll look forward to seeing you," Laila Agra said.

I hung up and put the phone back on the counter. Gabriel had the book open in his lap and his wide eyes on me, but when I met his stare he looked away, back at the pages. For a couple of seconds I just stood still, trying to decide what I was going to do, feeling like an intruder in my own home. I decided to sit in my easy chair again. Gabriel pretended to read.

I am on the verge of so much trouble, I realized. It was the closest I'd ever heard Laila come to telling me that my job was in jeopardy, maybe because this was, in fact, the closest I'd ever come to putting it there. I felt guilty about it too, and not just for the lies I'd told; I'd been a flake of late. In a way, I was surprised she'd taken this long to tell me enough was enough.

Gabriel turned a page, and his mouth curled into a smile at something he read.

I should just walk away from this whole thing, I told myself. Lisa made her bed, she should damn well lie in it.

But that was the problem, wasn't it? She *hadn't* made her bed, at least not entirely. She couldn't be blamed for her parents, her family, she couldn't be blamed for trying to make things better for herself and her son. And even if killing Vince had been a mistake, I couldn't help but think she'd been right when she said it had been self-defense. For her, it was; just not any sort of self-defense the law would understand.

She'd made bad mistakes. But she'd been a victim of worse. She'd been a victim all her life, and just when she was ready to change that, Vince had returned to set the record straight.

Vince had all but said that, try as she might, Lisa Schoof would always be a victim.

And I couldn't honestly believe that, if he'd lived, Vincent Lark wouldn't have come back at another time, and upon that return wouldn't have lashed out at Lisa and Gabriel.

In the end, didn't Lisa deserve one final, honest shot at being safe?

I blinked a couple of times and realized that Gabriel had closed his book. He smiled uncertainly at me.

"What would you do if your mother has to go to prison?" I asked.

"I don't know. Vera said that wasn't going to happen."

"There's going to be a trial, you know that."

Gabriel nodded.

"She could lose at trial, Gabe," I said. "She could be convicted for murder."

"Not if she's innocent."

"There are some people who think that she's guilty."

"But they're lying, right? And if she didn't do anything wrong, she'll be free to come home, right?"

"Right," I said, lying again.

"I miss her." His voice was turning thin.

"It's okay, she'll be home soon," I lied yet again, and it was too little, too late. Gabriel's eyes began to shimmer with rising tears. Then he got off the couch, dropping the book, and just like in his own home one month ago, as he had done to his own mother, he came to my chair and threw his arms around me.

"I want her to come home," he said.

I hugged him close and tight. There were no more lies I could tell him.

I put Gabe into a cab a little after four that afternoon with a kiss and told him to call me when he got to Vera's, to let me know that he'd arrived safely. I gave the driver ten bucks and directions, and made certain that he saw me note both his medallion number and the cab's license before letting him go.

Back in my apartment, I fixed myself a dinner that I didn't eat, then channel-surfed for an hour. Gabe called to say he'd arrived. I told him not to worry.

When I went to bed I had a headache.

Worse, I had the start of an idea.

"I need some personal time."

Laila Agra stared at me for a couple of seconds before saying, "How long?" Her dark eyes looked almost black.

"I don't know," I told her.

"This have anything to do with that shiner you're sporting?"

"No."

She kicked her chair back from behind her desk, rolling it into the wall. Over her head I could look out the window in her office, at an expensive view of the building that faced us on the other side of Madison Avenue. Laila was wearing a power suit today, the kind she wore when she was meeting with corporate customers, and she'd coiled her ponytail atop her head, so it looked like an ebony snake catching twenty winks.

"Starting when?" she asked.

"Immediately."

"I need more information."

"I don't have more information," I said. "I'm involved in something and I can't talk about it and I don't know how long it's going to take."

"Give me an idea, Bridgett."

"At least a month."

"Meaning I'll have you back by the middle of November?"

"Possibly."

"But this could take longer?"

"Yes."

She put two fingers to her right temple and massaged a small circle, frowning. "Are you aware how this sounds, honey?" she asked me. "I mean, do you have any idea how this looks? What you're asking?"

"Yes," I said.

"This is an extremely bad time to cut out on us, Bridgett. Martin and I have been scooping up your slack as it is, and now you're telling me this."

"I understand where this puts you," I said.

Her hand came down from her temple and she swiveled her chair so she could look out at the skyscraper across the street. "Do you understand where it puts *you*?

I thought you wanted to make partner by the end of the year, Bridgett."

"I'm still committed to the organization," I said. "I just have to take care of this business first. Once it's done I'll be back and you'll be able to count on me. But if I don't take the time now, it's just going to make the situation between us worse. I don't mean to do bad by you or Martin, Laila, but I don't want to string you along."

"But you can't tell me what it is you need to do, or why?"

"I really can't."

"Illegal?"

"Potentially."

"Something that puts your license in jeopardy?"

"Potentially," I repeated.

Laila swiveled the chair back to face me. "You understand that you may not have a job when you get back?"

"Yes."

She shook her head slightly, and the coil of hair on her head shimmered with the movement. She walked me to the door, and I felt like a client. Even more so when she offered me her hand.

"What, no hug?" I asked.

"Maybe when you get back, Bridgett."

"I don't want this to be good-bye."

"It isn't."

I took her hand and we shook and then she opened the door for me.

The last thing she said to me was, "Don't do anything stupid, honey."

I spent the next week working it out, either alone in my apartment or out on the streets. When I was out, I kept a low profile, a lot of shadowing from a distance, a lot of surveillance.

I saw a lot of people who neither Lisa nor I would call citizens. I saw a lot of drugs, dealt, used, sold.

Strangely, throughout the week, Mr. Jones was silent.

Maybe it was because we both knew what was coming.

I started packing and making phone calls, putting my belongings into boxes and then taking them out to a storage place just over the Harlem River in the Bronx. I made arrangements to have my mail held, and I contacted Bell Atlantic and Con Ed about my phone and power, respectively, to have service cut off the following week. I wrote the letters, one to my sister and one to Atticus.

Two weeks before Halloween, in the morning, I went to the bank and handled the money, withdrawing everything but five grand from my account and having it put into a cashier's check made out to Cashel. By eleven I was in the Porsche, and headed back to Rikers.

It took three hours before I could meet with Lisa, since I arrived unannounced and the guards had to make certain I was authorized. We met in a room identical to the others I'd seen before. I didn't bother to sit down.

She had hope all over her face when she came in, and as soon as the door shut, she asked, "You'll do it?"

"I'll do it," I said.

Her eyes squeezed shut and she blew out a breath of relief, and for a moment I could almost see the weight on her, the way it eased off her shoulders in that instant. Then it settled again and she asked, "How?"

"I can't tell you."

"What do you need me to do?"

"When the DEA offers you a deal, take it."

"What?"

"You heard me."

"When'd they get involved?"

"In about a month, if everything works out right."

"But . . . I mean, what sort of deal?"

"They'll want you to do something. Agree to it. I'll handle the rest."

"Bridgett—"

"One last thing," I said. "Don't tell anyone about this conversation. Not Glaser, not the DEA, no one. If somebody asks what we talked about today, tell them we talked about Gabriel, about plans in case you ended up doing time."

"Is someone going to ask?"

"There's a chance. There's a chance nothing will happen, that the DEA won't ever come by. I can't guarantee you anything, Lisa."

"But you've got hope?"

"Some."

"I'll do whatever it takes," Lisa said. "I have nothing to lose."

"No," I said. "I do."

From Rikers I went out to Forest Hills, in Queens, and dropped the Porsche off into the hands of someone I knew would treat the car almost as well as I did. Dale Matsui is a friend I met through Atticus, one of the protection people he works with, a guy who specializes in cars. This means that Dale Matsui knows how to drive quickly without dying. It also means he'd take a bullet for my 911.

"Take good care of her," I told him.

"You know I will. Where you off to?"

"Business trip to the Left Coast. I'll be out of town for a month or more."

"You told Atticus?"

"I'm going to call him when I get home."

"How are you and he doing?"

"I don't ask you about your love life."

"So it's love, then?"

"Dale," I warned.

"Gotcha. Take care. I'll see you when you get back."

He gave me a bear hug before I left, and I walked to the subway, then rode the train back into Manhattan. It was almost four when I got home, and it was strange walking into my apartment, when the emptiness hit me. For a fraction of a second, I felt lost, and that fraction was long enough for every doubt to stampede forward.

For a minute I really had to wonder if I was out of my mind.

I picked up my phone and was relieved to find that service hadn't been cut yet. I dialed and waited, sitting on the floor, and after three rings the Boy Scout answered.

"Hey, you," I said. "It's me."

"Hey," Atticus said, and I heard it in his voice, the wariness and the surprise. "Wasn't expecting to hear from you."

"I'm going out of town for a few weeks. Wanted to let you know. I'm hoping when I get back we can talk. Maybe even get together."

"How long will you be gone?"

"It's business, I don't know how long it will take. I'll call when I get back."

"I'll be looking forward to it," he said.

"Is Erika there?"

"She's at school right now. I'll let her know that you called."

"Do that," I said. "Also . . . she and I had a conversation a while ago, and . . . I don't know if you've talked to her about Christmas, but she wants a biker jacket. I was thinking we could go in on one for her together."

"You don't think it's a little early for Christmas shopping?"

"I just thought it would be a good present. There's a place on Christopher Street. Leather Man. If you want to go by there and pick one out for her, I'll split the cost with you."

"I can do that if you like," he said slowly. "You'll be back in time to give it to her, right?"

"Absolutely," I said.

I don't know what he heard in my voice, but something tipped him. "Business trip?" he asked.

"Yeah."

"Where?"

"San Francisco."

"No shit? My hometown. Where you going to be staying?"

"I don't know yet. I'll call you when I get in. Look, I got to go, finish packing. I'm flying out tonight. If you talk to Natalie, tell her I'll see her when I get back."

"I will. Bridgett?"

"Yeah?"

"Yeah, look . . . day or night, like I said. You know where I am."

"You keep saying things like that, I may take you up on the offer."

"The offer is always open."

"I'll remember that. Talk to you soon."

"Good-bye," he said.

"Good-bye, Atticus," I said.

By eight that night I'd just about finished with everything. I put the letters I'd written into a cardboard box along with the cashier's check, then left the apartment. After I locked up, I put my keys into the box as well, then sealed it shut with some strapping tape. I threw the roll of tape into the trash can on the corner, went to the nearest FedEx drop, and sent the box to my sister in the Bronx. Then I took my copy of the airbill and I put that into an envelope also addressed to my sister, and mailed that too.

It was dark now, and chilly, a true autumn wind zipping through the island, one with real teeth. My stomach was tight and twisting. I stood on the corner of Twentieth and Eighth and watched the traffic roll past, the lights. I saw a couple walking along the sidewalk, one of them pushing a stroller. The baby inside was wrapped like a caterpillar in a cocoon.

I started walking uptown, stopping along the way at an all-night pharmacy, where I bought a syringe. Then I switched to the subway, and rode the One all the way up to 168th Street. It was colder when I climbed back out of the ground, and the streets seemed larger, everything big and potentially frightening.

It took me less than ten minutes to find a steerer, working out of a doorway on Wadsworth Avenue, and I followed his directions to a Dominican gentleman in his midthirties who took my twenty dollars without comment and then disappeared down the street. Two minutes later a woman approached and handed me two decks, and I slid the glassines from her hardened palm and stowed them in a pocket.

"Good stuff," the woman told me. From the look of her, she'd been on the needle for years, skin tight across her bones, her face shiny as if molded from melted plastic. "You sure you know what to do with shit this nice?"

"I've got an idea," I said, and left her behind to deal with the next consumer. Radios on the street were blasting loud hip-hop remixes, and I saw other crews, sitting on stoops or leaning on cars. Men clustered outside of illegal bars, each nursing long-neck bottles of beer. It wasn't cold enough yet to drive them inside.

It was almost ten before I found the right address, before I found Carla's place. I checked my pockets a final time, found the lighter and the bottlecap and the syringe, the two decks of Alabacha stamped Goodness.

After you, Mr. Jones said.

"Don't mind if I do," I said, and went inside.

PART TWO

December 24 to December 27

CHAPTER ONE

"So, do you like him?" Erika asked.

"I have no idea who he is," I said.

"Grendel. He's a criminal genius, a sociopathic killer. He rules the underworld of Manhattan."

I blinked at her.

"He's a comic-book character, Atticus," Erika added patiently.

"Ah," I said, and looked at the doll once more. Grendel was nine inches tall, dressed all in black, with an imposing black mask that entirely encased his head. Long white vertical slits, presumably positioned as eyeholes, ran down either side of his helmet.

"This is his fork." Erika reached into the box and offered me the item in question. "Fits in his hand, see?"

The fork was more like a spear than an eating utensil, a long black pole ending in two silver prongs. The prongs looked sharp.

"Uses it a lot, does he?" I asked.

"Not as much as you'd think. Give me."

I handed over the doll and Erika fiddled with Grendel, slipping the weapon into his fist and then posing him on the living room floor. Light from the flickering menorah slipped appropriate shadows around the figure.

"Happy Hanukkah," Erika said.

"And merry Christmas."

"Not Christmas yet. Tomorrow."

"Then merry Christmas Eve," I amended.

We both looked at Grendel, where he stood ominously in the shadows on the floor.

"You don't like it," Erika decided.

"I didn't say that. All I said was that I didn't know who he was."

"Well, now you know, and you still haven't said that you like it."

"I like it," I said. "I think he's cool."

She searched my face intently for several seconds, and I tried to put the sincerity I felt into my expression. She sighed. "You're fucking awful to shop for, you know that?"

"I like it," I repeated. "You going to open yours now, or do I have to dance a little jig to prove that I am both happy and grateful for your gift?"

She gnawed on her bottom lip, then reached for the box I'd placed beneath the tiny shrub that acted as our Christmas tree. The shrub was on the opposite end of the table from my small menorah, more to reduce the danger of a fire than for any religious statement. The single string of tinsel Erika had draped off the shrub shimmered gold and black against the flames from the two burning candles.

We were doing our best to be egalitarian about how we celebrated the holidays.

Erika dealt with the paper quickly, shredding the gift-wrapping unceremoniously to reveal the cardboard box beneath.

"Heavy," she said. "What is it?"

"Open it and find out."

She hefted the box, tilting it from one side to the other, and then her eyes lit. Digging her fingers into the cardboard beneath the lid, she pulled against the tape, trying to force the box open. I considered offering to bring her some scissors, but then there was a snap as the tape broke free, and the box was open in her lap. Erika grinned, letting the tissue flutter dangerously close to the burning candles as she threw it away to reveal the black leather jacket within.

"If it doesn't fit, we can take it back," I said.

Erika got to her feet, kicking over Grendel as she did. His fork skittered into the corner, beneath the radiator. She slipped the jacket on and zipped it shut around her middle. The leather was shiny and new, and the scent of it was strong. "This is perfect, this is just the one I wanted. I didn't think you'd get it for me, I thought you'd completely missed my hints. How do I look?"

"Very nice."

"Fantastic," she said, and leaned over to where I was sitting on the couch to give me a hug. I hugged her back and Erika let me go, then spun in front of the window, using it as a makeshift mirror. The flames reflected her image. "Just like Bridgett's," Erika said.

"She told me where to find it," I said.

Erika turned her head from her reflection to look at me. "You've heard from her?" Her voice sharpened when she said it, almost ready to accuse me of withholding vital information.

"We talked about getting it for you before she left. Consider it a gift from both of us."

"It'd be better if she was here."

"It would."

"It would be better if she came back," Erika added after a second. "She's been gone a long time."

"Two months and two days." I gathered the torn wrapping paper from the floor, then headed for the kitchen, trying to ignore the new familiar lump in my stomach. The lump was Bridgett's; she'd planted it in October with a seed, and I'd watered it faithfully with concern for her and about a thousand other emotions for myself every hour since she'd left. In the last couple of weeks it had tripled in size, and cubed itself twice more with weight.

I opened the cabinet beneath the sink and put the paper in

the garbage can. I closed the cabinet, looked at the faucet, at a piece of my bent reflection on the water-spotted metal.

When I called her apartment, I got a message that said the number was no longer in service at this time. When I called Agra & Donnovan Investigations, I was told that Ms. Logan had taken a leave of absence, and that no one knew when she would be back. When I asked if she had left a number where she could be reached, I was told, quite baldly, no. When I said that I'd understood she was away on business, I was answered with a long pause, and then an almost sullen "Not to my knowledge."

I'd gone by her apartment five different times in as many weeks, and each time found nobody home, and neighbors who couldn't tell me where she'd gone. There was no mail jutting from her box, no slips of paper stuck half under the door.

It's Christmas Eve and she should be back by now, I thought. She should be back, or she should have called or something, and since she hasn't . . . well . . .

And here, as always, I ran out of steam. Try as I might, I didn't know what came next. There were all sorts of explanations for her absence I could come up with, covering the nefarious to the mundane. She could be away on business, professional or personal. She could be on some spectacular world cruise. She could be living in Kingston, Jamaica, working on her tan.

Or she could be in serious trouble.

I'd know if she were dead.

I hoped.

Her new jacket creaked as Erika came into the kitchen. I could feel her staring at my back. I turned around and fastened my it's-the-holidays smile in place, and she shot me one that was just as false in return. Then she reached for the phone and handed the receiver to me.

"I'll dial," she said, and did.

The phone rang three times before Dale Matsui answered. "God bless us, every one," he said.

"Hi, this is the Grinch," I said. "I'm looking for my dog,

Max. He's easy to recognize—he's got an antler tied to his head with a piece of string."

"Nobody here but us happy Whos of Who-ville," he said. "How you doing, Atticus? How's Erika?"

"We're fine, we're just indulging in some shared holiday melancholia. Think you can alleviate it?"

"She hasn't picked up the Porsche, Atticus."

I didn't say anything. Erika was watching me, and when I shook my head her face fell almost to the hardwood floor.

"And you haven't heard from her?"

"Nothing, man. Not since she dropped off the Porsche way back when. Shouldn't she be back by now?"

"That's what we're thinking."

"Worried?"

"Doesn't even cover it," I said. "How's your night?"

"Ethan and I are sipping mulled wine before the fire-place," Dale said. "Or shouldn't I have said that?"

"Don't worry about me. I've got pleasant enough company right here."

"Gonna see you tomorrow?"

"We'll be there for brunch," I promised, and got off the phone.

"What now?" Erika asked.

"I was thinking we could make some popcorn and watch *It's a Wonderful Life*."

"We could make popcorn and watch *Henry: Portrait of a Serial Killer*."

"You need your own television."

"For my birthday," Erika said, unzipping her new jacket and making for her room.

I looked out the window onto the alley for a moment longer, then reached for the big pot beneath the cupboard and got down the bottle of Wesson. I poured oil and threw in three kernels, set the pot on the burner and turned on the heat. I heard the door to Erika's room open again, and then the sound of the television being switched on in the living room.

The second of my three test kernels was exploding

when the buzzer from the intercom sounded. I went for the button. "Yes?"

"Atticus Kodiak?" The voice sounded possibly human, maybe in the last stages of tuberculosis.

"Speaking."

The voice made noise again.

"Sorry?"

"—a letter for you!"

"I'll buzz you in. Five F," I said, and pushed the button for the door, held it down while I counted to three, and then let it go. When I turned around, smoke was beginning to rise from the pot and the smell of burned popcorn had begun drifting through the apartment. I went back to the stove, promptly scorched my hand on the metal, swore, yanked again, and switched off the heat.

"Where's my popcorn?" Erika asked.

"On hold."

"Who was at the door?"

"Somebody with a letter for me. He's on his way up."

"At eight at night on Christmas Eve?"

"Special delivery," I said, and headed for the front door just as the first of four knocks fell. Erika followed me, standing back a couple of feet as I checked the spyhole. It's a testament to how bad the intercom system is in my building that the person outside was, in fact, not a man but a woman. It's a testament to how worried I was about Bridgett that, at first, I thought it was her standing outside my door.

I unfastened the locks in record time, pulling back on the door so fast that I scared her, and the woman was backing up half a step as I started to open my mouth. And then I realized that it wasn't her, that it wasn't Bridgett, and I felt the lump in my stomach expand a little more.

It was an understandable mistake. The woman was close to six feet tall, with the same black hair and almost-too-pale skin, the same nose, the same bones. Her eyes were more gray than blue, her mouth not as wide, her lips less generous. No piercing through the left nostril and only two earrings, one in each lobe, small little studs. She was dressed plainly, though not unattractively, navy blue corduroy pants and gray woolen jacket over a pink turtleneck. A white scarf was loose around her neck, and in one gloved hand she held a green, blue, and white stocking cap. In her other, she held a large manila envelope.

On her left lapel was fastened a rectangular pin, perhaps pewter or tarnished silver. Embossed on it was a relief of a hillside, a cross at the summit. Something was written in Latin along the edges, but I didn't want to stare, and the only word I caught was *amo*.

"You're Atticus Kodiak?" The woman didn't sound overly impressed. Even her voice was like Bridgett's, although not quite as low.

From my elbow, I heard Erika say, "Whoa!"

I said, "You're Cashel."

The woman nodded.

"Please, come in."

She squeezed through the space between Erika and myself and down our narrow hall, into the kitchen. I shut the door behind her, then followed, and now my stomach was doing something entirely different. I could feel the cold edge of nausea begin to work its way in.

"You're her sister?" Erika was asking Cashel Logan.

"Yes."

"Younger sister?"

"A year and a half."

"Erika," I said. "Will you give us a minute alone?"

"Huh?"

"Just a minute alone, okay?"

She looked at me warily, then at Cashel. Nothing in Cashel Logan's face had changed, and that gave my fear teeth.

Without another word, Erika headed down the hall, back to where the television babbled.

I pulled out one of the chairs from the table. "Have a seat."

"Thank you." She set the envelope and her cap on the table, unwrapped her scarf, then removed her gloves and put them alongside. When she unfastened her jacket, I saw a thin gold band around her left ring finger. She left the jacket on when she sat.

I knew that I was expecting very bad news, knew it from

the way my heart was thumping at my ears and the way I could hear Jimmy Stewart's voice from the next room. I moved to the windowsill and sat down, feeling the winter-chilled glass touch my back through my shirt.

"I'm here on behalf of my sister." She said it cautiously.

"I kind of guessed that. And if this is what I think it is, I'll save you the trouble and just ask you now, you know, so you don't have to work up to it." When I asked, it came out of my mouth like a rock. "Is she dead?"

Cashel Logan's head came back sharply, and she looked honestly stunned. "No, no, I don't think so. I pray not. I . . . You haven't heard from her?"

It wasn't a hell of a lot, I suppose, but it was enough. "No. I thought you . . ."

She followed my eyes to the envelope on the table, then reached for it and offered it to me. "I got this from her near the end of October. She sent me a box of papers, some other things. There was a letter."

The envelope was plain, unlabeled, and surprisingly heavy. It was thick too, as if another piece of paper slipped inside would be enough to tear it open from within.

"In the letter Bridgett sent to me were instructions," Cashel Logan said. "She asked that if I hadn't heard from her by the twenty-fourth of this month, I bring you that envelope. She left me your name and address. I assumed you would know what all of this is about."

"She told me she was going out of town, on business," I said.

"She also sent me the keys to her apartment. She sent me a cashier's check for over fifty thousand dollars. Why would she do that if she were only going out of town on business?"

"I don't know," I said. "Trust me, I'm as worried about her as you are, Mrs. . . . ."

"I'm not a Mrs.," Cashel said.

"I'm sorry, I saw the ring—"

"I'm a nun."

I stared at her.

"No wings, no halo," Sister Cashel Logan said. "Just a plain old Sister of Incarnate Love."

"I had no idea. I didn't mean any offense."

"None taken."

"You don't look like a nun."

"I wear my habit on special occasions."

I wasn't certain if she was joking or not, and there was an awkward pause that I used to move my attention back to the envelope. It didn't help.

"Do you know my sister well? I mean, didn't Bridgett ever mention me?"

"She's mentioned you," I said. "But she neglected the nun part."

Sister Cashel put her hands in her lap, crossed her legs at the ankles. "I suppose that shouldn't surprise me. I'd never heard of you until I got her letter. Do you work with her?"

"Sometimes," I said.

"Sometimes? So, you're another private investigator? Or are you a cop?"

"I'm in security. I protect people."

"In her letter to me, Bridgett said I must be certain I went to you. She said you were the only person who would do what she asked, no matter what."

"She's right," I said after a moment.

Sister Cashel looked at me closely, evaluating my features, searching out my eyes behind my lenses. I was glad that I'd shaved this morning, hoped that my scarred cheek didn't look too horrific, that the hoops in my left ear were neat and aligned. I wished I was in a nicer sweater, and slacks instead of jeans.

It was, after all, the first time I'd met Bridgett's family.

When she was done with her survey, Sister Cashel Logan gave me a small nod. She did not smile.

"Then you should probably open that envelope now," she said. "And find out what she asks of you."

CHAPTER TWO

There were perhaps forty pages of material: photographs, maps, typed notes, and lined pieces of legal paper covered with Bridgett's handwriting. I ignored all of them for the time being, because the letter was on top.

It was dated the twentieth of October, and read as follows:

Atticus,

Good evening, Mr. Phelps. . . .

You're probably pretty upset with me, pretty angry that I haven't been in touch, that I've dropped off the face of the planet. You've been by my apartment two or three times, and have discovered that the place is locked tight. You've called Agra & Donnovan, asked if they knew where I was, and have been told that they don't have a clue. Or that I've been fired. Or both. You've asked Natalie and Dale and Scott, and they don't know either.

And you're probably wondering how the hell I neglected to tell you that my sister is a Sister.

*But none of that's really important right now,
because since you're reading this, it means you're
wondering where the hell I've gone to.*

*Thing is, if you're reading this, it means I've gotten
myself into something that I can't find a way out of,
and I need your (here it comes, the moment we've all
been waiting for) . . . help.*

*Funny thing is, wherever I am now, I'm there for a
very similar reason—trying to give someone some help.*

So, here's what you need to know:

*I have not, in fact, gone to San Francisco or any
other strange and frightening city on business. I'm still
in New York (at least, I hope I'm still in New York).*

*I have gone undercover, inasmuch as a person such
as myself can when working alone. Meaning I'm
using my real name, so at least you've got that much
to help you out.*

*I am now—hopefully—a member of a drug-running
organization run by a man named Pierre Alabacha.*

*It's that last point that's the problem. It could be
that I've gotten myself in so deep that I just haven't
been able to work myself free. Could be that I've
gotten arrested. Could be that I was made, and we
both know what that would mean, so the less said
about that the better.*

*And now you're reading this, and I'm not there, so
I need you to come and get me. Attached is the
address of the place I've rented for the duration of
my little operation. Probably best if you look for me
there first.*

*Of course, I probably won't be there. In which
case, I don't really have much more to offer. I've
enclosed everything I gathered on Alabacha before my
departure, everything that could be of help to you in
finding me if I'm not where I should be. I tried to
make my notes clear. I sincerely hope it will be
enough. Among the names I've left you is that of
an old friend, Andrew Wolfe. He knew me pretty
well once upon a time. He gave me a hand when*

I started this whole thing, and he'll lend the same one to you.

As for the rest of our gang, I'd be grateful if you kept Dale and Natalie and Corry out of the loop. I'd be grateful if you could keep Erika out of the loop too, but doubt that'll be possible. You'll note that I've omitted Scott. I leave Scott to your discretion.

There's a final piece of information you should have, but I honestly can't bring myself to put it down on paper here. Odd, because I thought it would be easier to write it rather than to say it. But I can't, and have to therefore cop out and leave it to Cashel to explain.

When you finish this letter, ask my sister to tell you what I was like when I was sixteen years old. If she hedges, press her. You need to know. You need to know all of it.

And after you've heard what she has to say, if you can, forgive me. Not necessarily for what I've already done, but for what I may do.

This isn't meant to be a farewell letter, but I'd be a fool not to recognize that possibility. So I'll say now what I should have said to you on the phone that night we fought. I want for us to have another chance. I don't know if that'll even be possible, but you should know that much. It's an awful fucking cliché, but my intention has never been to hurt you. All my silence, that's been about me, not you. I forgave you long ago, Atticus. I forgave you the moment you called last July. I hope you'll be able to do the same for me.

I hope Erika likes the jacket. (You did remember to get her the jacket, didn't you?)
Love,
Bridie

When I finished, I flipped the letter over to the attached page. It was a photocopy of a short-term rental agreement, a service that provided apartments in Manhattan. Bridgett

Logan had made arrangements to stay in a studio apartment in the Flower District, off of Sixth Avenue. A phone number for the apartment was written on the bottom of the page.

I reached for the phone and dialed the number.

"Trying to reach her?" Cashel asked.

"She left a number," I said. The phone was ringing. I tried to keep my foot from tapping. It kept ringing.

I let it ring for a minute before giving up, then handed the letter to Cashel. "Read it," I said. I sounded about half as upset as I felt. "When you're done we should go over there and on the way you can tell me what the hell your sister is talking about."

She took the letter without comment, and I got up and headed for the living room.

Erika was on her back on the couch, plucking stuffing from a hole in the upholstery. The menorah had just about burned itself out, and on the television screen Jimmy Stewart was about to throw himself off a bridge. If memory served, Clarence the Angel would be showing up at any moment. I reached over her and took the remote, pressed the mute, and the sound cut out.

"What's going on?" Erika asked.

"Cashel gave me a letter from Bridgett," I said. "She and I need to discuss it."

"Is Bridgett okay?"

"I don't know. She's done something extremely stupid, and wants my help to get her out of it."

"What?"

I shook my head.

"No, you don't do that," Erika said, sitting up and bringing her right finger to bear. "You tell me. She's my friend too."

"Not yet. When I know more. Right now I need to have a private talk with Cashel, so she and I are going for a walk. I don't know how long we'll be out."

Erika glared at me. "You better tell me all of it."

"When I get back," I promised her.

Cashel had finished the letter and was pulling her gloves back on when I returned. I got my army jacket off its peg,

and my watch cap, and waited for her at the front door.
Erika watched us go from the end of the hall.

"Which way?" Sister Cashel asked. Her breath billowed
like she was exhaling cigar smoke.

"Sixth," I said, and headed west. The traffic on Lexington
Avenue was light, some cabs heading south, not much more,
and we didn't have to wait long to cross. Most of the store-
fronts were dark, and there was almost no one on the street.
Cashel walked at my side, no difficulty matching my pace.
We were crossing Park when she said, "I didn't understand
your relationship with my sister, that the two of you—"

"We're not," I said. "Or we are. I don't know. We've had
a lot of trouble over the past year."

"She's like that."

"Not her. I started it." I looked over at her, wondering
what sort of things one could say to a nun. Probably the
truth. "I cheated on her."

Sister Cashel gave me a slight nod of her head. "And that's
what she meant when she wrote that she'd forgiven you?"

"I hope so."

"Have you forgiven yourself?"

"I think, Sister, you're supposed to tell me what Bridgett
was like when she was sixteen now."

Cashel stopped on the island in the middle of the street
when the light changed. There was no real traffic to worry
about, but I stopped with her. Across the street, an old man
walking a Great Dane had stopped as well. The Great Dane
had a small Santa's cap on his head and looked decidedly
unjolly about the whole affair.

"That's not really what she wants me to tell you," Sister
Cashel said, and it surprised me, because I thought she
sounded angry. "She wants me to tell you that she was ad-
dicted to heroin."

The light changed and the man and the Great Dane began
moving, crossing toward us.

"My sister is a recovering junkie."

The man passed us, saying, "Merry Christmas." Sister Cashel responded in kind.

I didn't say anything.

It's not like she's going to lie to you, I thought. I mean, she's a nun. Why would she lie about something like this?

I managed to say, "Bridgett?"

"I was fourteen or so when she started using. I'm not sure how she started, probably through that guy she mentioned in the letter, Andrew. They were boyfriend/girlfriend."

Cashel resumed walking and adjusted her gloves. "Bridgett managed to keep her habit under control for a while, I guess. We were all blind to it, my Ma and Da and me. And then we couldn't be blind to it. It got out of control, and one day she didn't come home anymore. She'd been away for a day at a time, then two, then a week. And then she didn't come back at all."

Cashel halted about ten feet ahead of me, then turned and came back. We were under a section of construction scaffolding that had been erected along the side of a Chase Manhattan office, and it was darker and colder here. "You had no idea, I take it?"

I shook my head. "She was a junkie?"

"Was. Maybe still is. Do you ever really stop being one once you've started?"

I took off my glasses and rubbed my eyes, and when I did I could imagine a teenage Bridgett. I could see the syringe. But I couldn't picture the rest. The needle itself, putting it into her own body, her own arm, her own living vessels. The thought of doing it made me sick. The thought that Bridgett did it, did it willingly, that was beyond belief.

"Seems you don't know my sister as well as you thought, Mr. Kodiak," Cashel said.

I opened my eyes and replaced my glasses and looked at her. There was nothing on her face to indicate that she was mocking me.

"I never thought I did. How long . . . how long was she gone?"

"Three months. She came back once or twice, when she

knew my father was at work. For money." She moved her eyes from me, back toward the street, remembering. "Broke into our own home. Stole some things."

"She was on the street alone?"

"I don't know. She's never really talked about it, and Bridgett and I don't communicate as well as we used to."

We continued on, reaching Sixth. Macy's was still lit up, the window displays ornate and bright. Santa was guiding his sleigh through a series of white-and-red-striped hoops, high over a forest of candy canes.

"My mother used to take us to see Santa here. I think the last time we went I was eight or nine." Cashel dropped her hand and glanced at me, and there was a sadness that I thought, at first, was nostalgia. "Bridgett should have told you. She shouldn't have left this to me. It's a heavy secret to put between two hearts."

"It's not too surprising," I said, after a second. "Your sister is very proud."

"She's too proud sometimes," Cashel said. "Stubborn. You know how the Irish sometimes call themselves donkeys? My sister is, in the best and worst ways, a donkey."

I'd forgotten my gloves, and my hands were starting to hurt in the cold. I shoved them into my pockets. We walked down Sixth, passing shuttered florists and a closed Duane Reade pharmacy. A single grocery store was open, a young man from somewhere in the Middle East working the counter. He looked at us hopefully as we went by.

Cashel said, "The apartment should be over here, right?"

"Another couple of blocks. Tell me the rest. How'd she come home? I'm assuming she *did* come home?"

"She was brought home," Sister Cashel said, her voice very precise. "Da found her one day. He was a cop— you probably know that—and he and his partner brought her home. She was a mess, her clothes were filthy, she had cuts and bruises and was so thin. I mean, she was always tall and gangly, but when he brought her back she looked like a tree looks in winter. Dangerously thin. I barely recognized her. My Ma and Da, they cleared out their bedroom and put her inside. We spent the week with her, cleaning her out."

"Just the three of you?"

When she sighed, her breath flew out in a jet. "My parents were ashamed. They didn't want anyone to know what had happened to their daughter." She turned her head to me, checking for judgment in my expression. "It wasn't the best decision they ever made, but it's understandable, I think."

"Seems to me like it could only make things harder."

"It certainly wasn't easy. I've done a lot of substance abuse counseling since then, and heroin is always challenging. It works on people in different ways, and of course the psychological addiction is entirely different from the physical one. For some, after three days or so, they're physically right as rain, like they only had a bout of the flu. I've known others in recovery who needed two weeks before they felt healthy again."

"And Bridgett?"

"Physically? She'd been using heavily and her withdrawal was bad. And, of course, she made it sound worse than it really was." At that, I cast her a look, and Cashel caught it and shook her head gently. "I'm sorry if that doesn't sound kind. She was a junkie; she wanted more junk. She made a lot of noise about how we were killing her. Bridgett can be extremely manipulative."

I started to disagree, then shut my mouth, realizing where I was at the moment, what I was doing. What Bridgett had asked me to do.

"She was in counseling for a couple of years, through college, I think. It's always the psychological withdrawal that's worst, of course."

"Tell me something," I said. "Did she ever go back? I mean, has she used since then?"

"You know, Mr. Kodiak—"

"You should call me Atticus, Sister. You're telling me that Bridgett was a junkie; I think you should call me Atticus."

"I wish I could answer your question with certainty, Atticus, but I honestly can't. Since my father died, Bridgett and

I haven't seen much of each other. In my heart I believe she hasn't ever used again. But I don't really know."

My own breath fogged the lenses of my glasses. "But you think she's using again now?"

Her hesitation was an answer in itself. "If she's running around with drug dealers, the temptation is there. Some former addicts try to engineer situations where they can justify using again."

"She wouldn't do anything to blow her cover," I said.

Sister Cashel lowered her chin into the scarf around her neck until everything below her nose was hidden. "Have you ever known a junkie?" Her voice was muffled.

"I've met one or two."

"On the street?"

"Yes."

"Have you ever thought about the kind of addiction that brings people to that? The strength of it? Why someone would surrender everything they had—home, family . . . love—for the comfort at the end of a needle?"

"Sometimes."

"I've been counseling addicts for five years, and I don't understand it. I doubt anyone does. And that's really my point. Perhaps it's beyond reason." A cloud of her breath seeped out from the scarf. "Even if my sister isn't taking heroin right now, she's still a junkie. It's something that she's aware of at every moment, something that always influences her choices and her actions. Maybe, on a good day, she doesn't think about using at all. But on a bad day it's in her head all the time. If Bridgett has intentionally put herself into a situation where drugs are available, then she's put herself into a situation where she can use again. And a part of her craves that."

We'd reached the address listed on the rental papers. A Chinese restaurant, open and empty, took up half of the ground floor, but the rest seemed to be apartments. It wasn't much to look at. The building stood alone, six stories tall and narrow, facing the avenue on one side, a parking lot on the other. The run of Twenty-seventh Street, all the way over to Seventh, was dark and barren. No cars were parked along the street. Nobody but a bodyguard and a nun seemed to have business in the Flower District on Christmas Eve.

Cashel followed me across the street and to the front door, which was unlocked. The foyer was tiny and blocked by another door, glass, through which I could see a flight of stairs. It was warm in the foyer and cramped, and my glasses fogged completely as I stepped inside. The second door was locked.

There was an intercom, buttons beside each apartment listing, but no names. There seemed to be only two apartments on each floor. Looking over the top of my glasses, I identified the button for 2S and gave it a push.

Nothing happened.

"Now what?" Cashel asked.

"You know how to pick a lock?"

"No."

"Neither do I." I pressed the button for 2N and, after a moment, heard the intercom click on.

"Yes?"

"We're here for the Christmas party," I said loudly. "Come on, open up!"

"Go to hell," said the squawk box, then it clicked off.

Sister Cashel had the corner of a smile showing above her scarf. "That worked well."

"I'm not through yet," I said, and pressed the button for 3N. The response was similar, but ruder, and I doubted the speaker would have cursed me so colorfully if he had known I was in the company of a Sister of Incarnate Love.

I pressed the buttons for 3S, 4N, 4S, 5N, 5S, 6N, and 6S. Three of the apartments didn't answer. The rest gave me answers similar to the response I'd gotten from 2N. No one wished us a merry Christmas.

Cashel was looking at the bolt on the door. "You have a credit card?"

"I do," I said.

"May I?"

I got out my wallet and handed over my Visa, knowing exactly what she was planning and thinking that it wasn't going to work at all. She took the card and slipped the piece of plastic between the door and jamb, sliding it up until she hit the bolt.

"I could try kicking it open," I said. "That probably stands a better chance of succeeding."

Cashel's brow had furrowed in concentration, and she didn't look away from the lock, where she was now rocking my Visa card back and forth. I could see the card was rapidly becoming chewed and notched. "You try that," she said, "and you'll get broken glass all over yourself, or worse. And probably end up arrested too."

"But I'd have an intact credit card."

She smiled, but didn't look away. "That's why I asked for yours."

"Very noble of you, Sister."

The bolt clacked back, and Cashel's face lit in delight and surprise, looking more like Bridgett's. "Neat!"

I grabbed the handle, pushed the door open. Cashel stepped past me, to the bottom of the stairs, then offered me my card back. The top edge looked like a tiger had teethed on it, and one end was bent. I forced it back into my wallet.

The stairs were narrow, and she allowed me to lead the way up. The door to 2S was off the landing, directly opposite 2N. We looked at the door, and I think we both imagined the worst thing we could find on its other side. I'm pretty sure we imagined the same thing. It was very quiet, and the air smelled of bleach that had been used to mop the stairs at some point, and that was strong enough to mask any other scent. If there was decay or rot or death in 2S, the only way to find out was to enter.

"I may need your card again," Cashel said.

"Use your own." My levity sounded worse than hers; it seemed, even to me, that I sounded like an asshole when I said it. There was a plate screwed to the door, over the lock, with a section removed to reach the keyhole. There was no way to slip anything into the space between frame and door. "Won't work, anyway."

"Guess that means you can try kicking this one then."

I thought about it, then decided I'd test the knob first. It turned easily in my hand, and I pushed, expecting a second bolt to catch or maybe the security chain to stop me. The door swung open without resistance, revealing darkness. I sniffed the air and smelled oranges and remnants of Chinese food, maybe from the restaurant below.

"You might want to wait here," I said.

"Sure," Cashel said, and then followed right behind me as I stepped inside.

The floor was covered with thin carpeting that did nothing to cushion our steps, and the plaster wall was a little clammy under my hand as I felt for the light switch. It took five seconds of fumbling before I found it. The light that came on hung from a small track, and the fixture faced the wall and didn't do much to illuminate the room. I moved farther inside, and Cashel shut the door behind us.

The apartment was basically a narrow strip that ran the length of the building, almost as wide as a European street. The room was the architectural equivalent of a run-on sentence. On my immediate left, just inside the door, was the bathroom. Ten feet farther down was the kitchenette, consisting of a small section of tiled counter, a sink, and two electric burners. A Black & Decker coffeemaker and a toaster were on the counter. The kitchen stopped with a small refrigerator. Past that, a rickety circular table was pressed against the wall, just big enough to hold the bowl of fruit that rested on it. The bed was at the end of the room, not quite queen-size. I couldn't imagine Bridgett fitting in it. The bed was unmade. The room ended with a freestanding closet with a six-drawer bureau beside it. Both pieces of furniture looked like they were oak.

We started searching at opposite ends of the apartment, Cashel beginning with the bathroom, myself beginning with the bureau by the bed. The furniture wasn't really oak, but pressboard, laminated to look like oak. Four of the drawers were filled, two with linens, probably provided by the owner. Two extra blankets, two extra-large towels, a pillow, not much more. In drawer number three I found underwear, six pairs of Jockey for Her, three bras, two of them sports, six pairs of socks. In drawer number four I found three T-shirts and a sweater. One of the T-shirts was white and had Hot-head Paisan prancing across the center, holding hands with her cat. Hanging in the closet were three pairs of pants, two of them jeans, one of those two blue. The other pair was black. No shoes. A rolled-up duffel bag was shoved into the bottom corner of the closet.

"She was here," Cashel said behind me.

"Yeah," I said. "Her clothes."

She was looking at the unmade bed. "Recently?"

"I don't think so." I went back to the little table by the re-frigerator, examined the bowl of fruit. The scent from it was strong. I poked the orange resting on top, rolled it to reveal a growth of mold that had spread to the banana underneath. "Fruit's rotten. She wouldn't have kept it. Did you find a trash can?"

She shook her head, then helped me look for one. It didn't take long, because it was right where I thought it would be, beneath the sink. I pulled the can free and Cashel looked past my arm as I reached in and searched the garbage. I found a coffee filter, discarded long enough ago that the grounds had completely dried out. There were a couple of brown paper bags too, and at the bottom of one I found a receipt for what looked like take-out. Bridgett had paid in cash. I couldn't tell from the receipt where she had bought the meal. There was also a discarded copy of the *Daily News*, and the date across the top was from about three weeks back.

I handed the paper to Cashel, saying, "Hold this, please," then washed my hands in the sink. There was a square of fabric hanging from a hook beneath the cabinet, and I used that to dry my hands while Cashel shook the newspaper over the trash, trying to get the spilled coffee grounds out of its creases. I took the paper back from her and rolled it up, shoved it into a pocket. Then I put the trash back beneath the sink, closed the door, and took another look around.

"What are you thinking?"

I shook my head and scratched my nose. My finger smelled like old coffee. I opened the door to the fridge. Inside was a bottle of mineral water, a box of plain Thomas's English Muffins, and half a dozen miniature jars of strawberry jam, like you get when you order room service in a hotel. Nothing else.

I shut the door again, looked at Cashel. "Would you, uh, mind going door-to-door?"

"What?"

"Just go through the building, knocking on doors, ask if anyone's seen the woman who was staying here. Tell them that she's your sister. Tell them that you *are* a Sister. It should get you some cooperation."

"And where will you be?"

"I'll be here. I'm going to toss this place."

Cashel gave me an eyebrow raise that was almost identical to the one her sister would give, then nodded and went for the door.

I started with the toilet tank. Then I dismantled the rod for the shower curtain and checked that. I used my pocketknife to unscrew the light fixtures and checked inside them. I went through every drawer in the apartment, dumping the contents, turning them over, checking their undersides and backs. I looked to see if any of the furniture was hollow, and even pulled the fridge back from the wall, discovering only an old Roach Motel up against the baseboard. I pulled the electric coils on the stove out of their sockets, and checked the wells. I went, on my hands and knees, over every inch of carpet, looking for bulges or loose edges.

It took me over an hour, and Cashel returned well before I was done, saying, "I talked to four people, and none of them have seen her. Three of them haven't been staying here for more than a week."

"And the fourth?"

"He's been here for two months. Said he knew who I was talking about, but hasn't seen her since early December. He couldn't give me an exact date." She sat on the edge of the unmade bed, watched me wrestling with the air conditioner. "I don't think any of them were lying to me."

"Why not?"

"They all seemed lonely, wanted to keep talking."

"Christmas Eve," I said, straightening up.

Cashel looked at her watch. "I have a Mass to get to."

"We're done here, anyway," I said.

She rose and we went to the door, gave the apartment a last look. The space looked pretty much as it had when we'd entered. It didn't look the same, though. Now it looked desolate and cold.

I hit the lights and locked the door on my way out.

We headed back north on Sixth.

"You need a cab?"

"In a minute," Cashel said. "What are you going to do?"

"Go home. Erika's probably bouncing off the walls with worry, and I'm going to have to tell her something, calm her down."

"That's not what I meant to ask. Are you going to look for Bridgett?"

The question took me by surprise, probably because I hadn't considered the alternative. "Of course."

"Where will you start?"

"With the papers she gave me. I'll go through them tonight. Probably go see the ex-boyfriend tomorrow."

The corner of Cashel's mouth turned up in a smile, and then she hid it in her scarf.

"Sound jealous, do I?" I asked.

"Just a bit. It's funny, she pulls a stunt like this and you're still able to get jealous over an old boyfriend."

"According to you, this is the guy who got her hooked. Jealous might not cover it."

"And after you talk to Andrew?"

"Then I'll go where she takes me," I said.

"I'd like to come with you."

"I think that's a bad idea."

"Why? Because my sister has run off to join drug dealers? Because you'll be looking in dark, dangerous places?"

"Uh," I said.

"I'm a nun," Cashel said. "That doesn't make me naïve."

"It might be ugly, that's all."

"I've seen it all before, believe me. I'll call you in the morning. We'll go talk to Andrew together."

"It's Christmas tomorrow, Sister. I don't want to put you out."

She stopped and looked down the street, trying to spot a cab. "Bridgett is the one who's putting me out. If she thought I'd just drop off the letter for you and let it go then and there, she was deluding herself. She knows very well that I can't do that."

"You sound like her," I said.

"Do I?" Now she sounded surprised.

"Righteous indignation."

Down the block a cab veered across three lanes to reach our side of the street. One of its headlights was out. Cashel lowered her arm. "It's not indignation. It's anger. I'd think you'd have a little too."

"Oh, I do," I said. "I'm just keeping it out of my voice."

"You must tell me sometime how you do that."

"You don't want to know. It leads to ulcers."

The cab pulled to a stop beside us, and Cashel opened the passenger door, then reached into a coat pocket for her wallet. She pulled out a card and a pen and asked for my phone number. I gave it to her and she scribbled it on the back of the card, then put both away in the wallet.

"It was good to finally meet you," I told her. "I wish the circumstances had been better."

"Me too." She started to climb into the cab, then stopped and turned back to me. I was expecting a handshake, but Cashel surprised me with the dry press of her lips to my scarred left cheek. Then she got into the cab.

"Happy holidays, Mr. Kodiak," she said.

And then the cab pulled away, leaving me on Sixth Avenue, alone, my hands aching with the cold, wondering what I was supposed to do next.

CHAPTER THREE

Erika was at the kitchen table, the contents of Bridgett's envelope spread out in front of her. She was on the phone when I came through the door, and I heard her making her good-byes, as I came around into the room to catch her just as she hung up.

"Took you long enough," Erika said. "Was she there?"

I looked pointedly at the table, then pointedly at her.

"You left the envelope out, Atticus. What was I supposed to do, pretend nothing was going on? Did you go by the address, that apartment she rented?'

"She wasn't there." I pulled out the other chair and sat so I could face her, not even bothering to take off my jacket. "Probably hadn't been there for a week or two."

Erika nodded, as if she had expected this, then said, "I called Dude, told him what was up."

"Scott's in California."

"I know. I called him at his sister's."

"We don't have his sister's number," I said.

"I haven't spent the past year with you and Bridgett and not picked up a thing or two about gathering information. Dude said he wouldn't be back until the day after tomorrow, but in the meantime he'll make some calls, see if maybe Bridgett got arrested somewhere. He also said that this Pierre Alabacha guy is the real deal, some big-time drug lord in the city. He'll call us— What?"

"I underestimated you," I said. "Thought I'd get back here and have to break it to you slowly. Instead, you're ahead of me. Makes me proud of you."

"You still have to tell me the 'when-I-was-sixteen' part, what that was about," Erika said. "You did ask Cashel, right?"

"I asked."

"Now you tell."

I told, repeating most of what Cashel had said to me about Bridgett's habit. At first Erika didn't believe me, and her reaction looked a lot like I imagined mine had. For a minute after I finished talking she didn't say anything, sitting still, staring at the part of the baseboard that had separated from the wall. Every so often one of us would catch a mouse scurrying through the opening. There was no mouse tonight.

"Fucking bitch," Erika spat. "Lying, fucking bitch."

"I'm not sure that's quite—"

"What? Fair? You think I'm not being fair?" Anger splotched her cheeks. "She's lied to us all this time, and you think I'm not being fair? Jesus, Atticus, get some self-respect."

"You know Bridgett. She never talks about herself."

"Don't you see? That's where she is now! She's in some disgusting fucking hole, she's doing drugs, and she expects us to come and rescue her."

"Not necessarily," I said. "It could be worse than that."

"What could be worse than that?" she asked, angry.

"She could be dead," I said.

"That's not worse."

"Erika."

She headed for her room, stopping at the door to fire the parting shot. The light in the hallway made her eyes shimmer where the tears were starting to build.

"At least if she's dead, she's got some dignity," Erika said.

I was still at the table at one in the morning, nursing a cup of coffee and reading Bridgett's pile of papers, when the phone rang. Everything had been quiet for over an hour, even the street below our window had hushed, and when the bell splintered the peace, I spilled coffee all over the picture of Pierre Alabacha that rested in front of me. I swore a lot and picked up the phone with a dry hand, still swearing, wiping my wet one off on my pants leg.

"Merry fucking Christmas," Special Agent Scott Fowler said.

"And a happy fucking New Year to you too."

"Did you check the address?"

"Yeah. It was a bust."

"Anything at all?"

"She was there up until a couple weeks ago. Time of departure is dodgy, but I found a copy of the *News* from the eighth in the trash. The place looked okay, no mess, but the door was unlocked, so I think someone else had given the place a toss. No way for me to tell if anything was missing."

"So she could have moved on her own accord?"

"I suppose it's possible. There were no personal items aside from some clothes. No books, no bills, no magazines. Only that newspaper. She might have moved on."

"But you doubt it?"

"Yeah, I doubt it. I doubt it a lot," I said, leaning back. Erika had emerged from her room. I mouthed the word "Scott" at her, and she nodded, came to join me at the table. Her eyes held the remnants of a crying jag.

"I called a guy from the office," Scott said. "Had him run a check. As far as we can tell, no one named Bridgett Logan has been arrested or is in the system."

"Strike two," I said. "Not good."

"Most of the heroin that gets filtered through the boroughs is financed by the Alabacha Cadre. If she's pissed them off . . ."

"We would have heard something," I finished. "There would have been a body."

Scott didn't say anything for several seconds. Erika put her head against my shoulder and I wrapped an arm around her.

"She's not dead," I said.

"I'm not on the Taskforce," Scott said. "What I know about Alabacha is really limited. Former Nigerian law enforcement, fled the country when General Sani Abacha seized power. Didn't make any friends at Amnesty International while he was a cop, if you get my drift. Anyway, couple months back, there was this story going around the office about how the DEA had lost an undercover in someone's organization. Don't know for sure which organization it was, or even if the story was true, but it got everybody really upset for a week or two. I heard an agent mention Alabacha's name in connection with it."

"What happened?"

"You've got to understand the way undercover works, Atticus. Forget the movie bullshit, the agents are really tightly controlled and watched, and they almost never run without backup, and I mean immediate backup. The DEA doesn't even like to have their undercovers out of their sight during the operation. They're really careful about this, about putting their undercovers in danger, especially on big operations."

"Alabacha made an undercover in his organization?"

"It's just a rumor. But yeah. And Alabacha snagged the agent, got him away from his backup and controls. Took him out to the West Side Highway. Beat him pretty badly, some knife work, nothing that would kill him outright . . ."

I waited for Scott, listening to the phone, imagining him on the other end. There were three thousand miles between us, different coasts, but his voice was perfectly clear. It occurred to me that Erika could probably hear his voice over the receiver, and I moved slightly, disengaged my arm. After a second, Erika sat up straight, fixed the hair over her ear.

"They tied his hands behind his back, did his ankles too," Scott continued. "Used baling wire. And then they filled a plastic bag with kerosene and tied it around his head. They let it sit for a little bit, just so he could feel it eating at his skin. And then they lit the bag."

I looked at the picture on the table, at the dark-skinned man who hadn't known he was being photographed as he climbed out of his Mercedes-Benz. Bridgett had used a camera with a time stamp, and the date on the picture was 17 October, the photograph captured at 1832 hours. Pierre Alabacha looked like a retired businessman, nothing flashy about his clothes, about his personal appearance. The car gave some scale, and I didn't imagine that he was taller than five ten, and not more than 180 pounds. His hair was more gray than black, and the lines on his face were showing the length that comes from age. In the photograph, he was removing a pair of sunglasses, frowning at something down the street, looking past the photographer.

"Atticus?" Scott asked. "Still there?"

I cleared my throat, moved some of the papers on the table. "I've been going through the information Bridgett sent. She's got a lot of information on the business, notes on couriers and deliveries, timetables. I don't think any of this would stand up in court, but for her purposes it seems pretty solid. She's got names and addresses for Alabacha, couple of his lieutenants, even down to the street. Dealers and middlemen and muscle. Good surveillance work."

"Look, Atticus," Scott said slowly. "Pierre Alabacha is big-time drugs in New York City, you understand? He's organized, he's connected, he's professional, and he's clearly got seriously evil juice. I want you to wait until I get back, then we can work this thing together. You're going to want the law's help on this one."

"I know," I said.

"So you'll wait?"

I didn't answer. It occurred to me that I'd been doing a hell of a lot of waiting, at least where Bridgett was concerned.

"Atticus?"

"Not on your life," I said.

CHAPTER FOUR

At noon on Christmas Day I parked my motorcycle out-side of a two-story house on Tibbet Avenue in the Bronx, and Sister Cashel Logan pried her grip free from around my waist. She got off the bike first, and I killed the engine, then disconnected the leads running to our helmets and vests. By the time I got off the bike, she had removed her helmet. Her face was flushed and her gray eyes glimmered, and her grin was enormous.

"Told you you'd like it," I said.

She nodded and took an experimental step, as if to check that the earth was still beneath her feet. "My legs feel like water," Cashel said.

"Adrenaline."

She unfastened her coat with her free hand, then unzipped the heated vest underneath. The vest belonged to Erika, and I had given it to Cashel for the ride. I wore a similar one beneath my jacket. The vests worked well, keeping trunk temperature constant and comfortable, and even in the thirty-degree, over-cast weather, I felt fine.

From Cashel's face, she felt better than that.

Helmets in hand, we walked up the front steps to the house. It had been built on the side of a low hill, and the whole block was covered with identical homes on this side of the street. They all looked like they had gone up at the same time, perhaps in the late fifties. The house was painted beige, with dark brown trim, and in a large window overlooking the street, I could see the lights of a decorated Christmas tree. There was a spiky wreath of holly hanging in the center of the front door.

The woman who answered the bell was all of five feet two inches tall, wearing blue jeans and a bulky white sweater. Her hair was brown and short, and when she saw Cashel, she made a high-pitched sound like the whistle on a teakettle, flinging her arms around the other woman.

"Sister Cashel!"

"Hi, Kelly. Merry Christmas."

"Merry Christmas! This is a wonderful surprise, this is great!" The brown-haired woman let Cashel go, stepping back. "Look at you. The hog-riding nun!"

"It's actually his bike." Cashel used the helmet to indicate me. "This is Atticus Kodiak. He's a friend of Bridgett's. Atticus, this is Kelly Wolfe."

Kelly looked me over quickly, starting at my feet and then tilting her head back to look me in the eyes. "Merry Christmas, Atticus. Please, come in, both of you. We're just starting the feed."

We followed her inside the house, into warmth and spicy scent. I could smell turkey and cider, the odor of wax from burning candles. Kelly led us through the hall, into the big room with the Christmas tree, where a boy who couldn't have been older than three was playing on the floor with a Fisher-Price doctor's set. An older man sat on the couch, silver-haired and potentially shorter than Kelly herself, watching the child with a grandfather's eyes. Kelly introduced the man as her father, John, and the boy as Frankie, her son. John greeted us warmly. Frankie ignored us.

"Andrew's changing the baby," Kelly told us. "He'll be down in a second."

"How's little Eileen doing?" Cashel asked Kelly.

"Appetite like you wouldn't believe," she said proudly. "I didn't get to thank you for the baby clothes, by the way. It was sweet. She looks darling in them."

"I'm glad they were of use."

We were led into the kitchen, where I was introduced to Kelly's mother, Paige, who was working at the oven. Kelly offered us seats at the table and cups of hot apple cider, and she and Cashel began chatting minutiae almost immediately, sharing neighborhood news. I drank my cider and felt decidedly awkward, thinking about the party I was missing, the brunch at Dale's, where I'd dropped Erika off early that morning.

Cashel and Kelly had moved on to parish news when Andrew Wolfe came into the room, carrying a baby girl in his arms who was dressed in what looked like a big pink sock. Andrew was about my size, broader across the shoulders, hair closer to brown than blond and tied back in a short ponytail, with a narrow face and a nose that had been broken more than twice. His smile was big, and he was using it on his daughter as he came in.

"Andy, look who's here," Kelly said.

He saw Cashel and the big smile froze, then disintegrated as he realized that he had just walked into a potential condolence call. "Cashel."

"Merry Christmas, Andrew."

He looked at me. The baby gaped.

"Atticus Kodiak," I said. "I'm a friend of Bridgett's."

There was no recognition of my name in his eyes. "Yeah?"

"Yeah. We should talk."

"And where is she?"

"That's what we should talk about."

Andrew Wolfe looked to Cashel again, and whatever he was seeking in her face he found, because after a second he went to his wife and handed over the daughter in his arms. He gave the baby a kiss on the forehead. The child giggled, and then tried to grab his nose.

"We can talk in the office," he told me.

Cashel gave the preamble and I gave the speech, and Andrew Wolfe sat on the futon in his office, listening to us both. The office was more of a guest room than a work space, with a desk and computer and a futon that could open into a bed. From the looks of it, it didn't get a lot of use as either, and the air inside was a little dusty. Andrew was very still, very quiet, while I told him what little I knew. Beyond the closed door, someone had put Bing Crosby on the stereo.

Andrew waited until I'd finished, and then asked, "What do you need me to do?"

"Do you know where we can find her?"

"I can think of a couple of places we could ask."

"I'd like you to take me to them," I said.

Andrew Wolfe looked at his hands, then got up off the futon. "I'll get my coat."

When the door opened I got a whiff of glazed ham that made my stomach rumble.

"I think I'm ruining everyone's Christmas," I told Cashel.

She gave me a pat on the arm. "He wouldn't have volunteered if he wasn't willing to look."

I nodded and thought on that, wondering at Andrew Wolfe's motivations. If he had hesitated, if he had at least complained that he was going to miss his family and his holiday meal, I'd have felt—perversely—a little better about the whole thing. But as it was, his willingness made me question my own. Andrew had introduced Bridgett to heroin. I had cheated on her. And here we both were, all too willing to ride to her rescue.

It would have made Bridgett pissed off beyond belief.

Andrew returned, pulling on a dark green overcoat. "We can take my car."

"Fine," I said.

The car was at least ten years old, green like his overcoat, with rust spots and several dents. He unlocked the passenger side for me, moved around to his door, and I was about to get in when I realized Cashel was right behind me.

"You don't have to come, Sister," I said.

"You probably shouldn't," Andrew added, nodding.

"Why not?" she asked.

Neither of us could bring ourselves to open our mouths. She stood, still holding her helmet, looking quite pleased with herself. After five seconds I felt sufficiently foolish enough to tilt the front seat back far enough for her to squeeze into the car. She settled in the back without another word.

He took us to Washington Heights, crossing the Broadway Bridge out of the Bronx, onto the north end of Manhattan island. It was an overcast day, clouds high, and everything in the world seemed to have been sun-bleached centuries ago. Wien Stadium, Columbia University's big bowl of athleticism, looked as if it had been carved from slate.

Andrew was a good driver, the kind who kept both hands on the wheel and never, ever looked away from traffic. He reassured me more than his car itself; the Celica backfired and groaned, squeaking every time he used the brakes, shuddering every time he pressed down on the accelerator. While he drove he talked, telling Cashel and me about how Bridgett had contacted him, what she had asked him to do. He spoke slowly, and I could tell he was self-censoring, and it made the narrative disjointed. When he finished I still wasn't certain what help, exactly, he had given her.

"You just went canvassing?" I asked. "That was it?"

"Pretty much."

"Did she ever tell you why? Why she needed your help?"

His hand left the steering wheel long enough to downshift. The Celica's engine screamed as if he'd put a knife through its eye. "She said she wanted someone to watch her back."

"So she went to you?"

"Yeah. You have a problem with that?"

I shook my head. "But I'm wondering why you."

Andrew didn't say anything. Cashel leaned forward on the back seat, putting her head between ours. "Did she ever tell you what she was looking for, Andy?"

"Not really, no."

"And you didn't ask?"

"No, I didn't."

"Why not?" I asked.

He stopped at a light. His features were set, almost confrontational. "You wouldn't understand."

"Try me."

Andrew shook his head, and the light changed, and the Celica started up again with a shudder that I felt in my cervical vertebrae.

Sister Cashel cleared her throat. "You've got to have some idea, Andy. How many days did you spend with her?"

"Not days, nights. Three or four."

"So in three or four nights of work, you must have concluded something."

"I think she was investigating a murder." Andrew said it slowly and softly enough that I almost lost his words in the engine and road noise. "And I think the guy who got murdered was a dealer."

"A dealer she knew?" Cashel asked.

Andrew hesitated, then nodded.

Cashel sat back against her seat. In the rearview mirror, I saw enough of her to see that she had shut her eyes.

"It doesn't mean she was using," I said. "She could have run into this guy any number of places. We don't know the relationship."

Andrew almost sneered my way. "You're wrong."

"How do you know?" I asked. "You weren't sure why she was looking in the first place."

"Listen . . ."

"Atticus," I supplied, knowing full well that he hadn't forgotten my name.

"Atticus, yeah," Andrew said. "You didn't see her, you didn't see the way Bridgett was acting, hear what she was saying. But I did, and she was wired the whole time we were looking. She was taking all of it very personally."

"She takes almost everything personally."

"Not like this."

I closed my mouth, thinking that we were getting nowhere. We were in Washington Heights proper now, still on

Broadway, and all the stores lining the street were closed. There was almost nobody out. I thought I saw a couple Dominicans passing a bottle on the stairs down to a basement club, but when I turned my head to be sure, they were out of sight.

"Witnesses," Andrew said. "Bridie was looking for witnesses, best as I could figure. She said something about how the district attorney's office had a witness and that she needed to talk to this guy."

"Did this witness have a name?" I asked.

"Not that I remember."

"Did she ever find him?"

"I think so."

"And?"

"And I don't know. She probably met him without me, and that was around the last time I heard from her. That was in October sometime."

We turned off Broadway, down a block, then onto Wadsworth, where Andrew spotted a space between a black van and an old Chevy Malibu. The van had been decorated by its owner, and on the driver's side sported a fancy airbrushed painting of a red-skinned demon ravaging a buxom Latina whose dress left nothing to the imagination. Andrew curbed his wheels and set the parking brake, then shut off the engine and turned to look at me.

"You know how to take care of yourself?" Andrew asked.

"I can do my own laundry," I said.

Nothing in his face acknowledged my wit. Andrew looked away from me, across the street. I wasn't certain what he was trying to see. "There was this guy we talked to, first, second week of October, maybe. He was a dealer, and Bridgett went after him pretty hard."

"Hard how?"

"He wasn't very cooperative. He'd blown us off a few times, we weren't getting anywhere. Bridgett decided to lean on him."

"She beat him?" I asked.

"No."

"You beat him for her?"

Andrew didn't say anything.

"Andy?" Cashel asked.

"He was going to put a knife in your sister," Andrew told her. "Couldn't let that happen, could I?"

Cashel said nothing.

"I'm just saying there could be violence, that's all I'm saying," Andrew told me, then reached for the handle of his door. "Sister? You really might want to stay in the car."

"No," Cashel said firmly. "*You* really want me to stay in the car, but that's something very different. Go on, I'll follow you both."

We all got out and walked together across the street, Cashel between us. A wind had kicked up, knocking the temperature down another ten degrees. Scraps of trash skipped along the ground, pushed by the air. Somewhere, from one of the apartments in one of the buildings on the block, music was playing. From where we were, it sounded like angels whispering.

Andrew led, down half the block to the alley he'd indicated, stopping in the entrance. An assortment of litter carpeted the ground, and a very fat tabby was prowling the far end, but otherwise no one was there.

From behind us, across the street, came a piercing one-note whistle. I turned in time to see a man taking his fingers out of his mouth, and when I did he waved us over.

"That him?" I asked.

Andrew shook his head. "But he'll do."

We crossed back.

The whistler was Dominican, about my age, a couple of inches shorter than Cashel. He wore jeans and a denim coat over a gray sweatshirt, and his head was covered with a leather Greek fisherman's cap. He kept his head down as we crossed, but when we made the sidewalk, each of us got the eyeball in quick succession.

"Got business?" His accent was sharp, and it took me a moment to break through it.

"Looking for Goldy," Andrew answered. "He hooked me up last time."

"Goldy? Don't know, man, I can give you just as good as he ever did. You don't need Goldy's shit."

Andrew brushed me with an elbow, and I took the cue, reached for my wallet. As I produced a twenty, the dealer looked us over again, then fastened on Cashel. "Ho! Sister Logan, that you? Sister Logan, what you doing out here?"

"I'm sorry," Cashel said. "Have we met?"

"Sure, last year maybe, my little brother, you were counseling him at that, uh, that Covenant House, you know, downtown? Jaime Costas?"

Cashel's brow smoothed. "Summer before last?"

"That's right."

"So you must be Fernando?"

Fernando's smile was incandescent. "That's right, yeah, Fernando! You remember me!"

"Of course I remember you. You were his only family that came to visit. How's Jaime doing?"

"He's got a job, he drives a truck for a laundry company." Pride raised Fernando's voice slightly. "You're not really here to buy, are you, Sister? Tell me you're not. This stuff, it's bad for you."

Cashel's head shake was mild. "We're actually looking for someone."

"Goldy?"

"Goldy," Andrew confirmed. "Where can we find him?"

Fernando's excitement diminished as he gave Andrew the eyeball again, then switched it to me. "I've never seen you before," he said, then looked back at Andrew. "But you, I remember you. Asking questions around here, couple months back, working with some white girl."

"That was my sister," Cashel said. "She's who we're really looking for, but Andrew thinks Goldy might know where she is."

"That was your sister?"

"Yes. Bridgett."

"Should tell you something, that's a pushy girl. She ain't been making a lot of friends around here."

"Goldy had some information for us way back when," Andrew said. "Told us where we could find a junkie named Colin."

I clenched my jaw to stay silent, wondering how much

more information Andrew was keeping to himself. Fernando Costas removed his cap and revealed a layer of thinning hair. He scratched at the back of his scalp. His manner kept changing, amping up when talking to Cashel, dropping his guard, then replacing it when either Andrew or I spoke.

"Dr. Colin, that must be him," Fernando said. "Used to be at Carla's place on One Seventy-third. Maybe he's seen her, sure."

"Why do you say that?" I asked.

"She's been around."

"Recently?" Andrew asked.

"Maybe a month back." He replaced his cap, thinking, then turned his attention back to Cashel. "That girl, that Bridgett, she's really your sister?"

Cashel nodded. "You can speak your mind, Fernando. I'd like to hear what you have to say about her."

Fernando hesitated a moment longer, then shifted his posture, moving closer to Cashel, ready to reveal a confidence. "That girl put Miguelito in the hospital, end of November, Sister. He was late on a payment and she had no mercy."

None of us spoke.

"She gave him a beating," Fernando added softly. "Bad."

"Why?" Cashel asked.

"He'd cut some decks with Alabacha's stamp, stretched it real thin. The man wanted him brought back into line."

"Bridgett works for Alabacha?" I asked.

Fernando shot me a glance that spelled out exactly how stupid he thought I was, then said to Cashel, "Miguelito was just doing business, everybody does it."

"Do you know where she is right now?" Cashel asked. "It's really important, Fernando."

"I don't know, Sister, I'm sorry. If she was dealing with Colin, maybe he knows, but like I said, I ain't seen her."

Cashel looked at Andrew, and Andrew shook his head. "Thank you, Fernando," Cashel said. "You've been very helpful."

I reached for my wallet again, took out one of the new business cards I'd had made up, then offered it and the twenty to Fernando. "If you see her again, could you give me a call?"

He took both and separated the bill, stuffing it into a pocket while examining my card. His lips moved when he read. "I'll call," Fernando said.

"Tell Jaime I sent my love," Cashel said. "Tell him I'm very proud of him."

"I am, too, Sister."

Cashel raised an eyebrow. "And maybe he can get you a job too?"

Fernando laughed softly. "Jaime's happy driving a truck, Sister. But he's still poor as Jesus."

CHAPTER FIVE

The Celica groaned as Andrew turned us onto 171st Street, in search of Dr. Colin. I looked at the rows of stores as we drove, the same blocks, endlessly repeated with only minor variations. Bodega, hair salon, travel agency, hair salon, bodega, travel agency—the trinity of businesses established to launder drug money. Drugs were a fundamental part of the community, a provider of jobs in a service economy. All of the stores did some real business, but there was no way any of them did enough to keep them all open. I didn't know exactly what the percentages were, how many of the shops were fronts as opposed to legitimate, but guessed it had to be at least half.

Andrew stopped us at the end of the block, again parking with the same care, and again we all climbed out. The car was small enough that my legs ached each time I had to stretch them out again.

"It'll take me a while to find the place," Andrew said. "Could be anywhere along the block. Give me half an hour, okay?"

"We can come with you," I said.

Andrew just shook his head and went off down the street, leaving Cashel and me to wait beside the old car.

"What does it mean?" she asked. "What Fernando told us, what does it really mean?"

"It means Bridgett was alive and undercover up until the beginning of the month," I said. "Not much more."

"I don't think he was lying about her. About what she did."

"Neither do I."

Cashel adjusted the scarf around her neck. "Aren't you cold?"

"Not really." I could see Andrew almost two blocks down, speaking to someone on the front steps of an apartment building. The person was white, but that was the only thing I could tell from this distance.

"You don't like Andrew," Cashel said, following my gaze.

"Not much, no."

"He doesn't seem to like you either."

"Hadn't noticed."

"You shouldn't fib to a nun."

"No, I suppose I shouldn't. Thing is, I'm upset. I'm upset that Bridgett went to him instead of to me. I know why she did it, I know she didn't want to tell me she'd been a junkie, all of that. But it pisses me off."

"I expect it pisses him off too," Cashel said. "He's married, he's clean, he's worked very hard to put it all behind him. And then Bridgett shows up, and he really can't refuse her."

"I noticed."

"Not like that," Cashel admonished. "Andrew may well still love my sister, I suppose that's only to be expected. But it's not love that's gotten him out of his home, away from his family, on Christmas Day. It's guilt."

"Maybe."

"Something for you to think about."

"As if I needed more," I said.

Down the block, Andrew had disappeared. Cashel sighed and leaned back against the car. After a second I joined her. The Celica listed dangerously behind us, so I stood up again.

We continued to wait.

I was looking at my watch, calculating how much time we had wasted, when Andrew returned, coming up from the opposite end of the block. Walking with him was the thinnest, whitest man I'd ever seen, his pale skin made all the paler by the sheet of oily black hair that hung across his forehead. He was tall too, perhaps six feet four, and he shambled like a horror-flick zombie as he came down the street. The left sleeve of his jacket was folded up and pinned back against its upper arm, and I could see he was missing everything below the elbow.

"Found him," Andrew said. His face was a hard mask, and there was no joy in his discovery.

They came to a stop in front of us, and Cashel pushed off the Celica, standing beside me. I could hear the car rocking on shattered shocks.

"Man said you had money for me," Dr. Colin said.

I nodded and felt my stomach threaten. He had an odor that I'd only smelled before in the military, the stink of a body rotting apart. It was what I imagined leprosy to smell like. Somewhere inside his jacket, Dr. Colin was spoiled meat.

"How much do you need?" I asked.

"Take a hundred."

"For a hundred I want to hear what you have to say first," I said.

Colin gestured with his pinned sleeve at Andrew. "I know who he's talking about. Seen her."

"How recently?"

"Money," Colin said, extending his right hand. It was ungloved, dirty, and when he moved his arm, his sleeve climbed back, and I could see an angry red hole on his forearm. If what he looked like bothered him, it didn't show in his face.

I handed over a twenty, and Colin looked down at it in disdain. "More depending on what you say," I told him.

"Fair enough." Colin's smile was yellow, and so were his corneas. "Ask away."

"Bridgett Logan," I said. "Do you know her?"

"Surely do, sir. That get me another deuce?"

"Have you seen her?"

"Stands to reason if I know her, I've seen her." The yellow smile turned smug.

"When?"

"When the first time? Or when the last?"

"The last."

"December the eighth," he said.

"Sounds like a hard date. How do you know?"

"That's my methadone day at the clinic by Columbia Presbyterian. I always remember my methadone."

"What was she doing?"

"She was on her new job. Making the rounds."

"What job?" Cashel asked.

Colin squinted at her. "You look like her, you know that?"

"We're related. What was this new job, Colin?"

"Collections and deliveries. She was dropping off decks."

"Working for Alabacha?" I asked.

He rubbed at his nose with the back of his right hand, smearing lime-green snot on his already dirty sleeve. "That's the rumor. She didn't talk about it, but, yeah, they were his stamp."

"That was her new job?" Cashel asked. "What was her old one?"

Colin smiled and looked pointedly at me. I handed over another twenty. "First time I met her, she was asking about this shooting I saw."

"What shooting?"

"Guy named Lark, got himself dead couple blocks from here. That would've been back in September, I think." At my reaction, Colin grinned. "Shit, I guess I should have asked for more money before I told you that part, huh?"

I nodded, looking away and thinking fast, trying to understand what I thought I'd just discovered. September, that would have been when Bridgett called me, asking for a good lawyer. And when I'd given her Miranda Glaser's name, she had told me to butt out. And after that I had, and had promptly forgotten about it, but of course it made sense now. Whatever Bridgett was doing, why she had gone undercover, why she was working for Pierre Alabacha, it all had to relate to that call.

"Tell me about Vincent Lark."

"Cost you," Colin said.

"Tell me or I'll remove your other arm," I said.

He took a step back, and Cashel looked at me in shock. Andrew didn't blink, just put his hands on Colin's shoulders, holding him in place.

"Answer the man's question." Andrew said it softly.

"Shit," Colin muttered. "Look, I tell you what I told her, then just leave me the fuck alone, okay?"

"I'm waiting," I said.

"This girl, this blond chippy, she shot Vinnie, okay? That's it. Some girl, maybe she's in her twenties, fuck if I know. I'm in this gallery one day, up the stairs she comes, bang bang bang, dead dealer. Bridgett, she was asking me what I saw."

"Why?" I asked.

"Fuck do I know?"

Andrew gave him a rattle that wouldn't have moved a tree branch. It made Colin shake like he was living under an El.

"Police picked me as a witness in this case," Colin said angrily. "Nothing but trouble, they want me to testify against this blond chick. Maybe that's why, I don't know. She didn't tell me."

"You know the name of the girl? The one who did the shooting?"

"No, okay? She never told me, I never asked, and it doesn't matter noway, because I'm not going to testify."

Andrew looked at me for confirmation, then released Colin's shoulders. The other man shivered, adjusted his jacket. "That all?" he asked.

"That's all," I said, and handed over the remaining bills in my wallet. Colin counted the money hastily, then folded all the paper together and shoved it deep into his front pocket. He scraped the open wound on his hand when he did, but still his face showed no pain.

"Pleasure doing business with you all," he said. "Now I'm on my way, you don't mind."

"Hey. One more thing."

Colin stopped and turned, hostility pouring out of his eyes.

"When you saw Bridgett last," I said. "Was she using?"

Colin's smug smile reappeared. Then the smile got broader, and I thought he was going to speak, and then he started laughing, loud. It was almost jolly. It was almost the sort of laughter that, if he'd had a gut, would've gotten it shaking like a bowl full of jelly.

"You all have a merry Christmas," Colin told us, and then he continued on his way.

CHAPTER SIX

It was after six, and Erika was poring over Bridgett's papers at the kitchen table, her hair wet from a recent shower, wearing a sweatshirt and a pair of long underwear bottoms. She waited until I'd hung up my motorcycle gear before asking me how the day had gone, and I gave her my findings in broad strokes.

"What's Andrew like?" Erika asked.

"Confident," I said, and then avoided further questions by hiding in my room. I pulled off my boots and climbed onto my bed and looked at the water damage in the corner of my ceiling. I felt fatigued yet wired. Other things too. Some anger. Some fear. There was even, as I suspected, some small jealousy.

Atticus Kodiak, the gazpacho of emotion, I thought. Creamy and cold and a little tart, and sometimes served chunky.

———

At twenty-two minutes past nine, Erika knocked on my door and asked, "Are you coming out?"

"I suppose I'll have to eventually," I said. "Biology dictates it."

"Biology, huh? What are you doing in there? Going blind?"

"Only if I can ruin my eyes by staring at the ceiling."

"There's ceiling out here, you know. In fact, there's ceiling throughout this whole apartment."

"It's not the same," I said. "The ceiling in my room is better."

The door opened with a creak, and Erika took a step inside, confirming that I was, indeed, on my back and on my bed, and staring at the ceiling. Without a word she came around to the other side of the bed and climbed up next to me, taking a pillow for herself.

After a minute she said, "You're right. You've got the better ceiling."

"Don't I know it."

After another minute she said, "I'm really scared for her."

I put my hand on her head, gave her a pat.

"Me too," I said.

She fell asleep in my room, and I missed it at first, thinking that she was just being quiet and thinking like I was. Then I heard her snoring, and I told myself that I should try to sleep too, and so I shut my eyes, convinced I was embarking on an exercise in futility.

I kept seeing Washington Heights and Fernando and Colin's yellow smile. I kept seeing the look in Sister Cashel Logan's eyes. When I took the helmet back from Cashel outside of the home she shared with the other Sisters of her community, I saw the anguish, and again the anger, her struggle with both. She had seen me looking, taken a breath of the Bronx winter air, and summoned a smile from somewhere I couldn't access. I imagined it was what faith looked like when all else was failing.

At some point I actually managed to doze, only to be

awakened by my heart racing so fast I could feel my pulse beating in my head. The clock by the bed told me it was two thirty-seven, and I knew that grabbing any more sleep would be impossible.

Erika had rolled to one side while she slept, commandeering the center of my bed. I got up carefully, then covered her with the spare blanket that hung off the footboard. I grabbed my copy of Frank Bergon's latest book from where it was sitting on my desk, lying to myself that I could try to get some reading done, then tiptoed out into the kitchen. Erika had left the lights on.

I parked at the table and flipped through the papers there. I read the notes Erika had made. I looked at the maps, and I stared for a long time at the pictures of men I didn't know—Pierre Alabacha, Roley Butler, Anton Ladipo. The holy trinity of the Alabacha Cadre, the aging Pierre at the lead, Roley and Anton apparently his lieutenants. I tried to conjure some strong emotion about them, really felt that I should just hate them abstractly, and couldn't even manage that. They were just faces, the way people on the street, people you've never met, are just faces.

I made myself a cup of tea and moved into the living room. I stared out the window, at the dead street and the dark buildings. There was nothing to see.

In six or seven hours I'd call Miranda Glaser, try to find out what I could about the case Bridgett had been working. Then I'd wait for Scott Fowler to return from California, see what more he could offer. With those two calls, I was sure I'd have a lead, a direction. I'd have something I could do, and would feel useful, or at least not entirely useless.

There was plenty I could do.

Hours away.

You should be out there right now, I thought. You should be looking for her right now, not sulking because you can't sleep. You should act. You should find her.

It really, really bothered me that no one had seen Bridgett after the eighth.

At six I told myself it was still too early to call Miranda Glaser, and so went back to the kitchen for a fourth cup of tea. It had long since stopped tasting good, and now I was drinking it just to keep my bladder occupied. I was removing the tea bag when I remembered the newspaper I'd taken from Bridgett's rental, and cursed myself for forgetting about it in the first place. It took me three minutes of searching before I found it in my army jacket.

For the next hour I went through the edition carefully, reading it at the table, looking at each article, trying to attach significance to the *Daily News*. The cover story was about the serial rapist who had been haunting Queens for the last three months, complete with a police sketch, and there was another piece about a drunk driver who had flattened a father and son visiting from out of town while they crossed Varick Street. There was the normal editorial shrieking, and the standard sports bullshit about how New York needed better players who asked for less money. There was some ink about the MetroStars too, about how Alexi Lalas and Tab Ramos were most likely to be named to the U.S. Men's World Cup Team.

Good for them, I thought.

I was reading my way through the newsprint a second time when I realized I was missing pages, and began flipping the sheets back and forth, trying to discover which ones. Then I examined the table of contents, searching for a hint of what was missing. The contents revealed nothing. I went through the paper a third time, thinking that perhaps I was missing only a portion of a particular article or story, either the lead or the conclusion. I came up with nothing.

This is not necessarily important, I told myself. This does not necessarily qualify itself as a clue. The missing pages could have been advertising, for all you know. The paper's riddled with ads for holiday bargains.

I looked at the clock on the coffeemaker and saw that it was fourteen minutes past seven in the morning.

Fuck it, I thought, and reached for my address book and the phone.

After eleven rings Christiane Havel found her way to the receiver and snarled, ". . . the hell is this?"

"Chris? Morning. It's Atticus. Atticus Kodiak."

She made a honking noise as if she were calling geese. "Atticus?"

"Right."

"Kodiak?"

"Right again."

She mumbled something away from the handset, but I caught the word "cocksucker." Then she coughed a couple of times, and I realized she had a cold.

Chris Havel asked, "You know what time it is?"

"I need your help with something."

That helped clear her head. "Like the last time you needed help with something?"

"You got a book deal out of it."

"No thanks to you."

"This is safer. No one will shoot at you."

"I didn't actually get shot at, if you'll remember. Somebody tried to blow me up."

"Me too," I pointed out. "But you don't hear me complaining."

"Asshole." Chris Havel coughed again. "Look, I've got a fuck-awful flu and you jerked me from NyQuil nirvana, okay? I need ten minutes to pee and get my head on straight. I'll call you back, okay?"

"I'm at home."

"Ten minutes," she said, and banged the phone down.

I got up from the table and dumped my cold tea into the sink. It was starting to move past dawn into day. I told myself not to watch the clock.

All the same, when the phone rang, I answered, saying, "That was twenty minutes, not ten."

"You wanted my help, bozo," Havel said. "I'm not even awake yet. NyQuil is a fucking brick, you know that?"

"Yeah, it's great stuff," I agreed. "Listen, I've got a copy of the *Daily News* in front of me——"

"You can read?"

"It's from the eighth of this month, it's the early edition, and I'm missing pages thirty-three to forty-four. I need to know what was on those pages."

There was silence from her end, finally broken by another one of the goose-call honks. Then Havel asked, "You heard of the library?"

"Yes. But this is easier."

"For you, maybe."

"I need to know what's on those pages, and you're the only person I know at the *News*. Can you look this up for me?"

"I can," she said, and I heard the caginess in her cracked voice. "But I want something in return."

"Name it."

"I want that interview you promised me back at the end of July. You're the only one I'm missing—Herrera, Matsui, Trent the younger, they've all spoken to me and my tape recorder. You're the only one who's holding out."

"Okay," I said.

She continued without hearing me. "I'm going to be fair, you know that. I just want you to talk about the whole Drama-the-Assassin story."

"I said okay. I'll do it. Call me next week, we'll work it out."

"I'll have what you need by noon," Havel said.

When I sneaked back into my room for clean clothes, I woke Erika, who shrieked and bolted upright.

"Just me," I said.

She blinked at me for five seconds before recognition reached her brain. "Why are you in my room?"

"This is my room," I pointed out. "I'm just getting clothes. Go back to sleep."

She groaned and flopped back down.

I showered and shaved and dressed quickly, by which time it was almost eight, so I picked up the phone again and called Miranda Glaser at home. The phone rang four times before the machine answered, and the recording gave me no information other than that I had reached Miranda Glaser and should leave a message after the tone. I did, asking her to call me, then hung up. I grabbed my coat, tiptoed back into my room, and woke Erika as gently as possible. It didn't work, and she shrieked again.

"Stop doing that," I said.

"You surprised me," she accused.

I told her I was going out, that I didn't know when I'd be back, and if either Chris Havel or Scott Fowler called, to take messages. She was getting out of bed as I went out the door.

It's a ten-minute walk from my home to Miranda's office by Madison Square Park, and I tried to let it take exactly that long, but ended up doing it in six. It was cold out, the sky clear and the rising sunlight harsh, and I had a headache from the glare by the time I entered the lobby. I rode the elevator up to the third-floor offices of Glaser, Forenzo, Doolittle & Glaser and was stopped by the locked door leading from the hall to reception. I peered through the glass, decided that enough lights were on that someone was indeed in the office, and started banging on the door.

It took her three minutes, but Miranda came around from the receptionist's cubicle, looking irritated and suspicious. The suspicion disappeared when she recognized me, but the irritation compounded. It was the most casual I'd ever seen her—dirty sneakers, blue jeans, a blue hooded sweatshirt. I waited while she unlocked the door and pulled it back, just far enough to make it clear she wasn't planning on letting me inside.

"You," Miranda said.

"Hi. I need to talk to you."

"I'm trying to catch up on some work, Atticus. This is not a good time."

"It shouldn't take long. It's about Bridgett Logan."

She made a face. "You sure can pick them."

"Have you heard from her lately?"

Miranda moved her head back slightly, reappraising. "No. Have you?"

"That's what I need to talk to you about."

"You'd better come in." She moved out of my way, then

locked the door behind me and started back to the rear of the office. "You want coffee?"

"No, thanks," I said.

"I do," she said, and led me past her office, to the tiny kitchen lounge the firm maintained. An old Mr. Coffee was steaming on the counter, and Miranda got down two mugs, filled both of them, and offered one to me anyway. "You look like you need it."

I took the mug. "I need to know what the case was back in September, when I put the two of you together."

Miranda moved her mug to her lips, but didn't drink. Her eyebrows went up. "She didn't tell you?"

"No," I said.

"Then I'm not sure I should."

"Was she working with you?"

"On the case in question, yes, she was," Miranda said. "When did you last hear from her?"

"October. Then she went off the map."

"Hmm." Miranda sipped at her coffee, then set the mug down and added a spoonful of nondairy creamer. "I haven't heard from her since about then either."

I put my mug on the counter, the coffee untouched. "I need you to tell me about the case you were working on."

"Still working on, you mean. Your friend may have vanished and left me holding the bag, but I'm still working the case. Trial's in about three weeks."

"You've got to tell me about it."

"Do I?"

"Yes," I said, and then I explained exactly why.

CHAPTER SEVEN

Lisa Schoof was short and slight and had hair an eighth of an inch from being a skinhead, and she entered the interview room as if she were carrying twenty-to-life easily, and would carry another load just the same, without complaint or concern.

"Who is he?" she asked Miranda. Her voice was thin and rough.

"Atticus Kodiak," Miranda answered. "You want to sit down, Lisa?"

She shrugged, then took the offered chair. "You DEA?" she asked me.

I shook my head.

Lisa Schoof looked at Miranda. "Then I don't have anything to say to him."

"I need to talk to you about Bridgett," I said.

"Now I really don't have anything to say to you."

"I'm her friend," I said.

"No kidding? Me too. Thing is, she never said word one to me about you."

"Goes both ways," I said. "First I heard of you was from Miranda this morning."

"So what?"

"So Bridgett is in trouble, and she's there because of you. She's disappeared, you know that, Lisa? Gone undercover, trying to save your hide, but she hasn't come back. Some of us are starting to worry that she won't."

Lisa Schoof's sneer communicated buckets of disdain. She started to get up, saying, "I've got nothing to say—"

"Sit down." I didn't raise my voice. The command worked just the same. I waited until she was back in the chair. "I don't care what you did, I don't care a rat's ass about your case or your crime. I want to know what Bridgett told you, and I want to know where she is."

"How the fuck do I know?" Lisa asked. "Does it look like I've been getting visitors? Or news even?"

"She talked to you before she disappeared," Miranda interjected, sounding more sane than I did. "We checked the visitors' logs."

Lisa ran a hand through the shorn hair on her head.

"This is what I know," I said. "I know you're a recovering junkie. I know Bridgett is too. I know you're looking at trial for the murder of a dealer named Vincent Lark, and that Lark was connected with Pierre Alabacha's organization. I know that Bridgett got you your lawyer, I know that she was also helping on the case. I know that she's gone undercover, and that she's doing it to help a friend. Are you that friend, Lisa?"

"Could be."

"Then start acting like it."

"Eat me, prick."

"See, because if you are her friend, I'd think that'd earn her a little loyalty. I'd think if you are her friend, you'd want to be certain she was okay."

"Bridgett can take care of herself."

"Not this time," I said. "This time she's in trouble, and you put her there."

"Nothing to do with me."

"Nobody's seen her for nearly three months," I said. "Best

case, she's back on the needle. Worst case, she's dead. Either Alabacha's boys got her, or she shot something she shouldn't have. So your friend may be dead. How does that make you feel? Knowing that the woman you're counting on to save your ass may be dead?"

Her face stayed hard and cold, and I couldn't read what was in her eyes.

"Fuck," Lisa said softly. "Motherfuck."

"Let's hear it."

"She didn't tell me what she was going to do," Lisa said. "She just told me that the DEA would come and offer me a deal, and that when they did, I should take it."

Miranda's mouth dropped open a fraction. "Did she say why the DEA would do this?"

Lisa Schoof rubbed her eyes with both hands. None of us spoke.

"Why did she do this, Lisa? Why'd Bridgett go under-cover for you?" I asked.

Her hands came down and she looked as if she'd lost ten years since she'd walked into the interview room, was per-haps all of fourteen.

"Because I shot the son of a bitch," Lisa told me.

I couldn't tell if she was proud of what she'd done or not.

I got up and headed for the door without saying anything else, wondering how far friendships should stretch.

CHAPTER EIGHT

Erika paged me just as we got back to the law office, and Miranda steered me to her desk to use the phone, then headed off to deal with an irate assistant. I dialed and Erika answered immediately.

"Scott's back from L.A., he's on his way over. What should I do when he gets here?"

"Show him the file."

"Will do," Erika said. "Also, that Havel chicky messengered an envelope over. Can I open it?"

"Go ahead," I said, then heard Erika tearing at paper.

"Okay, it's a bunch of big photocopies and a note," Erika said. "The note says 'A—don't forget our deal.' The copies are of the newspaper."

"Just put them aside, I'll look at them when I get back."

"You tell me what to look for, I can start right now."

"I would tell you if I knew."

"Sounds par for the course."

"I'll be home soon," I said.

Erika hung up and I handed the receiver to Miranda as

she returned. She dropped it into its cradle, then folded herself into her chair, drawing her knees up beneath her and indicating one of the seats opposite her desk.

"Before today, did you know Schoof was guilty?" I asked.

Miranda shook her head. "Not guilty. I knew she shot Lark, but that's not murder."

My expression said it all.

"No, Atticus. This woman has extenuating circumstances like you wouldn't believe. She knew Lark, he'd been her dealer for years until she'd gone straight. He beat her, he abused her, he raped her. Then he showed up and threatened her and her son. She felt she was acting in self-defense, and I agree. Her life and the life of her boy were in danger from this man."

"She has a son?"

"Gabriel, he's ten."

"She can't be older than twenty-five," I said.

"Lisa is twenty-six. She had him when she was fifteen."

I pushed up my glasses and rubbed at my eyes. The lack of sleep was starting to catch up to me, and I was finding it harder to concentrate. "Was Lark the father?"

"Lisa claims she doesn't know who Gabriel's father is. I've wondered if it wasn't Lark too, but that's the Charles Dickens in me more than anything like evidence. At any rate, the boy's parentage has no bearing on the case. If Lisa goes to prison, her aunt will get legal custody of Gabriel."

"How likely is that to happen?"

"Her going to prison?" Miranda shrugged. "We're going to argue self-defense. Give me a jury full of minority single mothers, Lisa will walk. Otherwise, it's going to be tight. The DA's office will refute our defense by bringing up Lisa's drug use—she's untrustworthy, you see—and by arguing that she was stalking Lark before she actually killed him. And it's going to be very hard to prove the history of abuse at his hands—Lisa never went to the cops or filed a complaint because she was using and afraid they wouldn't believe her, or worse. If the jury thinks the crime was premeditated, they'll never buy our case."

I stopped rubbing my eyes and started rubbing my

temples. It helped a little. "That's why Bridgett's looking to cut a deal. The case is shit."

"I wouldn't say shit," Miranda objected. "I'd say difficult. Anyway, Bridgett would have to propose a hell of a deal to beat what the DA's office has already offered. I could call ADA Corwin right now and, with Lisa's permission, take a plea. They've offered. We could probably get away with man one."

"Then what's the difference between you doing it and Bridgett trying to orchestrate something?"

Her brow creased, and she pulled her legs free from beneath her, sitting straighter in the chair, and reached for the top center drawer of her desk. She removed a bottle of Tylenol and rattled it twice to make sure she had my attention before tossing it over.

"I'm not sure we should be having this conversation," Miranda said as I caught the bottle.

"Hypothetically." I shook out two gelcaps and swallowed them dry, then capped the bottle and sent it back through the air. Miranda caught it one-handed and replaced it in her desk drawer. "I told you she left me a packet of information, all of this stuff. But nowhere did she ever mention you, or Lisa, or Lark. She left all of that out."

Miranda looked at me and didn't speak.

"You can't say?"

She hummed a little tune to herself. It sounded like "I Had a Little Dreidel."

It took me almost a minute of thought to her musical accompaniment before I hit on it. "You said she's paying your bills, right?"

Miranda stopped humming and smiled.

Now it was my turn to nod. Bridgett hadn't left the connection because she *couldn't* leave the connection, couldn't leave any proof on paper that would explain her motivation. The phrase "obstruction of justice" came suddenly to mind. "Conflict of interest" was in hot pursuit.

So Bridgett had left that vital bit out. And, if worse came to worse, she could argue that going after Alabacha was something she'd undertaken entirely independent of Lisa

Schoof's impending trial. Without the paper proof, every suspicion about her motives would be circumstantial.

"It's something that she can offer in a deal that you can't," I told Miranda. "That's what this is all about."

"I'd think that's likely."

"But what?"

"It's a question of value," Miranda said. "An individual could conceivably bring the DEA something they like so much they'd be willing to cut a deal for a far lesser charge. A charge that wouldn't carry any time, for instance."

"Ah," I said, understanding.

"Lisa is extremely devoted to her son. Vera—that's the aunt—takes him to visit her as often as possible."

"And a single mother like Lisa Schoof . . ."

". . . would be very interested in not having to do time," Miranda finished. "I'll tell you, though: Whatever someone like Bridgett provided the DEA, it would have to be very big indeed to win Lisa no time, or even time served."

"Big how?"

"Pierre Alabacha big," Miranda replied.

Erika had cleared the kitchen table, moving all of Bridgett's papers into the living room, and then gone to work with thumbtacks. On the wall opposite the window she had posted each of the photographs, and street maps of upper and lower Manhattan, with Washington Heights surrounded in highlighted yellow. When I came in, she was on our decaying couch, the short stack of Havel's photocopies resting on her thighs, the same highlighter poised for attack. With his back to Erika, Special Agent Scott Fowler stood admiring her handiwork.

"Mr. President," he said, snapping off a pretty sloppy salute. "Welcome to the War Room."

"As you were," I said.

"Yes, sir! Thank you, sir!"

Erika smirked at our behavior, but didn't look up from her reading.

"Where've you been?" Scott asked me.

"Determining motive."

"Do tell."

Erika stopped reading the pages while I spoke, and gave me her whole attention. Scott listened while looking at the wall.

When I had finished, Scott said, "So, where to next?"

"I'm not certain. I'm not even sure that what I've learned today helps us. We still don't know where Bridgett is, and we still have a whole city to search."

"Not just the city."

"No."

Scott sighed and took a seat in the easy chair by the couch. He'd gotten a tan while in California, and his already blond hair had managed to get a tad more bleached in his week away. Against his skin and perhaps augmented by his eyeglasses, his eyes looked exceptionally blue.

"Seems to me the best way to do this is to contact the law here in town, see if she's reached out to someone there," he said. "We could make a call or two. I know a guy at Taskforce—"

"What?" Erika asked sharply.

Scott adjusted his glasses in a gesture reminiscent of Clark Kent. "The Joint Drug Taskforce."

Erika flipped through the pages on her lap, found the two she wanted, and thrust them towards us. "Like this Joint Drug Taskforce?"

The photocopies were oversize, clean and sharp, reproductions of pages 36 and 37 of the New York *Daily News* from December the eighth. There was a photograph of a group of law enforcement types, some NYPD, some FBI, some DEA, all posed beneath a banner that said 10,000 BUSTS AND GROWING. I grabbed the sheets and gave them a quick scan.

"That's where Bridgett went," Erika said as I read.

The article was mostly fluff, about what a wonderful thing the Drug Taskforce was, how the efforts of the men and women assigned to the job had cut distribution and use in half during the last five years. It went on to say that the Chinese had been all but shut down, and that the Taskforce was now focusing on the "Central African connection." The mayor was quoted near the end of the piece, praising the Taskforce's work. Nothing was mentioned about Pierre Alabacha or Bridgett Logan. All of the detectives and feds quoted in the piece did so without being identified.

I handed the pages over to Scott and waited for him to read them. Erika was on the edge of the couch now, knocking her heels repeatedly into the floor.

"Well?" she asked when he had finished.

Scott looked at me. "Let's go talk to the Taskforce."

Being with the Bureau, Scott got us pretty far, all the way to the Taskforce offices on Tenth Avenue, in fact. Scott surrendered his weapon at the metal detector, got it back on the other side, wangled a visitor's pass for me, and then we rode the elevator up seven floors to a waiting room that looked straight out of a doctor's office—a small couch, two chairs, never-thumbed magazines on a coffee table, an ugly and old plastic Christmas tree teetering in the far corner, a sliding glass partition where I expected to find a nurse in uniform. But there was no nurse, just a middle-aged black man in a turtleneck and blue jeans, and when he saw us, he pointed at the squawk box beside the sliding window.

Scott produced his badge and held it up, then pressed the button and said, "Agent Fowler. I'm wondering if Agent Runge is in?"

The man behind the glass spoke into a small microphone. "Runge's out. Are you expected, Agent Fowler?"

"No, it's a drop-in. You have somebody I can talk to about Pierre Alabacha?"

The man indicated me with his index finger, as if aiming an imaginary pistol. "Who's he?"

"He's with me. Civilian."

"But paper-trained," I added.

The man grinned. "Hold on." The speaker clicked off, and he disappeared from view.

Scott shrugged and I shrugged, and for a minute we just stood there, almost twiddling our thumbs. There were two doors out of the space, both without windows, and a sign on the wall informed us that no unauthorized visitors were permitted beyond this point. There were surveillance cameras too, one positioned in the corner by the door, the other just above the partition. I realized that the window wasn't glass, but Lexan.

From one of the doors came the solid thunk of a magnetic lock snapping back, and the agent we'd been speaking with leaned out and said, "Agent Fowler, you can come on back."

Scott looked at me and I shrugged again, said, "I'll wait."

He went through the door, and it closed and locked once more. I took a seat on the couch and, after a second, picked up the issue of *Forbes* that was staring at me. I turned it over and studied the ad for Land Rovers on the back. Then I studied the walls again. Then I got up and looked through the partition, thinking to ask the agent who had been there a question or two. He was gone. Behind where he had been standing was a bank of machines—a two-way radio console, a cellular frequency scanner, lots of electronics with lots of blinking lights.

I was starting to feel as if I'd been locked up like Lisa Schoof when the other door opened and the same agent gestured me inside. I entered and he told me to have a seat, that someone would be with me in a minute, then went out through the only other door. Again, locks clacked shut.

This room was half the size of the previous one, no windows, nothing on the walls, and a small rectangular table set lengthwise near the center. There were three chairs, only one on my side. The chairs were upholstered in what looked to be the same gray industrial carpet that covered the floors.

I sat down, thinking that now, in fact, I *was* locked up. My headache had returned too, and a stomachache had joined it. I told myself it was from lack of sleep. Then I told myself I was a liar. I checked my watch. It had already been two minutes.

After eleven minutes the other door opened, and Scott came in, carrying a folder. He shut the door behind him, then sat at the table opposite me.

"I'd like to exercise my right to an attorney," I told him.

He shook his head and didn't smile, just opened the

folder and turned it toward me. "This is classified and it's off the record and it doesn't leave this office," Scott said.

The folder was marked "Logan, Bridgett E." and there was a file code alongside her name, a long series of characters and numbers that meant nothing to me. Inside were several sheets of paper, typed reports, handwritten notes, a couple grainy eight-by-ten black-and-whites.

"Her case file," Scott supplied lamely, and I heard the edge in his voice, the other thing that he wouldn't yet say.

"How bad is it?" I asked.

"Keep reading."

The file had been opened on the twenty-eighth of October, with a note to the effect that Bridgett Logan had been seen in communication with members of Pierre Alabacha's organization. That was followed with other surveillance reports, putting her in the company of several names I didn't recognize from Bridgett's papers or photographs, and then one that I did—Roley Butler, one of the Alabacha lieutenants. The connection with Butler was recorded in early November, and at that point the tenor of the reports changed. At that point, Bridgett Logan was no longer an unknown; she'd become the enemy.

Surveillance photos showed her rubbing elbows with Butler, and with another man, black, who I thought might have been Anton Ladipo. Nothing incriminating but the company she kept.

But the reports refuted that, accused her of running drugs for Pierre Alabacha, and one was particularly damning. It described how Bridgett Logan had supposedly delivered payment to a group of Nigerians, in the country illegally, and in exchange, received ten kilos of uncut heroin. The date on the report was the twenty-second of November, and it was signed by Julian Runge, Supervisory Agent in charge. The report had been filed by someone who hadn't used a name, but a string of numbers.

"Who wrote this?" I asked Scott, showing him the report. My head was starting to scream for aspirin.

"Undercover," Scott said. "Anonymous."

"Can't be verified."

He shook his head, then reached across and rustled the pages until he found the one he wanted me to see. He pulled the report free, laid it out so I could read it.

The report was dated the eighteenth of December, and recommended that Bridgett Logan's file be placed inactive until further developments.

I looked at Scott.

"Last time anyone in Taskforce is sure they saw her was around the seventh or eighth of this month. They didn't realize she was gone until they started tracking a lot of activity among Alabacha's lieutenants, Butler and Ladipo. The undercover says that she vanished; he can't be sure it was of her own volition."

"What do they think?" I leaned a little on the last word of the question, heard my own impatience.

"They think it's too soon to close the file," Scott said evenly. "They need proof—testimony, something—before they can determine its . . . disposition."

Proof. Meaning her body. Meaning someone who could say, I saw Bridgett Logan shot, or stabbed, or beaten, or bound hands and feet with baling wire and with her head in a trash bag full of kerosene. Someone who could say, I lit the fire, threw the match myself, saw it done.

I could hardly breathe in that little room.

It's one thing to suspect, all by yourself, that the woman you love is dead. It's quite something else to hear that the DEA, the NYPD, and the FBI are inclined to agree with you.

I barely heard the magnetic locks snap, and then Scott was hurriedly placing papers back into the folder, turning to present the whole package to the same agent who'd talked to us before. I heard Scott thank him, and the other man say that he'd show us out. Scott said something and I made an agreeing noise. I have no idea what I was agreeing to.

The uniformed security guard on the first floor took my visitor's pass back without a word, and we stepped outside, into dusk. Scott said something about taking a cab back to my place, managed to hail one fairly quickly.

"It doesn't mean anything, really," Scott said before we got into the cab. "It doesn't mean Alabacha made her."

Well, no, it doesn't, I thought.

But it doesn't mean he didn't.

Scott gave up trying to talk to me, and we rode back to my apartment in silence. I paid before he could offer, and he followed me out and up the stairs and into my apartment, where I went straight to the living room. Erika had moved from the couch to the floor, and she read my expression the instant she saw me.

"What did they say?"

"Scott will explain," I said, and then turned my back and began studying the papers on the wall.

"Taskforce lost track of her," I heard Scott tell Erika. "About a week ago they put a hold on her file. I can't really say more. It's classified information."

"What does that mean, *they put a hold on her file*?" Her voice was beginning to climb. "What the hell does that mean?"

I didn't hear Scott's answer, and it didn't matter. On the wall, below the picture of Roley Butler, white and smug and with tattoos on two of his fingers, I found what I was looking for. I checked my watch, did the math, and what I was thinking seemed perfectly logical. I went quietly down the hall, leaving their voices behind me. In my bedroom closet I opened my gun locker and got out my pistol and holster and two clips. I put the holster on my waist and checked and loaded my gun, then chambered the first round. I put on my jacket and I grabbed the keys to the motorcycle, then waited until I heard both Erika's and Scott's voices, was certain they were deep in their words.

I left the apartment quietly, and after the door was shut, broke for the garage and my bike. It wasn't going to take Scott long to realize where I was going. Five minutes at the most. It wasn't a lot of time.

But if I was lucky, it would be more than enough to ram my gun down Pierre Alabacha's throat.

CHAPTER NINE

You can say a lot about Bridgett Logan, you can list faults until you're blue in the face. But one of the things you can absolutely not say is that she doesn't do her homework. One of the things you can absolutely not say is that Bridgett Logan doesn't know how to run a private investigation.

She'd located three domiciles for Pierre Alabacha in the five boroughs, one in Brooklyn, one in Queens, and one in Manhattan. According to her notes, the Manhattan apartment was his permanent residence, only two blocks from the Hayden Planetarium on the Upper West Side. Every day, according to her surveillance, Alabacha returned home by six in the evening, then left again for a dinner out at seven-thirty.

When I climbed onto the bike it was seven-seventeen.

I drove fast and unsafely, weaving through traffic and playing chicken with a squadron of cabs that were all changing lanes as I reached Central Park. The air was frigid on my exposed face, and I could feel the muscles below my cheeks tightening from the cold. There was a gap between two of the cars that I thought I could make, and I rolled the throttle back hard and shot through it, and got clipped on the rear wheel with somebody's fender. The motorcycle wobbled and threatened to go shiny-side down, but somehow I kept upright. If it was God's way of telling me to slow down, it didn't take. I was doing seventy when I came out on Eighty-first Street, slowed down enough to keep from dying as I turned onto Columbus, and then gunned it again, racing the blocks.

It was night now, streets lit by headlights and streetlamps, and cluttered with parked cars on either side, blocking the view of the sidewalk. I slowed, looking at addresses. A doorman was posted outside of Alabacha's building, uniformed in a black topcoat and black cap, both decorated with royal red piping. I shot past to the end of the block, then swung a tight turn and popped my wheels up onto the sidewalk, stopping, letting the bike idle. A young couple, walking hand in hand, told me I was an asshole. I ignored them and they went around.

A Mercedes-Benz was parked six cars down from where the doorman stood on post. It was silver and sleek, and looked like the one in the photograph of Alabacha.

I checked my watch, read seven twenty-eight. When I looked up again, the doorman had turned. The first man out was white, and looked enough like Butler that everything inside me dumped away, replaced by a cold rush. He was a big man, wearing a baseball jacket that made his shoulders look broader. He went to the Benz and unlocked the door, then turned to light a cigarette.

Alabacha followed him, dressed for the evening, in a cream-colored sweater and slacks. I didn't watch for more than one or two seconds, but the impressions came fast—age notwithstanding, he moved like a young man, his back straight, a soldier's bearing, certain but without swagger. One or two inches taller than Butler, perhaps five eleven, maybe even six feet. He went straight to the Benz, then stopped, letting the other man light his cigarette.

Ladipo came last, and one look told me what I needed to know. He was the strength of their protection, he was the one who knew how to look. He was the one who recognized what he saw when he looked my way, enough to earn me a double take.

I rolled the throttle and released the clutch, and pointed my front tire right at him.

He misread the situation, put a hand onto Alabacha's back, shoving him out of the way. Alabacha went into Butler, and then I was on them and my right leg swung out and I caught Ladipo in the gut with the toe of my boot. I felt the hit, felt him spin and fall away, braked hard and let the bike fall as I cleared it.

Ladipo was on his back on the sidewalk, hands on his belly, eyes up and open, and I didn't hear him making any noise. The doorman was frozen, trying to decide what to do, and Alabacha was still against the Benz, staring. Butler had managed a reaction and was beginning his move to intercept me, one hand going for the gun I could see hanging beneath his left shoulder.

I reached him before he got it, and Butler had started to curse me, had gotten as far as "Kill your—" before I nailed him in the stomach. The blow didn't sink far, but I followed it immediately with a knee between the legs and another two blows at his head. The second hit him in the side of the neck, and he was on his knees and still falling when I reached Alabacha.

Fight-or-flight had fired, and Pierre Alabacha was turning to open his driver's side door when I caught him by the throat and slammed him against the car. I drew my gun and forced the barrel against his forehead, and he craned his neck until the back of his skull rested on the roof of the Benz. I put my weight against him, my body on his, the HK in my hand concentrating pressure, and he was wincing when I spoke.

"Bridgett Logan," I said. "Where is she?"

He didn't speak. I pushed harder.

"Where the fuck is she?" I was shouting.

Pierre Alabacha forced the pain out of his expression. When he spoke, his accent was French.

"I have no idea who you mean." There was nothing in his voice that suggested bluff. "If you are going to fire, I'd do it now."

"Wrong," I said, and dipped the barrel three inches to the right and fired a round. The report was loud and in his ear and must have hurt like a bitch and Alabacha flinched, but that was all. I replaced the barrel on his forehead. "Where. Is. She?"

"You wasted your only chance," Alabacha said. His eyes went right, away from me, and I didn't bother to track the look. Using his throat as a grip, I wheeled him around in front of me, putting my back to the car and sliding the barrel to his temple. He was heavier than I'd thought he'd be, and I needed a lot of muscle for the move.

Ladipo was still on the ground, but had rolled, and was training his pistol on me, a serious-looking SIG-Sauer. Butler had gotten to his feet, and was doing much the same with a Smith & Wesson semiauto. The doorman scuttled for cover behind a potted plant just inside the doorway, like he knew the shooting was going to start any second. His stupid hat poked above the plant. I heard noise up and down the street.

And then Scott Fowler was standing between me and Alabacha's men, waving his badge in one hand, flapping his other like he was trying to put out a fire, and shouting, "Whoa! Whoa! Down with the guns! Everybody, *down* with the guns!"

Everybody went into freeze-frame.

"FBI," Scott said. "Now everybody calm the fuck down."

Butler and Ladipo lowered their weapons, but not to their holsters.

Rage flared in Scott's eyes when he looked at me. "Put it away," he said.

I didn't want to. I wanted an answer, just one answer, and it seemed it was a very simple question. It seemed it shouldn't be this difficult or this dangerous.

But I knew I wasn't going to get it here.

I loosened my grip on the HK, making it safe, and pulled the barrel away from Pierre Alabacha's head. Then I let go of his throat, dropped my arm away.

Alabacha straightened, coughed once softly into his hand, and stepped away from me. He glanced at Butler, then at

Ladipo, and both men holstered their weapons. Then he looked at Scott.

"Thank you," Alabacha said. "I think perhaps you should arrest this man? Assault? Menacing, maybe?"

"I think you should just forget about this whole thing," Scott said. "Unless you want your two friends arrested as well."

"My friends have acted only in self-defense. The law would support their actions."

"Then they won't mind if I run a check on their weapons."

Alabacha studied Scott's face. He put his left hand to his left ear, checking to see if there was blood, then looked at me. "Where I come from, I have seen tanks crush people in the streets. I have seen mass executions, the savagery of a military dictatorship out of control.

"But I have never been assaulted leaving my own home." His voice developed an edge that almost split skin. "If I lose my hearing, monsieur, you will pay."

Scott's look warned me not to speak. I put my gun into my holster.

Ladipo got to his feet slowly, guarding his belly with one hand. Alabacha waited until he was up, then motioned both men to the car. Scott reached out an arm and pulled me back toward him and out of their way. Alabacha climbed into the back of the vehicle without a word. Butler and I exchanged eyefucks as he got behind the wheel.

When everyone was in the Benz, the engine started, and the car pulled quietly away. I stared at it until it made its turn at the corner, then yanked myself free of Scott's grip and headed back down the block to where I'd left the bike. The motorcycle had stalled out, and I was trying to get it upright again when Scott lent a silent hand. After it was back on its two wheels, I kicked out the stand and crouched down, began checking it over. I had scraped the left side pretty badly, and some gasoline had leaked from the carburetor. To my eyes, it would still run.

Scott stood behind me, and I could feel his gaze. I didn't want to meet it right then.

I got up and put the stand up again, started walking the

bike down the block, to the opposite corner. It was heavy and clumsy and gave me something new to worry about.

We had reached the corner before Scott said, "Did he tell you?"

"No."

"So was it worth it? Do you feel better?"

All of the adrenaline had left, suddenly, and the headache and the stomachache and the lack of sleep, all of it soaked me to the core. A sudden weight rushed at my eyes. I just shook my head.

"Let's go get a drink," Scott said.

He gave me a hand with the bike, and we turned it, started walking down the block. We hadn't gone three steps before a black car squealed to a stop alongside us, popping its front two tires onto the sidewalk, and the doors were opening, and the two men with badges were pointing their guns at us, and another two men were throwing us into the side of a building.

Once again my motorcycle fell to the sidewalk.

"Nobody moves," one of the badges ordered. "You're both fucking under arrest."

"Julian," Scott Fowler was saying, "it's not what you think."

Agent Julian Runge of the DEA laughed in his face. Beside him, Detective James Shannon of the NYPD smiled to himself and closed his eyes, settling back in his chair. Maybe he was daydreaming about people who didn't interfere in Taskforce operations.

"I can have him arrested," Runge said, then added, for my benefit, "I can have you arrested. Illegal discharge of a firearm. Assault and battery. Attempted vehicular homicide. Anything else I can think of. What am I missing, Jimmy?"

Detective Shannon didn't open his eyes. "Criminal stupidity."

"I'm sorry," I said.

Runge laughed again. It wasn't an amused laugh, but then, he didn't look like a man who was amused by much. He was in his late thirties, maybe his early forties, of average height and perhaps a little too thin, with black hair that hadn't been cut very recently, or if it had, at least not cut very well. He had the mustache to match, with drooping ends that looked like they would curl into his mouth. His eyes were brown and big, and expressive like a hound's. There was no way to miss his opinion of me, and right now I figured he rated me marginally lower than rat shit.

James Shannon, on the other hand, seemed to find me a source of great entertainment, at least when he acted like we weren't disturbing his nap. Best as I could tell, Shannon was the optimist to Julian Runge's pessimist, and when his blue eyes were open, they showed more mirth than anything else. He was a big man, easily over six feet three, and bulky, what might have been fat but was probably more muscle underneath. His blond hair was thinning and going silver, and even in the artificial light of this Taskforce meeting room, I could see the redness on his scalp and face.

"Your apology doesn't mean dinky-dick to me," Runge continued. "The FBI shows up, starts fucking with a Taskforce surveillance—you *know* how sensitive this shit is, what we're up against—and this motherfucker just blows in there? What was he trying to do? Commit suicide?"

"Your operation is still solid," Scott said. "Your people never got involved."

"Only because you showed up!" Runge exploded. "We were halfway out of the van before you had the situation back under control. And having an FBI waving his badge around isn't the sort of thing drug dealers just forget, Scott! Now he's going to be even more paranoid . . ."

James Shannon opened his eyes slowly and put their full weight on me. It was a look that reminded me of my father's after I told him I was enlisting in the Army. He had paternal sorrow and disappointment down pat, and I glanced at Shannon's left hand, just to see if he was married. The ring finger was bare. Divorced, then, or widowed. I was certain he had sons of his own.

"You want to tell us what exactly you were doing, lad?" Detective Shannon asked me.

"I was trying to find someone. And Alabacha knows where she is."

"This someone, she's important enough to you that you'll threaten killers right on the street?"

Runge added, "What, she owe you money?"

I shook my head.

"This someone, she your girl?" Shannon asked.

"Something like that."

Runge moved the ends of his mustache out of his mouth so I could see his contempt clearly. "Your girl is running with Alabacha? Scott here should have let you catch the bullet."

"What's her name?" Shannon asked.

"Bridgett Logan."

In a way, I suppose it was funny. Even absent, her name caused waves. Runge looked sharply at Shannon, and for a moment Shannon's sleepy lids parted fully. The mirthful eyes seemed to lose some of their glimmer, to go flat. Runge looked back at me, then grumbled and took his seat.

"How do you know her?" Shannon asked me.

"She's a friend."

Runge leaned over to address Scott. "So . . . your friend is a friend of Pierre Alabacha's friends. What do you think of that?"

"She's my friend too," Scott replied softly. "And whatever you think is going on with Bridgett Logan, I guarantee you're wrong."

"We find her, we've got a case against her," Runge said. "A case that the U.S. attorney likes, I might add."

"It's not what you think," I said.

"No?" Shannon asked. "Logan's dealing smack for Alabacha. What else is there to think?"

I just shook my head. Even if what I'd determined about Bridgett's motives was correct, it wouldn't fly in the face of two members of Taskforce who believed their files said it all. And they weren't really mistaken—Bridgett probably had done exactly what the anonymous undercover had reported, she probably had bought for Alabacha. If Fernando Costas in Washington Heights was to be believed, she had done more, and maybe worse.

"Well?" Runge demanded.

"I have to find her," I said.

Shannon scratched a bushy eyebrow, looked like he was wrestling a yawn. "How'd you know she was connected with Alabacha?"

"She told me," I said.

"Logan just mentioned to you that she was dealing drugs?" Runge demanded, all sarcasm. "And you didn't bother to call the cops or us or anything like that?"

"He's legit," Scott said. "You can just forget that, okay, Julian? Atticus wouldn't know a controlled substance if it bit him."

"She told me she was working for him," I said.

Shannon's yawn won. When it finished, he asked, "When?"

"I got a letter from her on Christmas Eve."

"When was it mailed?"

"It wasn't, it was hand-delivered."

"By who?"

"Her sister."

Shannon managed to get both eyes all the way open once more, searched my face. "Take off the glasses," he told me.

I looked at Scott. "What's it going to hurt?" he asked me.

I took off my glasses.

"Look at me," Shannon said.

I looked at him. Even at a distance of three feet, he was a little blurry, but I figured he was trying to place my face, maybe from a mug shot. Out of the corner of my eye, Runge's mustache looked like a big dead moth resting on his upper lip. It felt like a long time before Shannon had seen enough.

"All right, put them back on."

I put my glasses on. Shannon had leaned his bulk to the side and was whispering in Runge's ear. Runge's expression remained peeved. Shannon leaned back and the two exchanged looks, then Runge got out of his chair.

"Come on," he told Scott.

"What's going on?" Scott asked.

"I want you two out," Shannon said. "I want to talk to Mr. Kodiak alone."

Runge was on his feet and at the door, waiting for Scott. Scott fiddled with the lower of the two posts in his left ear, then sighed. "He's sorry. Don't ring him up, Detective."

"Get out." Shannon said it mildly.

Scott rose, shot a last look at me, and then followed Agent Runge out the door. The latch sounded loud when it caught. At least it wasn't magnetic.

Detective James Shannon got out of his chair slowly, and it seemed he just kept going up for a while before he reached his full height. He looked down at me and then came around to my side of the table, moving behind my back. I felt a hand rest on my left shoulder.

"If I was the nervous sort, I'd be expecting a beating about now," I said.

"Not unless you're the type that likes that sort of thing," Shannon said. "We can make it look good, I can give you a parting shot, if you want."

I turned my head and tilted back to look at him, trying to figure out what he meant. Shannon grinned, let go of my shoulder, and took the seat beside me, moving in close.

"Do you know what Logan's up to?" Shannon asked.

"I might," I said. "I'm not certain."

"And you haven't seen her? You really don't know where she is?"

"No."

"Then why'd you go running at Alabacha and Ladipo and Butler? What was that really about?"

"It's what I said. I thought they knew where she was."

"They don't."

"You're certain?"

"They're looking for her too," Shannon said. "Have been for a while. Our suspicion is that she burned them. She got in good, managed to get some trust, and then ran with a couple kilos and a bag of cash, maybe."

I shook my head. "She didn't."

"How well do you know her?"

"Not as well as I should."

"But you don't think she'd do that?"

"I know she wouldn't do that."

James Shannon looked away from me, at the closed door. "Does she use drugs?"

"She did once."

"Maybe she still does."

"No."

"Addicts can hide their habits, at least for a while. Some of them, they can hide it for a good, long time."

I stared at Shannon, trying to figure him out.

"You know her," I realized.

Shannon didn't say anything. After a second, he got to his feet and crossed to the door. "You're free to go," he said.

"How do you know Bridgett?" I asked.

He stifled another yawn.

The conversation, such as it was, was over. Detective James Shannon needed to get more of his beauty rest. He held the door open so I could exit. Outside, I could see Scott talking with Runge. Both of them stopped their conversation and looked our way.

I was almost out of the room when Shannon lowered his head to my ear.

"Find her," he said.

It wasn't a request, I realized.

It was an order.

CHAPTER ELEVEN

It was almost two in the morning when I returned home, tired beyond belief, and fell into my bed already half asleep. I slept deeply, but poorly, with lots of vivid images from my subconscious, mostly replays of my day's stupidity. I awoke, feeling entirely unrested, to see Erika sitting on the edge of my bed, holding a mug of coffee, watching me.

I sat up and pulled the sheets around me, and Erika set the coffee on the nightstand and offered me my glasses. I put them on and she grinned.

"Sister Cashel's here, in the living room. I thought about letting her wake you, but didn't want to shock her with the sight of your naked form."

"I'm covered," I said.

"You weren't when I came in."

"Out," I commanded. "Scat!"

She giggled but went, and I slurped some of the coffee, then forced myself out of bed. I had a swollen-brain headache, the kind where it feels like a drill would be needed to relieve the pressure, and was surprised when the clock informed me it was after noon. Ten-plus hours of sleep hadn't taken my edge off.

I pulled on my clothes quickly, bolted down the rest of the coffee, and reached the living room with a refilled cup and my brain and body once again acknowledging their partnership, even if they weren't happy about it. Erika had disappeared into her bedroom, and Sister Cashel Logan, dressed in a long black skirt and a white turtleneck, was waiting patiently for me in the easy chair, looking at Erika's redecorated wall. She had her coat neatly folded across her knees.

"I thought you would have been awake by now," Cashel said.

"I needed to get up anyway. Would you like some coffee?"

"No, thank you, Erika already offered. I tried reaching you last night, but Erika said you had gone out. When I called she seemed quite upset. She said that you had just left without saying anything."

"I was in a hurry."

"Were you following a lead?"

"Trying to make one. I failed."

Cashel's expression patiently asked me to elaborate.

"I was stupid," I said. "I shoved a gun in Pierre Alabacha's face and demanded to know where your sister was. The only thing it got me was in trouble with the DEA."

"Sounds much like the day I had," Cashel said. "Andrew and I went looking for Bridgett again, mostly in Washington Heights. It didn't go well . . . he was antagonistic and got himself into two separate fights."

"That must have been fun."

Her expression darkened as if crossed by a shadow, and again the familial resemblance was strong, the look one I had seen Bridgett wear more than once. "I'm afraid it was, for Andrew. A means of working out frustration. I told him I thought he should stay home today, be with his wife and children. I don't know if he listened to me."

"Probably didn't," I said.

"And if I suggested that perhaps you should take a day to calm down, you'd ignore my advice too?"

"You're quite perceptive, Sister."

She shook her head. "Not really. I could use a day off, as well, but here I am, ready for more. Wondering what you've learned."

"I know why Bridgett went undercover. And I know that the DEA has a file on her. And I know that Pierre Alabacha and his men are not easily intimidated."

"Sounds reasonably productive." Cashel smoothed the coat folded across her knees. "Better than we did. We really only got confirmation of what Fernando told us—a couple of drug dealers admitted that they had 'done business' with her."

I finished my second cup of coffee, looking at the wall of paperwork, at the maps, at the big city. "Andrew was right about Bridgett working on a murder investigation. I spoke to the attorney your sister was working with, and to the client, a woman named Schoof. She's at Rikers right now. Her trial starts in just under four weeks."

"I'm sorry," Cashel said. "Do you mean Lisa Schoof?"

"You know her?"

"Not since I went to college. So it was Lisa who committed the crime, and Bridgett was trying to clear Lisa's name. Is that it?"

"That's how it looks."

"Lisa Schoof," Cashel said softly. "I haven't seen her in ages."

"You and Bridgett both knew her?"

"Oh, yeah. Bridgett better than I, of course, but I knew her pretty well too. I used to hate her guts." She moved her eyes from her hands to me, then grinned at my reaction. "Don't worry, I got over it. But at the time . . . I was jealous to death of her."

I thought about the small woman at Rikers in her gray prison jumpsuit, and couldn't imagine anything there of which Cashel Logan should be jealous. "Why?"

She took several seconds to formulate her answer, giving her words real thought before speaking. "Bridgett met Lisa in a therapy group," Cashel said. "She had been clean six, maybe seven months when Lisa joined. Bridgett was seventeen, Lisa was my age, fifteen. And she was pregnant. That's why she was trying to get clean—she wanted to have a healthy baby.

"Lisa and Bridgett got along very well—they bonded. Bridgett acted as Lisa's big sister. At that point I wanted desperately to be close to Bridgett again, to repair what had happened between us. I felt robbed, to say the least. And instead of admitting my anger, and Bridgett's fault, I blamed Lisa. Or tried to, at any rate."

"Not anymore?" I asked.

She hesitated, then spoke with care. "It hurts that my sister is more loyal to a woman she knows from rehab, to a friend from childhood, than she is to me. They share a closeness that I wish she and I had. But I'm old enough now, mature enough now, that I cannot be angry at Lisa."

"But with your sister?"

When she finally did speak this time, her voice was soft, and wrapped tight in the fight against the hurt that was still there.

"I love her," Sister Cashel said. "We haven't seen each other in two years, we live twenty minutes apart. I phone her, she doesn't return my calls. I try to visit, she isn't at home. After a while, you get the message. I love her. I want to forgive her. I'm a nun. I should be able to do it. With His grace and love, I should have forgiven her already. . . . But she makes it so hard."

She turned her face away. I was afraid she was crying, and couldn't be sure she wasn't. I didn't know what to say.

But I could think of something to do, and so I said, "I'll be right back." I don't think Cashel heard me.

I returned to the kitchen, dumped the dregs in my mug, and reached for the phone. I called Miranda Glaser's office, and in three minutes had the address I wanted. I hung up and turned back to the living room in time to hear the bathroom door in the hallway shut. The chair was empty, but Cashel's coat was draped over the back.

The sink ran in the bathroom just a short time, and then she came back out into the hall, her fair skin flushed, eyelashes matted. The look she met me with was apologetic.

"Don't," I said. "You don't need to."

"Confession," Cashel said, "is good for the soul."

The address I'd wangled from Miranda was that of Vera Grimshaw. I offered to take Cashel via motorcycle, but she suggested we use the subway. It was the right choice, because before we'd even made it to the train, the sky had darkened, and an icy rain had begun to fall.

It was twenty of three when we reached the building. There was no intercom system, no real security to speak of at all, and we climbed three flights of stairs to the apartment halfway down the hall. The hallway was rank with the scent of stale cigarette smoke.

I knocked, hearing television voices from within, and there was the rattle of a security chain being applied before the door got pulled back. In the space between the door and the frame, beneath the taut links, a sliver of middle-aged woman glowered at me.

"What do you want?"

"Vera Grimshaw?"

"Who's asking?"

Cashel leaned forward, presenting herself for inspection. "Ms. Grimshaw? I'm Cashel Logan, do you remember me?"

The one visible eyebrow arched. "My ass, you were just a scrawny thing last time I saw you, you weren't taller than my hip."

"It's me," Cashel said. "And this is Atticus Kodiak, he's a friend of my sister's."

Vera Grimshaw disconnected the security chain, let it drop with a jangle, then opened the door wide. "Your sister, huh? Haven't heard from her since they denied Lisa bail. Come on in, come on, there's room at the table. Have yourself seats."

The apartment opened into a kitchen and living space, and the table she had indicated was positioned in the center. Closer to the end of the room was a couch, its hideaway bed unfolded but neatly made. The television was in the corner, showing the latest adventures of Superman. I had reached the table before I saw the boy who had to be Gabriel, sprawled on his belly beyond the unfolded bed. He lay on the floor, in view of the television, pens and paper spread out in front of him, and he had propped himself up on his elbows to see us enter, curious.

"Who are they, Vera?" he asked.

"Friends of Bridgett's," Vera called back from the kitchen. "You go introduce yourself."

Gabriel pulled himself up using the bed and looked each of us over. The curiosity had given way to an almost utter lack of expression. "Hi," he said.

"Hi, I'm Atticus."

"Yeah."

Cashel hit him with a one-hundred-watt smile. "I'm Cashel, Gabriel. It's nice to see you again."

"I don't know you."

"I was there when you were born," Cashel said. The watts in the smile went to one-fifty.

Gabriel turned away, saying, "So what?" Then he flopped back onto the floor and resumed his drawing.

Vera came around from the kitchen with a plate of cookies in her hands, a cigarette smoldering between her lips, and a frown. "Gabe, don't be rude," she said.

Gabriel's response was lost behind the television.

Vera set the plate on the table, between a half-full ashtray and an open box of Lucky Charms. Her fingernails were painted bright red. "He's been like this all week," she confided. "Just plain rude. I think it's Christmas without his mother."

Cashel sat, thanking Vera for the hospitality, and said, "I just heard about Lisa. I'm sorry."

"That girl can't get a break," Vera said. "Your sister is the best thing that ever happened to Lisa, you know that? She's the only reason Lisa's still going, still holding out. Everybody should have a friend like Bridgett. Mr. Kodiak?"

I looked away from Gabriel, who was viciously attacking his paper with a green crayon. "Yes?"

"You know Bridgett too, huh?"

"Yeah, she's something." I looked back to where Gabriel was now on his knees, gathering up his art supplies. He shot us a hostile glare, then went out of the room, slamming the door as he left.

"Doing the best I can," Vera said softly. "But the kid's been with me three months now, and he wants to go home. If your sister can do everything she says she can, he'll be back in Lisa's arms before February."

"Actually, Bridgett's why we're here," Cashel said. "This may sound strange, Vera, but she's kind of disappeared. We were wondering if maybe you've seen her."

"Disappeared?" Vera Grimshaw trickled smoke like a leaky dragon. "Last time I saw Lisa, she said Bridgett was trying to clear her name. Lisa said she was helping get her defense all set for that lady lawyer."

"Glaser?" I asked.

"Yeah, the bossy bitchy one."

"Miss Glaser hasn't seen her either," I said.

"That can't be right."

"We think something may have happened to Bridgett," Cashel said softly.

There was a Matchbox car by one of the legs of the hide-away, a small black one that, when I picked it up, turned out to actually be blue. I looked at it in my palm as Vera and Cashel talked, and my headache finally went away.

"Mind if I talk to Gabriel?" I asked Vera, interrupting.

"Go right ahead," she said, snuffing out her cigarette in the ashtray. She already had another one lit and in her mouth.

Cashel looked at me and I shook my head, crossed over to the door and knocked. There was no answer, and I knocked again and got the same again, so I just opened it and went inside.

It had been Vera's bedroom before Gabriel moved in, and the space was a strange combination of middle-aged single woman and ten-year-old boy. Makeup shared space on the dresser with action figures. A print of a cat batting a ball of twine hung beside a poster of Michael Jordan getting down with Bugs Bunny. Some of Gabriel's crayon drawings were up too, fighter jets and ninjas and space aliens fighting with laser-blasting warriors. Some clothes were heaped in a corner, what I figured were the dirty ones.

Gabriel had abandoned his artistic endeavors for a career in construction, assembling orange plastic segments of a racetrack for his collection of miniature cars. It was an impressive setup he was working on, with loop-de-loops and high banking turns and a tunnel that looked like the mouth of a slavering beastie. One piece of the track was mechanized, with spinning disks that would propel the cars forward.

"Christmas present?" I asked.

"Yeah."

"It's pretty cool. Who's it from?"

"My mom. She told Aunt Vera to get it for me."

It took Gabriel another three minutes to finish the assembly, and then he sat up on his knees and switched the power on to the track, started searching around for a nearby car to race. He grabbed a tiny red Corvette and dropped it into place, and the car took off like a shot, banking through the turns and completing the first of the two loop-de-loops without any difficulty. On the second one, though, the Corvette jumped the track and clattered to the floor.

He reached for another car without a word, not even looking my way. This was a red Mustang convertible, one of the new models. He gave it a shove, and the car was off and running.

I sat down beside him, keeping my own silence.

The Mustang made it through the loops, but tanked at the tunnel, flipping just before it made the entrance. Gabriel frowned and reached for the next victim. In all, he ran another seven cars before completing the cycle, including a police cruiser, a VW Bug, and a Honda van. Only the Bug made it all the way, catching the spinning wheels to start its next lap unassisted. Then it ran out of momentum, and coasted to a stop just shy of the finish line.

"They're supposed to keep going around and around," Gabriel said. "They're supposed to do laps. But most of them can't make it."

"You should try this one," I said, and handed over the blue Porsche Boxster in my hand. "Built for speed."

He took it and looked at me, then quickly away and to the track. But it was enough, and I knew, and my headache stayed away, and my stomach started to tighten.

Gabriel placed the Matchbox Porsche onto the track, nudged it forward with his index finger until it caught the machinery, and then the car flew. It hugged the track tight on the first turn, flew through both loop-de-loops without trouble, and blasted its way through the tunnel and out the other side.

Gabriel stopped it with his hand before the Porsche crossed the finish line, switching off the power to the track. He moved the car to the floor and began rolling it back and forth.

"Where'd you see her?" I asked.

The car stopped moving.

"Was it recent?" I asked.

If I hadn't been looking for it, I would have probably missed his nod.

"This week?"

This nod was a little easier to spot.

"Where?"

Gabriel Schoof gave the miniature Porsche Boxster a savage shove with his finger, and the car shot off toward the wall. He pushed it so hard that it flew off its wheels, flipping onto its side, and then smashed into the baseboard with a loud whack. The impact scarred the wood.

"She's supposed to be helping my mom," he said. "She's supposed to be helping us. Why isn't she helping us like she said she was? She told me she was going to help, that it would be all right."

He glared at me, as if I knew the answer instead of only the question.

"Where was she?" I asked.

"Home."

"Her home?"

"*My* home!" His cheeks went flushed, and the words broke out of him fast and clumsily, like the way the Matchbox cars had wrecked one after another on the plastic orange track. "I . . . I went . . . back, okay, I went back to get my cars so I could have them, okay? So I could have them to play with on this stupid dumb crappy track. I went back and I went and she was there, okay? She was just there and she . . . she . . . she was *living* there okay? Okay?"

"Okay," I said.

He didn't listen. He'd been carrying the secret alone, its weight only adding to every other burden on his ten-year-old shoulders, and now that the pressure was off, everything else was fighting its way out too. He had gotten to his feet, his arms out, reaching for me, and he grabbed my sleeves, pulling on my jacket.

"Okay? Is that okay? That she's there? And my mom's not? And I asked her about Mom and she didn't say anything and . . . and . . . and I took the cars and she told me to leave and not to tell and—"

His mouth flapped, trying to get air. I worked my arms free and pulled him in, repeated, "It's okay, just breathe, it's okay. You've got to breathe." Vera and Cashel had come into the room, and Vera rushed to us, clucking for Gabriel.

"Gabe, baby, I'm here, honey." She pulled him free from my arms, but he fought her, trying to keep his grip on my coat, and Vera's eyes accused me. She didn't know what had happened, but her look made it certain I knew it was all my fault. "Come on, baby, Aunt Vera's here."

Gabriel let me go, falling back against Vera, and his face had turned bright red and puffy, the tears and snot leaking from his eyes and nose. He was giving the cry only a child can manage, the one that comes from frustration and fear, from the discovery that life is a game that changes its rules in the middle of your turn and constantly cheats.

The hiccups had begun by the time I reached Cashel and began to lead her to the door.

It was an ugly door in an ugly hall in an ugly building on an ugly corner, all of it built in an ugly part of Alphabet City. When I knocked, that sounded ugly too.

No answer and no noise came from within. Over the stench from the trash strewn in the hallway and on the stairs, I could smell dinner being fried up in one of the apartments farther down the hall.

Cashel looked at me and asked, "You have a credit card?" But this time she didn't smile.

I tested the knob, and it was locked. I gave the door a good looking-over. It was metal, but the frame was wood.

I stepped back and kicked, just above the knob. The door gave, wood splintering as it slammed open, and I stepped into what had been the main room of Lisa Schoof's apartment. There was a couch and a table and some trash on the floor, a paper bag from Burger King, other garbage. There was a kitchen space that was empty, and then another door, and through it, what must have been Gabriel's room.

Bridgett was there, on the bed, back against the wall. Her shirt was black and wrinkled, as if she hadn't removed it in days, and the rest of her things were strewn on the floor, her boots, her jacket, her gun. On the bed, on the floor, all around, were tiny little plastic squares, glassines like jewels in the light of her burning candle, and they were everywhere.

I said her name.

She looked up, mostly bored and maybe a little irritated by the interruption. Then her eyes sparked for a second beneath the broken curtain of her hair, and she recognized us. She let the end of the belt drop from her mouth, the loop still tight around her left arm.

"Hey, you. Hey, Sister sis."

"Bridgett," Cashel said.

"Hmm," Bridgett said. "Be right with you."

And then she fired the rest of the shot into her arm.

PART THREE

January 8 to January 19

CHAPTER ONE

I took my keys back from Dale Matsui, asking, "How's my girl?"

"Well fed, healthy, hearty, and hale." He smiled at me. "All in all, looking a hell of a lot better than you."

"I appreciate you taking care of her. It was an imposition."

He dismissed my line with a wave of his hand. "Not as big a one as your unexplained absence. You had people crawling the walls. Come on."

I followed him out of his kitchen, to the front door of his house in Queens, out onto the little path that bisected his square of frozen lawn. My nose started running again as we came off the porch, and I used my tattered wad of tissue for the third time in ten minutes.

Erika was still waiting outside, hands protected from the weather in the pockets of Atticus's army jacket, looking up at Ethan, who was scuttling along the roof. Dale stopped halfway to the garage to watch his lover fighting with the string of Christmas lights. His smile was loopy, and when he caught me looking, it changed to sheepish.

"My fella," Dale said. He unlocked the garage door, rolling it up on its tracks. "Here she is."

I looked at my Porsche, shielded in Dale's clean garage. "You washed her."

"I took her out once a week while you were gone. Put maybe two hundred miles on her total, that's all. But there's been salt on the roads, so I tried to keep her clean. You know how it is in winter."

"Looks great."

Beyond Dale's shoulder, I could see that Erika had switched her attention from Ethan to us, still working her naked suspicion of me. I tried to ignore it, reached for the checkbook in my inside jacket pocket, falling again into the shelter of Dale's concerned smile.

"What do I owe you?"

He looked deeply wounded. "You don't owe me anything, Bridgett. Favors among friends are free."

"Let me at least pay you for the gas."

He shook his head and furrowed his brow in distress, creating lines on his face when there wasn't any call for them. Dale's thirty, a glorious example of Japanese manhood, bigger than me, and with bones twice as thick. He has the generous spirit of a saint in a body that would shame the WWF.

"If you insist, you'll piss me off," he said. He looked at the car for a moment, then back to me. "Am I going to find out where you went? Atticus wouldn't say."

"I've been ill," I said. "I'm feeling better now."

"After you get settled in again, I expect a call. Ethan wants to have a dinner party near the end of the month."

"You two didn't get enough entertaining over the holidays?"

"New Year's was a bust," Dale said. "Natalie and Corry showed, but that was about it. We've been incapable of partying without you. Now that you're back, we should rectify the situation."

"I'll call," I promised. "Thanks again, Dale."

He gave me a hug. "We adore you, you know that?"

I nodded, which was easier than explaining why their adoration was a mistake.

At one point, I'd awoken to see Cashel by the side of the bed, washcloth in her hand and the nurse look on her face, and I'd thought I was sixteen again. There was a lot of ache running around inside me, having a hell of a time at my expense. If I had been sucking on sand for a week, I think my mouth would have been just a little less parched.

She'd put the washcloth to my brow, then performed a temperature check with the back of her hand against my cheek. She'd asked, "How you feeling, sis?"

I'd croaked at her, thinking that she looked older, that if she was growing up that fast, then I was too. Cashel had taken a glass of water from the nightstand and offered it to me, and when I'd tried to hold it, my hand wouldn't stop shaking. With her help I'd gotten some of the tepid water into my mouth, felt the sand slip farther down my throat. I'd wanted to vomit.

"Just a little," she'd cautioned. "We've got some Gatorade here too, if you want it."

I'd tried my question again, and was surprised by how strange my own voice sounded.

"Where's Da?"

I couldn't understand why she'd looked at me like that.

"Go back to sleep," Cashel had said.

We were on the Long Island Expressway when Erika finally spoke to me.

"You're a bitch," she said.

"I know."

"As long as we're clear on that." She made certain her cut ear was concealed, then turned to look out the window, at the light traffic we were keeping pace with.

A Toyota Corolla was blocking the lane in front of us, piddling along at all of forty miles an hour, and I could make out the silver hair jutting over the top of the driver's seat. I wanted to pass, but didn't feel up to it.

"You know what really makes me furious? You want to take a guess at that, Bridgett Logan, you fucking asshole she-bitch from hell?"

I took a fresh tissue from my pocket and wiped my nose again. "My selfishness."

The Toyota wobbled between lanes, nearly got clipped by a truck passing us on the right. I checked the mirrors and saw that it was clear, but still didn't pass.

"It's that none of them, Atticus, Cashel, they won't tell you what you were like. They'll never call you on it, what you said, what you did while we had to clean you out."

I wiped at my nose again.

"And they should," Erika declared.

"I was in withdrawal," I said.

"Is that supposed to be your lame-ass reason, or your lame-ass fucking excuse?"

"It's what it was . . . that's all."

"You told Atticus that the only reason he was helping you was to get a gratitude fuck," Erika said. "And then you of-fered him the same if he helped you to score, you climbed all over him, and when he tried to get you to settle down, you punched him in the face. You told Cashel to get the fuck back to Jesus because you sure as hell didn't want her around. You screamed and shouted and made so much noise that the neighbors called the police three different fucking times!"

"I remember," I said.

Erika turned away again, slammed herself back into her seat. "That only makes it worse."

It hit me as if I'd crashed the car, the need for a blast, the craving that forced everything else down. Just one shot would do the trick and shut Erika up. Just one shot would make the other noises fade away.

I'd passed the Toyota, and the speedometer was climbing beyond ninety. Erika had gone absolutely silent, as if I'd forced a sock into her mouth.

I slowed back to under fifty.

I'd awakened again in darkness, opening my eyes to the filtered nightlight that seemed unnaturally bright. There were explosions nearby, gunfire, and I knew Ladipo had found me, knew what I had done, and Butler was with him, sent by Pierre. They'd brought duct tape and Butler was excited and I was afraid. I'd bolted upright, feeling the sheets sticking to my body, feeling exposed, panicking in my disorientation and the noise.

Someone was in the room and he moved at me, and I tried to back away, but I fell back and smashed my head against something and lights strobed behind my eyes.

"It's okay," Atticus said. "Fireworks. Happy New Year."

I froze and he resolved, moving into more light. I realized who it was. I remembered where I was. And before I could feel ashamed or embarrassed, I only knew that I was so happy to see him.

"Feeling any better?" he asked.

I nodded, reached for him, felt my stomach rise, and I threw up all over the bed.

I put the Porsche into the garage, parking it carefully next to Atticus's BMW motorcycle. Erika didn't wait for me, racing to the stairs, and she was already in her own room when I reached the apartment. Atticus was turning from her shut door.

"How are you holding up?" he asked me.

"I'm tired."

"Maybe you should go back to bed."

I shook my head and regretted it immediately. I felt sweat on my back and arms, and knew that it was hot in the apartment, the radiator hissing from beneath the kitchen window, but I was cold all the same. I took most of a minute just to get out of my jacket, and felt the perspiration on my skin crawl and dry. When I tried to hang the jacket on the back of a chair, it slipped off and fell to the floor. I left it there. Then I took a fresh tissue from the box by the salt and pepper shakers and blew my nose again.

"Your sister and I both think you should be taking it easy," Atticus said.

"Too much to do," I said. "I wasted too much time."

He shook his head and turned to prepare the teapot, getting it down from the cabinet above the sink, then pulling out a tin of Irish Breakfast. He filled a sugar bowl and set it and a pint of half-and-half on the table.

I watched the little movements, stared without meaning to, realizing it had been over a year since I'd truly seen him at all. I remembered reading an account in a magazine, about how a man who had spent a year at the South Pole had returned home and spent his first week camping in a forest, staring at the greenness of the trees, enthralled with his return to the world of color.

I liked Atticus's color.

He caught the kettle just as it started to whistle, shutting off the burner. Then he brought the pot and two mugs to the table, took his seat near enough to touch. I forced my look away from him, chose the mugs as my next subject. They were big and decorated with classic art. One was a Seurat, the other a Picasso.

"How's Dale?" Atticus asked.

"Fine. He and Ethan were taking down their Christmas lights. They already had their tree out on the sidewalk."

"Isn't it about time?"

"When I was growing up, my Da kept the lights up until the end of January. The thought of taking them down only a week after New Year's Day was anathema to him."

Atticus smiled and poured the tea. He left me a lot of room for cream and sugar. "Did he ask where you'd been?"

I nodded, preparing my cup. "I lied by omission."

I looked over at Erika's closed door, felt another craving start to climb my spine. I told myself it would pass. Atticus was watching me carefully, and not doing a good job of hiding his concern.

"I'm okay," I said.

He smiled at my lie, but had the courtesy not to call me on it.

"Where's Cashel?"

"She's at work," he said. "She said she'd come by tonight to check on you."

"Work," I said. "I have to call them."

"You probably should, let them know when you'll be coming back."

"Not for a while."

"No?"

"I have to finish," I said.

Atticus moved the Picasso mug between his hands, watching the steam rise. "Do you?"

"I have to."

"I want to come with you. You shouldn't be alone."

"Scott said he'll accompany me when I talk to Taskforce," I said. "Jimmy Shannon knows me. It'll be all right."

"I mean after that."

"You can't come with me. I have to do it alone or they'll know something is up."

He looked up from the steam and frowned.

"I'll be okay," I said. "I'm back now, I won't go away again."

"I don't know why you went away in the first place," he said softly.

"Yeah, you do."

He shook his head. "I'm not talking about Lisa Schoof."

"I know what you're talking about."

"Then why'd you do it?" The way he asked the question, it made me think of Gabriel.

I pushed the Seurat away. "Because I'm a junkie."

"That's not what I mean."

"You mean why wouldn't I see you."

My left arm itched, the place where the skin was raw and pierced, where it was covered with a nice sterile square of gauze. The tape clung to my skin and right then I thought that I could feel my flesh suffocating. Out of Erika's room came the sounds of explosion and gunfire, and I knew she had started up a kill-'em-all game on her computer. I hoped she wasn't picturing me at the end of her computer-generated barrel, and knew that she was.

"I wanted to, Atticus," I said. "I wanted to the way I

wanted to do heroin, although I know it's not the same thing at all, not even close. But in my mind, you were another weakness."

He was just looking at me, still, trying to understand.

"It had to be on my terms. It had to be under my control."

"And that's why you hid in that apartment, shooting shit into your arms?" Atticus asked. "Because you wanted me to come to you? Those were your terms?"

"You give yourself a little more credit than you're due," I said. "I'm a bitch and an asshole, as Erika so gently put it to me in the car today, but I'm not a sadist. Me feeding my arm was something that started long before I ever met you."

"But you knew that I'd find you if you did go back to your habit. You counted on that."

I didn't respond.

"Your sister says that sometimes junkies will work themselves into situations so they can use. Is that what happened?"

I reached for a fresh tissue, wiped my nose. It was starting to hurt now, my skin feeling raw. The hole where I'd once worn a ring itched, still infected. I wasn't sure when I'd lost it, but when the ring had gone, I'd torn skin along with it.

"Just tell me if that's what it was, Bridgett," Atticus said. "If you wrote me that letter knowing how I'd find you."

"And if I did?" I asked, trying to keep my throat clear. I didn't want to be this upset. I wanted my nose to dry out and my body to act proper and for the sun to come out, to be warm again. "If I did it just so I could get high?"

His eyes never left me, growing darker as he brooded. I blew my nose again, felt the tissue shred in my hands. I got up, throwing the tatters into the trash by the sink, then ran the faucet and washed the snot off my fingers. I splashed two handfuls of water on my face. It took some of the cold away.

Atticus stayed at the table, waiting.

"It was everywhere," I said. "I couldn't open my eyes and not see a deck or a stack or a wrapped fucking brick, one kilo, two kilos, five, ten. Uncut or barely cut, white like a cloud. You can't imagine the amount of heroin these people are moving, and when you see it, you can't imagine there are junkies enough to buy it all.

"I was scared. I'd bought a new spike and some dope for Colin, brought them to him in the hope he'd help me find Goldy. And he did, and I grabbed Goldy's stash, and I brought it to Alabacha saying that he needed better people, that I was the answer to his prayers. Pierre, he laughed and told Butler to give me a job, and those first two weeks, they were all over me. I couldn't change clothes and not have one of Alabacha's boys peering down my pants.

"And then it changed, when I did that buy for them, twenty motherfucking kilos that Pierre sent me and Butler to fetch. They trusted me, I knew I was in, and I still couldn't stop being afraid.

"So I opened a deck and I chipped, just so I could sleep."

Atticus turned in his chair, and his expression hadn't changed.

"And none of that is an excuse," I told him. "I did it because I wanted to. I knew when I started there was a chance I'd use . . . for God's sake, I cleared out the apartment so I wouldn't be able to sell my life away. . . . I would have been a fool not to at least acknowledge the possibility."

He spoke like the words were made out of fragile crystal. "Possibility? Or inevitability?"

The noise from Erika's room had ceased, but I wasn't certain when it had stopped. From the street, through the window, I heard traffic, voices. Then they seemed to stop too. Everyone waiting for my answer.

"I told myself it would be okay, if I just did what I'd set out to do . . ." I said. "I could have my cake and eat it, you know? I'd written the letter. I knew you'd find me if you could.

"So, yes. I knew when I wrote it. Because when I wrote it, I already knew what I wanted to do."

Atticus got out of the chair and stepped over to where I stood. He touched my left cheek with his right hand, his fingers barely pressing into my skin. He moved forward again, his body almost on top of mine, and his lips rested on my forehead. I started to tell him not to do that, that I was clammy and cold and hot and gross, that I knew I tasted like the undercarriage of a dump truck.

I got as far as, "Don't—" before he shushed me.

Then he locked his arms around me, and didn't let me go for a long time.

CHAPTER TWO

I woke again alone in Atticus's bed to find that the box I had sent to my sister prior to my personal Stone Age was now waiting on his desk. I made it all the way to the bathroom, all the way to the shower and under the water, and I was washing the shampoo out of my hair before I even thought about trying to score.

A small victory, but I'd made it at least a full four minutes longer than I had the previous morning.

In the box I found some clean clothes and the keys to my own apartment. There wasn't any point in heading back home—moving back into my own life wasn't a step I felt quite up to yet. So I dressed in what I had, brushed my hair in the mirror, and stared just a little too long at my face. Then I made the bed and joined Atticus in the kitchen, where he was reading the *Times* at the table over a plate of freshly baked biscuits. There was butter and jam and honey, and even a fresh pot of coffee.

"Morning, sunshine," he said.

"Morning. All this for me?"

"You and Christiane Havel. She's coming by to interview me in about half an hour and I want her to treat me well."

"She that reporter that was writing about you and the gang last summer?"

"She's writing a book. I agreed to be interviewed."

I fixed myself a biscuit and a cup of coffee. "I'll get out of your hair. I have things I need to start doing, anyway."

Atticus gave me a cautioning look. "Don't push too hard."

"The hard part's over, remember? Now it's just watching the game play out and trying to get my life back in order."

Atticus grunted and handed me the Metro section of the paper. I skimmed it while I ate, and my stomach felt steady, but whether that was due to the quality of news or my own metabolism, I didn't know. My appetite, astonishingly, had returned.

"Erika and I had a little chat this morning, before she left for school," Atticus said when I was wiping crumbs from my mouth. "She's still angry with you, but I think she'll try to deal with it in more constructive ways."

"This is between her and me. You don't need to proxy for me."

He thought about that, refolding his paper and setting it beside the plate of biscuits.

"And the same goes for my sister," I said. "They're my relationships, I have to salvage them myself. Did Cashel say anything when she was here?"

"She left a number. She said she'll expect your call."

I finished the last of the coffee and got up, putting my dishes into the sink. "I'll see you later."

"Call if you need anything. I'll be in all day."

"I know. Atticus?"

"Yeah?"

"Doesn't Havel write for the *News*?"

"Uh, yeah?"

"Then you might want to hide the *Times*," I advised, and headed back to work.

———

I took the Porsche to the office, and when I walked in, Charice said, "Holy shit!"

"Yeah, I'm back," I said. "Laila in?"

Charice nodded. It seemed the best she could manage for the time being.

I knocked twice on Laila's door before opening it. Laila was behind her desk, a large and round white man filling the seat in front of her, and when I stuck my head in, the man turned too. It was a good thing; the expression on Laila's face wasn't one that would have inspired confidence in a client.

"I just wanted to let you know I'm back," I said. "I'll be in my office."

Laila wiped her surprise away, put her business face back on, nodded. "Stay there until I talk to you."

"Gotcha, boss," I said.

My office looked the same and smelled the same and disappointed me by not being dusty. The desk looked different than I had remembered it, though, as if someone had used it while I was away, and I straightened the papers on it, seeing names on reports that I didn't recognize. We had apparently been doing brisk business during my sabbatical. There was a pile of unanswered mail, and I stacked the letters together beside my computer monitor. When I was done with the tidying, I reached for the phone.

"So you're back," Miranda Glaser said when I identified myself. She didn't sound excited.

"Yeah, I'm back, and I need you to get me in to see Lisa just one more time."

"What's this about?"

"I need to talk to her about some things I discovered," I said.

"Things that might interest the DEA?"

The good thing about the telephone, I thought, is that it conceals one's surprise. "Atticus told you?"

"Lisa told both of us," Miranda said. "And I feel it necessary to repeat what I said to you way back when I first took her case, Miss Logan—I will not facilitate a miscarriage of justice, I will not compromise my ethics on this."

"Nothing's going to be miscarried or compromised."

"But you're trying to manufacture a deal on Lisa's behalf."

"How is that unethical?"

"On its face, it isn't. But I want to know the details."

"I need to talk to Lisa first," I said.

Miranda Glaser exploded. "No! No, no, no, dammit, absolutely not! You've been running around behind my back, you've been giving directions to my client that I feel are not in her best interest, and I cannot allow it to continue! Now you tell me exactly what it is you need to speak to her about, or that's it, you're not getting in to see her."

"I have to talk to Lisa first. Then I'll tell you everything."

"Like hell!"

"I can get in to see her without going through you." I said it mildly.

"But you can't see her in private without me. I'm tired of being at the end of your strings, Bridgett. If you want access to Lisa, you'll clear it with me first. Trial starts on Monday, that's in four days, and I'm through with your stupid games. Understand?"

I rocked in my chair, then began searching my desk drawers for a box of Kleenex.

"Do you understand?" Miranda repeated.

"When Lisa shot Lark, she stole the delivery he was carrying." I wiped my nose and threw the tissue into the trash can in the corner. "But Vince wasn't just carrying smack in his bag, he had something else, something the DEA would give a helluva lot to get their hands on."

"What?"

"I can't say yet."

I could practically feel the steam she was venting through my end of the phone.

"Believe me," I said, "it's worth your trust."

"Then tell me what she stole."

"Not until I talk to Lisa," I said.

The door to my office opened, and Laila Agra stepped inside, shutting it quietly behind her. I raised my eyebrows and she nodded, leaned against the wall, waiting. Today's power suit was navy blue.

"Tomorrow," Miranda Glaser said, anger in her voice. "Ten o'clock, and I'll be there too. You get five minutes alone with her, and that is it, and then I want everything."

"Done," I said, and hung up.

Laila folded her arms across her chest.

"Hi," I said.

She shook her head. Her mouth had turned into a crisp edge between her nose and chin.

"I'm sorry," I said.

Laila shook her head again. "Martin and I have been discussing whether or not to fire you. Should we?"

"I would, if I were you."

"If you wanted to quit, you should have just said as much. Sent us a letter of resignation, that would have done it. That would have been common courtesy, Bridgett."

"I don't want to quit."

"At least we know that much," she said.

"I put you and Marty in a bad position. I know that. I know what I did was rude and inexplicable, and that I've let you down. I know that I have a lot to make up for. I'm willing to."

She took one of the chairs on the other side of the desk, pulling her ponytail out from behind her so she wouldn't sit on it. "We heard some things while you were gone," Laila said. "Some things that had us worried."

I didn't say anything, watching Laila's eyes move over me, across my hands and up my arms and then, ultimately, stopping to match my gaze.

"Are you using drugs?" Laila asked.

"I was," I said.

There wasn't any surprise in her eyes, just a resignation that she had been correct all along. "Is that why you left?"

"No. I left to do what I had to do so I could help a friend."

Laila Agra worked the end of her black ponytail in one hand, digging her fingers into the glossy braid of hair. Then she stood up and sighed. "All right, Bridgett. As of now, your leave of absence is extended indefinitely. Our insurance will — cover a rehab program, and I suggest very strongly that if you want to continue in our profession and in this office, you admit yourself to one."

"I'm okay now," I said. "I'm over it."

"No. I don't trust your judgment on this, Bridgett, it's as simple as that. Marty and I will talk about it tonight, we'll decide what we want to do. But I think the three of us, my husband, myself, and you, need to think long and hard about what we really want for the future."

My arm itched. I felt my nose beginning to run again, and once again the craving threatened, Mr. Jones jumping up and down all along my spinal cord. I nodded.

"Can we reach you at home?" Laila asked.

I shook my head, hurriedly got a pen and clean sheet of notepaper out of the desk. I scribbled down Atticus's number, then stood up and handed the paper to her.

"We'll call," she told me.

I parked the Porsche in a lot maybe three blocks down from my rented apartment on Sixth Avenue, then walked north, bumped and jostled by the lunchtime crowd, stopping at a little hardware store to purchase a Phillips-head screwdriver. The flower markets were open and busy, and they cramped the sidewalk with plants standing on display. It was cold enough that the runoff from their waterings had frozen in places, and for most of a block, the footing was treacherous.

I had my keys out before I reached the door, and went through quickly, using the banister to help get me up the stairs. Inside the apartment, the scent of rotting fruit started my nose running again. Someone had searched the place, maybe a couple of someones. The drawers in the bureau had all been removed, my clothes dumped on the floor. The mattress to the bed had been flipped, and the blankets and sheets were wadded up with the pillows beneath the television, high on its hanging stand. The closet doors were open. My clothes had been pulled down from the hangers, dumped, their pockets turned inside out.

It had been a thorough toss. I just hoped it hadn't been successful.

I got out my screwdriver and dropped it on the bed, was

reaching for one of the chairs when the door at the end of the apartment opened, and Anton Ladipo came inside.

"Bridgett," he said. "We've been worried about you."

I let go of the chair as casually as possible. "Nothing to worry about, Anton."

He shut the door carefully, then turned back to look at me, clasping his hands in front of his waist. He looked as neat and clean and dangerous as he had the first time we'd met in that alley in Washington Heights.

"Where have you been?" he asked.

"I got sick," I said, and I tried to keep my voice from giving my fear away. "Took some time off to get myself well again."

"You should have told us." The concern in his words was false, like the plastic treats on a restaurant's dessert tray. "We would have taken care of you."

"I didn't want to put you boys out."

"Unfortunate that you didn't. That way we could be sure."

"What are you suggesting, Anton?"

He looked around the apartment as if he had never been inside before, as if he hadn't tossed the place himself, perhaps with Butler's help. Then he walked toward me, closing the distance and taking his time, smiling with closed lips. I stayed still, staring at him, thinking about the gun beneath my arm, thinking that if I had to kill him, it would ruin everything I'd worked for.

Anton Ladipo stopped five feet away.

"Maybe you weren't sick, Bridgett. Maybe you got yourself arrested."

I shook my head, pointed at my nose. "Sick, see? I was at my sister's."

"I didn't know you had a sister."

"You never asked."

"You wouldn't happen to have a brother as well?"

"No."

"Interesting." Anton Ladipo turned his head, gazing up at the television. I stepped a half inch to my right, trying to block his view of the screwdriver on the bed. His head swiveled back my way. "A man attacked Pierre the day after Christmas. He was asking where you were. He threatened Pierre's life."

I raised my eyebrows and showed my best surprised expression, which wasn't too hard, since he was giving me news I hadn't heard.

"Tall man, with glasses," Anton said. "Brown hair. Rode a motorcycle. Does any of this sound familiar?"

I shook my head.

"I'm not sure I believe you, Bridgett. But that doesn't matter really. It's a question of whether or not Pierre believes you."

"I'd be glad to explain it to him at some point," I said. "Maybe later?"

"Maybe now. Like I said, we've been worried. I think we should go see him. I think we should let him stop worrying."

"I'm kind of busy right now," I said. "I've got to clean this place up."

"I'm afraid I must insist."

We exchanged stares, each of us trying to prove how serious we were. Then I blinked and said, "All right, after you."

Anton's smile went broad. "Ladies first."

"You're a gentleman, Anton," I said, and started for the door. "You make me glad I'm back."

"Yes," he said. "Yes. It is good that we're together again, don't you think?"

CHAPTER THREE

"I missed you, sweetness," randy Roley Butler said, running his hands up the insides of my thighs. "I thought maybe you had dumped me for another guy."

"You know it's always been you," I said, trying to ignore his touch.

Butler put his right palm hard into my crotch, then pressed to the left, indicating he wanted me to turn. I did and he dropped his hand long enough for me to face the wall, then replaced it, sliding it slowly up over my ass. Ladipo stood by the door to Pierre Alabacha's office. His face was blank, and his eyes bored.

"You're a little creamy," Butler said over my shoulder, still moving his hand. "I figure maybe you missed me too."

"But my aim is getting better," I said.

He chuckled and both hands moved away from my hips, up my back. I felt his fingers in my hair, along my scalp, and then back down my neck. Then he ran both hands down the length of each leg. Finally Butler stepped back.

"No wire," he informed Ladipo. "Just the piece."

"I told you," I said.

"We'll hold on to your gun for now," Ladipo said, taking the weapon from Butler. "If that's all right?"

"Oh, sure," I said.

Ladipo motioned for Butler to let me move, and I straightened up and tucked my shirt back into my pants. Ladipo opened the door, and Butler gave me a little shove to follow.

Alabacha had on tan slacks and a light blue cardigan, and looked like he was waiting for his grandchildren to stop by for a visit.

"Bridgett!" he said. "We were so worried about you! Please, dear—have a seat."

I looked around at the office that I had never been to before, the sort of space that looked like it was used by realtors who did good business. The desk was gleaming wood, and the chair behind it was leather, everything executive-size, even the aquarium on the bookshelf. The fish were bright and tropical, happy to swim in luxury, and executive-size too. Venetian blinds covered the window on one wall, the metal slats tilted but not entirely closed. The room was maybe one or two lumens from being well lit.

We were somewhere in Queens, maybe Jackson Heights, but I wasn't certain. Ladipo had insisted on taking his car, and the route had been circuitous, and I had spent too much of the drive trying to guess what they knew rather than where we were going. My gun hadn't been taken until we'd reached the house, and I thought that was good, that it meant they weren't overly suspicious of me.

Either that, or they had nothing to fear.

I took the chair that Pierre indicated in front of him, saying, "Good to be back." Behind me, I heard Butler shutting the door. Ladipo positioned himself beside me, on my right.

"I am glad to hear you say that," Pierre Alabacha said, leaning forward. "It does my heart good to hear you say that. Please, say it again."

"It's good to be back, Pierre," I said.

He turned his head slightly, presenting me with his left ear. "Once more."

"What?"

"Say it again, Bridgett."

"It's good to be back, Pierre," I said slowly. Something very cold started to spread inside me.

Pierre Alabacha shook his head. "Sorry, I didn't hear you. Say it once more."

"What's this about?"

Alabacha looked at Ladipo, then at Butler, then back to me. This time, when he spoke, it was an order, and the Mr. Rogers act had turned to vapor. "Say it again."

"It's good to be back."

His right hand hit me open along the jaw, hard. My head snapped right, and the coldness spread, and something started buzzing in my ear.

"I can't hear you!" Alabacha shouted. "And do you know why I can't hear you, you fucking dumb cunt? Because some fucking dumb lunatic fired a pistol in my ear almost two weeks ago! Some fucking cocksucking motherfucker rode a motorcycle into Anton, then put a gun in my face and threatened to feed me lead if I didn't tell him where you were!"

I straightened in my seat, keeping my hands in my lap, meeting his eyes again. Alabacha had shut his mouth, but his breath was coming quick through his nose. I stared at him, trying to show him nothing through my eyes, wondering how bad a situation I had fallen into.

He unbuttoned his schoolteacher's cardigan, as if it was too tight around his middle. When he spoke again, his voice was level once more.

"An FBI agent showed up about then, put a stop to the whole thing. At least, I believe it was an FBI agent. He had a badge. But that may not mean anything. I'm not certain. I'd like to think I'm wrong. I'd like to think that the FBI isn't paying much attention to me at all."

I tasted copper in my mouth. I swallowed blood.

Alabacha put his hands into his trouser pockets, and looked at Ladipo.

"She says she doesn't know who he was," Anton told him.

"Is that right? You don't know who our lunatic motor-cyclist was?"

I shook my head.

Alabacha smiled at Anton. "See, she does know who he was. Tell me, Bridgett. Tell me who he was."

"He's nobody, just a guy I used to know," I said. "We used to deal together. I told him I didn't want to work with him anymore, that I was working with a better organization now."

I was certain Alabacha was looking through my lie. I could hear the bubbles popping in the aquarium. He kept looking at me, and I broke the gaze and put my eyes on his loafers, because that's what he wanted me to do.

"The only reason you're still alive, Bridgett, is that you didn't desert with any of my money or my merchandise. You realize that?"

I nodded.

"You came to me saying that my men were unprofessional, that they didn't know how to get the job done, do you remember? You told me how my men were skimming me, how you could keep them in line. You told me you could instill the discipline I required. I gave you a chance, and it turns out you were as bad as my boys on the street, just as unreliable."

"I was sick," I said. "I got really sick, so I pulled out for a while."

"Where did you go?"

"I was in the hospital, out in the Bronx, and then I was staying with my sister."

"Sick? What'd you have?"

"Pneumonia."

"And your sister, she took care of you?"

"After the hospital."

"What hospital was that, Bridgett?"

"Bronx-Lebanon." I looked up at him, pulled out all the innocence I could find. "I wouldn't fuck with you, Pierre. I know better than that."

"A month is a long time, Bridgett. A month is enough time for you to have been arrested and to have rolled over on me.

A month is long enough to get the FBI and the DEA and the NYPD all breathing down my neck."

"I didn't rat you out," I said. "I swear to God."

"Then I need to know where you were."

"I already told you."

"Tell me where your sister is, let us talk to her."

I shook my head.

Alabacha folded his hands behind his back, straightening, as if viewing a bad student. "We'll ask her if you're telling the truth. What's her phone number? We can call her right now, confirm your story."

The knot in my stomach was Gordian, and the cold had filled every limb. The sound of the bubbles was getting louder, and it seemed that Alabacha's voice was getting harder and harder to hear.

"Let's call her, Bridgett. Let's hear what she has to say about your illness."

"No," I said.

"We could find her. Roley, would you like to find Bridgett's sister? Maybe ask her sister a few questions?"

"Goddamn," Butler said, somewhere behind me. "I'd pay for the chance to meet her sister."

"She's got nothing to do with this," I said.

"A sister," Butler said. "Think she'll like me the way you like me?"

"Use the phone book," Pierre said. "Look under Logan, see what you find."

"I told you what happened," I said. "I'm telling you the truth."

"But I don't believe you, Bridgett. You're lying to me. And I have to know the truth, or you'll force me to employ techniques that are crude at best." He pointed his chin at Butler, granted him a single nod.

I started up, out of the chair, but I was too slow and it was already too late, and Butler had his forearm beneath my neck, one hand on my head, making the fulcrum. I kicked and missed everything, off-balance, and he held me against his chest, putting on more pressure, and Ladipo moved around to give him a hand, reaching. Panic floated up like the air in the fish tank, and I thrashed and knocked over the chair, but it didn't do any good. Butler pushed my neck into his arm harder, and the edges of my vision began to swim white.

Pierre moved back behind his desk, opening a drawer. His hand came out, holding a large pair of scissors.

With Butler restraining me, choking me, Ladipo yanked at my jacket, pulling it off. I tried to kick him, caught his shin, and he swore, and Butler pulled my hair until I could feel it starting to tear. Ladipo punched me in the stomach, then yanked the jacket free and the world went into a rush, what sounded like waves spilling into my brain, and then there was just a sudden silence, like the hush that follows a snowfall.

Butler rammed me into the desk so the edge caught my middle, and as I fell Ladipo grabbed my left hand, pinning it down, splaying my fingers. I tried one last time to rise, and Butler used my hair to bang my chin onto the desktop. I felt another rush of copper in my mouth.

Alabacha opened the shears and pushed the point of one blade against the thin skin between my thumb and my index finger.

"I'll only hurt you until I get the truth," he said. He smiled at me like he was my father. Then he bore down, like he was trying to put a staple through a thick stack of paper.

I almost put my teeth through my bottom lip trying to stay silent, suddenly seeing the holes in Colin Downing.

Ladipo said, "That's not going to do us any good."

I couldn't tell if he was talking to me or Alabacha.

Alabacha turned the blade, then pulled it out. I bit on my lip harder. Behind me, Butler had all of his weight on my back, and I could feel him.

Alabacha moved the scissors to my sleeve, saying, "Elbow."

Ladipo's grip shifted, and Alabacha made a long cut on my sleeve, then grabbed the fabric and ripped it with a quick snap all the way up my arm.

He saw the gauze below my bicep. He reached and tore the bandage off my arm.

Then he started laughing, and he dropped the scissors and said, "Let her go. It's all right, you can let her go."

Ladipo's grip went instantly, as if my skin was burning his hand, but Butler lingered, and then he saw my arm too, and I felt his body shaking against my back. He stayed a second longer, then moved away, and I slumped off the desk, onto my knees.

Now they were all laughing at me. Out of the corner of my eyes, I could see my jacket in a heap on the floor.

"Help her up, for God's sake," Alabacha said, then started laughing some more.

Butler's tattooed hand entered my field of vision, grabbing my left wrist. His voice told me to get up. When I was on my feet, not fast enough, he let go and picked up my jacket. Alabacha hadn't moved. I could see the small pit in the wood and the smear of blood on the desktop that had come from my hand.

Alabacha shook his head and pretended to wipe his eyes, sitting heavily in his big chair behind his big desk. He grinned like the joke he'd just heard was the best one ever told, like it would still bring him laughter far into his afterlife. Butler handed me my jacket, patting me on the back. The pain in my hand surged when he touched me.

"Why didn't you just say so?" Alabacha asked, and then he and Ladipo and Butler all exploded into laughter again. "You should have just told me, Bridgett. It would have saved you the pain. I would have understood."

"It wasn't your stuff," I managed to say. "I never stole your stuff."

He rubbed his chin, and when his hand came down, the amusement was still there. "Bought it, huh?" With an index finger, he rubbed my spilled blood into the notch on the desk.

I nodded.

"So we had an honest junkie working for us," he said to Ladipo. "So I wasn't entirely mistaken to trust her."

"Still a junkie," Ladipo pointed out.

"Indeed." Alabacha frowned my way. "So now what do I do with you? You're not a rat, you've got heart, you didn't scream. But you're like the rest of them on my corners, Bridgett. How do I deal with you?"

"I'm better," I said. When I moved my left thumb, the pain spiraled along the back of my hand.

"Oh, we can see that."

"No, I'm clean, Pierre." The pain in my throat wouldn't go away. I wished I had a Life Saver, an Altoid, something to suck on besides my tongue. "I had a problem, but it's over. I'm not going to use again. Let me come back to work."

He sighed and turned, leaving his chair and heading to the window with its venetian blinds. He parted two with his fingers, peering through. Cold winter sunlight slashed his face. Butler and Ladipo stood relaxed, watching their employer, waiting for his next order.

"You're a fucking junkie, Bridgett." Alabacha said it softly, and the disappointment was paternal and profound. "And I can't use a junkie. I just can't trust a junkie. On the street, sure, why not? On a corner, it's no problem. But not here, not when I need someone to handle volume. Not here, where I need people I can trust absolutely."

"It won't ever happen—"

Alabacha moved his fingers, and the slats slapped together again, and I shut my mouth.

"Maybe it's sentimental, but in a way, Bridgett, I am glad I don't have to kill you," he said. "Sure, you're clean now. But that does not mean clean tomorrow. And so, Bridgett Logan, I wish you a good life. May you find every happiness in all your pursuits. Anton? Please show Miss Logan out."

Ladipo reached for my arm. Butler was already at the door, holding it open.

I didn't move. "Pierre, please. I'm asking for another chance here."

He shrugged. "Make sure she doesn't come back."

"Pierre—"

Ladipo's grip tightened, and I tried to pull my arm away, and his fingers found a nerve, and then my arm went numb. I tried moving forward and he slapped me in the chest, and it seemed like a limp-wristed move, something without force when I saw it come up, and then it was like he'd punched a railroad spike between my breasts. I twisted and lunged, and then the real beating started, Ladipo hitting me with his hands, forearms, and elbows all at once, again and again. I saw the ceiling spiral by, felt a lock on the joint at my left shoulder, my whole arm pulled back and straight and opposite the pull of gravity. I went down under fists that pounded my side and back, tried to curl myself fetal in a last bid for safety, and got a kick to the lower back for my effort.

Then Butler joined in.

That's the last thing I remember clearly.

CHAPTER FOUR

They dragged me down the stairs, outside. They drove me maybe a block, and Butler said something about what a shame it would be to just let me go. Ladipo, behind the wheel, told him that they didn't have the time.

They dumped me on the side of the street, in the gutter, outside of a squat little bar, where the neon lights said that there was Guinness on tap. I thought the sign was funny, and when I laughed I blew blood out of my mouth, saw it dash against the curb like the beginnings of a spring rain. My lips felt torn. The pavement was deliciously cold.

Someone was making a lot of noise about that poor woman. I looked up to see a fat lady pointing and jabbering. Someone else was screaming about calling an ambulance. A black teenager was kneeling by my side, asking if he could help.

I grabbed at his shirt and my left hand felt as if it were spontaneously combusting. I managed to say, "Up."

"I got you," the kid said. "Get your arm around me, I got you."

When I tried to stand alone, my right knee wouldn't support my weight, and he had to catch me again.

"You need a hospital, lady," the kid said.

"Cab."

"No cab's going to let you ride."

Someone, the jabbering fatso, I think, told the kid to leave me alone. Fatso shrieked, "She could have AIDS!"

"Subway." Each word I spoke stung.

"You're fucking kidding me, lady."

"Please," I said.

The kid looked in my eyes, then started shouting for a taxi. Maybe because of the crowd of people who had gathered, one stopped, and the kid got the rear door open before the driver could pull away again. With his help, I fell into the back.

"Take her to a hospital," the kid told the driver, and then closed the door. The cab started forward with a lurch that made my wounded joints weep. The driver's dark eyes were big, watching me in the rearview mirror.

"Manhattan. Sixth and Twenty-seventh."

"You're bleeding . . ."

"I'll keep it off your upholstery."

He shook his head, but turned west, like I wanted. I tried to keep my promise, using my shirt to catch the blood running from my face.

We were back in Manhattan before I realized I was crying, that I had been for a long time now.

The cabby halted and I handed him a fistful of bills, knew that there was at least one twenty among them. He watched me get out of his cab like I was Medusa, using the mirrors and avoiding my gaze.

I fumbled with my keys and lurched my way up the stairs, and each time I tried to use my right leg my knee hurt so bad I started to cry again. I smeared blood from my hands all over the apartment door when I reached it, practically fell inside when the damn thing swung open. Using the wall, I made it into the bathroom, grabbed myself one of the three supplied towels. The whole place stank of rotten fruit and the Chinese food being cooked in the restaurant below.

I closed the toilet lid, lowered myself into a seated position, listing against the wall. The towel made a good pillow, and I rested my face on it, feeling it grow wet with my tears and blood. After a while I switched to a clean one, dropped the used terrycloth onto the floor. My blood had leached through the fabric, dark red on the bleached white.

My breathing finally slowed, but continued to be painful. The ringing in my head stopped, but the ache didn't die. My limbs stopped shaking, but my joints screamed each time I moved.

I listened to the sounds from the restaurant below, the growl of trucks moving up Sixth Avenue. A car alarm went off in the lot next door, then cut out abruptly.

Maybe an hour went by. I passed it staring at the piece of plastic mounted on the wall by my head, trying to remember what to do with it. Then I reached and pulled the telephone receiver off its hook. I punched the numbers I remembered, and got someone who was speaking in a foreign language I didn't recognize. Maybe it was Korean.

I dialed again, and got Erika Wyatt.

"Atticus," I said.

"He had to go out, he had a business dinner with a client," she said. "We thought you'd be back by now."

"I had trouble."

"You don't have to speak so slowly, I'm not an idiot."

"No," I said, trying to think, to prioritize. "I need help, Erika. I need you to come here."

"What happened?"

"It's on Sixth, the rental. I'm at the rental, it's—"

She hung up on me.

I looked at the phone, listening to the dead line. I tried to straighten up, but when I pulled the towel away from my face, the cut above my eye and the ones around my mouth started bleeding again. I used a clean corner, reapplied the pressure.

The bleeding didn't stop. Neither did the tears.

The banging on the door brought me back. It took an eternity to make it out of the bathroom, limping the twelve feet to the door. It had latched automatically when it swung shut, and I fought the handle to get it open, my hands sticky with drying blood.

"Oh my God," Erika said when she saw me. She spun on her Rollerblades in a tight turn inside, saying, "For God's sake, sit down, Bridgett."

I nodded and decided that right there was a good place to sit. Erika unlaced her skates and kicked them away, then shrugged the backpack off her shoulders, crouching down to look at me. Her expression told me how bad it was.

"Do you want me to call a doctor?" she asked, then added, "No, of course you don't or you would have done it already. What do you want me to do?"

"Help me up," I said.

Somehow she got me up again. She kept an arm around my waist as I crossed the length of the apartment, to the end with the bed and the television. Once we reached it, she let me down, and I flopped onto my back. The Phillips-head screwdriver dug into my spine beneath me. I pulled it free, handed it to her.

"Take the television off the mount," I said.

Erika looked at me, bewildered.

I pointed past her shoulder. It hurt to move my arm. "It's heavy," I said.

Erika unplugged the TV, looked around for the nearest chair, and ended up choosing the same one I'd grabbed before Ladipo had shown up. She positioned it beneath the bracket, then climbed onto the seat. It took her about a minute before she had the screw that anchored the TV unfastened.

"Take it down," I said. "Be careful."

She dropped the screwdriver, wrapped her arms around either side of the machine, slid it free of the bracket. The weight caught her by surprise despite my warnings; she hissed a sharp exhale, almost lost her footing on the chair, but didn't fall. She dropped the TV beside me on the bed, jouncing the mattress, and kicking up all of my pain again. I kept from screaming.

"Remove the back," I said. "Be careful not to touch anything inside. It's still got a charge."

This part took her a little longer, because there were more screws. She didn't say anything while working, chewing on her lower lip, absently brushing her hair into place. When she was done, she slid the cover off, away from the screen, and looked at the mass of parts she had exposed.

"Now what?"

"Inside the cover."

She turned the housing in her hand and saw the plastic bag I'd taped to the inside. With her fingernails she pulled the tape free and then presented me with the wrapped set of papers. I pushed the bundle back at her, not wanting to get blood on it.

"Put it in your backpack," I said.

She did. "What is it?"

"A Get Out of Jail Free card," I said.

With Erika's help I got undressed and into the tub. The dried blood peeled away in flakes. My skin had already discolored black and purple and red, and I could see the burst blood vessels beneath the surface. Erika viewed me in silence, her eyes lingering on the row of track marks.

"Scars," she said, and gestured to her ear.

"Scars," I agreed, grateful to her.

Erika left me to soak.

After fifteen minutes in the water, I managed to pull myself out and dry off with the only towel left that wasn't covered in my blood. It didn't last, because the hot water had removed the forming scab above my right eye. Erika brought me a pile of my clothes that had survived the search of the apartment. It took the better part of twenty minutes to get myself dressed.

I limped out of the bathroom to discover Erika scrubbing my smeared blood from the door.

"I tried to get it out of the carpet, but it already took," she said.

"Fuck it," I told her. "It's a rental."

I drove us back to the apartment in Murray Hill, again parking the Porsche in the garage beside Atticus's bike. Erika got out fast when I stopped, then came around to my side and offered me a hand. She put her arm around my waist once more when we reached the stairs, and kept supporting me all the way up.

Atticus still had his suit and tie on from dinner.

"What the hell happened?" he asked. "You said you weren't going near them yet, what the hell happened to you?"

Erika told him to calm down, waving him away from me, and then gently guided me to his bed, helping me off with my coat. Atticus followed a minute later, having lost his tie but gained a first-aid kit. He perched alongside me and opened the kit, began working on my care and feeding while shaking his head slightly, side to side.

"I ran into Ladipo. He took me to see Alabacha. Alabacha fired me." I gestured at my bruised body. "This is the severance package."

Erika opened her backpack and removed the bundled papers I'd given her. "Where do you want these?"

"Somewhere safe."

"Put it in my closet," Atticus said. "I'll lock it in the gun safe later."

Erika waited for my approval, then did as Atticus had said and came back to lend him a hand. He cut strips of tape and made butterfly sutures for the cut over my eye, sending Erika for Betadine from the bathroom cabinet. I winced when he smoothed the bandages into place.

"You're going to need a hospital," he said. "These should be stitched. And that one between your thumb and—"

"She won't go," Erika said. "I already told her."

Atticus muttered to himself that I was a donkey. It made me smile, which started my lips bleeding again.

"This is not funny," he said.

"Oh, come on," I said. "It's romantic."

"It'd be romantic if your lip wasn't twice the size of a golf ball and your mouth wasn't bleeding. It'd be romantic if I didn't worry that you've got a concussion. You need an aspirin?"

"Heroin is a better pain reliever."

"So I've heard." His voice was flat as a board. "Erika, would you get a glass of water?"

"Getting," Erika said, and went.

"Alone at last," I said.

"You shut up. And stop grinning. You have nothing to grin about."

"You're funny."

"And you're goddamn lucky, that's what you are. Jesus, Bridgett, what happened to your hand?"

"Alabacha pushed the end of a scissors through it. Then one of the others stomped on it."

"Can you feel that?"

"Yes."

"Move your fingers."

I did.

"And?"

"I'll play Chopin again."

Atticus scowled. "Wiggle it."

I wiggled. Blades of pain sliced up my hand.

"Probably broken," Atticus said.

"Nah."

"If the pain isn't better in the morning, I'm taking you to a doctor."

Erika returned, offering me water and aspirin. Atticus portioned out two pills and I managed to swallow without spilling. I was starting to feel silly, as well as bone-tired.

He caught it, and said, "All right, we'll leave you alone. Promise me you'll go to sleep."

"I'll pass out. I swear."

Atticus closed the first-aid kit and got up, saying, "I'll be right back." He scooped up the discarded wrappers and cut pieces of tape, took them with him back to the bathroom. Erika and I watched him go. We looked at each other. Then we giggled.

"He's such a *mother*," she said.

"Yeah. Thanks."

"I haven't forgiven you yet," Erika pointed out. "Just because I like you again doesn't mean I've forgiven you."

"Understood."

"Night."

When she left, I felt alone. I sat up gingerly, unlaced my boots, then used my toe to push each one off of each foot. My right knee seized during the process, and I had to use my hands as best as I could to finish it. Getting the leather away from my ankles made my eyes water.

Whatever the martial art was that Anton Ladipo had used, I never again wanted to be on its receiving end.

I lay back, listening for Atticus to return. After a time, I realized that he wasn't going to, so I called his name.

He was at the door in seconds. "What?"

"Where'd you go?"

"I was making up the couch."

"The couch can't be good for your back," I said.

One of his eyebrows crested over the rim of his glasses.

"No hanky-panky," I promised. "Company."

He appraised me thoughtfully, then looked over his shoulder, down the hall. I wasn't sure if he was looking at Erika's room, or at his awful old couch. Then he turned back to me.

"Let me brush my teeth," he said.

CHAPTER FIVE

With one look, Gabriel Schoof told me that he hated my guts.

Then he turned his back on me, leaving his aunt to pick up the slack.

"What the hell did you think you were doing, scaring the child like that?" One of Vera's painted nails flashed in front of my face. Her lipstick was red, and as hot as her voice. "A ten-year-old child, for the Lord's sake, and you scare him the way that you did."

The corrections officer in the waiting area cast us a glance, then went back to looking at his security monitor. He probably heard conflicts like this all the time, mothers yelling at fathers, brothers yelling at sisters, everybody trying to spread the blame for why their loved one was behind bars. Business as usual.

I hadn't known Vera and Gabriel were going to be at Rikers when I arrived, and it was just my dumb luck that I ran into them as they were leaving.

Their anger was all the worse because I didn't know what they were talking about.

"I don't understand," I said.

"You don't do that to a boy, not in his own home, not when he thinks you're his mother's only prayer! He told me, Bridgett Logan, he told me what he saw, and I am disgusted."

I moved stiffly over to Gabriel, trying to get him to look at me. It was difficult to crouch, and it hurt, but I wanted to be able to meet his eyes without me looking down.

"What did I say, Gabe?" I asked.

Vera growled. "You leave him alone."

"I don't remember," I told her. "I was high, and I don't remember."

"I know you were high." She barely stopped short of spitting on me.

"Whatever I said, Gabe, I didn't mean it. Whatever I said, I was wrong."

Gabriel Schoof put his hands in his pockets and looked at the linoleum floor, pitted and dirty.

"I apologize, Gabe," I said.

He went back to Vera, taking her free hand. She tugged him in and adjusted her pocketbook.

"You do what you said you were going to do," Vera ordered me, shooting me a final glare. "You just do that and leave us the hell alone."

At nine fifty-five Miranda Glaser came into the room, carrying her barrister's bag, dressed in a sleek dark suit. She looked my way and didn't acknowledge me, then looked again as she realized who it was beneath the torn skin and bruises.

"Well," she said. "Can't say I'm surprised."

I pushed myself up from the bench, joined her as she checked us in with the guard. We had to wait another ten minutes before Lisa was brought in to see us, and Glaser busied herself with papers from her bag, making it plain I was to leave her alone.

"Ready for you," the screw said.

"Five minutes," I told Glaser.

She didn't look up from her work. "And not one second more."

I was in and out in four.

"What happened to you?" Lisa asked. "Where have you been?"

"It doesn't matter."

"The fuck it doesn't."

"Tell me where you stowed Vince's bag."

Alarm rang up her face like a fire drill on a submarine. "Why?"

"I need to know. And you're going to have to tell the DEA when they ask."

"But why?"

"They're going to ask if you have something, a copy of a document. I don't know when, sometime in the next week, maybe. And when they ask, you're going to tell them yes, that it's with the heroin you took off Vince."

"But I don't—"

"I know, but you will. You've got the money list," I said.

The understanding broke like morning sunlight. "You're fucking kidding me."

"Can you handle it?"

Her nod was enthusiastic.

"Where?" I asked.

Lisa told me.

I left Rikers while Glaser was in talking with Lisa. It was a cheap dodge, and it was only going to make the attorney angrier with me, but I didn't want to spill the beans yet for fear that she would call the DEA before I was ready. I needed time to plant the money list, and she couldn't know that was what I had planned. Miranda Glaser had made it perfectly clear that she would not willingly attend any party I was throwing.

Lisa had stashed Vince's bag at a storage place across the river, and I got into it without trouble, using her code to get through the gate, using the combination she had given me to get past the lock. She had rented the smallest box available, and still it was much too big for her needs, Vince's bag the only item in the square of concrete and metal.

I had brought gloves, and though I doubted they'd be needed, I wore them. Getting one on my right hand was difficult, and it hurt to pull them on. My fingers weren't broken, but they hurt like they had been. Then I took a seat on the cold floor and unzipped the duffel bag Lark had been carting when he died.

There were four of them, hard bricks wrapped in foil, and though I knew they were only a kilo each, they felt heavier. I removed them from the canvas bag and then took my copy of the money list from the inside pocket of my jacket. I crumpled up the papers, smoothed them out again on the floor. I stood up and stomped on them, remembering a second too late to let my left leg hold most of my weight. Then I crumpled and smoothed them again and laid the six pages at the bottom of the bag. I replaced each of the bricks. I zipped the bag shut.

Then I opened it once more and removed one of the bricks. I checked the foil on it, how tightly it was wrapped. I gave the brick an experimental squeeze.

I hadn't seen Alabacha moving bricks wrapped in foil. He was a plastic-wrap kind of dealer—he liked to see his product.

After a minute I realized I was still holding on to the brick. I shoved it back into the bag, again ran the zipper closed.

And I got out of there before I could convince myself that no one would be the wiser if I took one sliver for myself, or even a whole kilo.

Scott Fowler was waiting for me at the offices of the Joint Drug Taskforce on Tenth Avenue. He gaped at my wounds and I assured him they weren't serious, that I could still see out of both eyes, that I could move under my own power.

"Runge's in a meeting," Scott told me. "He should be back any time."

"Dynamite," I said.

"They won't let me in when they talk to you," he warned. "You're approaching as a confidential source, and that makes you theirs. I won't have any juice with them once you're signed up."

"I know."

His look said that he believed I actually didn't. "You're going to have to give it all up, everything you did."

"I know that too."

"It amounts to a confession."

"It's okay, Scott. I'll be fine."

From inside the far wall came the sound of something clicking, and then one of the doors opened. Jimmy Shannon leaned out and said, "All right, we'll see her now."

I got up, ignoring Scott's offer of assistance, and limped my way over.

"You want me to wait?" Scott asked me.

"This could take a while," Jimmy told him, and then shut the door after me.

Jimmy led me down the hall, past a string of closed doors, stopping finally at one with a black plastic sign posted on the wall beside it. The sign read WAR ROOM, and he opened the door, again held it until I was inside.

There was an oval table surrounded by six mismatched chairs, a bulletin board and a dry-erase board, and a map of the boroughs on the wall. The smell of water-soluble ink was strong, but the bulletin and dry-erase boards were bare.

"Sit," Jimmy said.

I sat.

"I was contemplating tanning your hide," Jimmy Shannon said. "But it looks like someone beat me to it."

"How have you been?" I asked.

"Eating my fucking liver, Bridie. Sweet Jesus, do you have any idea the grief you've given me over the last three months?"

"Some," I admitted.

"I thought you'd fallen off the wagon. I thought you'd fallen off the wagon and gone over from the side of the an-gels, and it would have broken Dennis's heart, bless his memory. As it is, you're closer to arrest than anyone should feel comfortable being. Far as this office is concerned, you worked for Pierre Alabacha."

"Not anymore. I'm here as a CS."

"That's what that faggy FBI type said."

"Scott's straight."

"What's with the earrings, then?"

"Youth," I said.

Jimmy Shannon rolled his eyes toward the heavens in a silent lament about the state of law enforcement today, then pulled out one of the chairs at the end of the table and filled it completely.

"Julian doesn't know about your pop, that I was his partner," he said. "I'd advise you to keep your own silence about that too. What's between you and me, Julian doesn't need to know."

"I understand."

"He's going to kick your ass. Far as he's concerned, you're a perp. And I'm going to back him up. You'll get no half sovereign from me."

"My poem may be worth it, Uncle Jimmy."

Jimmy grunted and reached for the pad of paper lying on the table, pulled the ballpoint Bic from where it was clipped to his pocket. He scribbled some notes. Then he looked at me, and smiled like he had when I was eight and precious and Da had just told his favorite story about Thomas Moore and the bum, all Irish and sentimental.

"Glad you're back with us, Bridie. Now let's get started."

Agent Julian Runge joined us after forty minutes, in time for me to give the whole story again, about how I had approached Alabacha, gotten into his organization. It took another hour of names and dates and confession before Runge was willing to take me seriously, and a full hour again before they were satisfied. Then they left me alone in the room for twenty-five minutes while—I assume—they played "Come to Jesus" in the hall.

"Why are you willing to turn on Alabacha?" Runge asked after he'd taken his seat.

I pointed at my face with both hands.

His grin made his mustache twitch. "Yeah. Happens all the time."

Jimmy settled back into his seat, feet up on the table, closing his eyes. "What's this, fourth one this year?"

"Fourth or fifth," Runge agreed. "You get these folks, they think they're playing criminal and the world's their oyster, and then suddenly it goes bad and they always come crying to us, wanting to rat out the bastards."

"No kidding," I said.

"Happens every fucking day," Runge said. "Don't think you're special."

"If it happens so much, how come Alabacha's still walking free?"

When Runge frowned, his mustache drooped below his upper lip. "You're in no position to get smart. You're not getting anything anymore, without my written permission. You're working for us now, you understand?"

I nodded.

"You do exactly what we tell you, you help us, we'll guarantee you immunity for the crimes you've confessed to. That's dependent on your testimony, of course, and on the condition that you don't go fucking around on us. You step out of line, you deal, you buy, you use, you commit any crime at all—spit on the sidewalk, jaywalk, litter—and I'll yank this agreement so fast your head'll be spinning all the way to the joint. That clear?"

"Crystal," I said.

"While you're working with us, you'll have use immunity. You won't be charged for anything you do in pursuit of the investigation. Within limits, of course."

"So I don't get to shoot anyone?"

"You don't fucking even get a gun, my dear," Runge snarled. "We own you now, but don't think that makes you a police. It just means you're on the right side."

We stared at each other until I thought he thought I was intimidated enough, and then I nodded. "I know something else," I said.

Runge sighed and turned a bored eye to Jimmy. Jimmy's body did something close to a single, dull spasm, which I took for a laugh.

"Go on," Runge said.

"Like I said, I've got all these details about Alabacha and his crew. I can tell you where and when and how much, stuff like that. But I don't have all of it."

"Yes, we know."

"But I know . . . I mean, I heard . . . I heard something."

"What?"

"I have this friend, she's at Rikers. The cops say she killed this dealer, this guy named Vincent Lark."

Jimmy opened his eyes, looked from me to Runge. Runge's mustache wiggled.

"Lark worked for Alabacha," I said.

"Your friend kill him?" Runge asked.

"Lark? I don't know. . . . The cops say she did."

"Nothing we can do," Runge said. "Sorry."

I shook my head. "No, I know that, I mean, she doesn't have anything to do with this, right? But when I was working with Alabacha, when I was there, I heard some things about Lark, about how he had been making deliveries when he got capped. About how his bag of shit was never found."

"How much shit?"

"Three, four keys."

"Cut?"

"I think it was pure. I think Lark was taking it to the chemists when he was whacked."

"Four keys at one hundred percent?" Runge said. "No way to tie it to Alabacha, though. No good to us."

Jimmy had brought his feet down from the table, now eyeing me. "There's more, isn't there?"

"Word is that Alabacha, he was really upset, looking everywhere for that bag," I said. "And I figured, four keys, why bother? I mean, four keys are nothing to this guy. Had to be something else in that missing bag, right?"

Runge sighed again and began tapping the end of his pen on the tabletop.

"So I looked into it," I went on. "I asked one of the lieutenants, Butler, what they were looking for, why it was so important. And he told me."

"Any time." Runge said it wearily.

"The money list," I said. "Lark had made a copy. I think he was going to blackmail Alabacha with it. He was having money trouble, he'd been skimming, see? And he took the list, and I think he was going to shop it around. But he died before he could, and Lisa stole the bag."

Both men were giving me their full attention now.

"You're saying this Lisa friend of yours has a copy of the Alabacha money list?"

I sighed and began tapping my fingernails on the tabletop.

Runge ratcheted up his glare to full. "What's her name again?"

"Lisa Schoof." I spelled it. "She's at Rikers, like I said."

"And where is it, this copy?"

"I don't know."

Runge scribbled quickly, then set his pen down. He had a good cop's face, could make it utterly flat, impossible to read, and that was the look he was giving me now.

"Maybe you think I'm stupid," he said finally. "Is that it?"

"I don't think you're stupid, Agent Runge."

"No? But you want me to believe that you—who just happens to be offering herself as a CS on Alabacha—just happen to know this woman who just happens to have a copy of the Alabacha money list? Do I look stupid? Is it the mustache? Is that what it is? My wife says it's the mustache, but I don't think so."

I shook my head.

"This Lisa Schoof, you knew her before or after you started in with Alabacha?"

"I just know her."

"How? When?"

"She's a friend, like I said."

"She's such a friend, she whacks dealers? You have any friends like that, Jimmy?"

"Well, I know a lot of cops, so, yeah."

"That it?" Runge asked me. "She a police?"

"No."

"Then explain this to me. Explain this string of coincidences, Miss Logan. Please. I'm waiting."

"She's a recovered addict," I said. "And so am I, okay? That's how I know her. That's how she knew Lark. He used to deal to her."

Jimmy said, "It's a start. It's not enough."

"It's why I threw in with Alabacha in the first place. Trying to find out what really happened to Lark. But I started using again, okay? And I kind of lost it."

"So you joined Alabacha just trying to save your friend, is that it?"

I nodded.

"Bullshit," Runge said. "Total bullshit. You know why and I know why, and now that your habit's gotten away from you, you want us to pull you out. Fine. Fucking-A-peachy. But your 'friend,' this Lisa, she's something entirely different. We'll check on the money list, we'll see if you're right, if she's got it."

"She's a mother," I said. "She's got a kid. She's facing fifteen-plus years. She needs to make a deal."

Jimmy shook his head like he couldn't believe what I was saying.

"Do you really think you can just waltz in here and start dictating terms?" Runge was almost spitting. "For a woman who's down on a murder charge? Are you high right now? Is that it?"

"She gives you the money list, you guys lean on the Manhattan DA to cut her a deal," I said. "I know you can do it, you know you can do it. Cut her the deal, and I'll do whatever you want. Cut her free, and I'll dance to whatever tune you play for me."

Runge laughed. "Goddamn! Who the fuck do you think you are?"

"I can give you Alabacha," I said. "With me, with the money list, you've got your case. You guys are the *Joint* Taskforce. You can work it out."

Runge threw down his pencil, and it bounced off the table, onto the floor. I could see his anger at having been

used all over his face. Then he got out of his chair and exited
the room without a word.

"He's going to make you pay for the deal," Jimmy told
me, and then went out after Agent Runge.

I'd been alone in the War Room for over twenty minutes
when I felt the shakes start. My heartbeat quickened abruptly,
as if I'd taken a massive hit of caffeine, and I twisted in my
chair, trying to fight off the craving. I failed utterly, couldn't
get the thought out of my mind, couldn't stop wanting dope.
I told myself it would pass, and then told myself I was a liar. I
told myself to stay cool, to wait and see and just hold on. I
wiped my nose on the sleeve of my jacket, and tried to keep
from tapping my toes.

But it only got worse.

Then I told myself that if I just held on for a while longer,
I would score when I left. I told myself that it would be great,
and an irony to boot, if I went and scored after meeting with
the Joint Drug Taskforce.

And the craving went away, telling me that I would
be held to that promise, that I would pay if I didn't honor
my agreement.

I was thirsty but didn't want to drink anything for fear of
needing a bathroom when it might be hours before Runge
and Jimmy came back. They were talking it over now, I
knew, trying to figure out their relative gains to their potential losses. Trying to figure out if I really was telling the truth,
if Lisa Schoof was really at Rikers, if my story had legs.

If the money list I'd promised was more than just an addict's dream.

The memory of Runge's face made me smile, the way
his mustache had twitched and his eyes had shone at the
mention of the prize. If the whole joint case against Pierre
Alabacha was an unpickable lock, I'd just offered them
the key.

The money list spells out who owes how much for what. It
tells how much each dealer paid, and what each one got for

their crooked cash. It tracks the business in the most fundamental way. It is, in fact, the books.

And with the money list in hand, the DEA and the NYPD and whoever the hell else they wanted to invite could throw a party with Pierre Alabacha as the guest of honor. They'd start by arresting the small fry, the little dealers and chump-change buyers. They'd roust and ring them, put the fear of Bubba and homosexual rape and Sing-Sing into the suspects, then offer the deal. Talk and walk, or get used to wearing a dress.

It was the way the system worked. The Taskforce would make a deal with every motherfucking one of the dealers on that list, if in turn each dealer would testify against Alabacha. And thus they would have their case, and commendations could go around, and the U.S. attorney could run for public office, saying, hey, I took a big bite out of crime.

To my way of thinking, the money list was worth Lisa Schoof's freedom.

Runge returned, alone, kicking the door shut with a backward slap of his heel. I'd been waiting for six hours and eighteen minutes, and he found me drawing on his dry-erase board.

"That supposed to be me?"

"No, if it was you, it'd have fuzz under its nose, Agent Runge. It's one of Alabacha's boys, guy named Butler."

"You got a violent mind."

"It's therapeutic," I said, and put the finishing touches on the noose I'd drawn around the cartoon Butler's neck. "Can I go now?"

"Sit," Runge said sourly, dropping a stack of papers onto the table. While he sorted through them I returned to my chair, wondering why all law enforcement seemed to talk to people like they were actually disobedient dogs—sit, stay, roll over. Runge found the document he wanted in the middle of his stack, and slid it down to my end of the table along with a pen, then shoved the notepad after them.

"Name and address, a number where we can reach you, put it on the notepad."

I followed his instructions, gave Atticus's address and telephone number.

"Good, send it back."

I sent the notepad sliding back his way.

"Now read the other one."

It was seventeen pages documenting exactly what I had told Runge and Jimmy about my involvement in the Alabacha organization. I didn't read all of it, skimming once I realized what it was.

"That's your statement, your proffer," Runge said. "It establishes your relevant testimony. You sign it, you're obligated to make yourself available to the U.S. attorney should he convene a grand jury and require your presence."

I uncapped the pen and signed my name, wrote the date neatly in the provided space beside my signature. Then I slid both back to him.

"Now what?" I asked.

"Now you start thinking of a way to get back into Pierre Alabacha's good graces, Miss Logan," Runge said with a tight smile. "Because as soon as we're done with our paperwork, I'm boomeranging you right back to him. Only this time, you get to wear a wire."

"No way," I said.

Runge held up his hands as if to say he was sorry, but he was totally helpless.

"In case you hadn't noticed, I'm wearing how much Pierre Alabacha trusts me all over my mug," I said. "I put myself in his way again, he'll know I've turned rat."

"You'll find a way," Runge said. "You're good at arranging things, aren't you, Miss Logan? I mean, you've already managed to arrange this much."

"They'll kill me." It wasn't meant as hyperbole.

"Nah. We won't let that happen. We'll take good care of you."

"That doesn't actually make me feel too much better. Word is you lost one undercover in Alabacha's group already."

Agent Julian Runge stared at me, and when the

question came, it was coated in frost. "What do you know about that?"

"Nothing. Just talk."

"Just talk? Nothing more? You don't know anything more?" His cop mask had vanished, and his cheeks were getting pink. "Are you trying to fuck with me again, Miss Logan? Are you playing another game with me?"

"I just heard a rumor when I was with them, that's all," I said quickly. "Nothing more. I thought it was bullshit."

"You're going to find out different," Runge said. "That's why you're going to wear the wire. You're going to get his confession."

"I told you I can't—"

"Shut up. You can. You will. You'll do this. Or I'll see you do time for every fucking one of the crimes you've just confessed to on this piece of paper. You forget, Miss Logan, I own you now. You're mine. And if you want your end of the deal upheld, you'll stay in line and follow orders.

"So you'll be back to Pierre Alabacha when I tell you to. You'll wear the wire. And you'll get the confession."

He tore the top sheet off the notepad, where I'd written my contact information. Then he grabbed his stack of papers and got to his feet, heading for the exit.

"It'll take two or three days to get your paperwork sorted out." He turned, hand on the knob. "We like to make certain our confidential sources are well documented. When we're ready to let you run, we'll be in touch."

"I didn't come to you guys trying to plan my own murder."

Runge shook his head. "Someone will show you out."

He left me sitting there, feeling the craving start up once again.

Mr. Jones reminded me of my promise.

CHAPTER SIX

It was just past seven when I got back to Atticus's, and I had to use my set of keys to get inside. The apartment was empty, no one home but me. In the fridge I found some mineral water and some cranberry juice, and I mixed them together in a glass, then used the concoction to wash down another three aspirin. There were messages waiting on his answering machine. Maybe one was from Laila Agra, and maybe another was from Miranda Glaser. I didn't play them back.

Beside the machine was a small pad for notes, and on it was my sister's name and a phone number.

Who says I can't follow directions?

The phone was halfway through its second ring when it got picked up and a woman's voice said, "Good evening, this is Sister Janice."

"Good evening, Sister," I said. "I'm calling for Sister Cashel."

"She's just stepped out, I'm sorry. May I take a message?"

"Could you tell her Bridgett called? She'll know how to reach me."

"And will she know what this is about?"

"I'm another sister," I said. "She'll know."

I hung up. Then I dialed information and got the number for James Shannon, in the Bronx. Then I dialed that number. Jimmy let it ring four times before answering.

"Hey, Uncle Jimmy," I said.

"Wondering if you were going to call."

"You weren't in the office when Runge cut me loose. I looked for you."

"I was out confirming your story."

"And?"

"And Lisa Schoof took us to Lark's stash, and we found a couple of things, including the money list. Her trial starts in three days, but you already knew that. We'll be seeing her again tomorrow, and that you didn't know."

"Are you fixing a deal?"

Jimmy rumbled an amused chuckle. "The U.S. attorney doesn't like to work weekends, and since it's now Friday night, he's officially not to be bothered. He'll talk to the DA's office on Monday, and everybody will have a great big get-together to discuss what's to be done with Lisa Schoof. If the money list checks out the way we hope, I think something will fly. But nothing's in stone yet, so don't get your hopes up, kiddo."

"I need a favor from you, Jimmy. I need to know that you'll do all you can to help her out."

For a couple of seconds he was silent. Over the line, I heard the television, something that was a professional sport. Maybe he was watching a football game, and I remembered my Da and him watching games in our living room, getting drunk and yelling at the Jets. It seemed a very long time ago.

"Your friend . . . you think she really killed Lark?" Jimmy asked.

"You wouldn't believe me if I told you it was self-defense. She was trying to protect herself."

"Self-defense? Maybe public service. When I pulled the

paper on Lark, I told you he wasn't a nice boy. Big piece of me thinks that even if your friend did it, she should walk, deal or no."

"Can't think that way, Uncle Jimmy. Otherwise we're just like they are."

Jimmy grunted. It might have been agreement.

After a second, I asked, "Did Runge lose an undercover to Alabacha?"

"We all did. One of us. Julian tell you that?"

"Pretty much," I said. "Couple of Alabacha's ground crew were talking about it, but nobody ever admitted to anything. I was never sure if it was posturing or not."

"Last June," Jimmy said. "We had an undercover just gone inside, good guy, everything looked fine. Then he vanished. We found him a week later. Murdered the boy Haitian-style, kerosene and a plastic bag. He left three kids. Julian's been going apeshit since then, trying to find out who did it. It's been keeping him up nights, pretty much killed his marriage."

"He wants me to get Alabacha to confess to it," I said.

"Sure. One of the things he wants. One of the things we all want. Maybe with the money list we can find out how it happened, use it in leverage. It's not something any of us can forgive, you know?"

There was more silence for a bit, and I heard the announcers on Jimmy's television get louder, excited at a touchdown.

"You ever find out who ratted?" I asked.

"No. Figure it was someone on the street who saw something he shouldn't have and talked."

"So I could be blown the moment I show up. They could know the moment I arrive."

"Possible."

"Then they'll kill me."

"I won't let them."

The way he said it, I almost believed him.

Atticus and Erika returned together just past eight, each carrying a bag of groceries. They offered me greetings and smiles and promised a feast, and then Atticus noticed the messages waiting on his machine and played them back. There were only two, and both were for me.

Laila Agra asked me to call her at home.

Miranda Glaser asked for the same thing.

"Phone's all yours," Atticus told me.

"Maybe there's one I could use that's a little more private?"

"You can use mine," Erika said. "By my bed."

I went into Erika's room and shut the door. Her room reminded me of my own when I was entering college. It was devoid of girly frills, but there were posters on the wall for a couple of bands and one or two movies. Comic books were heaped by her closet. On the bed was a stuffed zombie, caricatured and plush, and it looked oddly comforting despite its undead bent.

I called Laila.

"Martin and I talked," she said. "We have the names of a couple of places we'd like you to look at."

"I don't want to go into rehab."

"And that's your choice, Bridgett. You've got until the end of the month to find a program you like, one that's covered by our medical insurance. If you admit yourself, we'll hold your job until you get back. That's our promise."

"And if I don't, I'm fired?"

"We'll have to replace you with someone we can trust."

"Sure," I said.

"We want you back," Laila said. "But you have to get help. It's as simple as that."

"Simple," I said, and hung up.

The phone rang immediately. I stopped myself from reaching for it, let it ring again. I heard Atticus shout, "You gonna get that?"

"It's your phone," I shouted back.

The ringing stopped. Then Erika opened the door and leaned in, saying, "It's your sister."

My stomach shrank, and with it the willingness to take part in the fight I knew would occur if I heard Cashel's voice. "Tell her I'll call back."

Erika frowned, then shrugged and shut the door again.

I waited, listening hard to the sound of Atticus's voice as he relayed my message. I couldn't make out the words, but he was on the line with Cashel for a couple of minutes before I decided he'd hung up.

I picked up the phone, heard the dial tone, and called Miranda Glaser. When I had identified myself, she said, "Wait."

I spent three minutes waiting.

"Okay," Miranda said.

"What was that?"

"Me controlling my temper," she said. "Now, you will be at my office at two Sunday afternoon. You will come alone, and you and I will talk. Is that a problem for you?"

"I'll be there."

"Good."

"Have you heard from Taskforce?" I asked.

"Good night, Bridgett," Miranda said, and slammed down the phone.

I didn't feel like talking to anyone for a while after that.

Neither Atticus nor Erika asked me any questions over dinner about my day, and after eating we watched television together for a couple of hours, then got ready for bed. Atticus hemmed and hawed and I told him that, if he didn't mind, we could share his bed again. We lay side by side for a while, both awake, before he got up the courage to put an arm around me. I liked that he did that.

I told him what Laila Agra had said.

"I think it's probably a good idea." He said it softly, speaking into my hair.

"It probably is a good idea."

"Then you should do it."

"If I go into rehab, everyone will know."

"Know what? That you've got a problem? That you have a substance abuse problem?"

"You're not a junkie."

"And you are. Nobody thinks what you're going through is easy, Bridie. No one thinks that needing help is wrong."

"It's weak."

Atticus's chest rose and fell with his sigh. "You've said that a lot to me, you know? I think maybe you've forgotten what strength is."

"This is different."

"Nah, it ain't. It's just the same. Weakness is the running away, and I know that from experience."

I didn't say anything.

"You should think about it," he said again.

"Maybe."

"Talk to your sister."

"Yeah."

He moved again, kissed me very gently, careful of my swollen lip. "No one who knows you thinks you are weak," he said.

CHAPTER SEVEN

Saturday passed like a snail on Quaaludes. Erika went out to the movies with a friend. I slept a lot. Atticus baked bread. He helped me change my bandages, and we were both relieved to see the hole in my hand had already sealed and was scabbing over. Once, he told me to call Cashel. I said I would, then didn't.

I didn't know what I was going to say to her yet, and maybe because of that, on Sunday morning I left early and went to Mass at the Church of the Sacred Hearts of Jesus and Mary, off of Second Avenue. I didn't confess myself and I didn't take communion, and I sat near the back where no one would bother me.

It had been two years since I'd attended Mass, and that was under exceptional circumstances. The time before that, I had been sixteen, and starting to take heroin.

When the service was over I lingered, taking in the quiet, trying to soothe away my fear in the silence and peace and the scent of incense. The priest returned, having shed his vestments, and came my way. I rose before he could close the gap, and left for Miranda Glaser's office before he could engage me in conversation.

"I'm going to get this out of the way up front," Miranda Glaser told me. "When this is over, I never want to see you again. You are unprofessional, you are unethical, you are quite possibly amoral. You're arrogant and selfish and whatever it is that Atticus and Lisa see in you is a mystery to me.

"You have manipulated me and used me. Just because I cannot prove that you planted the money list in that bag you led the Taskforce to does not mean that I do not know that's precisely what you did. Maybe you've fooled them, or maybe you haven't, and maybe they don't care either way because they're so happy to have the evidence you've supplied. But I know. And I don't trust you."

"You're very hot when you're righteous," I said.

"And you're not half as witty as you think you are."

She was across her desk from me, wearing a thick cardigan sweater the color of wheat. I hadn't been lying about her looking hot—behind all the paper and all her anger, without makeup and with her hair held back in a scrunchy, she looked like a repressed librarian, the kind who turns into a hellcat in the bedroom in seventies porno flicks.

"Opening statements in Lisa's trial are tomorrow," Miranda said. "The Taskforce won't be done checking the authenticity of the money list until then, at the earliest. It will be Tuesday before the U.S. attorney even tries to pressure the DA into a deal."

"How long will the trial last?"

"Not more than a week."

"So the deal has to be struck before then?"

"Before the jury returns with a verdict," Miranda said. "After that, the whole issue is moot."

"Maybe they'll acquit."

"It's doubtful. When the police went to retrieve the bag, they found the murder weapon."

"They what?"

"They found the gun Lisa used to blow out Vincent

Lark's brains." She leaned back in her chair, my reaction earning a reappraisal. "You didn't expect that?"

It didn't matter how bad I had been jonesing when I'd placed the money list, I would have remembered the gun. Especially if it was my father's revolver. It just hadn't been in the bag, and there was no way I could have missed it.

"And they're certain it was the murder weapon?" I asked.

"Detectives Ollerenshaw and Lee took the gun for a ballistics match. I haven't seen the results yet, but I'd be surprised if the test fire didn't match one of the rounds recovered at the scene."

I shook my head, and Miranda misinterpreted the gesture.

"It's not as bad as all that," she said. "I mean, Corwin was already arguing that Lisa did it, and frankly, so were we. Self-defense pretty much removed the issues around the gun."

"Have you talked to Lisa about this?"

"I saw her this morning to let her know what was happening."

"What did she say?"

"About the gun?"

"Yeah."

"Nothing. It didn't come up."

"So what did you talk to her about?"

She pushed her glasses up her nose, deciding whether or not to answer. "I explained the situation. Lisa seems to think that, if she gets a deal, it'll all be resolved. I told her that wasn't the case. She'll end up having to plea to a lesser charge. If we're lucky, she'll get probation."

"What would she plea to?"

"I'd push for involuntary manslaughter. But I'll urge her to take man two with a recommendation if that's the best we can get."

"That likely?"

"I don't know. A lot will depend on the U.S. attorney, what he can convince the DA's office to accept. Right now it's the money list and not the heroin that'll make the deal."

"But the heroin can't hurt," I said.

"It doesn't help as much as you might think. It turns out the junk had already been cut down to about fifty percent.

The way federal law works, that means that the U.S. attorney has only recovered two kilos of heroin, not four. It's all based on percents of purity."

"Two kilos is a lot. Two kilos is half a million dollars' worth."

Miranda shook her head. "They don't care about it, it's negligible. It's the money list that's important to them. If it turns out the DA's office is looking to share in the Taskforce's spoils, Lisa will fare okay. If the U.S. attorney is looking to hog the glory—say, because he's peeved about his heroin being cut—then the DA may decide he'll take whatever conviction they can get."

"It's not what I was hoping for," I said after a second.

"What did you think would happen? That the money list would be the end of it?"

"I thought it would be easier than this."

Miranda laughed. "This is the justice system."

I walked back to Atticus's apartment, taking the long way. It was another gray and cold day, another of winter's hangfires; that morning it had looked like snow, or at least sleet. By the afternoon it had become clear the promise wasn't going to be kept. It seemed to me that this winter had been full of days like this one—incomplete, unpleasant, and offering nothing as a reward.

Murray Hill was a nice neighborhood. I didn't see a single corner dealer, a single lurking fiend. Maybe I wasn't looking hard enough. It didn't much matter. If I walked farther east, just another few blocks, I knew I'd find someone willing to hook me up.

I kept thinking that I should go back, return to the safety of company that wouldn't let me score. Atticus had been good about keeping his fears and suspicions to himself. Whether it was faith or a resignation to the fact that, if I wanted to, I would, I didn't know. But I appreciated his restraint. It made me question my own.

I got back to the apartment a little after five, and Atticus was home alone, reading in the front room.

"Thought you'd be back sooner," he said.

"I was walking."

"Just walking or walking and thinking?"

"Is it possible to do one without the other?"

"In the Army I did it all the time."

I shucked my jacket and took the easy chair. Above him, on the wall, was the painting that Rubin Febres had done before he died. I hadn't known Rubin long or well. He had been Atticus's friend. As for the painting, I wasn't certain what I thought of it. The colors were nice, but the picture itself bugged me, a surreal representation of a murder in cold blood. I didn't know why Atticus kept it. Maybe as the last link to a friend who had left nothing else behind when he died.

"How'd it go?" he asked. "Miranda going to take care of Lisa?"

"Best as she can. I think I'm done, at least with that. I don't think there's anything more I can do. The Taskforce has the money list, the U.S. attorney will talk to the DA, it's just a question of everything falling into place."

"Which is usually where it all falls apart," he said.

"Kind of what I've been thinking of. Did anyone call?"

"You mean did Agent Runge call? No."

"I told you what they want me to do."

"Yeah. And I told you I don't think you should do it. It's too dangerous."

"Alabacha won't even let me get near him. He'll see my approach for exactly what it is."

"That's probably good. He'll refuse the approach and then you can tell Runge and Shannon and the rest that you tried your best, sorry, no dice."

I looked at him, wondering how he managed to maintain his naïveté.

"I'm under charges, Atticus. If I don't get the law to forgive and forget, I'll end up going to prison."

He closed the book on his lap and looked out the window, taking off his glasses. "I know a good lawyer," he said, after a second.

It earned a laugh. Not a big one, but a laugh nonetheless.

"Glaser told me that she never wanted to see me again once this was done," I said.

He looked back at me. His eyes looked a little bigger without the lenses between us. "Then you need to get them to clear the account."

"Alabacha refuses my approach, they'll just have me try again later. I've got to find a way to make him believe me. I've got to give him something up front that'll earn his trust."

He slid his glasses back into place slowly.

"You have an idea," he said.

"I have an idea," I admitted. "Nay, verily, I have a plan."

"Forsooth, fair maiden, I suspect such plan of grave risks."

"In faith, 'tis a plan most fraught with risk and peril, for which I require the assistance of a knight, good and true."

"I might know where you can find one," Atticus said. "Or two, if it came to that."

"One will suffice."

"Let's hear it."

I sighed and looked at the painted shattered head on the wall.

"It involves screwing over the Taskforce," I said.

CHAPTER EIGHT

Runge called at ten past three Monday afternoon, and Atticus answered the phone, then handed it to me, where I was waiting at the table. Downtown, in the Criminal Court Building, a judge was getting ready to call an end to the day's proceedings. Downtown, in the Criminal Court Building, Vera and Gabriel and Miranda Glaser were all preparing to leave Lisa behind as she was moved back to Rikers until the next day of trial.

And I was waiting for the last thing I could do, the one that could quite possibly kill me.

"Logan," I said.

"We want you to come in now," Runge said. "Do not pass Go, understand? We'll expect you in twenty minutes."

"I'm on my way." I hung up.

"Now?" Atticus asked.

"Give me an hour," I said.

He nodded and followed me to the door, and I hoped my expression wasn't anything like his. If I looked as worried as he did, Alabacha wouldn't buy me for an instant.

"You've got to relax," I told him.

"I was going to tell you the same thing."

"Me? I'm as cool as an ice floe."

He frowned.

I kissed him.

"Watch my back," I told him, and left.

A female agent named Dot Maguire fitted me for the wire, running the cable along the inside of my bra, taping the mike to the inside of my right breast.

"How's that?" she asked when she was finished.

The tape itched, and the whole setup felt uncomfortable, but I wasn't going to wear it for long. "It'll work," I said.

"Put your shirt back on."

I did as instructed, feeling her eyes on my bruises, on the damage I'd done with the needle. I tucked myself in and put my jacket on, squared my shoulders to present myself for inspection.

Dot Maguire looked me over with her hands on her hips, then nodded. "It'll do."

"And when they feel me up, what then?"

"Don't let them."

"I won't have a choice."

"Most of these boys won't grab the tits," she said. "They've still got a little decency to them."

"You don't know these boys like I know these boys."

"I guess that's why you're wearing the wire," Maguire said. "Come on, Runge wants you."

We went down the hall and into the War Room, where Runge sat waiting, along with Jimmy Shannon and another agent I'd never seen before. There was tension in the air and on every face, and when Maguire opened the door, Runge hurriedly shut the folder on the table in front of him.

"She's set," Maguire said.

"Thanks, Dot," Runge said. "Lionel and you should head on out and join the rest. We'll catch up."

"Gotcha."

The door closed again. I looked at Runge and Jimmy. "What's the rush?"

"Alabacha is on his way into the city from Queens," Runge said. "He's with Butler. We think they're headed back to the Upper West Side apartment, do you know where that is?"

I nodded.

"Good, so he won't be too surprised to see you there. We want you to pick him up, get him to take you wherever he's going."

"And you expect me to get a confession out of him in that time?" I asked.

Sweat was shining at Runge's temples. "Just get him to take you to his destination."

"And once I'm there, then what?"

Runge looked at Jimmy.

"Yesterday evening we lost contact with our current under-cover in Alabacha's clubhouse," Jimmy told me. "He made it in for a debriefing, left for his home, and then disappeared. We think he was made."

"We pulled Alabacha in for questioning and the fucker lawyered out before we could squeeze," Runge said. "We don't have anything we can run at him with, we haven't gotten anything from the rest of his crew. We're out of options."

"Given what we think happened to our last UC, we have reason to believe this one may still be alive," Jimmy said. "But if that's the case, it won't be for much longer. We need to find him."

"We're *going* to find him," Runge corrected. "That's what you're going to do."

"And how do I do that?"

"Get Alabacha to take you to him."

Bad to worse, I thought. "He won't trust me to begin with. How am I going to get him to take me to where this UC of yours is? And that's assuming, optimistically, that your guy is still breathing."

Runge slammed an open palm to the tabletop. "You do this! You do this, you lead us to our man, or so help me I'll find a way to pin this murder on you! You've played your game with us, girl, you got what you wanted, now you'll give us what we want, or I'll ruin you for the rest of your days!"

"He won't trust me!"

"You don't have a choice in this. Now you go down to your car and you go over to Alabacha's apartment and you wait for him to show up."

"We'll be watching," Jimmy told me. "We'll have you covered."

"Like you had your UC covered?"

Runge went for the door, yanking it open so hard it slammed back against the wall with a bang like a gunshot.

I looked at Jimmy.

After a second, Jimmy turned away.

"Junkie," Runge said, breathing hard. "Time to go to work."

When I was back in the car, I said, "I'm heading over there now."

There was no answer. I didn't expect there to be.

While I drove to Alabacha's apartment I thought about all the lies I had told.

I thought about how much my body ached, and how much my arm itched, and how badly I wanted a shot. The tape on my breast pinched, and I could feel sweat beginning to trickle down along the wire. The transmitter for the mike dug into my hip like a rock.

I never wanted to get high more than I did on that drive. I drove with Mr. Jones in the passenger seat, and he had ceased to be my enemy. Now he was a friend. A confidant.

He knew what I was going to do before I did, I thought.

He knew a lost cause when he saw one.

I parked around the block from Alabacha's apartment, with a view of the street, keeping the engine running. I gave the interior of the Porsche a final check, then unfastened my belt and unlocked both of the doors. I felt shaky again, didn't know if it was the craving or the adrenaline, or both, or something else. My nose felt like it was about to start running but when I swiped at it, nothing was on my sleeve.

I scanned the street, trying to spot the surveillance, the

promised Taskforce backup. No inconspicuous delivery vans, no cars with tinted windows. A truck from a glass store was double-parked across from the building where Alabacha lived, blocking most of the open lane. I didn't see any of Alabacha's cars, not his Benz, and not his Beemer.

In a blue Jeep Cherokee, six cars away from Alabacha's front door, two occupants were waiting. I wasn't sure, but one of them could easily have been Dot Maguire.

My skin was prickling.

I tried to concentrate, but kept thinking about needing heroin.

Butler's black Land Rover turned onto the street, passing me, then stopped, unable to get around the truck with its panes of glass. Butler leaned on the horn, blasting long, and the driver of the truck came running out of the building, flipping the bird as he climbed back into his cab. The truck pulled away, revealing a space, and Butler parallel-parked clumsily, tapping into the fenders both behind and in front of him.

Here goes nothing, I thought.

I popped into gear and raced down the block, braking to a stop as Butler began climbing out of his car. I got out fast.

"Where is he?" I shouted.

Butler moved around and caught me as I tried to get past him and around the car. Alabacha was coming out the other side.

"—told you to stay away," Butler was saying, pushing me back.

I slapped his hand down and stepped away to keep him from getting another grip, turning and using the same hand to indicate the Cherokee.

"They're here!" I shouted at him. "They're right on the fucking street!"

Alabacha stopped at the edge of the Land Rover, trying to manage enough time to consider.

"It's the goddamn DEA!" I reached past Butler, into the open car, grabbing the bottle of beer that was resting on the floorboard. I spun and put my back into the throw, and the bottle sailed, smashing the windshield of the Cherokee. A spray of Budweiser foamed over the webbed glass.

"What the fuck are you doing?" Butler hollered.

I grabbed at his arm, speaking as fast as I could, telling him that the DEA was all over him, that they were waiting, right on the street. Butler broke my grip, looking at Alabacha, who in turn was glaring at where the Cherokee's engine was kicking to life. Alabacha pointed and Butler started moving toward the Cherokee.

There were only two ways it could go now. The agents in the Cherokee could rush out and start making arrests, in their panic blowing the whole operation, realizing that I'd removed the wire, that they had no idea what was going on; or they could withdraw, hoping another team would pick up where they left off, and try to salvage what was left of the situation.

The Cherokee pulled out as Butler advanced, the engine racing like my heart, and for a moment I thought Maguire or whoever it was might try to run him down. Then the car stopped, there was the grinding of its gears, and the Cherokee reversed down the street, away from where I had blocked the route. A car came around the corner, onto the one-way street, then, and the horns started.

"We've got to go now," I implored Pierre Alabacha. "Before they get their second team here."

Butler came running back, saying, "She's right, one of them was on a radio. We gotta move."

I opened the passenger door of the Porsche, felt my sweaty fingers sliding on the metal. "Come on!"

Butler started to climb back inside his Land Rover.

Alabacha told him, "There's no time. We'll take her car. Get in."

Butler hesitated, dropped back out and slammed his door shut, then slid into the backseat of the Porsche. I ran around to the other side as Alabacha climbed in. I put the car into gear and started moving before he had shut his door. I made the turn onto the avenue and heard my tires squeal, then floored it and blew through two red lights on Columbus, one after the other. Butler was contorting himself in the back of the car, trying to fit into the space where no one was actually meant to sit.

"Slow down," Alabacha said. "You'll get us pulled over."

I nodded and decelerated, felt the leather of the steering wheel clinging to my palms.

"Now, what was all of that, Bridgett?" he said evenly.

"They wanted me to set you up," I said.

Alabacha nodded. "Left," he said.

I made the turn.

I could see Butler in the backseat, twisting away from the window, watching me in the rearview mirror. His weight pressed against my seat.

"Stop on the next block," Alabacha said. "Pull over."

I did, pulling to the side of the street, putting the car into neutral in the shadow of the projects that loomed on both sides of the block.

"Roley," Alabacha said.

Butler moved immediately, dropping a handgun into Alabacha's lap, then reached around the driver's seat, grabbed my chin in one hand, and yanked my head back and up, pulling me out of my seat as I struggled. Alabacha brought the gun up at his waist, pointed it at my middle.

"Easy, sweetness," Butler whispered.

His tattooed fingers dove into my shirt, down inside my bra, sweeping along each side. I tried to protest and he pulled my chin back until I was staring at the roof of the car, half an inch from my nose. His hand went down farther, and I closed my eyes and fought back tears as he felt across my belly, then down into my pants. He took too long, and I tried to stay still, not to do anything that he could use to imagine I liked his index finger. The hand came out again, moved back to my torso and sides, and then Butler shifted his grip and shoved me hard into the steering wheel face-first. He checked my back, again down my jeans, and then leaned over the seat farther, holding me down, and checked my legs.

Then he let me go.

"Nothing," he said. He sounded honestly surprised. "She's clean."

I sat upright and tried to stop shaking.

Alabacha still had the gun on me.

"Do I pass?" I asked. I hated how frightened I sounded.

"Why did you do this thing?" Alabacha asked.

I looked at my hands, put them on the wheel, made my grip tight. It didn't help. "I want to come back," I said.

"Dope-fucking-fiend," Butler muttered.

"So what? So I use, so what? I'm still the best fucking person you've ever had on your crew, man or woman, and you know it, Pierre. I made you money, I kept your corner boys straight, I made you profit. I saved your ass back there, I broke a DEA cover off you, you son of a bitch!"

Alabacha pursed his lips.

"I've earned another chance," I said. "If I didn't earn it from the work I did, from the beating I took, I earned it back there. I earned it just now when I let Roley finger-fuck me."

Roley got a disapproving glance from his employer. "You have no respect for women," Alabacha remarked.

"And they've got no respect for me."

"I want another chance," I said. "Give me one more chance."

I couldn't read anything beyond his eyes. At the most, Alabacha looked weary.

"As it so happens," he finally said, "I seem to have another vacancy in the organization."

Butler swore under his breath. "You aren't seriously going to trust this junkie bitch?"

"Bridgett has earned another chance," Alabacha said, eyes still on me. "Whether she's earned my trust again, that's still to be decided."

"You're making a big mistake," Butler said.

"Drive," Alabacha told me.

He guided me to the Bronx, but wouldn't tell me where I was going.

"I could get us there faster if you told me the destination," I said.

"No," Alabacha said. "Turn here."

"You want me to turn on Crotona?"

He smiled.

I muttered about the traffic on Crotona, complained louder when he had me turn south on Prospect. I hoped the radio beneath his seat was as sensitive as Atticus had claimed, that he and the Taskforce agents he hopefully had listening in were receiving me loud and clear. I knew they were behind us, maybe far behind.

Maybe even far enough to be out of radio range.

I dodged the late-afternoon traffic, the beginnings of the rush hour, keeping my speed safe and legal. When the Bruckner came into view, I had a good idea where we were going, and said as much.

"Hunts Point?"

Alabacha nodded.

"What's in Hunts Point?"

"Ladipo."

"We're meeting him?"

Butler laughed, and in the tiny car it was annoyingly loud.

"Yeah, in a way," Butler said.

"Mr. Ladipo—if that's truly his name—has betrayed my trust," Alabacha said. "But unlike yourself, Bridgett, he did not have a good excuse."

"Meaning he doesn't have a habit?"

"No, he does not. What Anton Ladipo has is a badge."

I didn't say anything.

"You're not surprised?"

"No," I said. "I'm surprised. I'd have thought Roley here was working for the feds, not Anton. He seemed a lot like you."

"I thought so too."

"How'd you find out?"

"Someone got a hold of our books. Someone gave our books to the authorities. It had to have been an inside job. I checked, and it turned out to be Anton who was talking out of turn."

The dry-mouth wasn't from withdrawal, psychological or otherwise.

"She doesn't look too good," Butler said.

"No, she doesn't. Are you disturbed by this, Bridgett?"

I shook my head, watching the road, the gray and dingy warehouses that lined the streets. "I need to fix," I said.

"Ah, well, we can help you with that," Alabacha said. "Business first. Pleasure later.

"Make the right up here."

The street was Ryawa, but I couldn't say it and not have one of them figure out what I was doing.

"Stinks," I said.

"That's the meat market."

"Not the meat market, it's the fucking sewage plant," Butler said. "Right on the fucking water, you believe that?"

"Pull over here," Alabacha ordered.

I pulled off on the deserted stretch of road, near the end of the block. There were three warehouses all within spitting distance and a couple of smaller, shoddy-looking shacks. One of the structures was weathered red brick, the others all painted a gray that matched the overcast sky. It was sixteen minutes past five o'clock, and all the business of the day was over, and it was still too early for the illegal clubs to open up. In another three hours the whores would be out, the locals on the job early, the girls bused in from Jersey joining them later. All the vices would be on sale, and the violence would follow.

When people talk about the ugly part of the Bronx, they're talking about Hunts Point.

The smell was powerfully bad, a combination of scents from the meat and produce markets to our east, and from the sewage and the East River to our south. Seagulls swooped in low from the water, and the road and buildings were streaked and stained with their droppings. Beyond the shore, obscured by the treatment plant, was Rikers Island. Lisa was probably already back in her cell.

I stopped the engine and pulled the keys, and Alabacha checked himself in the sun visor, to be certain that he looked his best. He finished, closed it, and then, instead of getting out of the car, he unfastened his seatbelt and turned to face me full on.

"You've won that second chance, Bridgett. Now I want your loyalty."

"And how do I prove that?" I asked.

"Ladipo is in there." He motioned at one of the squat buildings off the road.

"That one, that shack?"

He raised an eyebrow at me. "There was no need to be extravagant about this," he said. "I didn't need a warehouse."

"Sure," I said.

Roley Butler was resting his arms behind my head, on the seat back. I could hear his breathing in my right ear.

"This is your test," Alabacha said. "You're going to kill Anton for me."

The engine on the Porsche made clicking noises as it cooled. I could hear the gulls calling one another. I wondered if the microphone underneath Alabacha's seat was picking up those sounds too.

"You can do him however you like, it's up to you," Alabacha said. "Roley played with fire when he had his turn, and I understand the DEA is still talking about the message he sent. But when Anton's opportunity arose, he talked me out of it, said that it wasn't necessary. That was a mistake. Just like you, I want to correct my mistakes. Your second chance is my second chance."

I looked across the hood of my car, at the dead end of the wide road. Razor wire and chain-link fencing surrounded a couple of the buildings. Gang tags had been spray-painted on the walls. Some of the warehouses had broken windows. Outside the high fence surrounding the sewage treatment compound, the city had planted trees, all of them bare in the winter, maybe dead already.

"You made Roley do this too?" I asked.

"He didn't take much convincing."

"Fuck that," Butler said. "I was dying for a chance to earn my bones."

"It's quite simple, Bridgett. You kill Anton for me, and

when it's done, we can all go somewhere and celebrate," Alabacha said. "I'll have your favorite powder waiting."

The shiver caught me unaware, and I couldn't hide it. When I swallowed, my mouth tasted like paste.

"Lead on," I said.

CHAPTER NINE

They hadn't been kind to Anton Ladipo.

The shack was bigger than it looked from the street, wedged between warehouses, deep and dark, and it was freezing. One large open room, with no furniture and no machinery, not even electric lights. The floor was concrete, cracked so deep in places that weeds grew out of the ground. The streetlights had come on outside; they made gashes of light along the walls.

He was bound and gagged, on his side in the middle of the floor. His suit pants were torn and smeared with dirt, and his white dress shirt had a long oval stain of blood. His skin, so dark and beautiful, looked like it was slowly turning to gray.

When he saw me, his eyes sparked with hope.

He knew.

Then Alabacha handed me a gun and the hope in Ladipo's eyes died.

Give the junkie a gun and the promise of some smack, I thought. And she's all yours.

"I'd like to be back for my dinner at seven-thirty," Alabacha said.

It was my gun, the SIG-Sauer that Butler had taken off me four days earlier, prior to me receiving the beating of my life. It was smart of Alabacha, and cruel, and it didn't matter if he had known I was coming or not. Killing Ladipo with my gun would have tied me to the murder. Now that he had me to pull the trigger, so much the better.

I checked the breech and saw that a round was ready. Nice and shiny, a nine-millimeter bullet that wouldn't do anything but damage when it entered Anton Ladipo's body. I could put a round in his leg, and if he lived, he'd be crippled for life. I could do the same with his arm. I could kill him with a torso or head shot.

Behind me, Roley Butler shifted, and I heard the sound of metal sliding over metal. I didn't need to look to see that he had drawn his own weapon. I didn't need to see to know that he was pointing it at my back.

"What are you waiting for?" Alabacha asked. "Let's do this and seal the deal."

"No," I said.

Butler hissed. "Told you—"

"Not this way," I went on. "He hurt me. I'm wearing what he did to me, I'm feeling it every time I move. I want to hurt him first."

Alabacha appraised me, saw the sincere rage in my face. He extended his hand, and I realized he wanted me to hand the gun back. There was no way I could hold on to the weapon, I realized.

I handed the gun over and asked, "Either of you have a knife?"

Butler reached into a pocket and came out with a slim piece of black metal. I took it, pressed the button on its side, and the blade sprang out nearly silently. It was sharp and bright.

"Goddamn," Butler said. "You've really got a hard-on for the son of a bitch, don't you?"

I turned the knife in my hand, then looked down at

Ladipo, who was propping himself up on one elbow. The fear in his eyes made me sick.

My boots crunched on the broken ground, and that was the loudest noise, almost like it echoed in the far corners of the shack. I crouched down in front of him and held the knife out so he could see the narrow blade, making certain he got a good look. Ladipo's eyes found mine again, and the last plea was there, frustration mixing up into fear and confusion. He had to know I'd come in, talked to Runge and Jimmy. He had to know I'd signed on as a CS. He'd probably vouched for my worth.

They had worked his face hard, and it reminded me of my own, what Ladipo had done to me. A gash along his forehead was thick with oozing fluid. One of his cheeks had swollen to twice its natural size.

Butler was moving, his footsteps coming closer as he tried for a better view.

I moved the knife to Ladipo's face and let the tip rest on the crest of his chin.

Ladipo didn't flinch.

"Do it," Butler urged. I heard the snap of his lighter, smelled the tang of his cigarette smoke.

I ran my free hand over Ladipo's face, feeling my way with my fingers across his swollen skin and the tape across his mouth. The gash on his forehead was ugly and probably very painful, and when I pressed into it with my index finger, his eyes watered.

Alabacha was absolutely silent behind me. I heard seagulls crying.

I brought the knife up past his face, keeping the barest distance between Ladipo and the metal. I used my finger as a guide, and lay the blade along the gash. I wanted to look away, but knew if I did, it would only make it worse. Ladipo closed his eyes.

I turned the blade.

The gag didn't do much to stop his scream.

I moved back and held the knife flat against my thigh, pressing down. My breath quickened.

"Good cut," Butler said, choking on the smoke he'd had in his lungs when he began laughing.

Anton Ladipo was on his back, and his noises were of pain and pleading. I couldn't see his eyes anymore.

I could only hear the gulls, and I couldn't catch my breath.

Ladipo fell silent again, and again I felt Alabacha and Butler waiting.

I turned the knife in my hand.

"Cut him again," Butler said greedily. "Cut him in the gut."

Tears ran along with the blood that was spilling over Ladipo's face. My knife had deepened the wound. I didn't know how much blood he'd lost already; I doubted he could afford to lose much more.

Knives aren't the nice weapons people imagine. They discriminate more than a gun, but in that way, they are also crueler than bullets.

I thought about all the things I could do with the knife, all of the things that would look good to Alabacha and Butler, and I horrified myself by coming up with plenty. I could think of many ways to hurt him, to get more of the blood they wanted to see. But there wasn't anything I could do that wouldn't last, that wouldn't mark him for the rest of his life. There wasn't anything I could do with the knife in my hand that Anton Ladipo would ever be able to forget or forgive.

They weren't going to buy another balk, no matter how sadistic I made it appear.

They wouldn't accept another attack on an already open wound.

Alabacha wanted me to kill him now.

Alabacha wanted me to kill him for a single shot of heroin.

"I'm done," I said, and got to my feet.

"No, you're not," Alabacha objected. "He's still breathing."

I shook my head, pressed the button on the knife, folded the blade closed against my thigh.

Butler raised the barrel of his gun at me. "Goddamn, I knew it. I fucking knew you were wrong from the start."

I looked him in the eyes and didn't say anything. I wished

I had something to say before I died. I just couldn't think of anything that needed words.

The gulls had stopped crying.

Ladipo had frozen. Maybe he'd heard it too.

"I'm going to look up your sister when we're done," Butler told me. "Think I'll pay her a condolence call and—"

The doors broke in to the north and the south, and shouts and guns and the beams of flashlights all surged into the darkness. Butler started at the noise, swiveling his head to see the nearest door, and the gun tracked with him. I popped the blade again, reached out for his left shoulder, and pulled him back, stabbing. The knife broke through his coat and his shirt, and then his skin, and I looked down to see I had impaled him just left of his spine, in his lower back. I followed through, using him for leverage, pulled up, then jerked left, cutting my way out of him through his left kidney. He had kept his knife sharp, but it took a lot of effort anyway, and I had to shove him aside to free the blade.

"Stay away from my sister," I said.

Butler looked at me, dropped his gun, died, and fell to the floor.

His blood was all over me.

I heard Alabacha saying that he surrendered, that he was unarmed, that he had done nothing wrong, that he didn't know what had happened here.

And I heard Agent Dot Maguire say, "You solicited the murder of one federal agent and confessed to being an accessory in the death of another. We have it all on tape. You're dead to rights, motherfucker."

Alabacha said that he had been entrapped, that he wanted his attorney.

I dropped the blade and it splashed in the blood that had come out of Butler. I tried to walk to Ladipo, and someone was screaming at me not to move. I took another step, needing to reach where he was already surrounded by men and women, and I heard Runge shouting for an ambulance. I knew people were pointing guns at me, but until Jimmy grabbed hold of my arms I kept moving.

"Easy," Jimmy said. "You take it easy now, sweetheart. You're all right now."

"I have to tell him," I said.

"Ambulance is on the way. He'll be fine."

"I have to tell him."

"I'll let him know," Jimmy said, and he knew what I meant. "You stay, you settle. Your lad's here, he'll hold on to you."

Jimmy guided me left, around the crowd swarming on Ladipo. Alabacha was now in cuffs, and he had stopped talking. He tried to get me to look at him, but I didn't, couldn't stop trying to see the man I'd almost murdered.

Then Atticus was there, still wearing his white motorcycle helmet, grabbing my shoulders, holding me steady.

Runge moved back to look at where Butler was lying on the broken ground. I saw Ladipo, sitting with help. Someone had put a coat around his shoulders.

"I'm sorry," I said. "I'm sorry, I didn't want to do it and I tried not to . . . I'm sorry . . . I'm . . ."

And then I doubled over and puked my guts out.

On Friday morning, the third week of January, Lisa took the plea.

The judge asked, "You understand that by the terms of this agreement, you are required to state in detail the nature of your crime, manslaughter in the second degree. You understand that this is the same effect as a guilty verdict returned by the jury?"

Miranda whispered in Lisa's ear. Lisa said, "Yes, Your Honor."

"Please explain to the court exactly what you did."

Lisa looked at Miranda again, then cast a fast glance over her shoulder, reassuring herself that Vera and Gabriel were there. Then she said, "I stole the gun from my friend Bridgett Logan. I went to where I thought Vince would be and I . . . I started looking for him. Someone told me that he would be in the gallery on One Sixty-first and . . . and I waited for him. When he showed up I followed him inside and I told him to stay away from me . . . I told him . . . I thought he was going to hurt me again, and hurt my son, and I saw him and I started shooting. . . .

"I just started shooting. And then I ran."

The judge looked down from the bench at the assistant district attorney. "Is this acceptable?"

Corwin got to his feet. I couldn't see his face, but from his back, it wasn't. I couldn't blame him.

"Yes, Your Honor," Corwin lied.

"I have here a letter from the U.S. attorney," the judge said. "He says that Miss Schoof was instrumental in providing information in a major drug investigation. He says that the information she provided will lead to at least seventeen felony convictions, and assist in a murder trial against a man who murdered one federal agent and solicited the death of another."

None of the attorneys spoke. Where she stood at the table before the judge, Lisa adjusted her footing, looking down.

"With this in mind, and due to the nature of the crime, the extreme circumstances surrounding the case, and the cooperation of the defendant, I am sentencing Lisa Schoof to five years' probation, with time served. This case is dismissed, and Miss Schoof, you are free to go."

The gavel banged.

I waited for them outside of the courtroom, on the landing by the big marble stairs, watching the lawyers come and go. Miranda exited first, talking with Corwin, and she saw me and gestured for the ADA to go on ahead, that she would catch up.

"Thank you," I said before she could beat me to the punch. "You'll have my check as soon as I get your bill."

"Where should I send it?"

"Mail it to Atticus. I'll get it there."

"I'll do that." Miranda Glaser moved her barrister bag from one hand to the other, and it looked like she was gnawing on the inside of her cheek. "I understand you may be needing an attorney yourself."

"Where'd you hear that?"

"I get around."

"The U.S. attorney wants me before a grand jury at the end of the month," I said. "I don't think I'll be charged with anything. I'm supposed to have immunity."

"If you don't, and you end up looking at charges . . ."

"I'll be sure to forget I even know you," I said.

Glaser actually grinned. "I revise what I said to you on Sunday. I would be willing to see you again. Just not for a very long time." She offered me her hand and I shook it. "You'll have my bill by next week."

Then she went to catch up with Corwin.

Gabriel had come out of the courtroom and was looking at me from just beyond the doors. I tried a smile at him, and he didn't bounce back, but for once he didn't turn away. Vera and Lisa emerged. Both looked relieved, though nothing on Vera's face could match Lisa's delight at walking without cuffs around her wrists. They saw me too, and Lisa crouched and kissed, then hugged, then kissed Gabriel again, before joining me by the railing.

"I'll meet you at the car," she called to Vera.

Vera nodded and took Gabriel by the hand. Lisa watched them go. She couldn't stop smiling. When they were down the stairs, she managed to tear her eyes away from them.

"You are amazing," Lisa Schoof told me. "You did it."

"What are you going to do now?"

"Now? Home. I'm going to change my clothes. I'm going to eat some really good food. I'm going to figure out when the next EMT course starts and re-enroll, take the whole damn thing over again."

"Can't transfer your previous work?"

"They won't let me. Ever since the Fire Department took the program over, they keep changing the rules. But it's okay. I'll make it through this time."

"Yeah, this time I think you will."

Lisa straightened her blouse, and I saw it was an excuse to look at my arms. She couldn't see anything; I had my jacket on, and beneath it, my long sleeves. But she didn't need to see anything.

"I heard," she said. "Vera told me."

"Yeah."

"I'm sorry."

"For what? You didn't charge the needle and stick it in my arm."

"I know. But if it wasn't for me—"

"That's bullshit," I said. "And you know it, and I know it, so let's just stop. It was going to happen to me one way or another. You were just the excuse I used, Lisa. You shouldn't bear any guilt about that."

"You've done so much for me. I just . . . I owe you, Bridgett. I promise, I'll make it up to you."

"You really want to make it up to me, Lise?"

"Yeah, absolutely."

I reached out for her with my left arm, put my hand around her neck, pulling her in. She let me, then began to resist, and I realized what she thought I was going to do, and I said, "I'm not going to kiss you, relax."

She let me draw her in almost close enough to touch my bowed forehead to hers.

"There is something you can do," I whispered.

"Name it."

"Dump the smack you kept."

I felt the muscles along her neck and back tighten beneath my left hand. I adjusted my grip slightly.

"I know you cut it, Lise," I whispered. "That's why you were gone so long that day they arrested you. You know how to do it, hell—you used to do it for Vince, cutting his shit before packing the decks."

She tried to back away, and I pressed on her shoulder hard, and she stopped. She was looking at my chest, breathing through her nose.

"What I figure is, you took two of the bricks and kept them. Then you cut the other two by half, to fill them out again. You repackaged, stuffed them in the duffel, and thought you'd bought yourself some mad money, or maybe, like you said, Gabriel's future."

"Maybe I did," she said softly. "So what?"

"You want to be a citizen, those are your own words, Lise,

that's the song you've been singing all along. Well, love, citizens don't have two fucking keys stashed in case they need to raise some mad money."

I dropped my hand from her shoulder, stepped back. She straightened up immediately, adjusting her blouse yet again, then looking around to see if we had been overheard. If we had, no one was showing signs of interest.

"You keep that smack," I said, "and this is all for shit."

Then I headed for the stairs.

CHAPTER ELEVEN

Growing up, Sundays had belonged to St. John's Parish.

Our family would rise in the morning together, share a breakfast of eggs and sausages and thick home-baked bread. We would bathe and change into our really nice clothes and then we would drive to church and attend Mass.

Afterward we would pile back into Da's much-loved-and-tuned Alfa Romeo and he would drive us through the Bronx, out through Kingsbridge and then up to Riverdale, then south again along Palisade Avenue. Dennis Logan and his wife, Lilly, at his side, his two daughters in the backseat. We would look at the big and fancy town houses that had million-dollar views of the Hudson, and we would wonder at the people who lived in them. Da would remind us that the Bronx was a great place to live, that Babe Ruth had made his home there, and that we were indeed a blessed family. Then we'd stop for a bit at one of the parks, and we'd walk, and if it was summer, there would be ice cream.

Until I sat next to Cashel at St. John's that Sunday, I didn't know how angry I was at Da for leaving.

Andrew and Kelly were there with their children, and after the service, Cashel had dragged me over to them. The conversation between Andrew and me had been strained.

"You're okay?" he'd asked.

"I'm getting better," I'd answered.

Kelly had extended an offer of dinner, but I knew it was courtesy, nothing else. It was unspoken between us that we represented to each other a past we wished to forget. Encounters in the present would only serve to make us all uncomfortable.

Cashel had then introduced me to a couple of the Sisters of her community. All of them were older, the youngest by easily ten years, and they were all solicitous and charming and even witty. They said they were glad to meet me. They asked politely and kindly about my injuries. I told them I had been in a fight. Sister Janice asked if I kick-boxed. I told her I didn't, and she told me to try it.

It seemed Sister Janice was quite the kick-boxer.

But all that was an hour ago, and now we were sitting side by side in a pew, the church now empty, waiting for one of us to go first.

My sister the nun said, "You treat me like shit, Bridgett."

"It's nothing that you've done," I said, which was no answer at all.

She shook her head and kept her voice soft, but it echoed all the same in the empty church. "Even if I overlook all the times you've ignored me, look what you did over Christmas. You take me for granted."

"I've never taken you for granted," I said angrily. "Why do you think I came to you?"

"You came to me because you didn't want to tell Atticus you were a junkie. You wanted me to do it."

"You want an apology? I'm sorry. Every day I'm sorry, Cashel."

"Sure," she said. "Every day you're sorry for *yourself.*"

I rubbed the bandage over my eye, trying to soothe the itch from the knitting skin. The air still held the scent of the incense, of the perfumed and cleansed bodies that had filled every seat in the house.

Cashel sighed, looking up at the stained-glass window that showed John baptizing Jesus. "You make me so angry, Bridgett."

"It's a gift."

"God gives each of us one, I suppose."

"I don't presume to know."

"You think I do?"

"God called you to be a religious, remember? That was God's plan for you. It implies some communication."

Cashel opened her mouth, then stopped as we heard footsteps coming down the aisle. She waited until they had moved away again before saying, "I was called because of you. That was His plan."

"Then it's not a particularly nice plan," I said.

"We can't tell, Bridgett. We can only see parts, never the whole picture. That's where faith enters."

From the direction of the rectory came the murmur of voices, and then a burst of laughter. We watched as the priest emerged, still wearing his silk vestments, talking with another man, and they saw us and raised their hands in greeting, and Cashel waved.

The whole picture, I thought. With great big pieces missing that we just fill in all on our own, extrapolating and pretending, sometimes even lying to ourselves.

"You know I'm proud of you," I said. "You know I'm sorry. Sorry for what I've done to you and Ma and Da."

Cashel turned and looked at me.

"This has to be the last time," she said.

"Help me make it that," I said.

"How?"

I told her.

She agreed.

When we left St. John's we went for a drive around the Bronx. Then we got ice cream.

CHAPTER TWELVE

Detective Ollerenshaw almost convinced me that he was pleased to see me again. "Miss Logan, what a surprise! Heard your friend pled out."

"Yeah. Man two. She's on probation."

He settled behind his desk, shaking his head. "And they blame us for letting criminals roam the streets. What can I do you for?"

"Well, I think you guys have my gun. Or more specifically, my Da's gun."

Ollerenshaw scratched the end of his nose with a chewed nail on the end of a blunt finger. "Seem to recall we tried reaching you about such a weapon. Week or two ago, when we found it. Smith & Wesson .38? Old cop's style?"

"It's easy to identify," I said. "It's got a stainless steel side-plate, instead of a blued one."

"That would be the gun, then. We tried calling you, phone was disconnected. Went by your place, no answer."

"I've sort of been between homes lately."

"Well, I got a pile of paperwork for you to fill out. We process it, you can get your dad's gun back today."

"That would be great."

Ollerenshaw started searching his drawers, found the form he wanted and a pen.

"Was it empty when you found it?" I asked.

"Five spent, one ready."

"And in good shape?"

"Yeah, real clean. No prints on it or nothing. But the ballistics match was positive. Why?"

"Curiosity," I said.

Scott Fowler wasn't in, so I left a message with my questions, then went to pick up Da's gun at Evidence Control. By the time I finished, Scott had my answers.

"Why are you asking about this guy?" Scott asked over the phone. "Isn't he dead?"

"Like chivalry," I said. "Thanks for the help."

Jimmy Shannon lived alone not too far from Van Cortlandt Park in a bungalow that he'd bought for his bride, Caroline. It was a house I remembered well from my childhood, and it seemed shabbier when I saw it again, with the dirty snow piled on the sidewalk. I remembered visiting here, our family coming to spend time with Jimmy and his wife. Then the visits stopped, and I was too young to wonder why. It wasn't until I was in college that I realized it was because Caroline had left Jimmy.

When I had asked my Da about it he had said only, "He wanted kids."

It was after four in the afternoon, Monday, my last day of freedom, and I was running the last of my errands. In Manhattan, Cashel and Atticus and Erika were waiting for me to join them at dinner.

I parked the Porsche and crossed the pile of dirty snow, cradling the bottle of Scotch in my arm like it was a baby. My right knee was still giving me pain, sending stabs of fury that rode all the way up my leg to my hip.

The lights were on inside, and I heard the television talking as I rang the bell. It took most of a minute, but Jimmy came to the door, checking me through the peephole. Then I heard the locks turn, and he ushered me inside, big and delighted.

"Bridie!" His hug made me feel small.

"Hi, Uncle Jimmy. This is for you." I presented him with the brown paper bag.

He pulled out the bottle and grinned. "I'll get us glasses. Come on, have a seat. I was watching the game."

His den was dusty and cluttered, and made me feel immediately sad. It wasn't any one thing, but the room spoke of a lonely life, and I saw the old photos on the shelves of my father and mother, of myself and of Cashel, of Caroline, and wondered how many memories Jimmy spent his time recalling. He had a lot of books out, old paperbacks and new paperbacks, nonfiction, histories, mostly military. The seat of his couch still bore the imprint of his body and was peppered with broken potato chips. A six-pack of beer rested on the floor by where he'd propped his head on a small and surprisingly delicate-looking pillow. Two of the cans were crushed and empty.

I took off my jacket and cleared three books off a chair, sitting just as Jimmy returned. He handed one glass to me and poured into it, then splashed a couple of fingers into the other for himself.

He lifted his glass. "*Sláinte chuig na fir, agus go mairfidh na mná go deo.* Health to the men, and may the women live forever."

"*Sláinte,*" I replied. I looked at the amber liquid before drinking it, knowing that it wasn't the drug I wanted at all. Then I tossed it back.

We were both silent while the Scotch had its burn.

Jimmy uncapped the bottle again, and poured himself another two fingers, I declined a refill with a shake of my head.

"How's Ladipo?" I asked.

"Out of the hospital, back at home. Taking some of his time."

"I sent him flowers."

Jimmy smiled and drank more of his Scotch, this time savoring it. "He got them. Wanted to know if you were maybe going to ask him out on a date."

"You can tell him I'm flattered, but taken. He's going to be okay?"

"You're worried about what you had to do, don't be. You saved his life. He's strong. He'll be back." He pushed a button on the remote resting on the arm of the couch, and the television snapped off. It made the room suddenly a lot quieter. "That why you're paying your uncle Jimmy a visit? To find out about Ladipo?"

I shook my head.

"Didn't think so."

I held out my glass for him to refill, stopped him at a finger and a half. "I keep wondering what Da would have done, you know, if he had been in my position. How he would have handled things. Then I decide that he never would've been in my position at all."

"That's bullshit."

"You think?"

"As I understand it, you did what you did to help a friend."

"That's what I tell myself," I said. "That I owed Lisa, that I had to look out for her, and that maybe I didn't do such a good job in the past. That's how Andrew got involved. Atticus and Cashel too."

"Atticus and Cashel are involved?"

"Finish your drink, you dirty old man," I said.

Jimmy's couch creaked as he chuckled. "Dennis always went to the wall for his friends."

"So do you."

He reached for the bottle of Bushmills, poured another two fingers. This time, when he set the bottle down, he didn't cap it.

"You're family," Jimmy said. "Family's beyond friendship."

"Did you really think I tried to kill Vincent Lark?" I asked.

He didn't move when I asked it. The surface of the Scotch in his hand stayed steady. "Didn't think it was the ghost of your Da."

"And now you know."

"You want to tell it, and I'll fill in the blanks? Or should I just give you it all at once?"

"I'll tell you what I think happened, Jimmy, how about that?"

He took a gulp of the Scotch. It didn't seem to be touching him at all. "Tell me your story, Bridie."

"I called you in September, out of the blue. Shocked the hell out of you—I hadn't called in months, longer. I asked you about Lark, and either you knew who he was already or you found out fast. Lark had made some money for himself as an informant. Ten grand here and there, ratting out people professionally. It was his sideline work.

"You knew Lark dealt smack. So when I called, you got worried about me. You thought I was using again. That's fair. I don't like it, but it's fair."

"I was concerned," he said. "Dennis asked me to look after his girls."

"And that's why you met with Lark. Either he arranged it or you did. Because you were there that morning when Lisa showed up."

I stopped to drink some of my Scotch but it wasn't helping me any. "Lisa didn't see you, she only saw Vince. She opened fire, squeezed off four rounds. She doesn't know how to handle a gun, and she was scared, and she got lucky for even one of them to hit. That was the shoulder wound.

"Then she dropped the gun and ran.

"And you came out from wherever you were, and you saw the gun. And it was the gun that did it, because there's only one Smith & Wesson like Da's, and you were his partner for twenty years, and you knew it on sight.

"I had called you about Vincent Lark. Vincent Lark dealt smack. I was a junkie. And there was my father's gun on the floor.

"So you finished what you believed I had started. You thought I'd failed to kill Lark, that I'd get arrested, or worse,

Lark would come down on me hard. So you killed him to protect me.

"You kept the gun, thinking that it'd be hard to make a case against me without the murder weapon. You got out of there without trouble, really—couple people saw you, but everyone was worrying about the white girl who had been running, not the white man who was walking. Nobody paid you any mind.

"And when I told you it was Lisa Schoof who'd been the shooter, and you had seen she was going to try for a deal, you planted the gun with the stash. You cleaned it and dropped it there, and maybe it was you who later discovered it. Full circle, no loose ends. Clean. Da would have loved it."

"Lark had snitched for us before." Jimmy's eyes had closed, and his glass of Scotch was empty. "He said he had information. I took the contact because you had called about him. I wanted to make certain a skel like him knew better than to even think about touching a girl like you. He said he didn't know who you were, and I was certain he was full of shit. I was on my way out, heading down the back, when I heard the shots. Came back up, and the rest is what you say it is."

Jimmy opened his eyes. "There's only one thing your Da would want to know: What are you going to do now, Bridie?"

"If I wanted to prove you did it, I'd have to prove that you planted the gun in the bag. To do that, I'd have to admit that I'd seen the bag."

"And if you did that, it would mean you'd planted the money list." Jimmy managed a weary smile. "I'm not entirely off my game."

"No. No, you're still on the ball." I set my glass carefully on the edge of the end table beside my chair and stood up. "Thanks for the drinks, Uncle Jimmy."

"You're going so soon?"

"I've got plans for tonight. And tomorrow I go into rehab."

"Call me when you get back?"

"If you'll be around."

"Absolutely."

I started to leave, and he let me make it to the hall before he called my name.

"Your Da," he said, reaching for a refill as I turned to face him.

"What about him?"

"He'd be proud. He was right about you, you'd sure as hell have won that gold shield."

Atticus was preparing dinner when I got back to his place, a cloud of steam, rich with garlic, clinging to the plaster ceiling above him.

"Lisa Schoof called for you," he told me. "Her number's by the phone."

"I'll call after dinner."

"Fair enough. Now get out of my kitchen."

So I joined Erika and Cashel in the living room, where we all beat on one another with Erika's new PlayStation until dinner was ready.

When I left to meet Gabriel and Lisa, I took Da's gun with me.

They were waiting out front of their place, bundled up against the cold. Lisa clutched a paper shopping bag, its top rolled tightly down, protecting its contents. I braked and opened the car door, and Gabriel clambered into the back-seat, and then Lisa slid into the front.

"We thought the East River," she said. "Would the East River be all right?"

"Sounds good to me," I answered.

Traffic was light, and there was plenty of room to maneuver.

"Go faster," Gabriel urged.

"You sure?"

"Yeah, go faster."

I drove faster.

"That's cool."

Lisa held the bag in her lap and didn't say anything.

The drive didn't take long, and by eleven we had parked and were walking down towards the water. To the south the Williamsburg Bridge was lit with traffic, headlights traveling in from Brooklyn. Lisa led, Gabriel at her side, kicking at the small accumulations of filthy snow that had yet to melt away. When we reached the wall by the water, we stopped.

"Here?" Lisa asked.

"Sure," I said.

"I brought a knife."

"Wait first."

She looked at me, serious and expectant.

"I found out something," I said. "About how Vince died."

Lisa bent her head to look down at the water.

"You didn't kill him."

Gabriel looked up at me, confused. His mother sighed. "Yes, I did."

"No, you didn't," I said. "Someone else did. Someone who picked up the gun after you had dropped it."

Her eyes came back to me. "I thought . . . I thought I had dropped it, but . . . but at the trial they said it was in the bag, and I couldn't remember putting it there. . . ." Lisa put her right hand over her mouth. Her hand was in a mitten, pink and white with a mouse on the back. "Who . . . ?"

"It doesn't matter. Someone who thought he was doing the right thing for the right reasons."

Gabriel spun, kicking dirty snow onto his pant legs, my pant legs, and his mother's pant legs.

"Gabe, stop it," Lisa snapped.

He stopped it. "Aren't you happy?"

Her mittened hand came down and she nodded; then she reached for Gabe and wrapped her arms about him tight. I thought that maybe he had gotten taller in the past few weeks, but maybe that was just the snow he was standing on top of.

When Lisa let him go, she opened the shopping bag and removed the two bricks of heroin, still wrapped in their Alabacha plastic. Then she took out a small paring knife.

"Will you do the honors?" she asked.

I tested the wind, and was grateful to find it was calm. I took the knife and slit each brick lengthwise.

With Gabriel watching, his mother dumped the heroin into the East River.

It vanished in the bright waters instantly.

I thought of the hunk of metal in my pocket, the gun that was always Da's and never mine. I could almost hear his voice.

I couldn't have done better meself.

I liked that I saw the splash but didn't hear the noise.

ABOUT THE AUTHOR

Born in San Francisco, GREG RUCKA was raised on the Monterey Peninsula. He has worked at a variety of jobs, from theatrical fight choreographer to emergency medical technician. He and his wife, Jennifer, and son, Elliot, reside in Portland, Oregon, where he is at work on his next novel, *Critical Space*.